A
Garland Series

VICTORIAN
FICTION

NOVELS OF FAITH
AND DOUBT

A collection of 121 novels
in 92 volumes, selected by
Professor Robert Lee Wolff,
Harvard University,
with a separate introductory volume
written by him
especially for this series.

CATHARINE FURZE

CLARA HOPGOOD

William Hale White

Garland Publishing, Inc., New York & London

1976

PR
5795
W7x
1976

Library of Congress Cataloging in Publication Data

White, William Hale, 1831-1913.
  Catherine Furze ; Clara Hopgood.

  (Victorian fiction : Novels of faith and doubt)
  Reprint of two of the author's works originally
published by T. F. Unwin, London, in 1893 and 1896,
respectively.
  I. White, William Hale, 1831-1913. Clara Hopgood.
1976. II. Title: Catherine Furze. III. Series.
PZ3.W5862Cat15   [PR5795.W7]   823'.8   75-1516
ISBN 0-8240-1589-4

Printed in the United States of America

CATHARINE FURZE

Bibliographical note:

this facsimile has been made from a copy in the
British Museum
(012630.k4)

CATHARINE FURZE.

CATHARINE FURZE

BY

MARK RUTHERFORD

Edited by his Friend
REUBEN SHAPCOTT

IN TWO VOLUMES

VOL. I

London
T. FISHER UNWIN
Paternoster Square
MDCCCXCIII

CATHARINE FURZE.

CHAPTER I.

IT was a bright, hot, August Saturday in the
market town of Eastthorpe, in the eastern
Midlands, in the year 1840. Eastthorpe lay
about five miles on the western side of the Fens,
in a very level country on the banks of a river,
broad and deep, but with only just sufficient fall
to enable its long-lingering waters to reach the
sea. It was an ancient market town, with a
six-arched stone bridge, and with a High Street
from which three or four smaller and narrower
streets connected by courts and alleys diverged
at right angles. In the middle of the town was
the church, an immense building, big enough to
hold half Eastthorpe, and celebrated for its beau-

tiful spire and its peal of eight bells. Round the
church lay the churchyard, fringed with huge elms,
and in the Abbey Close, as it was called, which
was the outer girdle of the churchyard on three
sides, the fourth side of the square being the High
Street, there lived in 1840 the principal doctor, the
lawyer, the parson, and two aged gentlewomen
with some property, who were daughters of one
of the former partners in the bank, had been born
in Eastthorpe, and had scarcely ever quitted it.
Here also were a young ladies' seminary and an
ancient grammar school for the education of forty
boys, sons of freemen of the town. The houses
in the Close were not of the same class as the
rest ; they were mostly old red brick, with white
sashes, and they all had gardens, long, narrow,
and shady, which, on the south side of the Close,
ran down to the river. One of these houses was
even older, black-timbered, gabled, plastered, the
sole remains, saving the church, of Eastthorpe as it
was in the reign of Henry the Eighth.

Just beyond the church, going from the bridge,
the High Street was so wide that the houses on
either side were separated by a space of over two

hundred feet. This elongated space was the market-place. In the centre was the Moot Hall, a quaint little building, supported on oak pillars, and in the shelter underneath the farmers assembled on market day. All round the Moot Hall, and extending far up and down the street, were cattle-pens and sheep-pens, which were never removed. Most of the shops were still bow-windowed, with small panes of glass, but the first innovation, indicative of the new era at hand, had just been made. The druggist, as a man of science and advanced ideas, had replaced his bow-window with plate-glass, had put a cornice over it, had stuccoed his bricks, and had erected a kind of balustrade of stucco, so as to hide as much as possible the attic windows, which looked over, meekly protesting. Nearly opposite the Moot Hall was the Bell Inn, the principal inn in the town. There were other inns, respectable enough, such as the Bull, a little higher up, patronised by the smaller commercial travellers and farmers, but the entrance passage to the Bull had sand on the floor, and carriers made it a house of call. To the Bell the two coaches came which went through Eastthorpe, and there they changed horses. Both the Bull and the Bell had market dinners, but at the Bell the charge was three-and-sixpence; sherry was often drunk, and there the steward to the Honourable Mr. Eaton, the principal landowner, always met the tenants. The Bell was Tory and the Bull was Whig, but no stranger of respectability, Whig or Tory, visiting Eastthorpe could possibly hesitate about going to the Bell, with its large gilded device projecting over the pathway, with its broad archway at the side always freshly gravelled, and its handsome balcony on the first floor, from which the Tory county candidates, during election times, addressed the free and independent electors and cattle.

Eastthorpe was a malting town, and down by the water were two or three large malthouses. The view from the bridge was not particularly picturesque, but it was pleasant, especially in summer, when the wind was south-west. The malthouses and their cowls, the wharves and the gaily painted sailing barges alongside, the fringe of slanting willows turning the silver-gray sides of their foliage towards the breeze, the island in the middle of the river with bigger willows, the large expanse of sky, the soft clouds distinct in form almost to the far distant horizon, and, looking eastwards, the illimitable distance towards the fens and the sea—all this made up a landscape, more suitable perhaps to some persons than rock or waterfall, although no picture had ever been painted of it, and nobody had ever come to see it.

Such was Eastthorpe. For hundreds of years had the shadow of St. Mary's swept slowly over the roofs underneath it, and, of all those years, scarcely a line of its history survived, save what was written in the churchyard or in the church registers. The town had stood for the Parliament in the days of the Civil War, and there had been a skirmish in the place; but who fought in it, who were killed in it, and what the result was, nobody knew. Half a dozen old skulls of much earlier date and of great size were once found in a gravel pit two miles away, and were the subject of much talk, some taking them for Romans, some for Britons, some for Saxons, and some for Danes. As it was impossible to be sure if they were Christian, they could not be put in consecrated

ground ; they were therefore included in an auction
of dead and live stock, and were bought by the
doctor. Surnames survived in Eastthorpe with
singular pertinacity, for it was remote from the
world, but what was the relationship between the
scores of Thaxtons, for example, whose deaths
were inscribed on the tombstones, some of them
all awry and weather-worn, and the Thaxtons of
1840, no living Thaxton could tell, every spiritual
trace of them having disappeared more utterly
than their bones. Their bones, indeed, did not
disappear, and were a source of much trouble to
the sexton, for in digging a new grave they came
up to the surface in quantities, and had to be
shovelled in and covered up again, so that the
bodily remains of successive generations were
jumbled together, and Puritan and Georgian
Thaxtons were mixed promiscuously with their
descendants. Nevertheless, Eastthorpe had really
had a history. It had known victory and defeat,
love, hatred, intrigue, hope, despair, and all the
passions, just as Elizabeth, King Charles, Cromwell, and Queen Anne knew them, but they were
not recorded.

It was a bright, hot, August Saturday, as we have said, and it was market day. Furthermore, it was half-past two in the afternoon, and the guests at Mr. Furze's had just finished their dinner. Mr. Furze was the largest ironmonger in East-thorpe, and sold not only ironmongery, but ploughs and all kinds of agricultural implements. At the back of the shop was a small foundry where all the foundry work for miles round Eastthorpe was done. It was Mr. Furze's practice always to keep a kind of open house on Saturday, and on this particular day, at half-past two, Mr. Bellamy, Mr. Chandler, Mr. Gosford, and Mr. Furze were drinking their whiskey-and-water and smoking their pipes in Mr. Furze's parlour. The first three were well-to-do farmers, and with them the whiskey-and-water was not a pretence. Mr. Furze was a tradesman, and of a different build. Strong tobacco and whiskey at that hour and in that heat were rather too much for him, and he played with his pipe and drank very slowly. The conversation had subsided for a while under the influence of the beef, York-shire pudding, beer, and spirits, when Mr. Bellamy observed—

"Old Bartlett's widow still a-livin' up at the Croft?"

"Yes," said Mr. Gosford, after filling his pipe again and pausing for at least a minute, "Bartlett's dead."

"Bartlett wur a slow-coach," observed Mr. Chandler, after another pause of a minute, "so wur his mare. I mind me I wur behind his mare about five year ago last Michaelmas, and I wur well-nigh perished. I wur a-goin' to give her a poke with my stick, and old Bartlett says, 'Doan't hit her, doan't hit her; yer can't alter her.'"

The three worthy farmers roared with laughter, Mr. Furze smiling gently.

"That was a good 'un," said Mr. Bellamy.

"Ah," replied Chandler, "I mind that as well as if it wur yesterday."

Mr. Bellamy at this point had to leave, and Mr. Furze was obliged to attend to his shop. Gosford and Chandler, however, remained, and Gosford continued the subject of Bartlett's widow.

"What's she a-stayin' on for up there?"

"Old Bartlett's left her a goodish bit."

"She wur younger than he."

A dead silence of some minutes.

"She ain't a-goin' to take the Croft on herself," observed Gosford.

"Them beasts of the squire's," replied Chandler, "fetched a goodish lot. Scaled just over ninety stone apiece."

"Why doan't you go in for the widow, Chandler?"

Mr. Chandler was a widower.

"Eh!" (with a nasal tone and a smile)—"bit too much for me."

"Too much? Why, there ain't above fourteen stone of her. Keep yer warm o' nights up at your cold place."

Mr. Chandler took the pipe out of his mouth, put it inside the fender, compressed his lips, rubbed his chin, and looked up to the ceiling.

"Well, I must be a-goin'."

"I suppose I must too," and they both went their ways, to meet again at tea-time.

At five punctually all had again assembled, the additions to the party being Mrs. Furze and her daughter Catharine, a young woman of nineteen. Mrs. Furze was not an Eastthorpe lady; she came from Cambridge, and Mr. Furze had first seen her when she was on a visit in Eastthorpe. Her father was a draper in Cambridge, which was not only a much bigger place than Eastthorpe, but had a university, and Mrs. Furze talked about the university familiarly, so that, although her education had been slender, a university flavour clung to her, and the farmers round Eastthorpe would have been quite unable to determine the difference between her and a senior wrangler, if they had known what a senior wrangler was.

"Ha," observed Mr. Gosford, when they were seated, "I wur sayin', Mrs. Furze, to Chandler as he ought to go in for old Bartlett's widow. Now what do *you* think? Wouldn't they make a pretty pair?" and he twisted Chandler's shoulders round a little till he faced Mrs. Furze.

"Don't you be a fool, Gosford," said Chandler in good temper, but, as he disengaged himself, he upset his tea on Mrs. Furze's carpet.

"Really, Mr. Gosford," replied Mrs. Furze, with some dignity and asperity, "I am no judge in such matters. They are best left to the persons concerned."

" No offence, ma'am, no offence."

Mrs. Furze was not quite a favourite with her
husband's friends, and he knew it, but he was
extremely anxious that their dislike to her should
not damage his business relationships with them.
So he endeavoured to act as mediator.

" No doubt, my dear, no doubt, but at the same
time there is no reason why Mr. Gosford should
not make any suggestion which may be to our
friend Chandler's advantage."

But Mr. Gosford was checked, and did not
pursue the subject. Catharine sat next to him.

" Mr. Gosford, when may I come to Moat Farm
again ? "

" Lord, my dear, whenever you like ; you know
that. Me and Mrs. G. is always glad to see you.
*When*ever you please," and Mr. Gosford instantly
recovered the good-humour which Mrs. Furze had
suppressed.

" Don't forget us," chimed in Mr. Bellamy.
" We'll turn out your room and store apples in
it if you don't use it oftener."

" Now, Mr. Bellamy," said Catharine, holding up
her finger at him, " you'll be sick of me at last.

You've forgotten when I had that bad cold at your house, and was in bed there for a week, and what a bother I was to Mrs. Bellamy."

"Bother!" cried Bellamy—"bother! Lord have mercy on us! why the missus was sayin' when you talked about bother, my missus says, 'I'd sooner have Catharine here, and me have tea up there with her, notwithstanding there must be a fire upstairs and I've had to send Lucy to the infirmary with a whitlow on her thumb—yes, I would, than be at a many tea-parties I know.'"

Mrs. Furze gave elaborate tea-parties, and was uncomfortably uncertain whether or not the shaft was intended for her.

"My dear Catharine, I shall be delighted if you go either to Mr. Gosford's or to Mr. Bellamy's, but you must consider your wardrobe a little. You will remember that the last time on each occasion a dress was torn in pieces."

"But, mother, are not dresses intended to keep thorns from our legs; or, at any rate, isn't that *one* reason why we wear them?"

"Suppose it to be so, my dear, there is no reason why you should plunge about in thorns."

" No."

Catharine had a provoking way of saying "yes" or "no" when she wished to terminate a controversy. She stated her own opinion, and then, if objection was raised, at least by some people, her father and mother included, she professed agreement by a simple monosyllable, either because she was lazy, or because she saw that there was no chance of further profit in the discussion. It was irritating, because it was always clear she meant nothing. At this instant a servant opened the door, and Alice, a curly brown retriever, squeezed herself in, and made straight for Catharine, putting her head on Catharine's lap.

"Catharine, Catharine!" cried her mother, with a little scream, "she's dripping wet. Do pray, my child, think of the carpet."

But Catharine put her lips to Alice's face and kissed it deliberately, giving her a piece of cake.

" Mr. Gosford, my poor bitch has puppies—three of them—all as true as their mother, for we know the father."

"Ah!" replied Gosford, "you're lucky, then, Miss Catharine, for dogs, especially in a town——"

Mrs. Furze at this moment hastily rang the bell, making an unusual clatter with the crockery: Mr. Furze said the company must excuse him, and the three worthy farmers rose to take their departure.

CHAPTER II.

IT was Mr. Furze's custom on Sunday to go to sleep for an hour between dinner and tea upstairs in what was called the drawing-room, while Mrs. Furze sat and read, or said she read, a religious book. On hot summer afternoons Mr. Furze always took off his coat before he had his nap, and sometimes divested himself of his waistcoat. When the coat and waistcoat were taken off, Mrs. Furze invariably drew down the blinds. She had often remonstrated with her husband for appearing in his shirt-sleeves, and objected to the neighbours seeing him in this costume. There was a sofa in the room, but it was horsehair, with high ends both alike, not comfortable, which were covered with curious complications called anti-macassars, that slipped off directly they were touched, so that anybody who leaned upon them was engaged continually in warfare with them, picking them up from the floor or spreading them out again. There was also an easy chair, but it was not easy, for it matched the sofa in horsehair, and was so ingeniously contrived, that directly a person placed himself in it, it gently shot him forwards. Furthermore, it had special antimacassars, which were a work of art, and Mrs. Furze had warned Mr. Furze off them. " He would ruin them," she said, "if he put his head upon them." So a windsor chair with a high back was always carried by Mr. Furze upstairs after dinner, together with a common kitchen chair, and on these he slumbered. The room was never used, save on Sundays and when Mrs. Furze gave a tea-party. It overlooked the market-place, and, although on a Sunday afternoon the High Street was almost completely silent, Mrs. Furze liked to sit so near the window that she could peep out at the edge of the blind when she was not dozing. It is true no master nor mistress ever stirred at that hour, but every now and then a maidservant could be seen, and she was better than nothing for the purpose of criticism. A round table stood in the middle of the

room with a pink vase on it containing artificial
flowers, and on the mantelpiece were two other
pink vases and two great shells. Over the mantelpiece was a portrait of His Majesty King George
the Fourth in his robes, and exactly opposite
was a picture of the Virgin Mary, which was old
and valuable. Mr. Furze bought it at a sale with
some other things, and did not quite like it. It
savoured of Popery, which he could not abide ;
but the parson one day saw it and told Mrs. Furze
it was worth something ; whereupon she put it in
a new maple frame, and had it hung in a place
of honour second to that occupied by King
George, and so arranged that he and the Virgin
were always looking at one another. On the other
side of the room were a likeness of Mr. Eaton
in hunting array, with the dogs, and a mezzotint
of the Deluge.

Mr. Furze had just awaked on the Sunday
afternoon following the day of which the history
is partly given in the first chapter.

"My dear," said his wife, "I have been thinking a good deal of Catharine. She is not quite
what I could wish."

"No," replied Mr. Furze, with a yawn.

"To begin with, she uses bad language. I was really quite shocked yesterday to hear the extremely vulgar word, almost—almost—I do not know what to call it—profane, I may say, which she applied to her dog when talking of it to Mr. Gosford. Then she goes in the foundry; and I firmly believe that all the money which has been spent on her music is utterly thrown away."

"The thing is—what is to be done?"

"Now, I have a plan."

In order to make Mrs. Furze's plan fully intelligible, it may be as well to explain that, up to the year 1840, the tradesmen of Eastthorpe had lived at their shops. But a year or two before that date some houses had been built at the north end of the town and called "The Terrace." A new doctor had taken one, the brewer another, and a third had been taken by the grocer, a man reputed to be very well off, who not only did a large retail business, but supplied the small shops in the villages round.

"Well, my dear, what is your plan?"

"Your connection is extending, and you want more room. Now, why should you not move to the Terrace? If we were to go there, Catharine would be withdrawn from the society in which she at present mixes. You could not continue to give market dinners, and gradually her acquaintance with the persons whom you now invite would cease. I believe, too, that if we were in the Terrace Mrs. Colston would call on us. As the wife of a brewer, she cannot do so now. Then there is just another thing which has been on my mind for a long time. It is settled that Mr. Jennings is to leave, for he has accepted an invitation from the cause at Ely. I do not think we shall like anybody after Mr. Jennings, and it would be a good opportunity for us to exchange the chapel for the church. We have attended the chapel regularly, but I have always felt a kind of prejudice there against us, or at least against myself, and there is no denying that the people who go to church are vastly more genteel, and so are the service and everything about it—the vespers—the bells—somehow there is a respectability in it."

Mr. Furze was silent. At last he said, "It is a very serious matter. I must consider it in all its bearings."

It *was* a serious matter, and he did consider it—but not in all its bearings, for he did nothing but think about it, so that it enveloped him, and he could not put himself at such a distance that he could see its real shape. He was now well over fifty, and was the kind of person with whom habits become firmly fixed. He was fixed even in his dress. He always wore a white neckcloth, and his shirt was frilled—fashions which were already beginning to die out in Eastthorpe. His manner of life was most regular: breakfast at eight, dinner at one, tea at five, supper at nine with a pipe afterwards, was his unvarying round. He never left Eastthorpe for a holiday, and read no books of any kind. He was a most respectable member of a Dissenting congregation, but he was not a member of the church, and was never seen at the week-night services or the prayer-meetings. He went through the ceremony of family worship morning and evening, but he did not pray extempore, as did the elect, and contented himself with reading prayers from a book called "Family Devotions." The days were over for Eastthorpe when a man like Mr. Furze could be denounced, a man who paid his pew-rent regularly, and contributed to the missionary societies. The days were over when any expostulations could be addressed to him, or any attempts made to bring him within the fold, and Mr. Jennings therefore called on him, and religion was not mentioned. It may seem extraordinary that, without convictions based on any reasoning process, Mr. Furze's outward existence should have been so correct and so moral. He had passed through the usually stormy period of youth without censure. It is true he was married young, but before his marriage nobody had ever heard a syllable against him, and, after marriage, he never drank a drop too much, and never was guilty of a single dishonest action. Day after day passed by like all preceding days, in unbroken, level succession, without even the excitement of meeting-house emotion. Naturally, therefore, his wife's proposals made him uneasy, and even alarmed him. He shrank from them unconsciously, and yet his aversion was perfectly wise ; more so, perhaps, than any action for which he could have assigned a definite motive. With men like Mr. Furze the unconscious reason, which is partly a direction by past and forgotten experiences, and partly instinct, is often more to be trusted than any mental operation, strictly so-called. An attempt to use the mind actively on subjects which are too large, or with which it has not been accustomed to deal, is pretty nearly sure to mislead. He knew, or it knew, whatever we like to call it, that to break him from his surroundings meant that he himself was to be broken, for they were a part of him.

His wife attacked him again the next day. She was bent upon moving, and it is only fair to her to say that she did really wish to go for Catharine's sake. She loved the child in her own way, but she also wanted to go for many other reasons.

"Well, my dear, what have you to say to my little scheme?"

"How about my dinner and tea?"

"Come home to the Terrace. How far is it? Ten minutes' walk."

"An hour every day, in all weathers; and then there's the expense."

As to the expense, I am certain we should save in the long run, because you would not be expected to be continually asking people to meals."

"I am afraid that the business might suffer."

"Nonsense! In what way, my dear? Your attention will be more fixed upon it than it can be with the parlour always behind you."

There was something in that, and Mr. Furze was perplexed. He was not sufficiently well educated to know that something, and a great deal, too, can be said for anything, and he had not arrived at that callousness to argument which is the last result of culture.

"Yes, but I was thinking that perhaps if we leave off chapel and go to church some of our customers may not like it."

"Now, my good man, Furze, why you know you have as many customers who go to church as to chapel."

" Ah! but those who go to chapel may drop off."

" Why should they? We have plenty of customers who go to church. They don't leave us because we are Dissenters, and, as there are five times as many church people as Dissenters, your connection will be extended."

Mrs. Furze was unanswerable, but her poor husband, after all, was right. The change, when it took place, did not bring more people to the shop, and some left who were in the habit of coming. His dumb, dull presentiment was a prophecy, and his wife's logic was nothing but words.

" Then there are all the rooms here ; what shall we do with them ? "

" I have told you ; you want more space. Besides, you do not make half enough show. You ought to go with the times. Why, at Cross's at Cambridge their upstairs windows are hung full of spades and hoes and such things, and you can see it is business up to the garret. I should turn the parlour into a counting-house. It isn't the proper thing for you to be standing always at that poky little desk at the end of the counter with a pen behind your ear. Turn the parlour, I say, into a counting-house, and come out when Tom finds it necessary to call you. That makes a much better impression. The rooms above the drawing-room might be used for lighter goods, so as not to weight the floors too much."

Mr. Furze was not sentimental, but he shuddered. In the big front bedroom his father and he had been born. The first thing he could remember was having measles there, and watching day by day, when he was a little better, what went on in the street below. His brothers and sisters were also born there. He remembered how his mother was shut up there, and he was not allowed to enter; how, when he tried the door, Nurse Judkins came and said he must be a good boy and go away, and how he heard a little cry, and was told he had a new sister, and he wondered how she got in. In that room his father had died. He was very ill for a long time, and again Nurse Judkins came. He sat up with his father there night after night, and heard the church clock sound all the hours as the sick man lay waiting for his last. He rallied towards the end, and, being very pious, he made his son sit down by the bedside and read to him the ninety-first Psalm. He then blessed his boy in that very room, and five minutes afterwards he had rushed from it, choked with sobbing when the last breath was drawn. He did not relish the thought of taking down the old four-post bedstead and putting rakes and shovels in its place, but all he could say was—

"I don't quite fall in with it."

"*Why* not? Now, my dear, I will make a bargain with you. If you can assign a good reason, I will give it up; but, if you cannot, then, of course, we ought to go, because *I* have plenty of reasons for going. Nothing can be fairer than that."

Mr. Furze was not quite clear about the "ought," although it was so fair, but he was mute, and, after a pause, went into his shop. An accident decided the question. Catharine was the lightest sleeper in the house, notwithstanding her youth. Two nights after this controversy she awoke suddenly and smelt something burning. She jumped out of bed, flung her dressing-gown over her, opened her door, and found the landing full of smoke. Without a moment's hesitation she rushed out and roused her parents. They were both bewildered, and hesitated, ejaculating all sorts of useless things. Catharine was impatient.

"Now, then, not a second; upstairs through Jane's bedroom, out into the gutter, and through Hopkins's attic. You cannot go downstairs."

Still there was trembling and indecision.

"But the tin box," gasped Mr. Furze; "it is in the wardrobe. I must take it."

Catharine replied by literally driving them before her. They picked up the maid-servant, crept behind the high parapet, and were soon in safety. By this time the smoke was pouring up thick and fast, although no flame had appeared. Suddenly Catharine cried—

"But where is Tom?"

Tom was the assistant, and slept in an offset at the back. Underneath him was the kitchen, and beyond was the lower offset of the scullery. Catharine darted towards the window.

"Catharine!" shrieked her mother, "where are you going? You cannot; you are not dressed."

But she answered not a word, and had vanished

before anybody could arrest her. The smoke was
worse, and almost suffocating, but she wrapped
her face and nose in her woollen gown, and
reached Tom's door. He never slept with it
fastened, and the amazed youth was awakened by
a voice which he knew to be that of Miss Furze.
Escape by the way she had come was hopeless.
The staircase was now opaque. Fortunately
Tom's casement, instead of being in the side wall,
was at the end, and the drop to the scullery roof
was not above four feet. Catharine reached it
easily, and, Tom coming after her, helped her to
scramble down into the yard. The gate was
unbarred, and in another minute they were safe
with their neighbours. The town was now stirring,
and a fire-engine came, a machine which attended
fires officially, and squirted on them officially, but
was never known to do anything more, save to
make the road sloppy. The thick, brick party
walls of the houses adjoining saved them, but Mr.
Furze's house was gutted from top to bottom. It
was surrounded by a crowd the next day, which
stared unceasingly. The fire-engine still operated
on the ashes, and a great steam and smother arose.

A charred oak beam hung where it had always hung, but the roof had disappeared entirely, and the walls of the old bedchamber, which had seen so much of sweetness and of sadness, of the mysteries of love, birth, and death, lay bare to the sky and the street.

CHAPTER III.

THE stone bridge was deeply recessed, and in each recess was a stone seat. In the last recess but one, at the north end, and on the east side, there sat daily, some few years before 1840, a blind man, Michael Catchpole by name, selling shoelaces. He originally came out of Suffolk, but he had lived in Eastthorpe ever since he was a boy, and had worked for Mr. Furze's father. He was blinded by a splash of melted iron, and was suddenly left helpless, a widower with one boy, Tom, fifteen years old. His employer, the present Mr. Furze, did nothing for him, save sending him two bottles of lotion which he had heard were good for the eyes, and Mike for a time was confounded. His club helped him so long as he was actually suffering and confined to his house, but their pay did not last above six weeks. In these six weeks Mike learned much. He was brought face to face with a blank wall with the pursuer behind him—an experience which teaches more than most books, and he was on the point of doing what some of us have been compelled to do—that is to say, to recognise that the worst is inevitable, throw up the arms and bravely yield. But Mike also learned that this is not always necessary to a man with courage, and that very often escape lies in the last moment, the very last, when endurance seems no longer possible. His deliverance did not burst upon him in rainbow colours out of the sky complete. It was a very slow affair. He heard that an old woman had died who lived in Parker's Alley and sold old clothes, old iron, bottles, and such like trash. Parker's Alley was not very easy to find. Going up High Street from the bridge, you first turned to the right through Cross Street, and then to the right again down Lock Lane, and out of Lock Lane ran the alley, a little narrow gutter of a place, dark and squalid, paved with round stones, through which slops of all kinds perpetually percolated, and gave forth on the cleanest days a faint and sickening odour. Mike thought he could buy the stock for five shillings ; the rent was only half a crown a week, and with the help of Tom, a remarkably sharp boy, who could tell him in what condition the goods were which were offered him for purchase, he hoped he could manage to make way. It was a dreadful trial. The old woman had lived amongst all her property. She had eaten and drunk and slept amidst the dirty rags of Eastthorpe, but Mike could not. Fortunately the cottage was at the end of the alley. One window looked out on it, but the door was in a kind of indentation in it round the corner. On the right-hand side of the door was the room looking into the alley, and this Mike made his shop ; on the left was a little cupboard of a living-room. He kept the shop window open, so that no customer came through the doorway, and he begged some scarlet geranium cuttings, which, in due time, bloomed into brilliant colour on his sitting-room window-sill, proclaiming that from their possessor hope and delight in life had not departed. Alas ! the enterprise was a failure. Mike was no hand at driving hard bargains, and frequently, when the Jew from Cambridge came round to sweep up what Mike had been unable to sell in the town, he found himself the worse for his purchases. The unscalable wall was again in front of him, and his foe at his heels, closer than before, and raging for his blood. He had gone out one morning, Tom leading him, and was passing the bank, when the cashier ran out. Miss Foster, one of the maiden ladies, who it will be remembered, lived in the Abbey Close, had left a sovereign on the counter, and the cashier was exceedingly anxious to show his zeal by promptly returning it, for Miss Foster, it will also be remembered, was a daughter of a former partner in the bank, and still, as it was supposed, retained some interest in it. She had gone too far, however, and the cashier could not venture to leave his post and follow her. Knowing Mike and Tom perfectly well, he asked Mike to take the sovereign at once to the lady. He promptly obeyed, and was in time to restore it to its owner before it was missed. She was not particularly sensitive, but the sight of Mike and Tom standing at the hall entrance rather touched her, and she rewarded them with a shilling. She was also pleased to inquire how

Mike was getting on, and he briefly told her he
did not get on in any way, save as the most
unsuccessful happily get on, and so at last terminate their perplexities. Miss Foster, although
well-to-do, kept neither footman nor page, and a
thought struck her. She abhorred male servants,
but it was very often inconvenient to send her
maids on errands. She therefore suggested to
Mike that, if he and Tom could station themselves
within call, they would not only be useful, but
earn something of a livelihood. The bank wanted
an odd man occasionally, and she was sure that
other people in the town would employ him.
Accordingly Mike and Tom one morning established themselves in the recess of the bridge, after
having given notice to everybody who would be
likely to assist them, and Mike set up a stock of
boot-laces and shoe-laces of all kinds. He thus
managed to pick up a trifle. He wrapped sacking
round his legs to keep off the cold as he sat, and
had for a footstool a box with straw in it. He
also rigged up a little awning on some sticks to
keep off the sun and a shower, but of course when
a storm came he was obliged to retreat. He was

then allowed a shelter in the bank. The dust was a nuisance, for it was difficult to predict its capricious eddies, but he learnt its laws at last, and how to choose his station so as to diminish annoyance. At first he was depressed at the thought of sitting still for so many hours with nothing to do, but he was not left to himself so much as he anticipated. Two hours on the average were spent on errands; then there was his dinner: Tom talked to him; people went by and said a word or two, and thus he discovered that a foreseen trouble may look impenetrable, but when we near it, or become immersed in it, it is often at least semi-transparent, and even sometimes admits a ray of sunshine. Gradually his employment became sweet to him; he was a part of the town; he heard all its news; it was gentle with him; even the rough boys never molested him; he tamed a black kitten to stay with him, and a red ribbon and a bell were provided for her by a friend. When the kitten grew to be a cat she gravely watched under Mike's awning during his short absences with Tom, and not a soul ever touched the property she guarded. Country folk

who came to market on Saturday invariably
saluted Mike with their kind country friendliness,
and brought him all sorts of little gifts in the
shape of fruit, and even of something more substantial when a pig was killed. Thus with Mike
time and the hour wore out the roughest day.

Two years had now passed since his accident,
and Tom was about seventeen, when Miss Catharine crossed the bridge one fine Monday morning
in June with the servant, and, as was her wont,
stopped to have a word or two with her friend
Mike. Mike was always at his best on Monday
morning. Sunday was a day of rest, but he preferred Monday. It was a delight to him to hear
again the carts and the noise of feet, and to feel
that the world was alive once more. Sunday with
its enforced quietude and inactivity was a burden
to him.

" Well, Miss Catharine, how are you to-day ? "

" How did you know I was Miss Catharine ?   I
hadn't spoken."

" Lord, Miss, I could tell. Though it's only
about two years since I lost my eyes, I could
tell. I can make out people's footsteps. What

a lovely morning! What's going on now down below?"

Mike always took much interest in the wharves by the side of the river.

"Why, Barnes's big lighter is loading malt."

"Ah! what, the new one with the yellow band round it! that's a beautiful lighter, that is."

Mike had never seen it.

"What days do you dislike the most? Foggy, damp, dull, dark days?"

These foggy, damp, dull, dark days were particularly distasteful to Catharine.

"No, Miss, I can't say I do, for, you know, I don't see them."

"Cold, bitter days?"

"They are a bit bad; but somehow I earn more money on cold days than on any other; how it is I don't know."

"I hate the dust."

"Ah, now! that *is* unpleasant, but there again, Miss, I dodge it, and it's my belief that it wouldn't worry people half so much if they wouldn't look at it."

"How much have you earned this morning?"

" Not a penny yet, Miss, but it will come."

" I want two pairs of shoe-laces," and Miss Catharine, selecting two pairs, put down a four-penny-piece, part of her pocket-money, twice the market value of the laces, and tripped over the bridge. When she was at dinner with her father and mother that day she suddenly said—

" Father, didn't Mike Catchpole lose his sight in our foundry ? "

" Yes."

" Have you been talking with him again ? " interposed Mrs. Furze. " I wish you would not stop on the bridge as you do. It does not look nice for a girl like you to stay and gossip with Mike."

Catharine took no notice.

" Did you ever do anything for him ? "

" What an odd question ! " again interposed Mrs. Furze. " What should we do ? There was his club : besides, we sent him the lotion."

" Why cannot you take Tom as an apprentice ? "

" Because," said her father, " there is nobody to pay the premium ; you know what that means. When a boy is bound apprentice the master has a sum of money for teaching him the business."

Catharine did not quite comprehend, inasmuch as there were two boys in the back shop who were paid wages, and who were learning their trade. She was quiet for a few minutes, but presently returned to the charge.

" You *must* take Tom. Why shouldn't you give him what you give the other boys ? "

" Really, Catharine," said her mother, " why *must ?* "

" Must ! " cried the little miss—" yes, I say *must*, because Mike lost his eyes for you, and you've done nothing for him ; it's a shame."

" Catharine, Catharine! " said her father, but in accordance with his usual habit he said nothing more, and the mother, also in accordance with her usual habit, collapsed.

Miss Catharine generally, even at that early age, carried all before her, much to her own detriment. Her parents unfortunately were per-petually making a brief show of resistance and afterwards yielding. Frequently they had no pre-text for resistance, for Catharine was right and they were wrong. Consequently the child grew up accustomed to see everything bend to her own will,

and accustomed to believe that what she willed
was in accordance with the will of the universe—
not a healthy education, for the time is sure to
come when a destiny which will not bend stands
in the path before us, and we are convinced by the
roughest processes that what we purpose is to a
very small extent the purpose of Nature. The
shock then is serious, especially if the collision be
postponed till mature years. The parental opposition, such as it was, was worse than none, because
it enabled her to feel her strength. She continued
to press her point, and not only was victorious,
but was empowered to tell Mike that his son
would be taken into the foundry and paid five
shillings and sixpence a week—"a most special
case," as Mr. Furze told Mike, in order to stimu-
late his gratitude.

Mike was now able to find his way about by
himself, but before the date of the first chapter
in this history he had left the bridge, and Tom
supported him.

The morning after the fire beheld the Furze
family at breakfast with the hospitable Hopkins.
They had saved scarcely any clothes, but Tom

and his master were equipped from a ready-made
shop. The women had to remain indoors in
borrowed garments till they could be made pre-
sentable by the dressmaker. Mr. Furze was so un-
fitted to deal with events which did not follow in
anticipated, regular order, that he was bewildered.
He and Tom went out to look at the ruins, and everything which had to be done seemed to crowd in
upon him at once, one thing tumbling incessantly
over the other, and nothing staying long enough
before him to be settled. Although his business
had been fairly large, he had nothing of the
faculty of the captain or the manager, who can let
details alone and occupy himself with principles.
He had a stock of copper bolt-stave in the front
shop, and he poked about and pestered the men to
know if any of it could be found melted. Then it
occurred to him the next instant, and before the
inquiry about the bolt-stave could be answered,
that he had lost his account-books, and he began
to try to recollect what one of his principal
customers owed him. Before his memory was
fairly exercised on the subject it struck him that
the men in the foundry—which was untouched—

would not know what to do, and he hurried in, but came out again without leaving any directions. At last he became so confused that he would have broken down if Tom had not come to the rescue, and gently laid hold of his arm.

"Let us go into the Bell;" and into the Bell they went, into the large, empty coffee-room, very quiet at that time of the morning. "We are better here," said Tom, "if we want to know what we ought to do. The first thing is to write to the insurance company."

"Of course, of course!"

"We will do that at once; I will write the letter, and you sign it."

In less than ten minutes this stage of the business was passed.

"The next thing is to find a shop while they are rebuilding."

That was not quite so easy a matter. There was not one in the High Street to be let. At last an idea struck Tom.

"There is the Moot Hall—underneath it, I mean. We shall have to buy fittings, but I will have them so arranged that they will do for the new

building. All that is necessary is to obtain leave;
but we shall be sure to get it: only half of it is
wanted on market days, and that's the part that
isn't shut off. We'll then write to Birmingham
and Sheffield about the stock. We'd better have
a few posters stuck about at once, saying that
business will be carried on in the Hall for the
present."

Mr. Furze saw the complexity unravel itself,
and the knot in his head began to loosen, but he
did not quite like to reflect that he owed his relief
to Tom, and that Tom had seen his agitation.
Accordingly, when a proof of the poster was
brought, he was the master, most particularly the
master, and observed with much dignity and
authority that it ought not to have been set up
without the benefit of his revision; that it would
not do by any means as it stood, and that it had
better be left with him.

Mr. and Mrs. Hopkins insisted upon continuing
their hospitality until a new home could be found,
and Mrs. Furze urged her project of the Terrace
with such eagerness, that at last her husband
consented.

" I think," said Mrs. Furze, when the debate was concluded, " that Catharine had better go away for a short time until we are settled in the Terrace and the shop is rebuilt. She would not be of much use in the new house, and would only knock herself up."

That was not Mrs. Furze's reason. She had said nothing to Catharine, but she instinctively dreaded her hostility to the scheme. Mr. Furze knew that was not Mrs. Furze's reason, but he accepted it. Mrs. Furze knew it was not her own reason, but she also accepted it, and believed it to be the true reason. Such contradictions are quite possible in that mystery of mysteries, the human soul.

" My dear Catharine," quoth her mother that evening, " you look worried and done up. No wonder, considering what we have gone through. A change would do you good, and you had better go and stay with your aunt at Ely till we have a roof of our own over our heads once more. She will be delighted to see you."

Catharine particularly objected to her aunt at Ely. She was a maiden lady and elder sister to

Mrs. Furze. She had a small annuity, had turned herself into a most faithful churchwoman, and went to live at Ely because it was cheap and a cathedral city. Every day, morning and afternoon, was Aunt Matilda to be seen at the cathedral services, and frequently she was the only attendant, save the choir and officials.

"Why do you want me out of the way?" said Catharine, dismissing without the least notice the alleged pretext.

"I have told you, my dear."

"I cannot go to Ely. If you wish me to go anywhere, I will go to Mrs. Bellamy's."

"My dear, that is not a sufficient change for you. Ely is a different climate, and I cannot consent to quartering you on a stranger for so long."

"Mrs. Bellamy will not object. Will the new house be like the old one?"

"Well, really, my dear, nothing at present is quite determined; no doubt your father will take the opportunity of making a few improvements."

"My bedroom, I hope, will be what it was before, and in the same place."

"Oh, I—I trust there will be no serious

alteration, except what—what will be agreeable
to us all, but your father is so much bothered
now; perhaps you will have a room which is a
little larger, but I really do not know. I cannot
say anything; how can you *expect* me to say anything just at present, my dear child?"

Again there was the same contradiction. Mrs.
Furze knew this was wrong, but she believed it
was right. There was, however, a slight balance
in favour of what she knew against what she
believed, and she hastened to appease her conscience by a mental promise that, as soon as
possible, she would tell Catharine that, upon full
consideration, they had determined, &c., &c. That
would put everything straight morally. Had
Catharine put her question yesterday—so Mrs.
Furze argued—the answer now given would have
been perfectly right. She was doing nothing more
than giving a reply which was a trifle in arrear
of the facts, and, if she rectified it at the earliest
date, the impropriety would be nothing. It is
sometimes thought that it is those who habitually
speak the truth who are most easily deceived. It
is not quite so. If the deceivers are not entirely

deceived, they profess acquiescence, and perpetual acquiescence induces half-deception. It is, perhaps, more correct to say that the word deception has no particular meaning for them, and implies a standard which is altogether inapplicable. There is a tacit agreement through all society to say things which nobody believes, and that being the constitution under which we live, it is absurd to talk of truth or falsity in the strict sense of the terms. A thing is true when it is in accordance with the system and on a level with it, and false when it is below it. Every now and then at rarest intervals a creature is introduced to us who speaks the veritable reality and wakes in us the slumbering conviction of universal imposture. We know that he is not as other men are; we look into his eyes and see that they penetrate us through and through, but we cannot help ourselves, and we jabber to him as we jabber to the rest of the world. It was ridiculous that her mother should talk as she did to Catharine. Mrs. Furze was perfectly aware that she was not deluding her daughter; but she assumed that the delusion was complete.

" Well, mother, I say I cannot go to Ely."

Catharine again had her own way. She went to Mrs. Bellamy's, and Mrs. Furze, after having told Mrs. Bellamy what was going to happen, begged her not to say anything to Catharine about it.

CHAPTER IV.

MR. BELLAMY'S farm of Westchapel—
Chapel Farm it was usually called—
lay about half a mile from Lampson's Ford, and
about five miles from Eastthorpe. The road from
Eastthorpe running westerly and parallel with the
river, at a distance of about a mile from it sends
out at the fourth milestone a by-road to the
south, which crosses the river by a stone bridge,
and there is no doubt that before the bridge
existed there was a ford, and that there was
also a chapel hard by where people probably
commended their souls to God before taking
the water. In the angle formed by the main
road, the lane, and the river, lay Chapel Farm.
The house stood on a gentle slope, just enough
to lift it above the range of the worst of winter
floods, and faced the south. It was not in the

lane, but on a kind of private road or cart-track which issued from it; went through a gate and under a hedge; expanded itself in an open space of carefully weeded gravel just opposite the front door, and became a more insignificant and much rougher track on the other side, passing by the stacks into the field, and finally disappearing altogether. From the hand-post on the main road to the gate was half a mile, and from the gate to the farm nearly another half-mile. In driving from Chapel Farm you feel, when you reach the gate, you are in the busy world again, and when you reach the hand-post and turn to Eastthorpe you are in the full tide of life, although not a soul is to be seen. Opposite the house were the farm-buildings and the farm-yard. The gate to the right of the farm-buildings led into the meadow, and thus anybody sitting in the front rooms could see the barges slowly and silently towed from the sea to the uplands and back again, the rising ground beyond, and so on to Thingleby, whose little spire just emerged above the horizon. The river, deep and sluggish for the most part, was fringed with willows on the side opposite the towing-path. At the bridge, just where the ford used to be, it was broken into shallows, over which the stream slipped faster, and here and there there were not above two or three feet of water, so that sometimes the barges were almost aground. The farmhouse was not quite ideal. It was plain red brick, now grey and lichen-covered, about a hundred years old; the windows were white-painted, with heavy frames, and the only attempt at ornament was a kind of porch over the front door, supported by brackets, but with no sides to it. Nevertheless, it had its charms. Save on the northern side, where it was backed by the huge elms in the home-field, it lay bare to the winds, breezy, airy, full of light. In summer the front door was always open, and even when it was shut in cold weather no knocker was ever used. If a visitor came by daylight he was always seen, and if after dark he was heard. The garden, which lay on the west side of the house and at the back, was rather warm in hot weather, but was delicious. Under the wall on the north side the apricot and Orleans plum ripened well, and round to the right was the dairy, always cool, sweet, and clean, with the big elder trees before the barred window.

The mistress of the house, Mrs. Bellamy, was not a very robust woman. She was generally ailing, but never very seriously ill. She had had two children, but they had both died. Mrs. Bellamy's mind, unoccupied with parental cares, with politics, or with literature, let itself loose upon her house, her dairy, and her fowls. She established a series of precautions to prevent dirt, and the precautions themselves became objects to be protected. There was a rough scraper intervening on behalf of the black-leaded scraper; there was a large mat to preserve the mat beyond it; and although a drugget covered the stair carpet, Mrs. Bellamy would have been sorely vexed if she had found a footmark upon it. If a friend was expected she put some straw outside the garden gate, and she asked him in gentle tones when he dismounted if he would kindly "just take the worst off" there. The kitchen was scoured and scrubbed till it was fleckless. It was theoretically the living-room, and a defence for the parlour, but it also was defended in its turn like the scraper, and the back kitchen, which had a fireplace, was used for cooking, the fire in the state kitchen not being lighted in summer time. Partly Mrs. Bellamy's excessive neatness was due to the need of an occupation. She brooded much, and the moment she had nothing to do she became low-spirited and unwell. Partly also it was due to a touch of poetry. She polished her verses in beeswax and turpentine, and sought on her floors and tables for that which the poet seeks in Eden or Atlantis. It must not be imagined that because she was so particular she was stingy. She was one of the most open-handed creatures that ever breathed. She loved plenty. The jug was always full to overflowing with beer, and the dishes were always heaped up with good things, so that nobody was ever afraid of robbing his neighbour.

Catharine was never weary of Chapel Farm. She was busy from morning to night, and the living creatures on it were her especial delight Naturally, as is the case with all country girls the circumference of her knowledge embraced a region which a town matron would have veiled from her daughters with the heaviest curtains.

"How's the foal going on?" said Mrs. Bellamy to her husband one evening when he came in to supper.

"Oh, the foal's all right; he'll be just like his father—just the same broad hind-quarters. Lord! we shall hardly get him into the shafts. You remember, Miss Catharine, as I showed you what extrornary quarters King Tom had when he came here? It is a curious thing, there ain't one of his foals that hasn't got that mark of him. I allus likes a horse, I do, that leaves his mark strong. If you pay pretty heavy you ought to have something for your money. The mother, though, is in a bad way : my belief is she'll have milk-fever."

"That mare never seemed healthy to me," said Catharine.

"No, she was brought up anyhow. When she was about a fortnight old her mother died. They didn't know how to manage her, and half starved her."

" I don't believe in starvin' creatures when they are young," said Mrs. Bellamy, who was herself a very small eater.

" Nor I neither, and yet that mare, although, as you say, Miss Catharine, she was never healthy, has the most wonderful pluck, as you know. I remember once I had two ton o' muck in the waggon, and we were stuck. Jack and Blossom couldn't stir it, and, after a bit, chucked up. I put in Maggie—you should have seen her! She moved it, a'most all herself, aye, as far as from here to the gate, and then of course the others took it up. That's blood! What a thing blood is!—you may load it, but you can't break it. Never a touch of the whip would she stand, and yet it's quite true she isn't right, and never was. Maybe the foal will be like her; the shape goes after the father mostly, but the sperrit and temper after the mother."

The next morning Maggie was worse. Catharine was in the stable as soon as anybody was stirring, and the poor creature was trembling violently. She was watched with the most tender care, and when she became too weak to stand to eat or drink she was slung with soft bands and pads. Her groans were dreadful. After about a week of cruel misery she died. It was evening, and Catharine sat down and looked at what was left of her friend. She had never before even partly realised what death meant. She was too young to feel its full force. The time was yet to come when death would mean despair—when the insolubility of the problem would induce carelessness to all other problems and their solution. Furthermore, this was only a horse. Still, the contrast struck her between the corpse before her and Maggie with her bright eyes and vivid force. What had become of all that strength ; what had become of *her ?*—and the girl mused, as countless generations had mused before her. Then there was the pathos of it. She thought of the brave animal which she had so often seen, apparently for the mere love of difficulty, struggling as if its sinews would crack. She thought of its glad recognition when she came into the stable, and of its evident affection, half human, or perhaps wholly human, and imprisoned in a form which did not permit full expression.

She looked at its body as it lay there extended, quiet, pleading as it were against the doom of man and of beast, and tears came to her eyes as she noted the appeal—tears not altogether of sorrow, but partly of revolt.

Mr. Bellamy came in.

"Ah, Miss Catharine, I don't wonder at it. There's many a human as I should less have missed than Maggie. I can't make out at times why we should love the beasts so as perish."

"Perhaps they don't."

"Really, Miss, of course they do. What's the Lord to do with all the dead horses and cows?"

Catharine thought, "Or with the dead men and women," but she said nothing. The subject was new to her. She took her scissors and cut off a wisp of Maggie's beautiful mane, twisted it up, put it carefully in a piece of paper, and placed it in a little pocket-book which she always carried The next morning as soon as it was daylight a man came over from Eastthorpe; Maggie was hoisted into a cart, her legs dangling down outside, and was driven away to be converted into food for dogs.

One of Catharine's favourite haunts was a meadow by the bridge. She was not given to reading, but she liked a stroll ; and, as there were plenty of rats, the dog enjoyed the stroll too. Not a week after Maggie's death she had wandered to this point without her usual companion. A barge had gone down just before she arrived, and for some reason or other had made fast to the bank about a quarter of a mile below her on the side opposite to the towing-path. She sat down under a willow with her face to the water and back to the sun, for it was very hot, and in a few minutes she was half dozing. Suddenly she started, and one of the bargemen stood close by her."

"Hullo, my beauty ! Why you was asleep ! Wot's the time ? "

"I haven't a watch."

"Haven't a watch ! Now that's a shame ; if you was mine, my love, you should 'ave one o' gold."

"It is time I was at home," said Catharine, rising with as much presence of mind as she could muster ; "and I should think it must be your dinner-hour."

"Damn my dinner-hour, when I've got the chance of sittin' alongside a gal with sich eyes as yourn, my beauty. Why, you make me all of a tremble. Sit down for a bit."

Catharine moved away, but the bargee caught her round the waist.

"Sit down, I tell yer, jist for a minute. Who's a-goin' to hurt yer?"

It was of no use to resist, and she did not scream. She sat down, and his arm relaxed its hold to pick up his pipe which had fallen on the other side. Instantly, without a second's hesitation, she leaped up, and, before his heavy bulk could lift itself, she had turned and rushed along the bank. Had she made for the bridge, he would have over-taken her in the lane, but she went the other way. About fifty yards down the stream, and in the direction of Chapel Farm, was a deep hole in the river bed, about five feet wide. On the other side of it there were not more than eighteen inches of water at any point. Catharine knew that hole well, as the haunt of the jack and the perch. She reached it, cleared it at a bound, and alighted on the bit of shingle just beyond it. Her pursuer came up and stared at her silently, with his mouth half open.   Just at that moment the distant sound of wheels was heard, and he slowly sauntered back to his barge.   Catharine boldly waded over the intervening shallows, and was across just as the cart reached the top of the bridge, but her shoes remained behind her in the mud.   It proved to be her father's cart, and to contain Tom, who had been over to Thingleby that morning to see what chance there was of getting any money out of a blacksmith who was largely in Mr. Furze's debt.   He saw there was something wrong and dismounted.

"Why, Miss Catharine, you are all wet !   What is the matter ? "

" I slipped down."

She could not tell the truth, although usually so straightforward.   Tom looked at her inquiringly as if he was not quite sure, but there was something in her face which forbade further investigation.

" You've lost your shoes ; you cannot walk home ; will you let me give you a lift to Chapel Farm ? "

"They do not matter a straw : it is grass nearly the whole way."

"I'll fish them out, if you will show me where they are."

"Carried down by this time ever so far."

"But you will hurt your feet ; it isn't all grass ; you had better get in."

She thought suddenly of the bargee again, and reflected that the barge might still be moored where it was an hour ago.

"Very well, then, I will go."

She essayed to put her foot upon the step, but the mud on her stocking was greasy, and she fell backwards. Tom caught her in his arms, and a strange thrill passed through him when he felt that the whole weight of her body rested on him. Many a man there is who can call to mind, across forty years, a silly passage like this in his life. His hair has whitened ; all passion ought long ago to have died out of him ; thousands of events of infinitely greater consequence have happened ; he has read much in philosophy and religion, and has forgotten it all, and a slip on the ice when skating together, or a stumble on the stair, or the pressure of a hand prolonged just for a second in parting, is felt with its original intensity, and the thought of it drives warm blood once more through the arteries.

"Let me get in first," said Tom, putting some straw on the step.

He got into the cart, and he gently pulled her up, relinquishing her very carefully, and, in fact, not until after his assistance was no longer needed.

"How *did* you manage it?"

"You know how these things happen: it was all over in a minute: how are father and mother?"

"They are very well,"

There was a pause for a minute or two.

"Well, how are things going on at East-thorpe?"

"Oh, pretty well; the building is three parts done. I don't think, Miss Catharine, you'll ever go back to the old spot again."

"What do you mean?"

"I don't think your father and mother will leave the Terrace."

"Very likely," she replied, decisively. "It will

be better, perhaps, that they should not. I am sure that whatever they do will be quite right."

"Of course, Miss Catharine, but *I* shall be sorry. I wish my bedroom could have been built up again between the old walls. In that bedroom you saved my life."

"Rubbish! Even suppose *I* had done it, as you say, I should have done just the same for my silk-worms, and then, somehow when I do a thing on a sudden like that, I always feel as if *I* had not done it. I am sure I didn't do it."

The last few words were spoken in a strangely different tone, much softer and sweeter.

"I don't quite understand."

"I mean," said Catharine, speaking slowly, as if half surprised at what had occurred to her, and half lost in looking at it—"I mean that I do not a bit reflect at such times upon what I do. It is as if something or somebody took hold of me, and, before I know where I am, the thing is done, and yet there is no something nor somebody—at least, so far as I can see. It is wonderful, for after all it is I who do it."

Tom looked intently at her. She seemed to be

taking no notice of him and to be talking to herself. He had never seen her in that mood before,
although he had often seen her abstracted and
heedless of what was passing. In a few moments
she recovered herself, and the usual every-day
accent returned with an added hardness.

"Here we are at Chapel Farm. Mind you
say nothing to father or mother; it will only
frighten them."

Mrs. Bellamy came to the gate.

"Lor', bless the child! wherever have you
been ? "

"Slipped into the water and left my shoes
behind me, that's all ; " and she ran indoors,
jumping from mat to mat, and without even so
much as bidding Tom good-bye, who rode home,
not thinking much about his business, but lost
in a muddle of most contradictory presentations,
a constant glimmer of Catharine's ankles, wonder-
ment at her accident—was it all true ?—the
strange look when she disclaimed the honour of
his rescue and expounded her philosophy, and
the fall between his shoulders. When he slept,
his sleep was usually dreamless, but that night

he dreamed as he hardly ever dreamed before. He perpetually saw the foot on the step, and she was slipping into his arms continually, until he awoke with the sun.

CHAPTER V.

CATHARINE went home, or rather to the Terrace, soon afterwards, and found that there was no intention of removing to the High Street, although, notwithstanding their three months' probation in the realms of respectability, Mrs. Colston had not called, and Mrs. Furze was beginning to despair. The separation from the chapel was nearly complete. It had been done by degrees. On wet days Mrs. Furze went to church because it was a little nearer, and Mr. Furze went to chapel; then Mrs. Furze went on fine days, and, after a little interval, Mr. Furze went on a fine day. A fund had been set going to "restore" the church: the heavy roof was to be removed, and a much lighter and handsomer roof covered with slate was to be substituted; the stonework of many of the windows, which the

rector declared had begun to show "signs of
incipient decay," was to be cut out and replaced
with new, so as to make, to use the builder's
words, "a good job of it," and a memorial window
was to be put in near the great west window with
its stained glass, the Honourable Mr. Eaton
having determined upon this mode of commemo-
rating the services of his nephew, Lieutenant Eaton,
who had died of dysentery in India, brought on by
inattention to tropical rules of eating and drinking,
particularly the latter. Oliver Cromwell, it was
said, had stabled his horses in the church. This,
however, is doubtful, for the quantity of stable
accommodation he must have required throughout the country, to judge from vergers and guide-
books, must have been much larger than his armies
would have needed, if they had been entirely
composed of cavalry ; and the evidence is not
strong that his horses were so ubiquitous. It was
further affirmed that, during the Cromwellian
occupation, the west window was mutilated ; but
there was also a tradition that, in the days of
George the Third, there were complaints of din-
giness and want of light, and that part of the

stained glass was removed and sold. Anyhow, there was stained glass in the Honourable Mr. Eaton's mansion wonderfully like that at East-thorpe. It was now proposed to put new stained glass in the defective lights. Some of the more advanced of the parishioners, including the parson and the builder, thought the old glass had better all come out, "the only way to make a good job of it"; but at an archidiaconal visitation the archdeacon protested, and he was allowed to have his own way. Then there was the warming, and this was a great difficulty, because no natural exit for the pipe could be found. At last it was settled to have three stoves, one at the west end of the nave, and one in each transept. With regard to the one in the nave there was no help for it but to bore a hole through the wall. The builder undertook " to give the pipe outside a touch of the Gothic, so that it wouldn't look bad," and as for the other stoves, there were two windows just handy. By cutting out the head of Matthew in one, and that of Mark in another, the thing was done, and, as Mrs. Colston observed, " the general confused effect remained the same." There were one or two other improvements, such as pointing all over outside, also strongly recommended by the builder, and the shifting some of the tombs, and repairing the tracery, so that altogether the sum to be raised was considerable. Mrs. Colston was one of the collectors, and Mrs. Furze called on her after two months' residence in the Terrace, and intimated her wish to subscribe. Mrs. Colston took the money very affably, but still she did not return the visit.

Meanwhile Mrs. Furze was doing everything she could to make herself genteel. The Terrace contained about a dozen houses; the two in the centre were higher than the rest, and above them, flanked by a large scroll at either end, were the words, "THE TERRACE," moulded out of the stucco; up to each door was a flight of stone steps; before each front window on the dining-room floor and the floor above was a balcony protected by cast-iron filigree work, and between each house and the road was a little piece of garden surrounded by a dwarf wall and arrow-head railings. Mrs. Furze's old furniture had, nearly all, been discarded or sold, and two new carpets had

been bought. The one in the dining-room was
yellow and chocolate, and the one upstairs in the
drawing-room was a lovely rose-pattern, with large
full-blown roses nine inches in diameter in blue
vases. The heavy chairs had disappeared, and
nice light elegant chairs were bought, insufficient,
however, for heavy weights, for one of Mrs. Furze's
affluent customers being brought to the Terrace as
a special mark of respect, and sitting down with a
flop, as was his wont, smashed the work of art like
card-board and went down on the floor with a
curse, vowing inwardly never again to set foot in
Furze's Folly, as he called it. The pictures, too,
were all renewed. The "Virgin Mary" and
"George the Fourth" went upstairs to the spare
bedroom, and some new oleographs, "a rising
art," Mrs. Furze was assured, took their places.
They had very large margins, gilt frames, and
professed to represent sunsets, sunrises, and full
moons, at Tintern, Como, and other places not
named, which Mrs. Furze, in answer to inquiries,
always called "the Continent."

Mr. Furze had had a longish walk one morning,
and was rather tired. When he came home to

dinner he found the house upset by one of its periodical cleanings, and consequently dinner was served upstairs, and not in the half-underground breakfast-room, as it was called, which was the real living-room of the family. Mr. Furze, being late and weary, prolonged his stay at home till nearly four o'clock, and, notwithstanding a rebuke from Mrs. Furze, insisted on smoking his pipe in the dining-room. Presently he took off his coat and put his feet on a chair, Sunday fashion.

"My dear," said his wife, "I don't want to interfere with your comfort, but don't you think you might give up that practice of sitting in your shirt-sleeves now we have moved?"

"Why because we've moved?" interposed Catharine.

"Catharine, I did not address you; you have no tact, you do not understand."

"Coat doesn't smell so much of smoke," replied Mr. Furze, giving, of course, any reason but the true reason.

"My dear, if that is the reason, put on another coat, or, better still, buy a proper coat and a smoking-cap. Nothing could be more appropriate than some of those caps we saw at the restoration bazaar."

" Really, mother, would you like to see father in a velvet jacket and one of those red-tasselled things on his head? I prefer the shirt-sleeves."

" No doubt you do ; you are a Furze, every inch of you."

There is no saying to what a height the quarrel would have risen if a double knock had not been heard. A charwoman was in the passage with a pail of water and answered the door at once, before she could be cautioned. In an instant she appeared, apron tucked up.

" Mrs. Colston, mum," and in Mrs. Colston walked.

Mrs. Furze made a dash at her husband's clay pipe, forgetting that its destruction would not make matters better ; but she only succeeded in upsetting the chair on which his legs rested, and in the confusion he slipped to the ground.

" Oh, Mrs. Colston, I am so sorry you have taken us by surprise; our house is being cleaned ; pray walk upstairs—but oh dear, now I recollect, the drawing-room is also turned out ; what *will* you do, and the smell of the smoke, too ! "

" Pray do not disconcert yourself," replied the brewer's wife, patronisingly ; " I do not mind the smoke, at least for a few minutes."

Mrs. Colston herself had objected strongly to calling on Mrs. Furze, but Mr. Colston had urged it as a matter of policy, with a view to Mr. Furze's contributions to Church revenues.

" I have come purely on a matter of business, Mrs. Furze, and will not detain you."

Mr. Furze had retreated into a dark corner, and was putting on his waistcoat with his back to his distinguished guest. Catharine sat at the window quite immovable. Suddenly Mrs. Furze bethought herself she ought to introduce her husband and daughter.

" My husband and daughter, Mrs. Colston."

Mr. Furze turned half round, put his other arm into his waistcoat, and bowed. He had, of course, spoken to her scores of times in his shop, but he was not supposed to have seen her till that minute. Catharine rose, bowed, and sat down again.

"Take a chair, Mrs. Colston, take a chair," said

Mr. Furze, although he had again turned towards the curtain, and was struggling with his coat. Mrs. Furze, annoyed that her husband had anticipated her, pulled the easy-chair forward.

" I am afraid I deprived you of your seat," said the lady, alluding, as Mrs. Furze had not the slightest doubt, to his tumble.

" Not a bit, ma'am, not a bit," and he moved towards Catharine, feeling very uncomfortable, and not knowing what to do with his hands and legs.

" We are so much obliged to you, Mrs. Furze, for your subscription to the restoration fund. We find that a new pulpit is much required ; the old pulpit, you will remember, is much decayed in parts, and will be out of harmony with the building when it is renovated. Young Mr. Cawston, who is being trained as an architect—the builder's son, you know—has prepared a design which is charming, and the ladies wish to make the new pulpit a present solely from themselves." The smoke got into Mrs. Colston's throat, and she coughed. " We want you, therefore, to help us."

" With the greatest pleasure."

" Then how much shall I say? Five pounds ? "

" Would you allow me just to look at the sub-scription list? " interposed Mr. Furze, humbly; but before it could be handed to him Mrs. Furze had settled the matter.

" Five pounds—oh, yes, certainly, Mrs. Colston. Mr. Cawston is, I believe, a young man of talent ? "

" Undoubtedly, and he deserves encouragement. It must be most gratifying to his father to see his son endeavouring to raise himself from a com-paratively humble occupation and surroundings into something demanding ability and education, from a mere trade into a profession."

Catharine shifted uneasily, raised her eyes, and looked straight at Mrs. Colston, but said nothing.

Meanwhile Mr. Furze was perusing the list with both elbows on his knees. The difficulty with his hands and legs increased. He was conscious to a most remarkable degree that he had them, and yet they seemed quite foreign members of his body which he could not control.

" Well, ma'am, I think I must be going. I'll bid you good-bye."

"I have finished my errand, Mr. Furze, and I must be going too."

"Oh, pray, do not go yet," said Mrs. Furze, hoping, in the absence of her husband, to establish some further intimacy. Mr. Furze shook Mrs. Colston's hand with its lemon - coloured glove and departed. Catharine noticed that Mrs. Colston looked at the glove—for the ironmonger had left a mark on it—and that she wiped it with her pocket-handkerchief.

"I wish to ask," said Mrs. Furze, in her mad anxiety to secure Mrs. Colston, "if you do not think a new altar-cloth would be acceptable. I should be so happy—I will not say to give one myself, but to undertake the responsibility, and to contribute my share. The old altar-cloth will look rather out of place."

"Thank you, Mrs. Furze; I am sure I can answer at once. It will be most acceptable. You will not, I presume, object to adopting the design of the committee? We will send you a correct pattern. We have thought about the matter for some time, but had at last determined to wait indefinitely on the ground of the expense."

The expense ! Poor Mrs. Furze had made her proposal on the spur of the moment. She, in her ignorance, had not thought an altar-cloth a very costly affair, and now she remembered that she had no friends who were not Dissenters. Moreover, to be on the committee was the object of her ambition, and it was clear that not only had nobody thought of putting her on it, but that she was to pay and take its directions.

" I believe," continued Mrs. Colston, " that the altar-cloth which we had provisionally adopted can be had in London for £20."

A ring at the front bell during this interesting conversation had not been noticed. The charwoman, still busy with broom and pail outside, knocked at the door with a knock which might have been given with the broom-handle and announced another visitor.

" Mrs. Bellamy, mum."

Catharine leaped up, rushed to meet her friend, caught her round the neck, and kissed her eagerly.

" Well, Miss Catharine, glad to see you looking so well ; still kept the colour of Chapel Farm.

This is the first time I've seen you in your new house, Mrs. Furze. I had to come over to East-thorpe along with Bellamy, and I said I *must* go and see my Catharine, though—and her mother—though they *do* live in the Terrace, but I couldn't get Bellamy to come—no, he said the Terrace warn't for him; he'd go and smoke a pipe and have something to drink at your old shop, or rather your new shop, but it's in the old place in the High Street—leastways if you keep any baccy and whiskey there now—and he'd call for me with the gig, and I said as I knew my Catharine—her mother—would give me a cup of tea ; and, Miss Catharine, you remember that big white hog as you used to look at always when you went out into the meadow ?—well, he's killed, and I know Mr. Furze likes a bit of good, honest, country pork—none of your nasty town-fed stuff—you never know what hogs eat in towns—so Bellamy has a leg about fourteen pounds in the gig, but I thought I'd bring you about two or three pounds of the sausages myself in my basket here," and Mrs. Bellamy pointed to a basket she had on her arm. She paused and became aware that there was a stranger sitting near the fireplace. "But you've got a visitor here; p'r'aps I shall be in the way."

"In the way!" said Catharine. "Never, never; give me your basket and your bonnet; or stay, Mrs. Bellamy, I will go upstairs with you, and you shall take off your things."

And so, before Mrs. Furze had spoken a syllable, Catharine and Mrs. Bellamy marched out of the room.

"Who is that—that person?" said Mrs. Colston. "I fancy I have seen her before. She seems on intimate terms with your daughter."

"She is a farmer's wife, of humble origin, at whose house my daughter — lodged — for the benefit of her health."

"I must bid you good-day, Mrs. Furze. If you will kindly send a cheque for the five pounds to me, the receipt shall be returned to you in due course, and the drawing of the altar-cloth shall follow. I can assure you of the committee's thanks."

Mrs. Furze recollected she ought to ring the bell, but she also recollected the servant could not appear in proper costume. Accordingly she opened the dining-room door herself.

"Let me move that ere pail, mum, or you'll tumble over it," said the charwoman to Mrs. Colston, "and p'r'aps you won't mind steppin' on this side of the passage, 'cause that side's all wet. 'Ere, Mrs. Furze, don't you come no further, I'll open the front door;" and this she did.

Mrs. Furze felt rather unwell, and went to her bedroom, where she sat down, and, putting her face on the bedclothes, gave way to a long fit of hysterical sobbing. She would not come down to tea, and excused herself on the ground of sickness. Catharine went up to her mother and inquired what was the matter, but was repulsed.

"Nothing is the matter—at least, nothing you can understand. I am very unwell; I am better alone; go down to Mrs. Bellamy."

"But, mother, it will do you good to be down-stairs. Mrs. Bellamy will be so glad to see you, and she was so kind to me; it will be odd if you don't come."

"Go *away*, I tell you; I am best by myself; I can endure in solitude; you cannot comprehend these nervous attacks, happily for you ; go *away*, and enjoy yourself with Mrs. Bellamy and your sausages."

Catharine had had some experience of these nervous attacks, and left her mother to herself. Mrs. Bellamy and Catharine consequently had tea alone, Mr. Furze remaining at his shop that afternoon, as he had been late in arrival.

" Sorry mother's so poorly, Catharine. Well, how do you like the Terrace ? "

" I hate it. I detest every atom of the filthy, stuck-up, stuccoed hovel. I hate——" Catharine was very excited, and it is not easy to tell what she might have said if Mrs. Bellamy had not interrupted her.

" Now, Miss Catharine, don't say that ; it's a bad thing to hate what we must put up with. You never heard, did you, as Bellamy had a sister a good bit older than myself ? She *was* a tartar, and no mistake. She lived with Bellamy and kept house for him, and when we married, Bellamy said she must stay with us. She used to put on him as you never saw, but he, somehow, seemed never to mind it ; some men don't feel such things, and some do, but most on 'em don't when it's a woman, but I think a woman's worse. Well, what was I saying?—she put on me just in the same way and come between me and the servant-girl and the men, and when I told them to go and do one thing, went and told them to do another, and I was young, and I thought when I was married I was going to be mistress, and she called me 'a chit' to her brother, and I mind one day I went upstairs and fell on my knees and cried till I thought my heart would break, and I said, ' O my God, when will it please Thee to take that woman to Thyself!' Now to wish anybody dead is bad enough, but to ask the Lord to take 'em is awful; but then it was so hard to bear 'cause I couldn't say nothing about it, and I'm one of them as can't keep myself bottled up like ginger-beer. You don't remember old Jacob? He had been at Chapel Farm in Bellamy's father's time, and always looked on Bellamy as his boy, and used to be very free with him, notwithstanding he was the best creature as ever lived. He took a liking to me, and I needn't say that, liking of me, he didn't like Bellamy's sister. Well, I came

down, and I went out of doors to get a bit of fresh
air—for I'm always better out of doors—and I
went up by the cart-shed, and being faint a bit,
sat down on the waggon shafts. Old Jacob, he
came by ; I can see him now ; it was just about
Michaelmas time, a-getting dark after tea, though
I hadn't had any, and he said to me, 'Hullo,
missus, what are you here for ? and you've been
a-cryin',' for I had my face toward the sky and
was looking at it. I never spoke. 'I know what's
the matter with you,' says he ; 'do you think
I don't ? Now if you go on chafing of yourself, you'll worrit yourself into your grave, that's
all. Last week there was something the matter
with that there dog, and she howled night
after night, and I never slept a wink. The first
morning after she'd been a-yelping I was in a
temper, and had half a mind to kill her. I felt
as if she'd got a spite against me ; but it come to
me as she'd got no spite against *me*, and then all
my worriting went away. I don't say as I slept
much till she was better, but I didn't *worrit*. Now
Bellamy's sister don't mean nothing against you.
That's the way God-a-mighty made her.' I've

never forgot what Jacob said, and I know it made a difference, but the Lord took her not long afterwards."

"But I don't see what that has to do with me. It isn't the same thing."

"Yes, that's just what Bellamy says. He says I always go on with anything that comes into my head; but then it has nothing to do with anything he is saying, and maybe that's true, for one thing seems always to draw me on to another, and so I go round like, and I don't know myself where I am when I've finished. A little more tea, my dear, if you please. And yet," continued Mrs. Bellamy, when she had finished half of her third cup, "what I meant to say really has to do with you. It's all the same. You wouldn't hate the Terrace so much if you knew that nobody meant to spite you, as Jacob said. Suppose your father was driven to the Terrace and couldn't help it, and there wasn't another house for him, you wouldn't hate it so much then. It isn't the Terrace alto-gether. Now, Miss Catharine, you won't mind my speaking out to you. You know you are my girl," and Mrs. Bellamy turned and kissed her;

"you mustn't, you really mustn't. I've seen what was coming for a long time. Your mother and you ain't alike, but you mustn't rebel. I'm a silly old fool, and I know I haven't got a head, and what is in it is all mixed up somehow, but you'll be ever so much better if you leave your mother out of it, and don't, as I've told you before, go on dreaming she came here because you didn't want to come, or that she set herself up on purpose against you. And then you can always run over to Chapel Farm just whenever you like, my pet, and there's your own room always waiting for you."

An hour afterwards, when Mrs. Bellamy had left, Mr. Furze came home. Mrs. Furze was still upstairs, but consented to be coaxed down to supper. She passed the drawing-room ; the door was wide open, and she reflected bitterly upon the new carpet, the oleographs, and the schemes erected thereon. To think on what she had spent and what she had done, and then that Mrs. Colston should be received by a charwoman with a pail, should be shown into the room downstairs, and find it like a public-house bar ! If Mr. Furze had been there alone it would not so much have mattered, but the presence of wife and daughter sanctioned the vulgarity, not to say indecency. Mrs. Colston would naturally conclude they were accustomed to that sort of thing—that the pipe, Mrs. Bellamy and the sausages, the absence of Mr. Furze's coat and waistcoat, were the " atmosphere," as Mrs. Furze put it, in which they lived.

" That's right ; glad to see you are able to come down," said Mr. Furze.

" I must say that Catharine is partly the cause of my suffering. When Mrs. Colston called here Catharine sat like a statue and said not a word, but when her friend Mrs. Bellamy came she precipitated herself—yes, I say precipitated herself —into her arms. I've nothing to say against Mrs. Bellamy, but Catharine knows perfectly well that Mrs. Colston's intimacy is desired, and *that's* the way she chose to behave. Mrs. Bellamy was the last person I should have wished to see here this afternoon ; an uneducated woman, a woman whom we could not pretend to know if we moved in Mrs. Colston's circle ; and what we have done was all done for my child's benefit. She, I presume, would prefer decent society to that of peasants."

Catharine stopped eating.

"Mrs. Bellamy was the last person *I* should have wished to see here."

"I don't know quite what you mean, but it is probably something disobedient and cruel," and Mrs. Furze became slightly hysterical again.

Catharine made no offer of any sympathy, but, leaving her supper unfinished, rose without saying good-night, and appeared no more that evening.

CHAPTER VI.

"MY dear," said Mrs. Furze to her husband the next night when they were alone, " I think Catharine would be much better if she were sent away from home for a time. Her education is very imperfect, and there are establishments where young ladies are taken at her age and finished. It would do her a world of good."

Mr. Furze was not quite sure about the finishing. It savoured of a region outside the modest enclosure within which he was born and brought up.

" The expense, I am afraid, will be great, and I cannot afford it just now. There is no denying that business is no better; in fact, it is not so good as it was, notwithstanding the alterations."

" You cannot expect it to recover at once. Something must be done to put Catharine on a level with the young women in her position,

and my notion is that everything which will help
to introduce us into society will help you. Why
does Mrs. Butcher go out so much? It is because
she knows it is a good investment."

" An ironmonger is not a doctor."

"Who said he was?" replied Mrs. Furze,
triumphant in the consciousness of mental superiority. "Furze," she once said to him, when
it was proposed to elect him a guardian of the
poor, "take my advice and refuse. Your *forte*
is not argument: you will never hold your own in
debate."

" I know an ironmonger is not a doctor," she
continued; "*I* of all people have reason to know
it; but what I do say is, that the more we mix
with superior people, the more likely you are to
succeed, and that if you bury yourself in these
days you will fail."

The italicised " I " was an allusion to a fiction
that once Mrs. Furze might have married a doctor
if she had liked, and thereby have secured the pre-
eminence which the wife of a drug-dispenser
assumes in a country town. The grades in
Eastthorpe were very marked, and no caste

distinctions could have been more rigid. The
county folk near were by themselves. They
associated with none of the townsfolk, save with
the rector, and even in that relationship there
was a slight tinge of ex-officiosity. Next to
the rector were the lawyer and the banker and
the two maiden banker ladies in the Abbey Close.
Looked at from a distance these might be supposed to stand level, but, on nearer approach,
a difference was discernible. The banker and
the ladies, although they visited the lawyer,
were a shade beyond him. Then came the
brewer. The days had not arrived when brew-
ing—at least, on the large scale—is considered
to be more respectable than a learned profession,
and Mrs. Colston, notwithstanding her wealth,
was incessantly forced by the lawyer's wife to
confess subordination. The brewer kept three
or four horses for pleasure, and the lawyer kept
only one ; but " Colston's Entire " was on a dozen
boards in the town, and he supplied private
families and sent in bills. The position of Mrs.
Butcher was perhaps the most curious. She
visited the rector, banker, lawyer, and brewer,

and was always well received, for she was clever, smart, young, and well behaved. She had established her position solely by her wits. She did not spend a quarter as much as Mrs. Colston, but she always looked better. She was well shaped, to begin with, and the fit of her garments was perfect. Not a wrinkle was to be seen in gown, gloves, or shoes. Mrs. Colston's fashion was that imposed on her by the dressmaker, but Mrs. Butcher always had a style peculiarly her own. She knew the secret that a woman's attractiveness, so far as it is a matter of clothes, depends far more upon the manner in which they are made and worn than upon costliness. It was always thought that she ruled her husband and had just a spice of contempt for him. She gained thereby in Eastthorpe, at least with the men, for her superiority to him gave her an air which was slightly detached, free, and fascinating. She always drove when she went out with him, and it was really a sight worth seeing: she bolt upright with her hands well down, her pretty figure showing to the best advantage, the neat turn-out—for she was very particular on this point and understood horses thoroughly—and Butcher leaning back, submissive but satisfied. She had made friends with the women too. She was much too shrewd to incur their hostility by openly courting the admiration of their husbands. She knew they did admire her, and that was enough. She was most deferential to Mrs. Colston, so much so that the brewer's wife openly expressed the opinion that she was evidently well bred, and wondered how Butcher managed to secure her. Furthermore she was useful, for her opinion, when anything had to be done, was always the one to be followed, and without her the church restoration would never have been such a success. Eastthorpe, like Mrs. Colston, often marvelled that Butcher should have been so fortunate. It mostly knew everything about the antecedents of everybody in the town, but Mrs. Butcher's were not so well known. She came from Cornwall, she always said, and Cornwall was a long way off in those days. Her maiden name was Treherne, and Mrs. Colston had been told that Treherne was good Cornish. Moreover, soon after the marriage she found on the table, when she called on Mrs. Butcher, a letter which she could not help partly reading, for it lay wide open. All scruples were at once removed. It had a crest at the top, was dated from Helston, addressed Mrs. Butcher by a nickname, and was written in a most aristocratic hand—so Mrs. Colston averred to her intimate friends. She could not finish the perusal before Mrs. Butcher came into the room; but she had read enough, and the doctor's elect was admitted at once without reservation. Eastthorpe was slightly mistaken, but Mrs. Butcher's history cannot be told here.

So much by way of digression on Eastthorpe society.

Mrs. Furze carried her point as usual. As for Catharine, she did not object, for there was nothing in Eastthorpe attractive to her. The Limes, Abchurch, was the "establishment" chosen. It was kept by the Misses Ponsonby, Abchurch being a large village five miles further eastward. It was a peculiar institution. It was a school for girls, but not for little girls, and it was also an educational home for young ladies up to one-

or two-and-twenty whose training had been neglected or had to be completed beyond the usual limits. It was widely known, and, as its purpose was special, it had little or no competition, and consequently flourished. Many parents who had become wealthy, and who hardly knew the manners and customs of the class to which they aspired, sent their daughters to the Limes. The Misses Ponsonby—Miss Ponsonby and Miss Adela Ponsonby—were of Irish extraction, and had some dim connection with the family of that name. They also preserved in their Calvinistic evangelicalism a trace of the Cromwellian Ponsonby, the founder of the race. There was a difference of two years in the age of the two ladies, but no perceptible difference in their characters. The same necessity to conceal or suppress all individuality on subjects disputable in their own sect had been imposed on each. Both had the same "views" on all matters religious and social, and both of them confessed that on many points their "views" were "strict" —whatever that singular phrase may have meant. Nevertheless, they displayed remarkable tact in

reconciling parents with the defects and peculiarities of their children. There were always
girls in the school of varying degrees of intelli-
gence, from absolute stupidity to brilliancy, but
the report at the end of the term was so fashioned
that the father and mother of the idiot were not
offended, and the idiocy was so handled that it
appeared to have some advantages. If Miss
Carter had been altogether unable to master
the French verbs, or to draw the model vase
until the teacher had put in nearly the whole
of the outline, there was a most happy counterpoise, as a rule, in her moral conduct. In these
days of effusive expression, when everybody thinks
it his duty to deliver himself of everything in
him—doubts, fears, passions—no matter whether
he does harm thereby or good, the Misses Ponsonby would be considered intolerably dull and
limited. They did not walk about without their
clothes—figuratively speaking—it was not then
the fashion. They were, on the contrary, heavily
draped from head to foot, but underneath the
whalebone and padding, strange to say, were real
live women's hearts. They knew what it was

to hope and despair; they knew what it was to reflect that with each of them life might and ought to have been different; they even knew what it was sometimes to envy the beggar-woman on the doorstep of the Limes who asked for a penny and clasped a child to her breast. We mistake our ancestors who read Pope and the *Spectator.* They were very much like ourselves essentially, but they did not believe that there was nothing in us which should be smothered or strangled. Perhaps some day we shall go back to them, and find that the " Rape of the Lock " is better worth reading and really more helpful than magazine metaphysics. Anyhow, it is certain that the training which the Misses Ponsonby had received, although it may have made them starched, prim, and even uninteresting, had an effect upon their character not altogether unwholesome, and prevented any public crying for the moon, or any public charge of injustice against its Maker because it is unattainable.

The number of girls was limited to thirty. The house was tall, four-square, built of white brick about the year 1780, had a row of little pillars

running along the roof at the top, and a Grecian
portico. It was odd that there should be such
a house in Abchurch, but there it was. It was
erected by a Spitalfields silk manufacturer, whose
family belonged to those parts. He thought to
live in it after his retirement, but he came there
to die. The studies of the pupils were super-
intended by the Misses Ponsonby and sundry
teachers, all female, except the drawing-master
and the music-master. The course embraced the
usual branches of a superior English education,
French, Italian, deportment, and the use of the
globes, but, as the Misses Ponsonby truly stated
in their prospectus, their sole aim was not the
inculcation of knowledge, but such instruction as
would enable the young ladies committed to their
charge to move with ease in the best society, and,
above everything, the impression of correct principles in morality and religion. In this impression
much assistance was given by the Reverend
Theophilus Cardew, the rector of the church in
the village. The patronage was in the hands of
the Simeonite trustees, and had been bought by
them in the first fervour of the movement.

The thirty pupils occupied fifteen bedrooms, although each had a separate bed, and to Catharine was allotted Miss Julia Arden, a young woman with a pretty, pale face, and black hair worn in ringlets. Her head was not firmly fixed on her shoulders, and was always in motion, as if she had some difficulty in balancing it, the reason being, not any physical defect, but a wandering imagination, which never permitted her to look at any one thing steadily for an instant. Nine-tenths of what she said was nonsense, but her very shallowness gave occasionally a certain value and reality to her talk, for the simple reason that she was incapable of the effort necessary to conceal what she thought for the moment. In her studies she made not the slightest progress, for her memory was shocking. She confounded all she was taught, and never could recollect whether the verb was conjugated and the noun declined, or whether it was the other way round, to use one of her favourite expressions, so that her preceptors were compelled to fall back, more exclusively than with her school-fellows, on her moral conduct, which was out-

wardly respectable enough, but by the occupant
of the other bed might perhaps have been reported on in terms not quite so satisfactory as
those in the quarterly form signed by Miss
Ponsonby.

Catharine's mother came with her on a Saturday
afternoon, but left in the evening. At half-past
eight there were prayers. The girls filed into the
drawing-room, sat round in a ring, of which the
Misses Ponsonby formed a part, but with a break
of about two feet right and left, the servants
sitting outside near the door: a chapter was
read, a prayer also read, and then, after a
suitable pause, the servants rose from their
knees, the pupils rose next, and the Misses
Ponsonby last; the time which each division,
servants, pupils, and Ponsonbys remained kneeling being graduated exactly in proportion to
rank. A procession to the supper-room was
then formed. Catharine found herself at table
next to Miss Arden, with a spotless napkin
before her, with silver forks and spoons, and a
delicately served meal of stewed fruits, milk-
puddings, bread-and-butter, and cold water.

Everything was good, sweet, and beautifully clean, and there was enough. At half-past nine, in accordance with the usual practice, one of the girls read from a selected book. On Saturday a book, not exactly religious, but related to religion as nearly as possible as Saturday is related to Sunday, was invariably selected. On this particular Saturday it was Clarke's " Travels in Palestine." Precisely as the clock struck ten the volume was closed and the pupils went to bed.

" I am sure I shall like you," observed Miss Arden, as they were undressing. " The girl who was here before was a brute, so dull and so vulgar. I hope you will like me."

" I hope so too."

" It's dreadful here : so different to my mother's house in Devonshire. We have a large place there near Torquay—do you know Torquay? And I have a horse of my own, on which I tear about during the holidays, and there are boats and sailing matches, and my brothers have so many friends, and I have all sorts of little affairs. I suppose you've had your affairs. Of course you won't say. We never see a man here, except Mr. Cardew. Oh, isn't he handsome? He's only a parson, but he's such a dear; you'll see him to-morrow. I can't make him out: he's lovely, but he's queer, so solemn at times, like an owl in daylight. I'm sure he's well brought up. I wonder why he went into the church: he ought to have been a gentleman."

"But is he not a gentleman?"

"Oh, yes, of course he's a gentleman, but you know what I mean."

"No, I don't."

"There, now, you are one of those horrid creatures, I know you are, who never *will* understand, and do it on purpose. It is so aggravating."

"Well, but you said he was not a gentleman, and yet that he was a gentleman."

"You *are* provoking. I say he is a gentleman —but don't some gentlemen keep a carriage?— and his father is in business. Isn't that plain? You know all about it as well as I do."

"I still do not quite comprehend."

Catharine took a little pleasure in forcing people to be definite, and Miss Arden invariably fell back on "you understand" whenever she herself did not understand. In fact, in exact proportion to her own inability to make herself clear to herself, did she always insist that she was clear to other people.

"I cannot help it if you don't comprehend. He's lovely, and I adore him."

Next morning, being Sunday, the Limes was, if possible, still more irreproachable; the noise of the household was more subdued; the passions appeared more utterly extinguished, and any indifferent observer would have said that from the Misses Ponsonby down to the scullery-maid, a big jug had been emptied on every spark of illegal fire, and blood was toast and water. Alas! it was not so. The boots were cleaned overnight to avoid Sunday labour, but when the milkman came, a handsome young fellow, anybody with ears near the window overhead might have detected a scuffling at the back door with some laughter and something like "Oh, don't!" and might have noticed that Elizabeth afterwards looked a little rumpled and adjusted her cap. Nor was she singular, for many of the young women who were supposed to be studying a brief abstract of the history of the kingdoms of Judah and Israel, in parallel columns, as arranged by the Misses Ponsonby, were indulging in the naughtiest thoughts and using naughty words as they sat in their bedrooms before the time for departure to church. At a quarter-past ten the girls assembled in the dining-room, and were duly marshalled. They did not, however, walk two-and-two like ordinary schools. In the first place, many of them were not children, and, in the second place, the Misses Ponsonby held that even walking to church was a thing to be taught, and they desired to turn out their pupils so that they might distinguish themselves in this art also as well-bred people. It was one of the points on which the Misses Ponsonby grew even eloquent. How, they said, are girls to learn to carry themselves properly if they march in couples? They will not do it when they leave the Limes, and will be utterly at fault. There is no day in the week on which more general notice is taken than on Sunday ; there is no day on which differences are more apparent. The pupils therefore walked irre-

gularly, the irregularity being prescribed. The
entering the church ; the leaving the pews ; the
loitering and salutations in the churchyard ; the
slow, superior saunter homewards were all the
result of lecture, study, and even of practice
on week-days. " Deliberation, ease," said Miss
Ponsonby, " are the key to this, as they are to so
much in our behaviour, and surely on the Sabbath
we ought more than on any other day to avoid
indecorous hurry and vulgarity."

Catharine's curiosity, after what Miss Arden
had said, was a little excited to know what kind
of a man Mr. Cardew might be, and she imagined
him a young dandy.   She saw a man about thirty-
five with dark brown hair, eyes set rather deeply in
his head, a little too close together, a delicate, thin,
very slightly aquiline nose, and a mouth with
curved lips, which were, however, compressed as
if with determination or downright resolution.
There was not a trace of dandyism in him, and he
reminded her immediately of a portrait she had
seen of Edward Irving in a shop at Eastthorpe.

He stood straight up in the pulpit reading from
a little Testament he held in his hand, and when

he had given out his text he put the Testament down and preached without notes. His subject was a passage in the life of Jesus taken from Luke xviii. 18 :—

18. *And a certain ruler asked Him, saying, Good Master, what shall I do to inherit eternal life ?*

19. *And Jesus said unto him, Why callest thou Me good ? None is good, save one, that is God.*

20. *Thou knowest the commandments, Do not commit adultery, Do not kill, Do not steal, Do not bear false witness, Honour thy father and mother.*

21. *And he said, All these have I kept from my youth up.*

22. *Now when Jesus heard these things, He said unto him, Yet lackest thou one thing : sell all that thou hast and distribute unto the poor, and thou shalt have treasure in heaven : and come, follow Me.*

Mr. Cardew did not approach his theme circuitously or indifferently, but seemed in haste to be on close terms with it, as if it had dwelt with him and he was eager to deliver his message.

" I beseech you," he began, " endeavour to make this scene real to you. A rich man, an official, comes to Jesus, calls Him Teacher—for so the word is in the Greek—and asks Him what is to be done to inherit eternal life. How strange it is that such a question should be so put! how rare are the occasions on which two people approach one another so nearly! Most of us pass days, weeks, months, years in intercourse with one another, and nothing which even remotely concerns the soul is ever mentioned. Is it that we do not care? Mainly that, and partly because we foolishly hang back from any conversation on what it is most important we should reveal, so that others may help us. Whenever you feel any promptings to speak of the soul or to make any inquiries on its behalf, remember it is a sacred duty not to suppress them.

" This ruler was happy in being able to find a single authority to whom he could appeal for an answer. If anybody wishes for such an answer now, he can find no oracle sole and decisive. The voices of the Church, the sects, the philosophers are clamorous but discordant, and we are bewildered. And yet, as I have told you over and over again in this pulpit, it is absolutely necessary that you should have one and one only supreme guide. To say nothing of eternal salvation, we must, in the conduct of life, shape our behaviour by some one standard, or the result is chaos. We must have some one method or principle which is to settle beforehand how we are to do this or that, and the method or principle should be Christ. Leaving out of sight altogether His Divinity, there is no temper, no manner so effectual, so happy as His for handling all human experience. Oh, what a privilege it is to meet with anybody who is controlled into unity, whose actions are all directed by one consistent force !

"Jesus, as if to draw from this ruler all that he himself believed, tells him to keep the Law. The Law, however, is insufficient, and it is noteworthy that the ruler felt it to be so. To begin with it is largely negative : there are three negatives in this twentieth verse for one affirmative, and negations cannot redeem us. The law is also external. As a proof that it is ineffectual, I ask, Have you ever *rejoiced* in it? Have you ever been kindled by it? Have all its precepts ever moved you like one single item in the story of the

love of Jesus? Is the man attractive to you who
has kept the law and done nothing more? Would
not the poor woman who anointed our Lord's feet
and wiped them with her hair be more welcome to
you than the holy people who had simply never
transgressed?

"We are struck with the magnitude of the
demand made by Jesus on this ruler. To obtain
eternal life he was to sell all he had, give up house,
friends, position, respectability, and lead a vagrant
life in Palestine with this poor carpenter's son.
Alas! eternal life is not to be bought on lower
terms. Beware of the damnable doctrine that it is
easy to enter the kingdom of heaven. It is to be
obtained only by the sacrifice of *all* that stands in
the way, and it is to be observed that in this, as in
other things, men will take the first, the second,
the third—nay, even the ninety-ninth step, but the
hundredth and last they will not take. Do you
really wish to save your soul? Then the sur-
render must be absolute. What! you will say, am
I to sell everything? If Christ comes to you—
yes. Sell not only your property, but your very
self. Part with all your preferences, your loves,

your thoughts, your very soul, if only you can gain Him, and be sure too that He will come to you in a shape in which it will not be easy to recognise Him. What a bargain, though, this ruler would have made! He would have given up his dull mansion in Jerusalem, Jerusalem society, which cared nothing for *him*, though it doubtless called on him, made much of him, and even professed undying friendship with him; he would have given this up, nothing but this, and he would have gained those walks with Jesus across the fields, and would have heard Him say, 'Consider the lilies!' 'Oh, yes, we would have done it at once!' we cry. I think not, for Christ is with us even now."

Curiously enough, the exordium was a piece of the most commonplace orthodoxy, lugged in, Heaven knows how, and delivered monotonously, in strong contrast to the former part of the discourse.—M. R.

These notes, made by one who was present, are the mere ashes, cold and grey, of what was once a fire. Mr. Cardew was really eloquent, and consequently a large part of the effect of what he said is not to be reproduced. It is a pity that no record is possible of a great speaker. The writer of this history remembers when it was his privilege to listen continually to a man whose power over his audience was so great that he could sway them unanimously by a passion which was sufficient for any heroic deed. The noblest resolutions were formed under that burning oratory, and were kept, too, for the voice of the dead preacher still vibrates in the ears of those who heard him. And yet, except in their hearts, no trace abides, and when they are dead he will be forgotten, excepting in so far as that which has once lived can never die.

Whether it was the preacher's personality, or what he said, Catharine could hardly distinguish, but she was profoundly moved. Such speaking was altogether new to her ; the world in which Mr. Cardew moved was one which she had never entered, and yet it seemed to her as if something necessary and familiar to her, but long lost, had been restored. She began now to look forward to Sunday with intense expectation ;

a new motive for life was supplied to her, and a new force urged her through each day. It was with her as we can imagine it to be with some bud long folded in darkness which, silently in the dewy May night, loosens its leaves, and, as the sun rises, bares itself to the depths of its cup to the blue sky and the light.

CHAPTER VII.

THE Misses Ponsonby speedily came to a conclusion about Catharine, and she was forthwith labelled as a young lady of natural ability, whose education had been neglected, a type perfectly familiar, recurring every quarter, and one with which they were perfectly well able to deal. All the examples they had had before were ticketed in exactly the same terms, and, so classed, there was an end of further distinction. The means taken with Catharine were those which had been taken since the school began, and special attention was devoted to the branches in which she was most deficient, and which she disliked. Her history was deplorable, and her first task, therefore, was what were called dates. A table had been prepared of the kings and queens of England—when they came to the throne, and when they died ; and another table gave the years of all the battles. A third table gave the relationship of the kings and queens to each other, and the reasons for succession. All this had to be learned by heart. In languages, also, Catharine was singularly defective. Her French was intolerable and most inaccurate, and of Italian she knew nothing. Her dancing and deportment were so "provincial," as Miss Adela Ponsonby happily put it, that it was thought better that the dancing and deportment teacher should give her a few private lessons before putting her in a class, and she was consequently instructed alone in the rudiments of the art of entering and leaving a room with propriety, of sitting with propriety on a sofa when conversing, of reading a book in a drawing-room, of acknowledging an introduction, of sitting down to a meal and rising therefrom, and in the use of the pocket-handkerchief. She had particularly shocked the Misses Ponsonby on this latter point, as she was in the habit of blowing her nose energetically, "snorting," as one of the young ladies said colloquially, but with truth, and the deportment mistress had some difficulty in reducing her to the whisper, which was all that was permitted in the Ponsonby establishment, even in cases of severe cold. On the other hand, in one or two departments she was far ahead of the other girls, particularly in arithmetic and geometry.

It was the practice on Monday morning for the girls to be questioned on the sermons of the preceding Sunday, and a very solemn business it was. The whole school was assembled in the big schoolroom, and Mr. Cardew, both the Misses Ponsonby being present, examined *viva voce*. One Monday morning, after Catharine had been a month at the school, Mr. Cardew came as usual. He had been preaching the Sunday before on a favourite theme, and his text had been, "So then with the mind I myself serve the law of God, but with the flesh the law of sin," and the examination at the beginning was in the biography of St. Paul, as this had formed a part of his discourse. No fault was to be found with the answers on this portion of the subject, but presently the class was in some difficulty.

"Can anybody tell me what meaning was assigned to the phrase, ' The body of this death ' ? "

No reply.

"Come, you took notes, and one or two interpretations were discarded for that which seemed to
be more in accordance with the mind of St. Paul.
Miss Arden "—Miss Arden was sitting nearest to
Mr. Cardew—"cannot you say ? "

Miss Arden shook her ringlets, smiled, and
turned a little red, as if she had been complimented by Mr. Cardew's inquiries after the body
of death, and, glancing at her paper, replied—

" The death of this body."

" Pardon me, that was one of the interpretations
rejected."

" This body of death," said Catharine.

" Quite so."

Mr. Cardew turned hastily round to the new
pupil, whom he had not noticed before, and looked
at her steadily for a moment.

" Can you proceed a little and explain what that
means ? "

Catharine's voice trembled, but she managed to
read from her paper : " It is strikingly after the
manner of St. Paul. He opposes the two natures
in him by the strongest words at his command—

death and life. One *is* death, the other *is* life, and he prays to be delivered from death ; not the death of the body, but from death-in-life."

"Thank you ; that is very nearly what I intended."

Mr. Cardew took tea at the Limes about once a fortnight with Mrs. Cardew. The meal was served in the Misses Ponsonby's private room, and the girls were invited in turn. About a fortnight after the examination on St. Paul's theory of human nature, Mr. and Mrs. Cardew came as usual, and Catharine was one of the selected guests. The company sat round the table, and Mrs. Cardew was placed between her husband and Miss Furze. The rector's wife was a fair-haired lady, with quiet, grey eyes, and regular, but not strikingly beautiful, features. Yet they were attractive, because they were harmonious, and betokened a certain inward agreement. It was a sane, sensible face, but a careless critic might have thought that it betokened an incapability of emotion, especially as Mrs. Cardew had a habit of sitting back in her chair, and generally let the conversation take its own course until it came very close to her. She had a sober mode of statement and criticism, which was never brilliant and never stupid. It ought to have been most serviceable to her husband, because it might have corrected the exaggeration into which his impulse, talent, and power of pictorial representation were so apt to fall. She had been brought up as an Evangelical, but she had passed through no religious experiences whatever, and religion, in the sense in which Evangelicalism in the Church of England of that day understood it, was quite unintelligible to her. Had she been born a few years later she would have taken to science, and would have done well at it, but at that time there was no outlet for any womanly faculty, much larger in quantity than we are apt to suppose, which has an appetite for exact facts.

Mr. Cardew would have been called a prig by those who did not know him well. He had a trick of starting subjects suddenly, and he very often made his friends very uncomfortable by the precipitate introduction, without any warning, of remarks upon serious matters. Once even, shocking to say, he quite unexpectedly at a tea-party made an observation about God. Really, however, he was not a prig. He was very sincere. He lived in a world of his own, in which certain figures moved which were as familiar to him as common life, and he consequently talked about them. He leaned in front of his wife and said to Catharine—

"Have you read much, Miss Furze?"

"No, very little."

"Indeed! I should have thought you were a reader. What have you read lately? any stories?"

"Yes, I have read Rasselas."

"Rasselas! Have you really? Now tell me what you think of it."

"Oh! I cannot tell you all."

"No, it is not fair to put the question in that way. It is necessary to have some training in order to give a proper account of the scope and purpose of a book. Can you select any one part which struck you, and tell me why it struck you?"

"The part about the astronomer. I thought all that is said about the dreadful effects of uncontrolled imagination was so wonderful."

"Don't you think those effects are exaggerated?"

She lost herself for a moment, as we have already seen she was in the habit of doing, or rather, she did not lose herself, but everything excepting herself, and she spoke as if nobody but herself were present.

"Not in the least exaggerated. What a horror to pass days in dreaming about one particular thing, and to have no power to wake!"

Her head had fallen a little forward; she suddenly straightened herself; the blood rose in her face, and she looked very confused.

"I should like to preach about Dr. Johnson," said Mr. Cardew.

"Really, Mr. Cardew," interposed the elder Miss Ponsonby, "Dr. Johnson is scarcely a sacred subject."

"I beg your pardon; I do not mean preaching on the Sabbath. I should like to lecture about him. It is a curious thing, Miss Ponsonby, that although Johnson was such a devout Christian, yet in his troubles his remedy is generally nothing but that of the Stoics—courage and patience."

Nobody answered, and an awkward pause followed. Catharine had not recovered from the shock of self-revelation, and the Misses Ponsonby were uneasy, not only because the conversation had taken such an unusual turn, but because a pupil had contributed. Mrs. Cardew, distressed at her husband's embarrassment, ventured to come to the rescue.

" I think Dr. Johnson quite right ; when I am in pain, and nothing does me any good, I never have anything to say to myself, excepting that I must just be quiet, wait and bear it."

This very plain piece of pagan common sense made matters worse. Mr. Cardew seemed vexed that his wife had spoken, and there was once more silence for quite half a minnte. Miss Adela Ponsonby then rang the bell, and Catharine, in accordance with rule, left the room.

" Rather a remarkable young woman," carelessly observed the rector.

" Decidedly ! " said both the Misses Ponsonby, in perfect unison.

" She has been much neglected," continued Miss Ponsonby. " Her manners leave much to be desired. She has evidently not been accustomed to the forms of good society, or to express herself in accordance with the usual practice. We have endeavoured to impress upon her that, not only is much care necessary in the choice of topics of conversation, but in the mode of dealing with them. I thought it better not to encourage any further remarks from her, or I should have pointed out that, if what you say of Dr. Johnson is correct, as I have no doubt it is, considering the party in the church to which he belonged, it only shows that he was unacquainted experimentally with the consolations of religion."

" Isn't Mr. Cardew a dear ? " asked Miss Arden, when she and Catharine were together.

" I hardly understand what you mean, and I have not known Mr. Cardew long enough to give any opinion upon him."

" How exasperating you are again ! You *do* know what I mean ; but you always pretend never to know what anybody means."

" I do *not* know what you mean."

" Why, isn't he handsome ; couldn't you doat on him, and fall in love with him ? "

" But he's married."

" You fearful Catharine! of course he's married; you do take things so seriously."

" Well, I'm more in the dark than ever."

" There you shall stick," replied Miss Arden, lightly shaking her curls and laughing. " Married! —yes, but they don't care for one another a straw."

" Have they ever told you so ? "

" How very ridiculous! Cannot you see for yourself ? "

" I am not sure: it is very difficult to know whether people really love one another, and often equally difficult to know if they dislike one another."

" What a philosopher you are! I'll tell you one thing, though : I believe he has just a little liking for me. Not for his life dare he show it. Oh, my goodness, wouldn't the fat be in the fire! Wouldn't there be a flare-up! What would the Ponsonbys do? Polite letter to papa announcing that my education was complete! That's what they did when Julia Jackson got in a mess. They couldn't have a scandal : so her education was complete, and home she went. Now the first time we are out for a walk and he passes us and bows, you watch."

Miss Julia Arden went to sleep directly she went to bed, but Catharine, contrary to her usual custom, lay awake till she heard twelve o'clock strike from St. Mary, Abchurch. She started, and thought that she alone, perhaps, of all the people who lay within reach of those chimes had heard them. Why did she not go to sleep? She was un- used to wakefulness, and its novelty surprised her with all sorts of vague terrors. She turned from side to side anxiously while midnight sounded, but she was young, and in ten minutes afterwards she was dreaming. She was mistaken in supposing that she was the only person awake in Abchurch that night. Mrs. Cardew heard the chimes, and over her their soothing melody had no power. When she and her husband left the Limes he broke out at once, with all the eagerness with which a man begins when he has been repeating to himself for some time every word of his grievance—

" I don't know how it is, Jane, but whenever I say anything I feel you are just the one person on whom it seems to make no impression. You have a trick of repetition, and you manage to turn everything into a platitude. If you cannot do better than that, you might be silent."

He was right so far, that it is possible by just a touch to convert the noblest sentiment into commonplace. No more than a touch is necessary. The parabolic mirror will reflect the star to a perfect focus. The elliptical mirror, varying from the parabola by less than the breadth of a hair, throws an image which is useless. But Mr. Cardew was far more wrong than he was right. He did not take into account that what his wife said and what she felt might not be the same; that persons, who have no great command over language, are obliged to make one word do duty for a dozen, and that, if his wife was defective at one point, there were in her whole regions of unexplored excellence, of faculties never encouraged, and an affection to which he offered no response. He had not learned the art of being happy with her : he did not know that happiness is an art : he rather did everything he could do to make the relationship intolerable. He demanded payment in coin stamped from his own mint, and if bullion and jewels had been poured before him he would have taken no heed of them.

She said nothing. She never answered him when he was angry with her. It was growing dark as they went home, and the tears came into her eyes and the ball rose in her throat, and her lips quivered. She went back—does a woman ever forget them?—to the hours of passionate protestation before marriage, to the walks together when he caught up her poor phrases and refined them, and helped her to see herself, and tried also to learn what few things she had to teach. It was all the worse because she still loved him so dearly, and felt that behind the veil was the same face, but she could not tear the veil away. Perhaps, as they grew older, matters might become worse, and they might have to travel together estranged down the long, weary path to death. Death ! She did not desire to leave him, but she would have lain down in peace to die that moment if he could be made to see her afterwards as she knew she was—at least in her love for him. But then she thought what suffering the remembrance of herself would cost him, and she wished to live. He felt that she moved her hand to her pocket, and he knew why it went there. He pitied her, but he pitied himself more, and though her tears wrought on him sufficiently to prevent any further cruelty, he did not repent.

CHAPTER VIII.

MRS. CARDEW met Catharine two or three times accidentally within the next fortnight. There were Dorcas meetings and meetings of all kinds at which the young women at the Limes were expected to assist. One afternoon, after tea, the room being hot, two or three of the company had gone out into the garden to work. Catharine and Mrs. Cardew sat by themselves at one corner, where the ground rose a little, and a seat had been placed under a large ash tree. From that point St. Mary's spire was visible, about half a mile away in the west, rising boldly, confidently, one might say, into the sky, as if it dared to claim that it too, although on earth and finite, could match itself against the infinite heaven above. On this particular evening the spire was specially obvious and attractive, for it divided the sunset clouds, standing out black against the long, narrow interspaces of tender green which lay between. It was one of those evenings which invite confidence, when people cannot help drawing nearer than usual to one another.

" Is it not beautiful, Miss Furze ? "

" Beautiful ; the spire makes it so lovely."

" I wonder why."

" I am sure I do not know ; but it is so."

" Catharine—you will not mind my calling you by your Christian name—you can explain it if you like."

Catharine smiled. " It is very kind of you, Mrs. Cardew, to call me Catharine, but I have no explanation. I could not give one to save my life, unless it is the contrast."

" You cannot think how I wish I had the power of saying what I think and feel. I cannot express myself properly—so my husband says."

" I sympathise with you. I am so foolish at times. Mr. Cardew, I should think, never felt the difficulty."

"No, and he makes so much of it. He says I do not properly enjoy a thing if I cannot in some measure describe my enjoyment—articulate it, to use his own words."

He had inwardly taunted her, even when she was suffering, and had said to himself that her trouble must be insignificant, for there was no colour nor vivacity in her description of it. She did not properly even understand his own short-comings. He could pardon her criticism, so he imagined, if she could be pungent. Mistaken mortal! it was her patient heroism which made her dumb to him about her sorrows and his faults. A very limited vocabulary is all that is necessary on such topics.

" I am just the same."

" Oh, no, you are not ; Mr. Cardew says you are not."

" Mr. Cardew ?—he has not noticed anything in me, I am certain, and if he has, why nobody could be less able to talk to him than I am."

Catharine knew nothing of what had passed between husband and wife—one scene amongst many—and consequently could not understand the peculiar earnestness, somewhat unusual with her, with which Mrs. Cardew dwelt upon this subject.

We lead our lives apart in close company with private hopes and fears unknown to anybody but ourselves, and when we go abroad we often appear inexplicable and absurd, simply because our friends have not the proper key.

"Do you think, Catharine—you know that, though I am older than you and married, I feel we are friends." Here Mrs. Cardew took Catharine's hand in hers. "Do you think I could learn how to talk? What I mean is, could I be taught how to say what is appropriate? I *do* feel something when Mr. Cardew reads Milton to me. It is only the words I want—words such as you have."

"Oh, Mrs. Cardew!"—Catharine came closer to her, and Mrs. Cardew's arm crept round her waist —"I tell you again I have not so many words as you suppose. I believe, though, that if people take pains they can find them."

"Couldn't you help me?"

"I? Oh, no! Mr. Cardew could. I never heard anybody express himself as he does."

"Mr. Cardew is a minister, and perhaps I should find it easier with you. Suppose I bring the

' Paradise Lost ' out into the garden when we next meet, and I will read, and you shall help me to comment on it."

Catharine's heart went out towards her, and it was agreed that "Paradise Lost" should be brought, and that Mrs. Cardew would endeavour to make herself " articulate " thereon. The party broke up, and Catharine's reflections were not of the simplest order. Rather let us say her emotions, for her heart was busier than her head. Mrs. Cardew had deeply touched her. She never could stand unmoved the eyes of her dog when the poor beast came and laid her nose on her lap and looked up at her, and nobody could have persuaded her of the truth of Mr. Cardew's doctrine that the reason why a dog can only bark is that his thoughts are nothing but barks. Mrs. Cardew's appeal, therefore, was of a kind to stir her sympathy ; but—had she not heard that Mr. Cardew had observed and praised her ? It was nothing—ridiculously nothing ; it was his duty to praise and blame the pupils at the Limes ; he had complimented Miss Toogood on her Bible history the other day, and on her satisfactory account of the scheme of Redemption.

He had done it publicly, and he had pointed out the failings of the other pupils, she, Catharine, herself being included. He had reminded her that she had not taken into account the one vital point, that, as we are the Almighty Maker's creatures, His absolutely, we have no ground of complaint against Him in whatever way He may be pleased to make us. Nevertheless, just those two or three words Mrs. Cardew reported were like yeast, and her whole brain was in a ferment.

The Milton was produced next week. Since Catharine had been at the Limes she had read some of it, incited by Mr. Cardew, for he was an enthusiast for Milton. Mrs. Cardew was a bad reader ; she had no emphasis, no light and shade, and she missed altogether the rhythm of the verse. To Catharine, on the other hand, knowing nothing of metre, the proper cadence came easily. They finished the first six hundred lines of the first book.

" You have not said anything, Catharine."

" No ; but what have you to say ? "

" It is very fine ; but there I stick ; I cannot say any more ; I want to say more ; that is where I always am. I can *not* understand why I cannot go on as some people do; I just stop there with ' very fine.' "

"Cannot you pick out some passage which particularly struck you ? "

"That is very true, is it not, that the mind can make a heaven of hell and a hell of heaven ? "

"Most true; but did you not notice the description of the music ? "

Catharine was fond of music, but only as an expression of her own feelings. For music as music—for a melody of Mozart, for example—that is to say, for pure art which is simply beauty, superior to our personality, she did not care. She liked Handel, and there was a choral society in Eastthorpe which occasionally performed the " Messiah."

"Don't you remember what Mr. Cardew said about it—it was remarkable that Milton should have given to music the power to chase doubt from the mind, doubt generally, and yet music is not argument ? "

"Oh, yes, I recollect, but I do not quite comprehend him, and I told him I did not see how music could make me sure of a thing if there was not a reason for it."

" What did he say then ? "

" Nothing."

Mr. Cardew called that evening to take his wife home.   He was told that she was in the garden with Miss Furze, and thither he at once went.

" Milton ! " he exclaimed.   " What are you doing with Milton here ? "

" Miss Furze and I were reading the first book of the ' Paradise Lost ' together."

Mrs. Cardew looked at her husband inquiringly, and with a timid smile, hoping he would show himself pleased.   His brow, however, slightly wrinkled itself with displeasure.   He had told her to read Milton, had said, " Fancy an English-woman with any pretensions to education not knowing Milton ! " and now, when she was doing exactly what she was directed to do, he was vexed. He was annoyed to find he was precisely obeyed, and perhaps would have been in a better temper if he had been contradicted and resisted.   Mrs. Cardew turned her head away.   What was she to do with him? Every one of her efforts to find the door had failed.

"What has struck you particularly in that book, Miss Furze?"

Catharine was about to say something, but she caught sight of Mrs. Cardew, and was arrested. At last she spoke, but what she said was not what she at first had intended to say.

"Mrs. Cardew and I were discussing the lines about doubt and music, and we cannot see what Milton means. We cannot see how music can make us sure of a thing if there is not good reason for it."

Catharine used the first person plural with the best intention, but her object was defeated. The rector recognised the words at once.

"Yes, yes," he replied, impatiently; "but, Miss Furze, you know better than that. Milton does not mean doubt whether an arithmetical proposition is true. I question if he means theological doubt. Doubt in that passage is nearer despondency. It is despondency taking an intellectual form and clothing itself with doubts which no reasoning will overcome, which re-shape themselves the moment they are refuted." He stopped for a moment. " Don't you think so, Miss Furze ? "

She forgot Mrs. Cardew, and looked straight into Mr. Cardew's face bent earnestly upon her.

" I understand."

Mrs. Cardew had lifted her eyes from the ground on which they had been fixed. " I think," said she, " we had better be going."

" We can go out by the door at the end of the garden, if you will go and bid the Misses Ponsonby good-bye."

Mrs. Cardew lingered a moment.

" I have bidden them good-bye," said her husband.

She went, and Miss Ponsonby detained her for a few minutes to arrange the details of an important quarterly meeting of the Dorcas Society for next week.

" What do you think of the subject of the ' Paradise Lost,' Miss Furze ? "

" I hardly know ; it seems so far away."

" Ah ! that is just the point. I thought so once, but not now. Milton could not content himself with a common theme ; nothing less than God and the immortal feud between Him and Satan would suffice. Milton is representative to me of what I may call the heroic attitude towards existence. Mark, too, the importance of man in the book. Men and women are not mere bubbles—here for a moment and then gone—but they are actually important, all-important, I may even say, to the Maker of the universe and His great enemy. In this Milton follows Christianity, but what stress he lays on the point! Our temptation, notwithstanding our religion, so often is to doubt our own value. All appearances tend to make us doubt it. Don't you think so?"

Catharine looked earnestly at the excited preacher, but said nothing.

"I do not mean our own personal worth. The temptation is to doubt whether it is of the smallest consequence whether we are or are not, and whether our being here is not an accident. Oh, Miss Furze, to think that your existence and mine are part of the Divine eternal plan, and that without us it would be wrecked! Then there is Satan. Milton has gone beyond the Bible, beyond what is authorised in giving such a distinct, power-

ful, and prominent individuality to Satan.   You
will remember that in the great celestial battle—

> " ' Long time in even scale
> The battle hung.'

But what a wonderful conception that is of the
great antagonist of God !   It comes out even more
strongly in the 'Paradise Regained.'   Is it not a
relief to think that the evil thought in you or me
is not altogether yours and mine, but is foreign ;
that it is an incident in the war of wars, an attack
on one of the soldiers of the Most High ? "

Mr. Cardew paused.

" Have you never written anything which I could
read ? "

" Scarcely anything.   I wrote some time ago a
little story of a few pages, but it was never
published.   I will lend you the manuscript, but
you will please remember that it is anonymous,
and that I do not wish the authorship revealed.   I
believe most people would not think any the better
of me, certainly as a clergyman, if they knew it was
mine."

" That is very kind of you."

Catharine felt the distinction, the confidence. The sweetest homage which can be offered us is to be entrusted with something which others would misinterpret.

"I should like, Miss Furze, to have some further talk with you about Milton, but I do not quite see " (musingly) " how it is to be managed."

"Could you not tell us something about him when you and Mrs. Cardew next have tea with us at the Limes?"

"I do not think so. I meant with you, yourself. It is not easy for me to express myself clearly in company—at any rate, I should not hear your difficulties. You seem to possess a sympathy which is unusual, and I should be glad to know more of your mind."

"When Mrs. Cardew comes here, could you not fetch her, and could we not sit out here together?"

He hesitated. They were walking slowly over the grass towards the gate, and were just beginning to turn off to the right by the side path between the laurels. At that point, the lawn being levelled and raised, there were two stone steps. In descending them Catharine slipped, and he caught her arm.

She did not fall, but he did not altogether release her for at least some seconds.

"Mrs. Cardew has no liking for poetry."

Catharine was silent.

"It is quite a new thing to me, Miss Furze, to find anybody in Abchurch who cares anything for that which is most interesting to me."

"But, Mr. Cardew, I am sure I have not shown any particular capacity, and I am very ignorant, for I have read very little."

"It does not need much to reveal what is in a person. It would be a great help to me if we could read a book together. This self-imprisonment day after day and self-imposed reticence is very unwholesome. I would give much to have a pupil or a friend whose world is my world."

To Catharine it seemed as if she was being sucked in by a whirlpool and carried she knew not whither. They had reached the gate, and he had taken her hand in his to bid her good-bye. She felt a distinct and convulsive increase of pressure, and she felt also that she returned it. Suddenly something passed through her brain swift as the flash of the swiftest blazing meteor: she dropped his hand, and, turning instantly, went back to the house, retreating behind the thick bank of evergreens.

"Where is Miss Furze?" said Mrs. Cardew, who came down the path a minute or two afterwards.

"I do not know : I suppose she is indoors."

"A canting, hypocritical parson, type not uncommon, described over and over again in novels, and thoroughly familiar to theatre-goers." Such, no doubt, will be the summary verdict passed upon Mr. Cardew. The truth is, however, that he did not cant, and was not a hypocrite. One or two observations here may perhaps be pertinent. The accusation of hypocrisy, if we mean lofty assertion, and occasional and even conspicuous moral failure, may be brought against some of the greatest figures in history. But because David sinned with Bathsheba, and even murdered her husband, we need not discredit the sincerity of the Psalms. The man was inconsistent, it is true, inconsistent exactly because there was so much in him that was great, for which let us be thankful. Let us take notice, too, of what lies side by side quietly in our own souls. God help us if all that is good in us is to be invalidated by the presence of the most contradictory evil.

Secondly, it is a fact that vitality means passion. It does not mean avarice or any of the poor, miserable vices. If David had been a wealthy and most pious Jerusalem shopkeeper, who subscribed largely to missionary societies to the Philistines, but who paid the poor girls in his employ only two shekels a week, refusing them ass-hire when they had to take their work three parts of the way to Bethlehem, and turning them loose at a minute's warning, he certainly would not have been selected to be part author of the Bible, even supposing his courtship and married life to have been most exemplary and orthodox. We will, however, postpone any further remarks upon Mr. Cardew : a little later we shall hear something about his early history, which may perhaps explain and partly exculpate him. As to Catharine, she escaped. It is vexatious that a complicated process in her should be represented by a single act which was transacted in a second. It would have been much more intelligible if it could have written itself in a dramatic conversation extending over two or three pages, but, as the event happened, so it must be recorded. The antagonistic and fiercely combatant forces did *so* issue in that deed, and the present historian has no intention to attempt an analysis. One thing is clear to him, that the quick stride up the garden path was urged not by any single, easily predominating impulse which had been enabled to annihilate all others. Do not those of us, who have been mercifully prevented from damning ourselves before the whole world, who have succeeded and triumphed—do we not know, know as we know hardly anything else, that our success and our triumph were due to superiority in strength by just a grain, no more, of our better self over the raging rebellion beneath it? It was just a tremble of the tongue of the balance: it might have gone this way, or it might have gone the other, but by God's grace it was this way settled—God's grace, as surely, in some form of words, everybody must acknowledge it to have been. When she reached her bedroom she sat down with her head on her hands, rose, walked about, looked out of window in the hope that she might see him, thought of Mrs. Cardew; forgot

her ; dwelt on what she had passed through till
she almost actually felt the pressure of his hand ;
cursed herself that she had turned away from
him ; prayed for strength to resist temptation, and
longed for one more chance of yielding to it.

The next morning a little parcel was left for
Miss Furze.   It contained the promised story,
which is here presented to my readers :—

"Did he Believe ?

" Charmides was born in Greece, but about the
year 300 A.D. was living in Rome.   He had come
there, like many of his countrymen, to pursue his
calling as sculptor in the imperial city, and he
cherished a great love for his art.   He knew too
well that it was not the art of the earlier days of
Athens, and that he could never catch the spirit of
that golden time, but he loved it none the less.   He
was also a philosopher in his way.   He had read
not only the literature of Greece, but that of his
adopted land, and he was especially familiar with
Lucretius and his pupil Virgil.   His intellectual
existence, however, was not particularly happy.

Rome was a pleasant city ; his occupation was one in which he delighted ; the thrill of a newly noticed Lucretian idea or of a tender touch in Virgil were better to him than any sensual pleasure, but his dealings with his favourite authors ended in his own personal emotion, and it was sad to think that the Hermes on which he had spent himself to such a degree should become a mere decoration to a Roman nobleman's villa, valued only because it cost so much, and that nobody who looked at it would ever really care for it. Once, however, he was rewarded. He had finished a Pallas Athene just as the sun went down. He was excited, and after a light sleep he rose very early and went into the studio with the dawn. There stood the statue, severe, grand in the morning twilight, and if there was one thing in the world clear to him, it was that what he saw was no inanimate mineral mass, but something more. It was no mere mineral mass with an outline added. Part of the mind which formed the world was in it, actually in it, and it came to Charmides that intellect, thought, had their own rights, that they were as much a fact as the stone, and that what he had done was simply to realise a Divine idea which was immortal, no matter what might become of its embodiment.   The weight of the material world lifted, an avenue of escape seemed to open itself to him from so much that oppressed and deadened him, and he felt like a man in an amphitheatre of overhanging mountains, who should espy in a far-off corner some scarcely perceptible track, and on nearer inspection a break in the walled precipices, a promise, or at least a hint, of a passage from imprisonment to the open plain.   It was nothing more than he had learned in his Plato, but the truth was made real to him, and he clung to it.

"Rome at the end of the third century was one of the most licentious of cities.   It was invaded by all the vices of Greece, and the counterpoise of the Greek virtues was absent. The reasoning powers assisted rather than prevented the degradation of morals, for they dissected and represented as nothing all the motives which had hitherto kept men upright.   The healthy and uncorrupted instinct left to itself would have been a sufficient restraint, but sophistry argued and said, *What is there in it?*—and so the very strength and prerogative of man hired itself out to perform the office of making him worse than a beast. Charmides was unmarried, and it is not to be denied that though his life as a whole was pure, he had yielded to temptation, not without loathing himself afterwards. He did not feel conscious of any transgression of a moral law, for no such law was recognised, but he detested himself because he had been drawn into close contact with a miserable wretch simply in order to satisfy a passion, and in the touch of mercenary obscenity there was something horrible to him. It was bitter to him to reflect that, notwithstanding his aversion from it, notwithstanding his philosophy and art, he had been equally powerless with the uttermost fool of a young aristocrat to resist the attraction of the commonest of snares. What were his books and fine pretensions worth if they could not protect him in such ordinary danger? Thus it came to pass that after a fall, when he went back to his work, it was so unreal to him, such a mockery, that days often elapsed before he could do anything. It was a mere toy, a dilettante dissipation, the embroidery of corruption. Oh, for a lawgiver, for a time of restraint, for the time of Regulus and the republic! Then, said Charmides to himself, my work would have some value, for heroic obedience would be behind it. He was right, for the love of the beautiful cannot long exist where there is moral pollution. The love of the beautiful itself is moral—that is to say, what we love in it is virtue. A perfect form or a delicate colour are the expression of something which is destroyed in us by subjugation to the baser desires or meanness, and he who has been unjust to man or woman misses the true interpretation of a cloud or falling wave.

"One night Charmides was walking through the lowest part of the city, and he heard from a mere hovel the sound of a hymn. He knew what it was—that it was the secret celebration of a religious rite by the despised sect of the Jews and their wretched proselytes. The Jews were especially hateful to him and to all cultured people in Rome. They were typical of all the qualities which culture abhorred. No Jew had ever produced anything lovely in any department whatever—no picture, statue, melody, nor poem. Their literature was also barbaric : there was no consecutiveness in it, no reasoning, no recognition in fact of the reason. It was a mere mass of legends without the exquisite charm and spiritual intention of those of Greece, of bloody stories and obscure disconnected prophecies by shepherds and peasants. Their god was a horror, a boor upon a mountain, wielding thunder and lightning. Aphrodite was perhaps not all that could be wished, but she was divine compared with the savage Jehovah. It was true that a recent Jewish sect professed better things and recognised as their teacher a young malefactor who was executed when Tiberius was emperor. So far, however, as could be made out he was a poor crack-brained demagogue, who dreamed of restoring a native kingdom in Palestine. What made the Jews especially contemptible to culture was that they were retrograde. They strove to put back the clock. There is only one path, so culture affirmed, and that is the path opened by Aristotle, the path of rational logical progress from what we already know to something not now known, but which can be known. If our present state is imperfect, it is because we do not know enough. Every other road, excepting this, the king's highway, leads into a bog. These Jews actually believed in miracles; they had no science, and thought they could regenerate the world by hocus-pocus. They ought to be suppressed by law, and, if necessary, put to death for they bred discontent.

"Nevertheless, Charmides decided to enter the hovel. He was in an idle mood, and he was curious to see for himself what the Jews were like. He pushed open the door, and when he went in he found himself in a low, mean room very dimly lighted and crowded with an odd medley of Greeks, Romans, tolerably well-dressed persons, and slaves. The poor and the slaves were by far the most numerous. The atmosphere was stifling, and Charmides sat as near the door as possible. Next to him was a slave-girl, not beautiful, but with a peculiar expression on her face very rare in Rome at that time. The Roman women were, many of them, lovely, but their loveliness was cold—the loveliness of indifference. The somewhat common features of this slave, on the contrary, were lighted up with eagerness : to her there was evidently something in life of consequence—nay, of immense importance. There were few of her betters in Rome to whom anything was of importance. A hymn at that moment was being sung, the words of which Charmides could not catch, and when it was finished an elderly man rose and read what seemed the strangest jargon about justification and sin. The very terms used were in fact unintelligible. The extracts were from a letter addressed to the sect in Rome by one Paul, a disciple of that Jesus who was crucified. After the reading was over came an address, very wild in tone and gesture, and equally unintelligible, and then a prayer or invocation, partly to their god, but also, as it seemed, to this Jesus, who evidently ranked as a dæmon, or perhaps as Divine. Charmides was quite unaffected. The whole thing appeared perfect nonsense, not worth investigation, but he could not help wondering what there was in it which could so excite that girl, whom he could hardly conclude to be a fool, and whose earnest-

ness was a surprise to him. He thought no more
about the affair until some days afterwards when
he happened to visit a friend. Just as he was
departing he met this very slave in the porch.
He involuntarily stopped, and she whispered to
him.

"'You will not betray us?'

"'I! Certainly not.'

"'I will lend you this. Read it and return it to
me.'' So saying, she vanished.

" Charmides, when he reached home, took out
the manuscript. He recognised it as a copy of
the letter which he had partly heard at the
meeting. He was somewhat astonished to find
that it was written by a man of learning, who
was evidently familiar with classic authors, but
surely never was scholarship pressed into such
a service! The confusion of metaphor, the sud-
denness of transition, the illogical muddles were
bad enough, but the chief obstacle to comprehension was that the author's whole scope and
purpose, the whole circle of his ideas, were outside
Charmides altogether. He was not attracted any
more than he was at the meeting, but he was a

little piqued because Paul had certainly been well educated, and he determined to attend the meeting again. This time he was late, and did not arrive till it was nearly at an end. His friend was there, and again he sat down next to her. When they went out it was dark, and he walked by her side.

"' Have you read the letter?'

"' Yes, but I do not understand it, and I have brought it back.'

"' May Christ the Lord open your eyes!'

"' Who is this Christ whom you worship?'

"' The Son of God, He who was crucified; the man Jesus; He who took upon Himself flesh to redeem us from our sins; in whom by faith we are justified and have eternal life.'

"It was all pure Hebrew to him, save the phrase 'Son of God,' which sounded intelligible.

"' You are Greek,' he said, for he recognised her accent although she spoke Latin.

"' Yes, from Corinth: my name is Demariste;' and she explained to him that, although she was a slave, she was partly employed in teaching Greek to the children of her mistress.

"'If you are Greek and well brought up, you must know that I cannot comprehend a word of what you have spoken. It is Judaism.'

"'To me, too,' she replied, speaking Greek to him, 'it was incomprehensible, but God by the light which lighteth every man hath brought me into His marvellous light, and now this that I have told you is exceedingly clear—nay, clearer than anything which men say they see.'

"'Tell me how it happened.'

"'When I first came to Rome I had a master who desired to make me his concubine, and I hated him; but what strength had I?—and I was tempted to yield. My parents were dead; I had no friends who cared for me—what did it matter! I had read in my books of the dignity of the soul, bnt that was a poor weapon with which to fight, and moreover sin was not exceeding sinful to me. By God's grace I was brought amongst these Christians, and I was convinced of sin. I saw that it was not only transgression against myself, but against the eternal decrees of the Most High, against those decrees which, as one of our own poets still dear to me has said—

" ' Ου γάρ τι νῦν γε κἀχθὲς, ἀλλ' ἀεί ποτε
ζῇ ταῦτα, κοὐδεὶς διδεν ἐξ ὅτου 'φάνη.' [1]

" ' I saw that all art, all learning, everything
which men value, were as straw compared with
God's commands, and that it would be well to
destroy all our temples, and statues, and all that
we have which is beautiful, if we could thereby
establish the kingdom of God within us, and so
become heirs of the life everlasting. Oh, my
friend, my friend in Christ, I hope, believe
me, Rome will perish, and we shall all perish,
not because we are ignorant, but because we
have not obeyed His word. But how was I
to obey it? Then I heard told the life of Christ
the Lord : how God the Father in His infinite
pity sent His Son into the world ; how He lived
amongst us and died a shameful death upon
the cross that we might not die ; and all His
strength passed into me and became mine through
faith, and I was saved ; saved for this life ; saved
eternally ; justified through Him ; worthy to

[1] " Not now nor of yesterday are they, but for ever they live, and
no one knows whence to date their appearance."—*Sophocles*,
" *Antigone.*"

wait for Him and meet Him at His coming, for He shall come, and I shall be for ever with the Lord.'

"Demariste stood straight upright as she spoke, and the light in her transfigured her countenance as the sun penetrating a grey mass of vapour informs it with such an intensity of brightness that the eye can scarcely endure it. It was a totally new experience to Charmides, an entire novelty in Rome. He did not venture to look in her face directly, for he felt that there was nothing in him equal to its sublime, solemn pleading.

"'I do not know anything of your Jesus,' he said at last, timidly; 'upon what do you rest His claims?'

"'Read His life. I will lend it to you; you will want no other evidence for Him. And was He not raised from the dead to reign for ever at His Father's right hand? No, keep the letter for a little while, and perhaps you will understand it better when you know upon what it is based.'

"A day or two afterwards the manuscript was

sent to him secretly with many precautions. He was not smitten suddenly by it. The Palestinian tale, although he confessed it was much more to his mind than Paul, was still *rude*. It was once more the rudeness which was repellent, and which almost outweighed the pathos of many of the episodes and the undeniable grandeur of the trial and death. Moreover, it was full of superstition and supernaturalism, which he could not abide. He was in his studio after its first perusal, and he turned to an Apollo which he was carving. The god looked at him with such overpowering, balanced sanity, such a contrast to Christian incoherence and the rhapsodies of the letter to the Romans, that he was half ashamed of himself for meddling with it. He opened his Lucretius. Here was order and sequence ; he knew where he was ; he was at home. Was all this nought, were the accumulated labour and thought of centuries to be set aside and trampled on by the crude, frantic inspiration of clowns ? The girl's face, however, recurred to him; he could not get rid of it, and he opened the biography again. He stumbled upon what now stand as

our twenty-third and twenty-fourth chapters of
Matthew, containing the denunciation of the
Pharisees, and the prophecy of the coming of
the Son of Man. He was amazed at the new
turn which was given to life, at the reasons
assigned for the curses which were dealt to
these Jewish doctors. They were damned for
their lack of mercy, judgment, faith, for their
extortion, excess, and because they were full
of hypocrisy and iniquity. They were fools and
blind, but not through defects which would have
condemned them in Greece and Rome at that
day, but through failings of which Greece and
Rome took small account. Charmides pondered
and pondered, and saw that this Jew had given
a new centre, a new pivot to society. This, then,
was the meaning of the world as nearly as
it could be said to have a single meaning.
Read by the light of the twenty-third chapter,
the twenty-fourth chapter was magnificent. 'For
as the lightning cometh out of the east, and
shineth even unto the west, so shall the coming
of the Son of Man be.' Was it not intelligible
that He to whom right and wrong were so

diverse, to whom their diversity was the one fact for man, should believe that Heaven would proclaim and enforce it ? He read more and more, until at last the key was given to him to unlock even that strange mystery, that being justified by faith we have peace with God through our Lord Jesus Christ. Still it was idle for him to suppose that he could ever call himself a Christian in the sense in which those poor creatures whom he had seen were Christians. Their fantastic delusions, their expectation that any day the sky might open and their Saviour appear in the body, were impossible to him ; nor could he share their confidence that once for all their religion alone was capable of regenerating the world. He could not, it is true, avoid the reflection that the point was not whether the Christians were absurd, nor was it even the point whether Christianity was not partly absurd. The real point was whether there was not more certainty in it than was to be found in anything at that time current in the world. Here, in what Paul called faith, was a new spring of action, a new reason for the blessed

life, and, what was of more consequence, a new
force by which men might be enabled to persist
in it. He could not, we say, avoid this reflection ;
he could not help feeling that he was bound
not to wait for that which was in complete
conformity with an ideal, but to enlist under the
flag which was carried by those who in the main
fought for the right, and that it was treason to
cavil and stand aloof because the great issue
was not presented in perfect purity. Nevertheless,
he was not decided, and could not quite decide.
If he could have connected Christianity with
his own philosophy; if it had been the out-
come, the fulfilment of Plato, his duty would
have been so much simpler; it was the complete rupture—so it seemed to him—which was
the difficulty. His heart at times leaped up
to join this band of determined, unhesitating
soldiers ; to be one in an army ; to have a
cause ; to have a banner waving over his head ;
to have done with isolation, aloofness, specula-
tion ending in nothing, and dreams which profited
nobody ; but even in those moments when he
was nearest to a confession of discipleship he

was restrained by faintness and doubt. If he
were to enrol himself as a convert his conversion
would be due not to an irresistible impulse, but
to a theory, to a calculation, one might almost
say, that such and such was the proper course
to take.

"He went again to the meeting, and he went
again and again. One night, as he came home,
he walked as he had walked before, with Demariste.
She was going as far as his door for the manuscript which he had now copied for his own use.
As they went along a man met them who raised
a lantern, and directed it full in their faces.

"'The light of death,' said Demariste.

"'Who is he?'

"'I know him well; he is a spy. I have often
seen him at the door of our assembly.'

"'Do you fear death?'

"'I? Has not Christ died?'

"Charmides had fallen in love with this slave,
but it was love so different from any love which
he had felt before for a woman, that it ought to
have had some other name. It was a love of the
soul, of that which was immortal, of God in her;

it was a love, too, of no mere temporary phenomenon, but of reality outlasting death into
eternity. There was thus a significance, there
was a grandeur in it wanting to any earthly love.
It was the new love with which men were henceforth to love women—the love of Dante for
Beatrice.

" She waited at the door while he went inside
to fetch the parchment. He brought it out and
gave it to her, and as he stood opposite to her
he looked in her face, and her eyes were not
averted. He caught her hand, but she drew
back.

" ' 'Tis but for a day or two,' she said ; ' a week
will see the end.'

" ' A week!' he cried.   ' Oh, my Demariste,
rather a week with thee than an age with anything less than thee ! '

" ' You will have to die too. Dare you die ?
The spirit may be willing, but the flesh may be
weak.'

" ' Death ! Yes, death, if only I am yours ! '

" ' Nay, nay, my beloved, not for me, but for
the Lord Jesus.'

"He bent nearer to her; his head was on her neck, and his arms were round her body. Oh, son and daughter of Time! oh, son and daughter of Eternity!

"He had hardly returned to his house, when he was interrupted by his friend Callippus, just a little the worse for wine.

"'What new thing is this?' said Callippus. 'I hear you have consorted with the Jews, and have been seen at their assembly.'

"'True, my friend.'

"'True! By Jupiter! what is the meaning of it? You do not mean to say that you are bitten by the mad dog?'

"'I believe.'

"'Oh, by God, that it should have come to this! Are you not ashamed to look him in the face?' pointing to the Apollo statue. 'Ah! the old prophecy is once more verified!—

"'Tutemet a nobis iam quovis tempore vatum
terriloquis victus dictis desciscere quæres.' [1]

---

[1] "You, yourself, some time or other, overcome by the terror-speaking tales of the seers, will seek to fall away from us."— *Lucretius,* "*De Rerum Natura.*"

But I must be prudent. I saw somebody watching your house on the other side of the street. If I am caught they will think I belong to the accursed sect too. Farewell.'

"The morning came, and about an hour after Charmides had risen two soldiers presented themselves. He was hurried away, brought before the judges, and examined. Some little pity was felt for him by two or three members of the court, as he was well known in Rome, and one of them condescended to argue with him and to ask him how he could become ensnared by a brutal superstition which affirmed, so it was said, the existence of devil-possessed pigs, and offered sacrifices to them.

"'You,' said he, 'an artist and philosopher— if it be true that you are a pervert, you deserve a heavier punishment than the scum whom we have hitherto convicted.'

"'For Christ and His cross!' cried Charmides.

"'Take him away!'

"The next day Charmides and Demariste met outside the prison gates. They were chained together in mockery, the seducer, Demariste, and the seduced, Charmides. They were marched through the streets of Rome, the crowd jeering them and thronging after them to enjoy the sport of their torments and death. Charmides saw the eyes of Demariste raised heavenwards and her lips moving in prayer.

"'He has heard me,' she said, 'and you will endure.'

"He pressed her hand, and replied, with unshaken voice, 'Fear not.'

"They came to the place of execution, but before the final stroke they were cruelly tortured. Charmides bore his sufferings in silence, but in her extremest agony the face of Demariste was lighted with rapture.

"'Look, look, my beloved, there, there!' trying to lift her mangled arm, 'Christ the Lord! One moment more and we are for ever with Him.'

"Charmides could just raise his head, and saw nothing but Demariste. He was able to turn himself towards her and move her hand to his lips, the second, only the second and the last kiss.

"So they died. Charmides was never considered a martyr by the Church. The circumstances were doubtful, and it was not altogether clear that he deserved the celestial crown."

CHAPTER IX.

THE school broke up next week for the summer holidays, and Catharine went home. Her mother was delighted with her daughter. She was less awkward, straighter, and her air and deportment showed the success of the plan. The father acquiesced, although he did not notice the change till Mrs. Furze had pointed it out. As to Mrs. Bellamy, she declared, when she met Catharine in the street the first market afternoon that " she had all at once become a woman grown." Mrs. Furze's separation from her former friends was now complete, but she had, unfortunately, not yet achieved admission into the superior circle. She had done so in a measure, but she was not satisfied. She felt that these people were not intimate with her, and that, although

she had screwed herself with infinite pains into
a bowing acquaintance, and even into a shaking
of hands, they formed a set by themselves, with
their own secrets and their own mysteries, into
which she could not penetrate. Their very polite-
ness was more annoying than rudeness would
have been. It showed they could afford to be
polite. Had she been wealthy, she could have
crushed all opposition by sheer weight of bullion ;
but in Eastthorpe everybody's position was known
with tolerable exactitude, and nobody was deluded
into exaggerating Mr. Furze's resources because
of the removal to the Terrace. Eastthorpe, on
the contrary, affirmed that the business had not
improved, and that expenses had increased.

When Catharine came home a light suddenly
flashed across Mrs. Furze's mind. What might
not be done with such a girl as that ! She
was good-looking — nay, handsome ; she had
the manners which Mrs. Furze knew that
she herself lacked, and Charlie Colston, aged
twenty-eight, was still disengaged. It was Mrs.
Furze's way, when she proposed anything to
herself, to take no account of any obstacles,

and she had the most wonderful knack of be-
littling and even transmuting all moral objections.
Mr. Charlie Colston was a well-known figure in
Eastthorpe. He was an only son, about five feet
eleven inches high, thin, unsteady on his legs,
smooth-faced, unwholesome, and silly. He had
been taken into his father's business because there
was nothing else for him, and he was a mere
shadow in it, despised by every cask-washer.
There was nothing wicked recorded against him ;
he did not drink, he did not gamble, he cared
nothing for horses or dogs ; but Eastthorpe
thought none the better of him for these negative
virtues. He was not known to be immoral,
but he was for ever playing with this girl or the
other, smiling, mincing, toying, and it all came to
nothing. A very unpleasant creature was Mr.
Charlie Colston, a byword with women in Eastthorpe, even amongst the nursery-maids. Mrs.
Furze knew all about this youth ; but she brought
out her philosopher's stone and used it with effect.
She did not intend to mate Catharine with a
fool, and make her miserable. If she could not
have persuaded herself that the young man was

everything that could be desired she would have thought no more about him. The whole al-chemical operation, however, of changing him into purest gold occupied only a few minutes, and the one thought now was how to drop the bait. It did cross her mind that Catharine herself might object ; but she was convinced that if her daughter could have a distinct offer made to her, all opposition might somehow be quenched.

Fate came to her assistance, as it does always to those who watch persistently and with patience. One Sunday evening at church it suddenly began to rain. The Furze family had not provided themselves with umbrellas, but Mrs. Furze knew that Mr. Charlie Colston never went out without one. Her strategy, when the service was over, was worthy of Napoleon, and, with all the genius of a great commander, she brought her forces into exact position at the proper moment. She herself and Mr. Furze detained the elder Mr. Colston and his wife, and kept them in check a little way behind, so that Catharine and their son were side by side when the entrance was reached. Of course he could do nothing but offer Catharine

his umbrella, and his company on the way homewards, but to his utter amazement, and the confusion of Mrs. Furze, who watched intently the
result of her manœuvres, Catharine somewhat
curtly declined, and turned back to wait for her
parents. Mr. Charlie rejoined his father and
mother, who naturally forsook the Furzes at the
earliest possible moment in such a public place
as a church porch. In a few minutes the shower
abated. Mrs. Furze could not say anything to
her daughter ; she could not decently appear to
force Charlie on her by rebuking her for not
responding to his generosity, but she was disappointed and embittered.

On the following morning Catharine announced
her intention of going to Chapel Farm for a few
days. Her mother remonstrated, but she knew
she would have to yield, and Catharine went.
Mrs. Bellamy poured forth the pent-up tale of
three months—gossip we may call it if we wish
to be contemptuous ; but what is gossip? A
couple of neighbours stand at the garden gate
on a summer's evening and tell the news of the
parish. They discuss the inconsistency of the

parson, the stony-heartedness of the farmer, the behaviour of this young woman and that young man ; and what better could they do ? They certainly deal with what they understand—something genuinely within their own circle and experience ; and there is nothing to them in politics, British or Babylonian, of more importance. There is no better conversation than talk about Smith, Brown, and Harris, male and female, about Spot the terrier or Juno the mare. Catharine had many questions to answer about the school, but Mr. Cardew's name was not once mentioned.

One afternoon, late in August, Catharine had gone with the dog down to the riverside, her favourite haunt. Clouds, massive, white, sharply outlined, betokening thunder, lay on the horizon in a long line ; the fish were active ; great chub rose, and every now and then a scurrying dimple on the pool showed that the jack and the perch were busy. It was a day full of heat, a day of exultation, for it proclaimed that the sun was alive ; it was a day on which to forget winter with its doubts, its despairs, and its indistinguishable grey ; it was a day on which to believe in immortality. Catharine was at that happy age when summer has power to warm the brain; it passed into her blood and created in her simple, uncontaminated bliss. She sat down close to an alder which overhung the bank. It was curious, but so it was, that her thoughts suddenly turned from the water and the thunderclouds and the blazing heat to Mr. Cardew, and it is still more strange that at that moment she saw him coming along the towing-path. In a minute he was at her side, but before he reached her she had risen.

"Good morning, Miss Furze."

"Mr. Cardew! What brings you here?"

"I have been here several times; I often go out for the day; it is a favourite walk."

He was silent, and did not move. He seemed prepossessed and anxious, taking no note of the beauty of the scene around him.

"How is Mrs. Cardew?"

"She is well, I believe."

"You have not left home this morning, then?"

"No; I was not at home last night."

"I think I must be going."

"I will walk a little way with you."

"My way is over the bridge to the farmhouse, where I am staying."

"I will go as far as you go."

Catharine turned towards the bridge.

"Is it the house beyond the meadows?"

"Yes."

It is curious how indifferent conversation often is just at the moment when the two who are talking may be trembling with passion.

"You should have brought Mrs. Cardew with you," said Catharine, tearing to pieces a water lily, and letting the beautiful white petals fall bit by bit into the river.

Mr. Cardew looked at her steadfastly, scrutinisingly, but her eyes were on the thunderclouds, and the lily fell faster and faster. The face of this girl had hovered before him for weeks, day and night. He never for a moment proposed to himself deliberate love for her—he could not do it, and yet he had come there, not, perhaps, consciously in order to find her, but dreaming of her all the time. He was literally possessed. The more he thought about her, the less did he see and hear of the world outside him, and no motive for action found access to him which was not derived from her. Of course it was all utterly mad and unreasonable, for, after all, what did he really know about her, and what was there in her to lay hold of him with such strength ? But, alas ! thus it was, thus he was made ; so much the worse for him. Was this a Christian believer ? was he really sincere in his belief ? He was sincere with a sincerity, to speak arithmetically, ot the tenth power beyond that of his exemplary churchwarden Johnson, whose religion would have restrained him from anything warmer than the extension of a Sunday black-gloved finger-tip to any woman save " Mrs. J." Here he was by the riverside with her ; he was close to her ; nobody was present, but he could not stir nor speak ! Catharine felt his gaze, although her eyes were not towards him. At last the lily came to an end, and she tossed the naked stalk after the flower. She loved this man ; it was a perilous moment : one touch, a hair's breadth of oscillation, and the two would have been one. At such a crisis the least external disturbance is often decisive. The first note of the thunder was heard, and suddenly the image of Mrs. Cardew presented itself before Catharine's eyes, appealing to her piteously, tragically. She faced Mr. Cardew.

" I am sorry Mrs. Cardew is not here. I wish I had seen more of her. Oh, Mr. Cardew ! how I envy her ! how I wish I had her brains for scientific subjects ! She is wonderful. But I *must* be going; the thunder is distant : you will be in Eastthorpe, I hope, before the storm comes. Good-bye," and she had gone.

She did not go straight to the house, however, but went into the garden and again cursed herself that she had dismissed him. Who had dismissed him ? Not she. How had it been done ? She could not tell. She crept out of the garden and went to the corner of the meadow where she could see the bridge. He was still there. She tried to make up an excuse for returning ; she tried to go back without one, but it was impossible. Something, whatever it was, stopped her ; she struggled and wrestled, but it was of no avail, and she saw Mr. Cardew slowly retrace his steps to the town. Then she leaned upon the wall and found some relief in a great fit of sobbing. Consolation

she had none; not even the poor reward of
conscience and duty. She had lost him, and she
felt that, if she had been left to herself, she would
have kept him. She went out again late in the
evening. The clouds had passed away to the
south and east, but the lightning still fired
the distant horizon far beyond . Eastthorpe and
towards Abchurch. The sky was clearing in the
west, and suddenly in a rift Arcturus, abou* to
set, broke through and looked at her, and in a
moment was again eclipsed. What strange confusion ! What inexplicable contrasts ! Terror and
divinest beauty ; the calm of the infinite inter-
stellar space and her own anguish ; each an
undoubted fact, but each to be taken by itself as
it stood : the star was there, the dark blue depth
was there, but they were no answer to the storm
or her sorrow.

She returned to Eastthorpe on the following day
and immediately told her mother she should not
go back to the Misses Ponsonby.

CATHARINE
FURZE

BY

MARK RUTHERFORD

EDITED BY HIS FRIEND

REUBEN SHAPCOTT

IN TWO VOLUMES

VOL. II

London

T. FISHER UNWIN

PATERNOSTER SQUARE

MDCCCXCIII

CATHARINE FURZE.

CHAPTER X.

THE reader has, doubtless, by this time judged
with much severity not only Catharine, but
Mr. Cardew. It is admitted to the full that they
are both most unsatisfactory and most improbable.
Is it likely that in a sleepy Midland town, such as
Eastthorpe, knowing nothing but the common
respectabilities of the middle of this century, the
daughter of an ironmonger would fall in love with
a married clergyman? Perhaps to their present
biographer it seems more remarkable than to his
readers. He remembers what the Eastern Midlands were like fifty years ago and they do not.
They are thinking of Eastthorpe of the present
day, of its schoolgirls who are examined in Keats

and Shelley, of the Sunday morning walks there, and of the, so to speak, smelling acquaintance with sceptical books and theories which half the population now boasts. But Eastthorpe, when Mr. Cardew was at Abchurch, was totally different. It knew what it was for parsons to go wrong. It had not forgotten a former rector and the young woman at the Bell. What talk there was about that affair! Happily his friends were well connected: they exerted themselves, and he obtained a larger sphere of usefulness two hundred miles away. Mr. Cardew, however, was not that rector, and Catharine was not the pretty waitress, and it is time now to tell the promised early history of Mr. Cardew.

He was the son of a well-to-do London merchant, who lived in Stockwell, in a large, white house, with a garden of a couple of acres, shaded by a noble cedar in its midst. There were four children, but he was the only boy. His mother belonged to an old and very religious family, and inherited all its traditions of Calvinistic piety and decorum. Her love for this boy was boundless, and she had a double ambition for him, which was that he might become a minister of God's Word, and in due time might marry Jane Berdoe, the only daughter of the Reverend Charles Berdoe, M.A., and Euphemia, her dearest friend. Mrs. Cardew had heard so much of the contamination of boys' schools that Theophilus was educated at home and sent straight from home to Cambridge. At the University he became a member of the ultra-evangelical sect of young men there, and devoted himself entirely to theology. He thus passed through youth and early manhood without any intercourse with the world so called, and he lacked that wholesome influence which is exercised by healthy companionship with those who differ from us and are not afraid to oppose us. Of course he married Jane Berdoe. His mother was always contriving that Jane should be present when he was at home: he was young: he had never known what it was to go astray with women, and he was unable to stand at a distance from her and ask himself if he really cared for her. He fell in love with himself, married himself, and soon after discovered that he did not know who his wife was. After his marriage he became wholly unjust to

her, and allowed her defects to veil the whole of
her character.

The ultra-evangelical school in the Church preserved at that time the religious life of England,
although in a very strange form. They believed
and felt certain vital truths, although they did not
know what was vital and what was not. They
had real experience, and their roots lay, not upon
the surface, but went deep down to the perennial
springs, and the articles of their creed became a
vehicle for the expression of the most real
emotions. Evangelicalism, however, to Mr. Cardew was dangerous. He was always prone to
self-absorption, and the tendency was much increased by his religion. He lived an entirely
interior life, and his joys and sorrows were
not those of Abchurch, but of another sphere.
Abchurch feared wet weather, drought, ague,
rheumatism, loss of money, and, on Sundays,
feared hell, but Mr. Cardew's fears were spiritual
or even spectral. His self-communion produced
one strange and perilous result, a habit of prolonged evolution from particular ideas uncorrected
by reference to what was around him. If any-

thing struck him it remained with him, deduction followed deduction in practice unfortunately as well as in thought, and he was ultimately landed in absurdity or something worse. The wholesome influence of ordinary men and women never permits us to link conclusion to conclusion from a single premiss, or at any rate to act upon our conclusions, but Mr. Cardew had no world at Abchurch save himself. He saw himself in things, and not as they were. A sunset was just what it might happen to symbolise to him at the time, and his judgments upon events and persons were striking, but they were frequently judgments upon creations of his own imagination, and were not in the least apposite to what was actually before him. The happy, artistic, Shakespearian temper, mirroring the world like a lake, was altogether foreign to him.

When he saw Catharine a new love awoke in him instantaneously. Was it legitimate or illegitimate? In many cases of the same kind the answer would be that the question is one which cannot be put. No matter how pure the intellectual bond between man and woman may be, it is

certain to carry with it a sentiment which cannot
be explained by the attraction of mere mental
similarity.   A man says to a man, "Do you really
believe it ?" and, if the answer is "yes," the two
become friends ; but if it is a woman who responds
to him, something follows which is sweeter than
friendship, whether she be bound or free.   It cannot be helped ; there is no reason why we should
try to help it, provided only we do no harm to
others, and indeed these delicate threads are the
very fairest in the tissue of life.   With Mr. Cardew
it was a little different.   Undoubtedly he was
drawn to Catharine because her thoughts were
his thoughts.   St. Paul and Milton in him saluted
St. Paul and Milton in her.   But he did not
know where to stop, nor could he look round
and realise whither he was being led.   Any
other person in six weeks would have noticed
the milestones on the road, and would have
determined that it was time to turn, but he
gaily walked forward with his head in the clouds.
If anybody at that particular moment when he
left the bridge could have made him comprehend that he was making love to a girl ; that

what he was doing was an ordinary, common-place criminal act, or one which would justifiably be interpreted as such, he not only would have been staggered and confounded, but would instantly have drawn back. As it was, he was neither staggered nor confounded, and went home to his wife with but one image in his brain, that of Catharine Furze.

Catharine was one of those creatures whose life is not uniform from sixteen to sixty, a simple progressive accumulation of experiences, the addition of a ring of wood each year. There had come a time to her when she had suddenly opened. The sun shone with new light, a new lustre lay on river and meadow, the stars became something more than mere luminous points in the sky, she asked herself strange questions, and she loved more than ever her long wanderings at Chapel Farm. This phenomenon of a new birth is more often seen at some epochs than at others. When a nation is stirred by any religious movement it is common, but it is also common in a different shape during certain periods of spiritual activity, such as the latter part of the eighteenth century

and the first half of the nineteenth in England
and Germany. Had Catharine been born two
hundred years earlier, life would have been easy.
All that was in her would have found expression
in the faith of her ancestors, large enough for any
intellect or any heart at that time. She would
have been happy in the possession of a key which
unlocks the mystery of things, and there would
have been ample room for emotion. How impatient she became of those bars which nowadays
restrain people from coming close to one another!
Often and often she felt that she could have leaped
out towards the person talking to her, that she
could have cried to him to put away his circumlo-
cutions, his forms and his trivialities, and to let her
see and feel what he really was. Often she knew
what it was to thirst like one in a desert for
human intercourse, and she marvelled how those
who pretended to care for her could stay away so
long: she could have humiliated herself if only
they would have permitted her to love them and
be near them. Poor Catharine! the world as it is
now is no place for people so framed! When life
runs high and takes a common form men can walk

together as the disciples walked on the road to Emmaus. Christian and Hopeful can pour out their hearts to one another as they travel towards the Celestial City and are knit together in everlasting bonds by the same Christ and the same salvation. But when each man is left to shift for himself, to work out the answers to his own problems, the result is isolation. People who, if they were believers, would find the richest gift of life in utter confidence and mutual help are now necessarily strangers. One turns to metaphysics; another to science; one takes up with Rousseau's theory of existence, and another with Kant's; they meet; they have nothing to say; they are of no use to one another in trouble; one hears that the other is sick; what can be done? There is a nurse; he does not go; his old friend dies, and as to the funeral—well, we are liable to catch cold. Not so, Christian and Hopeful! for when Christian was troubled " with apparitions of hobgoblins and evil spirits, even on the borderland of Heaven—oh, Bunyan! Hopeful kept his brother's head above water, and called upon him to turn his eyes to the Gate and the men standing by it to receive him."

My poor reader-friend, how many times have you in this nineteenth century, when the billows have gone over you—how many times have you felt the arm of man or woman under you raising you to see the shining ones and the glory that is inexpressible?

Had Catharine been born later it would have been better. She would perhaps have been able to distract herself with the thousand and one subjects which are now got up for examinations, or she would perhaps have seriously studied some science, which might at least have been effectual as an opiate in suppressing sensibility. She was, however, in Eastthorpe before the new education, as it is called, had been invented. There was no elaborate system of needle points, Roman and Greek history, plain and spherical trigonometry, political economy, ethics, literature, chemistry, conic sections, music, English history, and mental philosophy, to draw off the electricity within her, nor did she possess the invaluable privilege of being able, after studying a half-crown handbook, to unbosom herself to women of her own age upon the position of Longland as an English poet.

Shakespeare or Wordsworth might have been of some use to her, but to Shakespeare she was not led, although there was a brown, dusty, one-volume edition at the Terrace ; and of Wordsworth nobody whom she knew in Eastthorpe had so much as heard. A book would have turned much that was vague in her into definite shape; it would have enabled her to recognise herself ; it would have given an orthodox expression to cloudy singularity, and she would have seen that she was a part of humanity in her most extravagant and personal emotions. As it was, her position was critical because she stood by herself, affiliated to nothing, an individual belonging to no species, so far as she knew. She then met Mr. Cardew. It was through him the word was spoken to her, and he was the interpreter of the new world to her. She was in love with him—but what is love ? There is no such thing : there are loves, and they are all different. Catharine's was the very life of all that was Catharine, senses, heart, and intellect, a summing-up and projection of her whole self-hood. He was more to her than she to him—was any woman ever so much to a man as a man is to

a woman?   She was happy when she was near him.
When she was in ordinary Eastthorpe society she
felt as a pent-up lake might feel if the weight of
its waters were used in threading needles, but
when Mr. Cardew talked to her, and she to him,
she rejoiced in the flow of all her force, and that
horrible oppression in her chest vanished.

Nevertheless, the fear, the shudder, came to her
and not to him ; the wrench came from her and
not from him.   It was she and not he who watched
through the night and found no motive for the
day, save a dull, miserable sense that it was her
duty to live through it.

CHAPTER XI.

IT was a fact, and everybody noticed it, that since the removal to the Terrace, and the alteration in their way of living, Mr. Furze was no longer the man he used to be, and seemed to have lost his grasp over his business. To begin with, he was not so much in the shop. His absences in the Terrace at meal-times made a great gap in the day, and Tom Catchpole was constantly left in sole charge. Mr. Bellamy came home one evening and told his wife that he had called at Furze's to ask the meaning of a letter Furze had signed, explaining the action of a threshing - machine which was out of order. To his astonishment Furze, who was in his counting-house, called for Tom, and said, "Here, Tom, this is one of your letters ; you had better tell Mr. Bellamy how the thing works."

"I held my tongue, Mrs. Bellamy, but I had my thoughts all the same, and the next time I go there, *if* I go at all, I shall ask for Tom."

Mr. Furze was aware of Tom's growing importance, and Mrs. Furze was aware of it too. The worst of it was that Mr. Furze, at any rate, knew that he could not do without him. It is very galling to the master to feel that his power is slipping from him into the hands of a subordinate, and he is apt to assert himself by spasmodic attempts at interference which generally make matters worse and rivet his chains more tightly. There was a small factory in Eastthorpe in which a couple of grindstones were used which were turned by water-power at considerable speed. One of them had broken at a flaw. It had flown to pieces while revolving, and had nearly caused a serious accident. The owner called at Mr. Furze's to buy another. There were two in stock, one of which he would have taken; but Tom, his master being at the Terrace, strongly recommended his customer not to have that quality, as it was from the same quarry as the one which was faulty, but that another should be ordered. To this he assented.

When Mr. Furze returned Tom told him what had happened. He was in an unusually irritable, despotic mood. Mrs. Furze had forced him to yield upon a point which he had foolishly made up his mind not to concede, and consequently he was all the more disposed to avenge his individuality elsewhere. After meditating for a minute or two he called Tom from the counter.

"Mr. Catchpole, what do you mean by taking upon yourself to promise you would obtain another grindstone?"

"Mean, sir! I do not quite understand. The two out there are of the same sort as the one that broke, and I did not think them safe."

"Think, sir! What business had you to think? I tell you what it is, you are much too fond of thinking. If you would only leave the thinking to me, and do what you are told, it would be much better for you."

Tom's first impulse was to make a sharp reply, and to express his willingness to leave, but for certain private reasons he was silent. Encouraged by the apparent absence of resistance, Mr. Furze continued—

" I've meant to have a word or two with you several times. You seem to have forgotten your position altogether, and that I am master here, and not you. You, perhaps, do not remember where you came from, and what you would have been if I had not picked you up. Let there be no misunderstanding in future."

" There shall be none, sir. Shall I call at the factory and explain your wishes about the grindstone ? I will tell them I was mistaken, and that they had better have one of those in stock."

" No, you cannot do that now ; let matters remain as they are ; I must lose the sale of the stone and put up with it."

Tom withdrew. That evening, after supper, Mr. Furze, anxious to show his wife that he possessed some power to quell opposition, told her what had happened. It met with her entire approval. She hated Tom. For all hatred, as well as for all love, there is doubtless a reason, but the reasons for the hatreds of a woman of Mrs. Furze's stamp are often obscure, and perhaps more nearly an exception than any other known fact in nature to the rule that every effect must have a cause.

"I would get rid of him," said she. "I think that his not replying to you is ten times more aggravating than if he had gone into a passion."

"You cannot get rid of him," said Catharine.

"Cannot! What do you mean, Catharine—cannot? I like that! Do you suppose that I do not understand my own business—I who took him up out of the gutter and taught him? Cannot, indeed!"

"Of course you *can* get rid of him, father; but I would not advise you to try it."

"Now, do take *my* advice," said Mrs. Furze: "send him about his business at once, before he does any further mischief, and gets hold of your connection. Promise me."

"I will," said Mr. Furze, "to-morrow morning, the very first thing."

Morning came, and Mr. Furze was not quite so confident. Mrs. Furze had not relented, and as her husband went out at the door she reminded him of his vow.

"You will, now? I shall expect to hear when you come home that he has had notice."

"Oh, certainly he shall go, but I am doubtful whether I had better not wait till I have somebody in my eye whom I can put in his place."

"Nonsense! you can find somebody easily enough."

Mr. Furze strode into his shop looking and feeling very important. Instead of the usual kindly "Good morning," he nodded almost imperceptibly and marched straight into his counting-house. It had been his habit to call Tom in there and open the letters with him, Tom suggesting a course of action and replies. Today he opened his correspondence in silence. It happened to be unusually bulky for a small business, and unusually important. The Honourable Mr. Eaton was about to make some important alterations in his house and grounds. New conservatories were to be built, and an elaborate system of hot water warming apparatus was to be put up both for house and garden. He had invited tenders to specification from three houses—one in London, one in Cambridge, and from Mr. Furze. Tom and Mr. Furze had gone over the specification carefully, but Tom had preceded and originated, and Mr. Furze had followed, and, in order not to appear slow of comprehension, had frequently assented when he did not understand—a most dangerous weakness. To his surprise he found that his tender of £850 was accepted. There was much work to be done which was not in his line, but had been put into his contract in order to save subdivision, and consequently arrangements had to be made with sub-contractors. Materials had also to be provided at once, and there was a penalty of so much a day if the job was not completed by a certain time. He did not know exactly where to begin; he was stunned, as if somebody had hit him a blow on the head, and, after trying in vain to think, he felt that his brain was in knots. He put the thing aside, looked at his other letters, and they were worse. One of his creditors, a blacksmith, who owed him £55 for iron, had failed, and he was asked to attend a meeting of creditors. A Staffordshire firm, upon whom he had depended for pipes, in case he should obtain Mr. Eaton's order, had sent a circular announcing an advance in iron, and he forgot that in their offer their price held good for another week. He was trustee under an old trust, upon which no action had been taken for years ; he remembered none of its provisions, and now the solicitors had written to him requesting him to be present at a most important conference in London that day week. There was also a notice from the Navigation Commissioners informing him that, in consequence of an accident at one of their locks, it would be fully a fortnight before any barge could pass through, and he knew that his supply of smithery coal would be exhausted before that date, as he had refrained from purchasing in consequence of high prices. To crown everything a tap came at the door, and in walked his chief man at the foundry to announce that he would shortly leave, as he had obtained a better berth. Mr. Furze by this time was so confused that he said nothing but " Very well," and when the man had gone he leaned his head on his elbows in despair. He looked through the glass window of the counting-house and saw Tom quietly weighing some nails. He would have given anything if he could have called him in, but he could not. As to dismissing him, it was out of the question now, and yet his sense of dependence on him excited a jealousy nearly as intense as his wife's animosity. When a man cannot submit to be helped he dislikes the benevolent friend who offers assistance worse than an avowed enemy. Mr. Furze felt as if he must at once request Tom's aid, and at the same time do him some grievous bodily harm.

The morning passed away and nothing was advanced one single step. He went home to his dinner excited, and he was dangerous. It is very trying, when we are in a coil of difficulty, out of which we see no way of escape, to hear some silly thing suggested by an outsider who perhaps has not spent five minutes in considering the case. Mrs. Furze, knowing nothing of Mr. Eaton's contract, of the blacksmith's failure, of the advance in iron, of the trust meeting, of the stoppage of the navigation, and of the departure of the foundryman, asked her husband the moment the servant had brought in the dinner and had left the room—

"Well, my dear, what did Tom say when you told him to go?"

" I haven't told him."

" Not told him, my dear! how is that?"

" I wish with all my heart you'd mind your own affairs."

"Mr. Furze! what is the matter? You do not seem to know what you are saying."

" I know perfectly well what I am saying. I wish you knew what *you* are saying. When we came up here to the Terrace—much good has it done us—I thought I should have no interference with my business. You understand nothing whatever about it, and I shall take it as a favour if you will leave it alone."

Mrs. Furze was aghast. Presently she took out her pockethandkerchief and retreated to her bedroom. Mr. Furze did not follow her, but his dinner remained untouched. When he rose to leave, Catharine went after him to the door, caught hold of his hand and silently kissed him, but he did not respond.

During the dinner-hour Tom had looked in the counting-house and saw the letters lying on the table untouched. Mr. Eaton's steward came in with congratulations that the tender was accepted, but he could not wait. As Mr. Furze passed through the shop Tom told him simply that the steward had called.

" What did he want ? "

" I do not know, sir."

Mr. Furze went to his papers again and shut the door. He was still more incapable of collecting his thoughts and of determining how to begin. First of all came the contract, but before he could settle a single step the navigation presented itself. Then, without any progress, came the rise in the price of iron, and so forth. In about three hours the post would be going, and nothing was done. He cast about for some opportunity of a renewal of intercourse with Tom, and looked anxiously through his window, hoping that Tom might have some question to ask. At last he could stand it no longer, and he opened the door and called out—

" Mr. Catchpole "—not the familiar " Tom."

Mr. Catchpole presented himself.

" I wish to give you some instructions about these letters. I have arranged them in order. You will please write what I say, and I will sign in time for the post to-night. First of all there is the contract. You had better take the necessary action and ask the Staffordshire people what advance they want."

"Yes, sir, but"—deferentially—"the Staffordshire people cannot claim an advance if you accept at once: you remember the condition ? "

" Certainly; what I mean is that you can accept their tender. Then there is the meeting of creditors."

" I suppose you wish Mr. Eaton's acceptance acknowledged and the sub-contractors at once informed ? "

" Of course, of course ; I said necessary action —that covers everything. With regard to the creditors' meeting, my proposal is—— " A pause.

" Perhaps it will be as well, sir, if you merely say you will attend."

" I thought you would take that for granted. I was considering what proposal I should make when we meet."

" Probably, sir, you can make it better after you hear his statement."

" Well, possibly it may be so ; but I am always

in favour of being prepared. However, we will postpone that for the present. Then there is the trustee business. That is a private matter of my own, which you will not understand. I will give you the papers, however, and you can make an abstract of them. I cannot carry every point in my head. If you are in any doubt come to me."

"You wish me to say you will go, sir?"

"I should have thought there was no need to ask. You surely do not suppose that I am to give instructions upon every petty detail! Then about the navigation : I *must* have some coal, and that is the long and the short of it."

The "how" was probably a petty detail, for Mr. Furze went no further with the subject, and was inclined to proceed with the man at the foundry.

"It will be too late if we wait till the lock is repaired, sir. I understand it will be three weeks really. Will you write to Ditchfield and tell them five tons are to come to Millfield Sluice? We will then cart it from there. That will be the cheapest and the best way."

"Yes, I do not object; but we *must* have the coal—that is really the important point. As to Jack in the foundry, I will get somebody else. I suppose we shall have to pay more."

"How would it be, sir, if you put Sims in Jack's place, and Spurling in Sims' place? You would then only want a new labourer, and you would pay no more than you pay now. Sims, too, knows the work, and it might be awkward to have a new man at the head just now."

"Yes, that may do; but what I wish to impress on you is that the vacancy *must* be filled up. That is all, I think; you can take the letters."

Tom took them up and went to his little corner near the window to re-peruse them. There was much to be done which had not been mentioned, particularly with regard to Mr. Eaton's contract. He took out the specification, jotted down on a piece of paper the several items, marked methodically with a cross those which required prompt attention, and began to write. Mr. Furze, seeing his desk unencumbered, was very well satisfied with himself. He had "managed" the whole thing perfectly. His head became clear, the knots were untied, and he hummed a few bars of a hymn. He then went to his safe, took out the trust papers without looking at them, handed them over to Tom with a remark that he should like the abstract the next morning, and at once went up to the Terrace. He was hungry : he had left Mrs. Furze unwell, and, in his extreme good-humour, had relented towards her. She had recovered, but did not mention again the subject of Tom's discharge. He had ham with his tea, but it was over sooner than usual, and he rose to depart.

" You are going early, father," said Catharine.

" Yes, my dear ; it has been a busy day. I have been successful with my tender for Mr. Eaton's improvements ; iron has advanced ; the navigation has stopped ; Castle, the blacksmith, has gone to smash ; I have to go to a trustees' meeting under that old Fothergill trust ; and Jack in the foundry has given notice to leave."

" When did you hear all this ? "

" All within an hour after breakfast. I have been entirely occupied this afternoon in directing Tom what to do, and I must be off to see that he has carried out my instructions. What a coil it is! and yet I rather like it."

Catharine reflected that her father did not seem to like it at dinner-time, and went through the familiar operation of putting two and two together. She accompanied him to the front gate, and as he passed out she said—

" You have not given Tom notice ? "

" No, my dear, not yet. It would be a little inconvenient at present. I *could* do without him easily, even now ; but perhaps it will be better to wait. Besides, he is a little more teachable after the talking-to I have given him."

Mr. Furze signed his letters. He did not observe that many others, of which he had not thought, remained to be written, and when Tom brought them the next day he made no remark. The assumption was that he had noticed the day before what remained to be done, saw that it was not urgent, and consented to the delay. The curious thing was that he assumed it to himself. It is a fact—not incredible to those who know that nobody, not the most accomplished master in flattery, can humbug us so completely

as we can and do humbug ourselves—that **Mr.**
Furze, ten minutes after the letters were posted,
was perfectly convinced that he had foreseen the
necessity of each one—that he had personally and
thoroughly controlled the whole day's operations,
and that Tom had performed the duties of a
merely menial clerk. As he went home he
thought over Catharine's attitude with regard to
Tom. She, in reality, had been anxious to
protect her father; but such a motive he could
not be expected to suggest to himself. A horrid
notion came into his head. She might be fond
of Tom! Did she not once save his life? Had
she not, even when a child, pleaded that something ought to be done for him? Had she not
affirmed that he was indispensable? Had she
not inquired again about him that very day?
Had she not openly expressed her contempt
for that most eligible person, Mr. Colston? He
determined to watch most strictly, and again he
resolved to dismiss his assistant. A trifling increase in his attention to small matters would
enable him to do this within a month or two.
It would be as well for Mrs. Furze to watch

too.　After supper Catharine went to bed early,
and her father hung out the white flag, to which
friendly response was given directly the subject
of his communications was apparent.　It became
a basis of almost instantaneous reconciliation, and
Mrs. Furze, mindful of the repulse of the brewer's
son and the ruin of her own scheme thereon built,
hated Tom more than ever.　It was Tom, then,
who had prevented admission into Eastthorpe
society. .

CHAPTER XII.

MR. TOM CATCHPOLE had never had any schooling. What he had learned he had learned by himself, and the books he had read were but few, and chosen rather by chance. He had never had the advantage of the common introduction to the world of ideas which is given, in a measure, to all boys who are systematically taught by teachers, and consequently, not knowing the relative value of what came before him, his perspective and proportion were incorrect. His mind, too, was essentially plain. He was perfect in his loyalty to duty ; he was, as we have seen, very good in business matters, had a clear head, and could give shrewd advice upon any solid, matter-of-fact difficulty, but the spiritual world was non-existent for him. He attended chapel regularly, for he was a Dissenter, but his reasons

for going, so far as he had any, were very simple.
There was a great God in heaven, against whom
he had sinned and was perpetually sinning. To
save himself from the consequences of his trans-
gressions certain means were provided, and he was
bound to use them. On Monday morning chapel
and all thoughts connected with it entirely disappeared, but he said his prayers twice a day
with great regularity. There are very few, however, of God's creatures to whom the supernatural
does not in some way present itself, and no man
lives by bread alone. To Tom, Catharine was
miracle, soul, inspiration, religion, enthusiasm,
patriotism, immortality, the fact, essentially identical, whatever we like to call it, which is not bread
and yet is life. He never dared to say anything
to her. He felt that she lived in a world beyond
him, and he did not know what kind of a world
it was. He knew that she thought about things
which were strange to him, and that she was
anxious upon subjects which never troubled him.
She was often greatly depressed when there was
no cause for depression, so far as he could see,
and he could not comprehend why a person should

be ill when there was nothing the matter. If he felt unwell—a rare event with him—he always took two antibilious pills before going to bed, and was all right the next morning. He wished he himself could be ill without a reason, and then perhaps he would be able to understand Catharine better. Her elation and excitement were equally unintelligible. He once saw her sitting in her father's counting-house with a book. She was not a great reader—nobody in Eastthorpe read books, and there were not many to read—but she was so absorbed in this particular book that she did not lift her eyes from it when he came in, and it was not until her father had spoken twice to her, and had told her that he was expecting somebody, that she moved. She then ran upstairs into a storeroom, and was there for half an hour in the cold. The book was left open when she went away, and Tom looked at it. It was a collection of poems by all kinds of people, and the one over which she had been poring was about a man who had shot an albatross. Tom studied it, but could make nothing of it, and yet this was what had so much interested her! "O

God!" he said to himself, passionately, "if I could, if I did but know! She cares not a pin for me; this is what she cares for." Poor Tom! he did not pride himself on the absence of a sense in him, but knew and acknowledged to himself that he was defective. It is quite possible to be aware of a spiritual insensibility which there is no power to overcome—of the existence of a universe in which other favoured souls are able to live, one which they can report, and yet its doors are closed to us, or, if sitting outside we catch a glimpse of what is within, we have no power to utter a single sufficient word to acquaint anybody with what we have seen. Catharine respected Tom greatly, for she understood well enough what her father owed to him, but she could not love him. One penetrating word from Mr. Cardew thrilled every fibre in her, no matter what the subject might be. Tom, in every mood and on every topic, was uninteresting and ordinary. To tell the truth, plain, common probity taken by itself was not attractive to her. Horses, dogs, cows, the fields were more stimulant than perfect integrity, for she was young and did not know how precious it was; but, after all, the reason of reasons why she did not love Tom was that she did not love him.

It was announced one day by small handbills in the shop windows that a sermon was to be preached by Mr. Cardew, of Abchurch, in East-thorpe, on behalf of the County Infirmary, and Catharine went to hear him. It was in the evening, and she was purposely late. She did not go to her mother's pew, but sat down close to the door. To her surprise she saw Tom not far off. He was on his way to his chapel, when he noticed Catharine alone, walking towards the church, and he had followed her. Mr. Cardew took for his text the parable of the prodigal son. He began by saying that this parable had been taken to be an exhibition of God's love for man. It seemed rather intended to set forth, not the magnificence of the Divine nature, but of human nature—of that nature which God assumed. The determination on the part of the younger son to arise, to go to his father, and above everything to say to him simply "Father, I have sinned," was as great as God is great : it was God—God moving in us ; in a sense it was far more truly God—far greater than the force which binds the planets into a system. But the splendour of human nature—do not suppose any heresy here; it is Bible truth, the very gospel—is shown in the father as well as in the son. "When he was yet a great way off." We are as good as told, then, that day after day the father had been watching. How small were the probabilities that at any particular hour the son would return, and yet every hour the father's eyes were on that long, dusty road! When at last he saw what he was dying to see, what did he say? Was there a word of rebuke? He stopped his boy's mouth with kisses, and cried for the best robe and the ring and the shoes, and proclaimed a feast—the ring, mark you, a sign of honour!

> "Say nothing of pardon ; the darkness hath gone :
> Shall pardon be asked for the night by the sun ?
> No word of the past ; of the future no fear :
> 'Tis enough, my beloved, to know thou art here."

"Oh, my friends," said the preacher, "just consider that it is this upon which Jesus, the Son of God, has put His stamp, not the lecture, not chastisement, not expiation, but an instant unquestioning embrace, no matter what the wrong may have been. If you say this is dangerous doctrine, I say it is *here*. What other meaning can you give to it? At the same time I am astonished to find it here, astonished that priest-craft and the enemy of souls should not have erased it. Sacred truth! Is it not moving to think of all the millions of men who for eighteen hundred years have read this parable, philosophers and peasants, in every climate, and now are we reading it to-day! Is it not moving—nay, awful— to think of all the good it has done, of the sweet stream of tenderness, broad and deep, which has flowed down from it through all history? History would all have been different if this parable had never been told."

Mr. Cardew paused, and after his emotion had a little subsided he concluded by an appeal on behalf of the infirmary. He inserted a saving clause on Christ's mediatorial work, but it had no particular connection with the former part of his discourse. It was spoken in a different tone, and it satisfied the congregation that they had really heard nothing heterodox.

Tom watched Catharine closely. He noted her eager, rapt attention, and that she did not recover herself till the voluntary was at an end. He went out after her ; she met Mr. and Mrs. Cardew at the churchyard gates ; he saw the excitement of all three, and he saw Catharine leave her friends at the Rectory, for they were evidently going to stay the night there. Mrs. Cardew went into the house first, but Catharine turned down Fosbrooke Street, a street which did not lead, save by a very round-about way, to the Terrace. Presently Mr. Cardew came out and walked slowly down Rectory Lane. In those days it was hardly a thoroughfare. It ended at the river bank, and during daylight a boat was generally there, belonging to an old, super-annuated boatman, who carried chance passengers over to the mill meadows and saved them a walk if they wanted to go that side of the town. A rough seat had been placed near the boat moorings for the convenience of the ferryman's customers. At this time in the evening the place was deserted. Tom followed Mr. Cardew, and presently overtook him. Mr. Cardew and he knew one another slightly, for there were few persons for miles round who did not now and then visit Mr. Furze's shop.

" Good evening, Mr. Cardew."

" Ah ! Mr. Catchpole, is that you ? What are you doing here ? "

" I have been to hear you preach, sir, and I thought I would have a stroll before I went home."

" I thought I should like a stroll too."

The two went on together, and sat down on the seat. The moon had just risen, nearly full, sending its rays obliquely across the water, and lighting up the footpath which went right and left along the river's edge. Mr. Cardew seemed disinclined to talk, was rather restless, and walked backwards and forwards by the bank. Tom reflected that he might be intruding, but there was something on his mind, and he did not leave. Mr. Cardew sat down again by his side. They both happened to be looking in the same direction eastwards at the same moment.

" If that lady thinks to cross to-night," said Tom, " she's mistaken. I'd take her over myself, though it is Sunday, if the boat were not locked."

" What lady ? " asked Mr. Cardew—as if he were frightened, Tom thought.

" The lady coming down there just against the willow."

Mr. Cardew was short-sighted, and could not see her. He made as if he would go to meet her, but he stopped, returned, and remained stånding. The figure approached, but before Tom could discern anything more than that it was a woman, it disappeared behind the hedge up the little by-path that cut off the corner into Rectory Lane.

" She's gone," said Tom. " I suppose she was not coming here after all."

" Which way has she gone?" asked Mr. Cardew, looking straight on the ground and scratching it with his stick.

" Into the town."

" I must be going, I think, Mr. Catchpole ; good-night."

" I'll walk with you as far as your door, sir. There's something I want to say to you."

Mr. Cardew did not reply, and meditated for a moment.

" It is a lovely evening. We will sit here a little longer. What is it ?"

" Mr. Cardew, as I said, I have been to hear you

preach, and I thank you with all my heart for your sermon, but I want to ask you something about it. What you said about the Mediator was true enough, but somehow, sir, I feel as if I ought to have liked the first part most, but I couldn't, and perhaps the reason is that it was poetry. Oh, Mr. Cardew, if you could but tell me how to like poetry!"

"I am afraid neither I nor anybody else can teach you that; but why are you anxious to like it? Why are you dissatisfied with yourself?"

"I do not think I am stupid. When I am in the shop I know that I am more than a match for most persons, and yet, Mr. Cardew, there are some people who seem to me to have something I have not got, and they value it more than anything besides, and they have nothing to say really, *really*, I mean, to those who have not got it, although they are kind to them."

"It is not very easy to understand what you mean."

"Well, now to-night, sir, when you talked about God moving in us, and the force which binds the planets together, and all that, I am sure you felt it, and I am sure it is true, and yet I was out of doors, so to speak."

"Perhaps I may be peculiar, and it is you who are sane and sound."

"Ah, Mr. Cardew, if you were alone in it, and everybody were like me, that might be true, but it is not so ; it is I who am alone."

"Who cares for it whom you know ? You are under a delusion."

"Oh, no, I am not. Why there—there." Tom stopped.

"There was what ? "

"There was Miss Furze—she took it in."

"Indeed ! " Mr. Cardew again looked straight on the ground, and again scratched it with his stick. It was a night of nights, dying twilight long lingering in the north-west, the low golden moon, the slow, placid, shining stream, perfect stillness. Tom was not very susceptible, but even he was overcome and tempted into confidence.

"Mr. Cardew, you are a minister, and I may tell you : I know you will not betray me. I love Miss Furze ; I cannot help it. I have never loved any girl before. It is very foolish, for I am only her father's journeyman ; but that might be got over. She would not let that stand in her way, I am sure. But, Mr. Cardew, I am not up to her ; she is strange to me. If I try to mention her subjects, what I say is not right, and when I drove her home from Chapel Farm, and admired the view I know she admired, she directly began to speak about business, as if she did not wish to talk about better things ; perhaps it is because I never was taught. I had no schooling ; cannot you help me, sir ? I shall never set eyes on anybody like her. I would die this instant to save her a moment's pain."

Mr. Cardew was silent. It was characteristic of him that often when he himself was most person- ally affected, the situation became an object of reflection. What a strange pathos there was in this recognition of superiority and in the inability to rise to it and appropriate it ! Then his thoughts turned to himself again, and the flame shot up clear and strong, as if oil had been poured on the fire. She understood him ; she alone.

" I am very sorry for you, Mr. Catchpole, more sorry than I can tell you. I will think over what you have said, and we will have another talk about it. I must be going now."

Mr. Cardew, however, did not go towards Rectory Lane, but along the side path. Tom mechanically accompanied him, but without speaking. At last Mr. Cardew, finding that Tom did not leave him, retraced his steps and went up the lane. In about two minutes they met Mrs. Cardew.

" I wondered where you were. I was coming down to the ferry to look for you, thinking that most likely you were there. Ah, Mr. Catchpole ! is that you ? I am glad my husband has had company. Let me go back and look at the water."

" Certainly."

Tom stopped and took his leave.

The two went back to the river and sat on the seat.

Mrs. Cardew took her husband's hand in her own sweet way, kissed it, and held it fast. At last, with a little struggle, she said—

" My dear, you have never preached—to me, at least—as you have preached to-night."

" You really mean it ? "

She kissed his hand again, and leaned her head
on his shoulder. That was her reply. He clasped
her tenderly, fervently, more than fervently, and
yet ! while his mouth was on her neck, and his
arms were round her body, the face of Catharine
presented itself, and it was not altogether his wife
whom he caressed.

Meanwhile Tom, pursuing his way homewards,
overtook Miss Furze, to his great surprise.

" Tom, where have you been ? "

" I have just left Mr. and Mrs. Cardew."

Catharine, on her way home, hesitating—for it
was Catharine whom Tom and Mr. Cardew saw—
had met Mrs. Cardew just about to leave the house.

" Why, Catharine ! you here ? "

" I was tempted by the night."

" Catharine, did you ever hear my husband
preach better than he did to-night ? "

" Never ! "

" I was so proud of him, and I was so happy,
because just what touched him touched me too.
Come back with me : I know he has gone to the
ferry."

"No, thank you ; it is late."

"I am sure he will see you home."

"I am sure he shall not. What! walk up to the Terrace after a day's hard work!"

So they parted. What had passed between Catharine and Mrs. Cardew when they lingered behind at the Rectory gate, God and they only know, but what we call an accident prevented their meeting. Accident! my friend Reuben told me the other day his marriage was an accident. The more I think about accidents, the less do I believe in them. By chance he had an invitation to go to Shott Woods one afternoon, and there he saw the girl who afterwards became his wife and the mother of children with a certain stamp upon them. They in turn will have other children, all of them moulded after a fashion which would have been different if his wife had been another woman. Nay, *these* children would not have existed if this particular marriage had not taken place. Thus the whole course of history is altered, because of that little note and a casual encounter. But, putting aside the theory of a God who ordains results absolutely inevitable, although to us it seems as if they might have been different, it may be observed that the attraction which drew Reuben to his dear Camilla was not quite fortuitous. What decided her to go? It was perfect autumn weather; it was just the time of year she most loved; there would be no crowding or confusion, for many people had gone away to the seaside, and so she was delighted at the thought of the picnic. What decided him to go? The very same reasons. They had both been to Shott during the season, and he had talked and laughed there with some delightful creatures before she crossed his path and held him for ever. Why had he waited? Why had she waited? We have discarded Providence as our forefathers believed in it; but nevertheless there is a providence without the big P, if we choose so to spell it, and yet surely deserving it as much as the Providence of theology, a non-theological Providence which watches over us and leads us. It appears as instinct prompting us to do this and not to do that, to decide this way or that way when we have no consciously rational ground for decision, to cleave to this person and shun the

other, almost before knowing anything of either :
it has been recognised in all ages under various
forms as Demon, Fate, or presiding Genius.   But
still further.   Suppose they both went to Shott
Woods idly ; suppose—which was not the case—
they had never heard of one another before, is it
not possible that they were brought together by a
law as unevadable as gravity ?   There would be
nothing more miraculous in such attraction than
there is in that thread which the minutest
atom of gas in the Orion nebula extends across
billions of miles to the minutest atom of dust on
the road under my window.   However, be all this
as it may, it would be wrong to say that the
meeting between Catharine and Mr. Cardew was
prevented by accident.   She loitered : she went
up Fosbrooke Street : if she had gone straight to
Mr. Cardew she might have been with him before
Tom met him.   Tom would not have interrupted
them, for he ventured to speak to Mr. Cardew
merely because he was alone, and Mrs. Cardew
would not have interrupted them, for they would
have gone further afield.   Tom's appearance even
was not an accident, but a thread carefully woven,
one may say, in the web that night.

"I saw you at church to-night, Miss Catharine," said Tom, as they walked homewards.

"Why did you go? You do not usually go to church."

"I thought I should like to hear Mr. Cardew, and I am very glad I went."

"Are you? What did you think of him? Did you like him?"

"Oh, yes; it was all true; but what he said about Christ the Mediator was so clearly put."

"You did not care for the rest then?"

"I did indeed, Miss Catharine, but it is just the same with our minister: I get along with him so much better when he seems to follow the catechism, but "—he looked up in her face—" I know that is not what you cared for. Oh, Miss Catharine," he cried suddenly, and quite altering his voice and manner, "I do not know when I shall have another chance; I hardly dare tell you; you won't spurn me, will you? My father was a poor workman; I was nothing better, and should have been nothing better if it had not been for you; all my schooling almost I have done myself; I know nothing compared with what you know ; but, Miss Catharine, I love you to madness : I have loved no woman but you ; never looked at one, I may say. Do you remember when you rode home with me from Chapel Farm ? I have lived on it ever since. You are far above me : things come and speak to you which I don't see. If you would teach me I should soon see them too."

Catharine was silent, and perfectly calm. At last she said—

"My dear Tom."

Tom shuddered at the tone.

"No, Miss Catharine, don't say it now ; think a little ; don't cast me off in a moment."

"My dear Tom, I may as well say it now, for what I ought to say is as clear as that moon in the sky. I can *never* love you as a wife ought to love her husband."

"Oh, Miss Catharine ! you despise me, you despise me ! Why in God's name ? " Tom rose above himself, and became such another self that Catharine was amazed and half staggered. "Why in God's name did He make you and me after such a fashion, that you are the one person in the

world able to save me, and you cannot! Why did
He do this! Why did He put me where I saw you
every day and torment me with the hope of you,
knowing that you would have nothing to do with
me! He maimed my father and made him a
beggar: He prevented me from learning what
would have made me fit for you, and then He
drove me to worship you. Do not say 'never'!"

They were close to her father's door at the
Terrace. She stopped, looked at him sadly, but
decisively, straight in the face, and said—

"Never! never! Never your lover, but your
best friend for ever," and she opened the gate
and disappeared.

CHAPTER XIII.

M R. and Mrs. Furze were not disturbed because their daughter was late. A neighbour told them that she had gone to the Rectory with Mr. and Mrs. Cardew, and Mrs. Furze was pleased that Eastthorpe should behold her daughter apparently on intimate terms with a clergyman so well known and so respectable. But it was ten o'clock, and they wished to be in bed. Mrs. Furze had gone to the window, and had partly pushed aside the blind, watching till Catharine should appear. Just as the clock struck she saw Catharine approaching with somebody whom she of course took for Mr. Cardew. The pair came nearer, and, to her astonishment, she recognised Tom. Nay more, she saw the couple halt near the gate, and that Tom was speaking very earnestly. Mrs. Furze was so absorbed that she did not recover herself until the interview was at an end, and before she could say a word to her husband, who was asleep in the armchair, her daughter was at the door. Mrs. Furze went to open it.

"Why, Catharine, that surely wasn't Tom!"

"Yes, it was, mother. Why not?"

"To-om!" half shrieked Mrs. Furze.

"Yes, Tom: I suppose father has gone to bed? Good-night mother," and Catharine kissed her on the forehead and went upstairs.

Mrs. Furze shut the door and rushed into the room.

"My dear! my dear!" shaking him, "Catharine has come, and Tom brought her, and they stood ever so long talking to one another."

Mr. Furze roused himself and took a little brandy-and-water.

"Rubbish!"

"Rubbish! it's all very well for you to say rubbish' when you've been snoring there!"

"Well, where is she? Make her come in; let us hear what she has to say."

"She's gone to bed. Now take my advice:

don't speak to her to-night, but wait till to-morrow; you know what she is, and you had better think a bit."

Mrs. Furze, notwithstanding her excitement, dreaded somewhat attacking Catharine without preparation.

"There's no mistake about it," observed Mr. Furze, rousing himself, "that I have had my suspicions of Master Tom, but I never thought it would come to this; nor that Catharine would have anything to say to him. It was she, though, who said I could not do without him."

"It was she," added Mrs. Furze, "who always stuck out against our coming up here, and was rude to Mrs. Colston and her son. I do not blame her so much, though, as I do that wretch of a Catchpole. What he wants is plain enough : he'll marry her and have the business, the son of a blind beggar who used to go on errands! Oh me! to think it has come to this, that my only child should be the wife of a pauper's son, and we've struggled so hard! What will the Colstons say, and all the church folk, and all the town, for the matter of that!"

Here Mrs. Furze threw herself down in a chair and became hysterical. Poor woman! she really cared for Catharine, loved her in a way, and was horrified for her sake at the supposed engagement, but her desire for her daughter's welfare was bound up with a desire for her own, a strand of one inter-laced with a strand of the other, so that they could not be separated. It might be said that the union of the two impulses was even more intimate, that it was like a mixture of two liquids. There was no conflict in her. She was not selfish at one moment, and unselfishly anxious for her child the next ; but she was both together at the same instant, the particular course on which she might determine satisfying both instincts.

Mr. Furze unfastened his wife's gown and stay-laces and gave her a stimulant. Presently, after directing him with a gasp to open the window, she recovered herself.

"I'll discharge Mr. Tom at once," said her husband, "and tell him the reason."

"Now, don't be stupid, Furze ; pull down that blind, will you ? Fancy leaving it up, and the moon staring straight down upon me half un-

dressed! Don't you admit anything of the kind
to Tom. I would not let him believe you
could suspect it. Besides, if you were to dismiss
him for such a reason as that, you would make
Catharine all the more obstinate, and the whole
town would hear of it, and we should perhaps be
laughed at, and lots of people would take Tom's
part and say we might go further and fare worse,
and were stuck up, and all that, for we must remember that all the Furzes were of humble origin,
and Eastthorpe knows it. No, no, we will get rid
of Tom, but it shall not be because of Catharine—
something better than that—you leave it to me."

"Well, how about Catharine?"

"We will have her in to-morrow morning, when
we are not so flurried. I always like to talk to
her just after breakfast if there is anything wrong;
but do not you say a word to Tom."

Mrs. Furze took another sip of the brandy-and-
water and went to bed. Mr. Furze shut the
window, mixed a little more brandy-and-water,
and, as he drank it, reflected deeply. Most vividly
did that morning come back to him when he had
once before decided to eject Mr. Catchpole.

"I do not know how it is with other people," he groaned, "but whenever I have settled on a thing something is sure to turn up against it, and I never know what to be at for the best. My head, too, is not quite what it used to be. Half a dozen worries at once do muddle me. If they would but come, one up and one down, nobody could beat me." He took another sip of the brandy-and-water. "Want of practice—that's all. I have been an idiot to let him do so much. He shall go;" and Mr. Furze put out the candles.

Catharine was down before either her father or mother, and stood at the window reading when her father came in. She bade him good morning and kissed him, but he was ill at ease, and pretended to look for something on the side-table. He felt he was not sufficiently supported by the main strength of his forces; he was afraid to speak, and he retreated to his bedroom, sitting down disconsolately on a rush-bottom chair whilst his wife dressed herself.

"She's there already," he said.

"Then it is as well you came back."

"I think you had better begin with her; you

are her mother, and we will wait till breakfast is over. Perhaps she will say something to us. How had we better set about it ? "

" I shall ask her straight what she means."

" How shall we go on then ?"

" How shall we go on then ?   What ! won't *you* have a word to put in about her marrying a fellow like that, your own servant with such a father ?   And how are they to live, pray ?   Am I to have him up here to tea with us, and is Phœbe to answer the front door when they knock, and is she to wait upon him, *him* who always goes down the area steps to the kitchen ?   I do not believe Phœbe would stop a month, for with all her faults she does like a respectable family. And then, if they go to church, are they to have our pew, and is Mrs. Colston to call on me and say, ' How is Catharine, and how is your *son-in-law ?* '   And then—oh dear, oh dear !—is his father to come here too, and is Catharine to bring him, and is he to be at the wedding breakfast ? And perhaps Mrs. Colston will inquire after him too.   But there, I shall not survive *that !*   Oh ! Catharine, Catharine ! "

Mrs. Furze dropped on the chair opposite the looking-glass, for she was arranging her back hair while this monologue was proceeding, although the process was interrupted here and there when her emotions got the better of her. Her hair fell into confusion again, and it seemed as if she would again be upset even at that early hour. Her husband gave her a smelling-bottle, and she slowly recommenced her toilette.

"Would it not," he said, "be as well to try and soften her a bit, and remind her of her duty to her parents?"

"You might finish up with that, but I don't believe she'd care; and what are we to do if she owns it all and sticks out—that's what I want to know?"

Mr. Furze was silent.

"There you sit, Furze; you *are* provoking! Pick up that hairpin, will you? You always sit and sit whenever there's any difficulty. You never go beyond what I have in my own head, and when I *do* stir you up to think it is sure to be something of no use."

"I'll do anything you want," said the pensive

husband, as his wife rose and put on her cap. "I've told you before I'll get rid of Tom, and then perhaps it will all come round!"

"At it again! What *did* I tell you last night?—and yet you go on with your old tune. All come round, indeed! Would it! She's your daughter, but you don't know her as I do."

Here there came a tap at the door. It was Phœbe: Miss Catharine sent her to say it was a quarter-past eight: should she make the coffee?

"Look at that!" said Mrs. Furze: "shall she make the coffee!—after what has happened! That's the kind of girl she is. It strikes me you had better have nothing to do with her and leave her to me."

Phœbe tapped again.

"Certainly not," replied Mrs. Furze. "I'll begin," she added to her husband, "by letting her know that at least I am not dead."

"Well, we'd better go. You just tackle her, and I'll chime in."

The couple descended, but their plan of campaign was not very clearly elaborated, and even the one or two lines of assault which Mrs. Furze had prepared turned out to be useless. It is all very well to decide what is to be done with a human being if the human being will but comport himself in a fairly average manner, but if he will not the plan is likely to fail.

Mr. Furze was very restless during his meal. He went to the window two or three times, and returned with the remark that it was going to be wet; but the observation was made in a low, mumbling tone. Mrs. Furze was also fidgety, and, in reply to her daughter's questions, complained of headache, and wondered that Catharine could not see that she had had no sleep. At last the storm broke.

"Catharine," said Mrs. Furze, "it *was* Tom, then, who came home with you last night."

"It was Tom, mother."

"Tom! What do you mean, child? How—how did he—where did you meet him?"

Mr. Furze retired from the table, where the sun fell full upon him, and sat in the easy-chair, where he was more in the shade.

"He overtook me somewhere near the Rectory."

"Now, Catharine, don't answer your mother like

that," interposed Mr. Furze ; " you know what you
heard, or might have heard, last Sunday morning,
that prevarication is very much like a lie ; why
don't you speak out the truth ? "

Catharine was silent for a moment.

" I have answered exactly the question mother
asked."

" Catharine, you know perfectly well what I
mean," said Mrs. Furze ; " what is the use of pretending you do not ! Tom would never dare to
walk with you in a public street, and at night, too,
if there were not something more than you like to
say. Tom Catchpole ! whose father sold laces on
the bridge ; and to think of all we have done for
you, and the money we have spent on you, and
the pains we have taken to bring you up respect-
ably ! I will not say anything about religion, and
all that, for I daresay that is nothing to *you*, but
you might have had some consideration for your
mother, especially in her weak state of health,
before you broke her heart, and yet I blame myself, for you always had low tastes—going to
Bellamy's, and consorting with people of that kind
rather than with your mother's friends. Do you

suppose Mrs. Colston will come near us again! And it all comes of trying to do one's best, for there's Carry Hawkins, only a grocer's daughter, who never had a sixpence spent on her compared with what you have, and she is engaged to Carver, the doctor at Cambridge. Oh, it's a serpent's tooth, it is, and if we had never scraped and screwed for you, and denied ourselves, but left you to yourself, you might have been better; oh dear, oh dear!"

Catharine held her tongue. She saw instantly that if she denied any engagement with Tom she would not be believed, and that in any case Tom would have to depart. Moreover, one of her defects was a certain hardness to persons for whom she had small respect, and she did not understand that just because Mrs. Furze was her mother she owed her at least a deference, and, if possible, a tenderness due to no other person. However weak, foolish, and even criminal parents may be, a child ought to honour them as Moses commanded, for the injunction is, and should be, entirely unconditional.

"Catharine," said Mr. Furze, "why do you not answer your mother?"

"I cannot ; I had better leave."

She opened the door and went to her room. After she had left further debate arose, and three points were settled : First, that no opposition should be offered to a visit to Chapel Farm, which had been proposed for the next day, as she would be better at the Farm than at the Terrace ; secondly, that Tom and she were in love with one another ; and thirdly, that not a word should be said to Tom. "Leave that to me," said Mrs. Furze again. Although she saw nothing distinctly, a vague, misty hope dawned upon her, the possibility of something she could not yet discern, and, notwithstanding the blow she had received, she was decidedly more herself within an hour after breakfast than she had been during the twelve hours preceding.

CHAPTER XIV.

IN Mr. Furze's establishment was a man who
went by the name of Orkid Jim, "Orkid" sig-
nifying the general contradictoriness and awkward-
ness of his temper. He had a brother who was
called Orkid Joe, in the employ of a builder in the
town, but it was the general opinion that Orkid
Jim was much the orkider of the two. He was a
person with whom Mr. Furze seldom interfered.
He was, it is true, a good workman in the general
fitting department, in setting grates, and for jobs
of that kind, but he was impertinent and disobedient. Mr. Furze, however, tolerated his
insults, and generally allowed him to have his own
way. He was not only afraid of Orkid Jim, but
he was a victim to that unhappy dread of a quarrel
which is the torment and curse of weak minds. It
is, no doubt, very horrible to see a man trample

upon opinions and feelings as easily and carelessly
as he would upon the grass, and go on his way
undisturbed, but it is more painful to see faltering,
trembling incapacity for self-assertion, especially
before subordinates.   Mr. Furze could not have
suffered more than two or three days' inconvenience
if Orkid Jim had been discharged, but a vague
terror haunted him of something which might
possibly happen.   Partly this distressing weakness
is due to the absence of a clear conviction that we
are right ; it is an intellectual difficulty ; but frequently it is simple mushiness of character, the
same defect which tempts us, when we know a
thing is true, to whittle it down if we meet with
opposition, and to refrain from presenting it in all
its sharpness.   Cowardice of this kind is not only
injustice to ourselves, but to our friends.   We
inflict a grievous wrong by compromise.   We are
responsible for what we see, and the denial or the
qualification should be left to take care of itself.
Our duty is, if possible, to give a distinct outline to
what we have in our mind.   It is easy to say we
should not be obstinate, pig-headed, and argue for
argument's sake.   That is true, just as much as

every half truth is true, but the other half is also true.

Mr. Furze, excepting when he was out of temper, never stood up to Orkid Jim. He needed the stimulus of passion to do what ought to have been done by reason, and when we cannot do what is right save under the pressure of excitement it is generally misdone. Orkid Jim had a great dislike to Tom, which he took no pains to conceal. It was difficult to ascertain the cause, but partly it was jealousy. Tom had got before him. This, however, was not all. It was a case of pure antipathy, such as may often be observed amongst animals. Some dogs are the objects of special hatred by others, and are immediately attacked by them, before any cause of offence can possibly have been given.

Jim had called at the Terrace on the morning after the explosion with Catharine. He came to replace a cracked kitchen boiler, and Mrs. Furze, for some reason or other, felt inclined to go down into the kitchen and have some talk with him. She knew how matters stood between him and Tom.

"Well, Jim, how are you getting on now? I have not seen you lately."

"No, marm, I ain't one as comes to the front much now."

"What do you mean? I suppose you might if you liked. I am sure Mr. Furze values you highly."

Jim was cautious and cunning; not inclined to commit himself. He consequently replied by an "Ah," and knocked with great energy at the brickwork from which he was detaching the range.

"Anything been the matter, then, Jim?"

"No, marm; nothing's the matter."

"You have not quarrelled with Mr. Furze, I hope? You do not seem quite happy."

"Me quarrel with Mr. Furze, marm!—no, I never quarrel with *him*. He's a gentleman, he is."

Mrs. Furze was impatient. She wanted to come to the point, and could not wait to manœuvre.

"I am afraid you and Tom do not get on together."

"Well, Mrs. Furze, if we don't it ain't my fault."

"No, I dare say not; in fact, I am sure it is not. I dare say Tom is a little overbearing. Consider-

ing his origin, and the position he now occupies, it
is natural he should be."

" He ain't one as ought to give himself airs,
marm. Why——"

Jim all at once dropped his chisel and his mask
of indifference and flashed into ferocity.

" Why, my father was a tradesman, he was, and
I was in your husband's foundry earning a pound
a week when Master Tom was in rags. Who
taught him, I should like to know ? "

" Jim, you must not talk like that ; although,
to tell you the truth, Tom is no favourite of mine.
Mr. Furze, however, relies on him."

" Relies on him, does he ? Leastways, I know
he does ; just as if scores of others couldn't do jist
as well, only they 'aven't 'ad his chance ! Relies on him, as yer call it ! But there, if I wur
to speak, wot 'ud be the use ? "

It is always a consolation to incapable people
that their lack of success is due to the absence
of chances. From the time of Korah, Dathan,
and Abiram—who accused Moses and Aaron of
taking too much upon themselves, because every
man in the congregation was as holy as his God-

selected leaders — it has been a theory, one may even say a religion, with those who have been passed over, that their sole reason for their supersession is an election as arbitrary as that by the Antinomian deity, who, out of pure wilfulness, gives opportunities to some and denies them to others.

"What do you mean, Jim? What is it that you see?"

"You'll excuse me, missus, if I says no more. I ain't a-goin' to meddle with wot don't concern me, and get myself into trouble for nothing : wot for, I should like to know? Wot good would it do me?"

"But, Jim, if you are aware of anything wrong it is your duty to report it."

"Maybe it is, maybe it isn't ; but wot thanks should I get?"

"You would get my thanks and the thanks of Mr. Furze, I am sure. Look here, Jim." Mrs. Furze rose and shut the kitchen door. Phœbe was upstairs, but she thought it necessary to take every precaution. "I know you may be trusted, and therefore I do not mind speaking to you. Tom's conduct has not been very satisfactory of late. I need not go into particulars, but I shall really be glad if you will communicate to me anything you may observe which is amiss. You may depend upon it you shall not suffer."

She put two half-crowns into Jim's hand. He turned and looked at her with one eye partly shut, and a curious expression on his face—half smile, half suspicion. He then looked at the money for a few seconds and put it deliberately in his pocket, but without any sign of gratitude.

"I'll bear wot you say in mind," he replied.

At this instant the kitchen door opened, and Phœbe entered. Mrs. Furze went on with the conversation immediately, but it took a different turn.

"How do you think the old boiler became cracked?"

He was taken aback; his muddled brain did not quite comprehend the situation, but at last he managed to stammer out that he did not know, and Mrs. Furze retired.

Jim was very slow in arranging his thoughts, especially after a sudden surprise. A shock, or a quick intellectual movement on the part of anybody in contact with him, paralysed him, and he recovered and extended himself very gradually. Presently, however, his wits returned, and he concluded that the pretext of the shop and business mismanagement was but very partially the cause of Mrs. Furze's advances. He knew that although Mr. Furze was restive under Tom's superior capacity, there was no doubt whatever of his honesty and ability. Besides, if it was business, why did the mistress interfere? Why did she thrust herself upon him?—"coming down 'ere a purpose," thought Mr. Orkid Jim. "No, no, it ain't business," and, delighted with his discovery so far, and with the conscious exercise of mental power, he smote the bricks with more vigour than ever.

"Good-bye, Phœbe," said Catharine, looking in at the door.

"Good-bye, Miss," said Phœbe, running out; "hope you'll enjoy yourself: I wish I were going with you."

"Where is she a-goin'?" asked Jim, when Phœbe returned.

" Chapel Farm."

" Oh, is she ? Wot, goin' there agin ! She's oftener there than here. Not much love lost 'twixt her and the missus, is there ? "

Phœbe was uncommunicative, and went on with her work.

" I say, Phœbe, has Catchpole been up here lately ? "

" Why do you want to know? What is it to you ? "

" Now, my beauty, wot is it to me? Why, in course it's nothin' to me ; but you know he's been here."

" Well, then, he hasn't."

Phœbe, going to bed, had seen Tom and Catharine outside the gate.

" Wy, now, I myself see'd 'im out the night afore last, and I'd swear he come this way afore he went home."

" He did not come in ; he only brought Miss Catharine back from church : she'd gone there alone."

Jim dropped his chisel. The three events presented themselves together—Tom's escort of

Catharine, the interview with Mrs. Furze, and the departure to Chapel Farm. He was excited, and his excitement took the form of a sudden passion for Phœbe.

"You're ten times too 'ansom for that chap," he cried, and, turning suddenly, he caught her with one arm round her waist. She strove to release herself with great energy, and in the struggle he caught his foot in his tool basket and fell on the floor, cutting his head severely with a brick. Phœbe was out of the kitchen in an instant.

"You damned cat!" growled he, "I'll be even with you and your Master Tom! I know all about it now."

CHAPTER XV.

A S Jim walked home to his dinner he became
pensive. He was under a kind of pledge
to his own hatred and to Mrs. Furze to produce
something against Tom, and he had nothing.
Even he could see that to make up a charge
would not be safe. It required more skill than
he possessed. The opportunity, however, very
soon came. Destiny delights in offering to the
wicked chances of damning themselves. It was
a few days before the end of the quarter. The
builder—in whose service Jim's brother, Joe, was—
sent Joe to pay a small account for ironmongery,
which had been due for some weeks. When he
entered the shop Tom was behind his desk, and
Jim was taking some instructions about a job.
Mr. Furze was out. Joe produced his bill, threw
it across to Tom, and pulled the money out of

his pocket. It was also market day; the town was crowded, and just at that moment Mr. Eaton drove by. Tom looked out of the window on his left hand and saw the horse shy at something in the cattle pens, pitching Mr. Eaton out. Without saying a word he rushed round the counter and out into the street, the two men, who had not seen the accident, thinking he had gone to speak to Mr. Eaton. He was absent some minutes.

" A nice sort of a chap, this," said Jim ; " he's signed your bill, and he ain't got the money."

" S'pose I must wait, then."

" Look 'ere, Joe: don't you be a b——y fool ! You take your account. If he writes his name afore he's paid, that's *his* look-out."

Joe hesitated.

" Wot are you a-starin' at ? You've got the receipt, ain't yer ? Isn't that enough ? You ain't a-robbin' of him, for you never giv him the money, and I tell yer agin as he's the one as ought to lose if he don't look sharp arter people. That's square enough, ain't it ? "

Joe had a remarkably open mind to reasoning

of this description, and, without another word, he took up the bill and was off. Jim also thought it better to return to the foundry. Mr. Eaton, happily, was not injured, for he fell on a truss of straw, but the excitement was great; and, when Tom returned, Joe's visit completely went out of his head, and did not occur to him again, for two or three customers were waiting for him, and, as already observed, it was market day.

Now, it was Mr. Furze's practice always to make out his accounts himself. It was a pure waste of time, for he would have been much better employed in looking after his men, and any boy could have transcribed his ledger. But no, it was characteristic of the man that he preferred this occupation—that he took the utmost pains to write his best copybook hand, and to rule red-ink lines with mathematical accuracy. Two days after the quarter a bill went to the builder, beginning, "To account delivered." The builder was astonished, and instantly posted down to the shop, receipt in hand, signed, "For J. Furze, T. C." Mr. Furze looked at his ledger again called for the day-book, found no entry, and then sent for Tom. The history of that afternoon flashed across him in an instant.

"That's your signature, Mr. Catchpole," said Mr. Furze.

"Yes, sir."

"But here's no entry in the day-book, and, what's more, there weren't thirty shillings that night in the till."

"I cannot account for it, unless I signed the receipt before I had the money. It was just when Mr. Eaton's accident happened, and I ran out of the shop while Joe was waiting. When I came back he had gone."

"Which is as much as to say," said the builder, "that Joe's a thief. You'd better be careful, young man."

"Well, Mr. Humphries," said Mr. Furze, loftily, "we will not detain you: there is clearly a mistake somewhere; we will credit you at once with the amount due for the previous quarter, and if you will give me your account I will correct it now."

Mr. Furze took it, and ruled through the first line, altering the total.

"This is very unpleasant, Mr. Catchpole," observed Mr. Furze, after the builder had departed. "Was there anybody in the shop besides yourself and Joe?"

"Jim was there."

Mr. Furze rang a bell, and Jim presently appeared.

"Jim, were you in the shop when your brother came to pay Mr. Humphries' bill about a week ago?"

"I wor."

"Did he pay it? did you see him hand over the money?"

"I did, and Mr. Catchpole took it and put it in the till. I see'd it go in with my own eyes."

"Well, what happened then?"

"He locked the till all in a hurry, put the key in his waistcoat pocket; let me see, it wor in his left-hand pocket—no, wot am I a-sayin'?—it wor in his right-hand pocket—I want to be particklar, Mr. Furze—and then he run out of the shop. Joe, he took up his receipt, and he says, says he, 'He might a given me the odd penny,' and says I, 'He ain't Mr. Furze, he can't give away none of the guvnor's money.' If it wor the guvnor himself he'd a done it, and with that we went out of the shop together."

"That will do, Jim ; you can go."

"Mr. Catchpole, this assumes a very—I may say —painful aspect."

"I can only repeat, sir, that I have not had the money. It is inexplicable. I may have been robbed."

"But there is no entry in the day-book."

It did not occur to Tom at the moment to plead that if he was dishonest he would have contrived not to be so in such a singularly silly fashion : that he might have taken cash paid for goods bought, and that the possibility of discovery would have been much smaller. He was stunned.

"It is so painful," continued Mr. Furze, "that I must have time to reflect. I will talk to you again about it to-morrow."

The truth was that Mr. Furze wished to consult his wife. When he went home his first news was what had happened, but he forgot to mention the corroboration by Jim.

"But," said Mrs. Furze, "Joe may have been

mistaken ; perhaps, after all, he did not pay the money."

"Ah ! but Jim was in the shop at the time. I had Jim in, and he swears that he saw Joe give it to Tom, and that Tom put it in the till."

Mrs. Furze seemed a little uncomfortable, but she soon recovered.

"We ought to have proof beyond all doubt of Tom's dishonesty. I do not see that this is proof. At any rate, it would not satisfy Catharine. I should wait a month. It is of no use making two faces about this business ; we must take one line or the other. I should tell him that, on recon-sideration, you cannot bring yourself to suspect him ; that you have perfect confidence in him, and that there must be some mistake somewhere, though you cannot at present see how. That will throw him off his guard."

Mr. Furze acknowledged the superiority of his wife's intellect and obeyed. Tom came to work on the following morning in a state of great ex-citement, and with an offer of restitution, but was appeased, and Orkid Jim, appearing in the shop, was astonished and dismayed to find Tom and his master on the same footing as before. He went up to the Terrace, the excuse being that he called to see how the new boiler was going on. Phœbe came to the door, but he wanted to see the mistress.

"What do you want her for? She knows nothing about the boiler. It is all right, I tell you."

"Never you mind. It wor she as give me the directions, worn't it, when I was 'ere afore?"

Accordingly the mistress appeared, and Phœbe, remaining in the kitchen, was sent upstairs upon some unimportant business, much cogitating upon the unusual interest Mrs. Furze took in the kitchen range, and the evident desire on her part that her instructions to Jim should be private.

"Well, Jim, the boiler is all right."

"That's more nor some things are."

"Why, what has happened?"

"I s'pose you know. Joe paid Humphries' bill, and Mr. Catchpole swears he never had the money, but Joe's got his recept."

"You were in the shop and saw it paid?"

"Of course I was. I s'pose you heerd that too?"

"Yes. We do not think, however, that the case is clear, and we shall do nothing this time."

"I don't know wot you'd 'ave, Mrs. Furze. If this 'ere ain't worth the five shillin' yer gave me, nothin' is—that's all I've got to say."

"But, Jim, you must see we cannot do anything unless the proof is complete. Now, if there should happen to be a second instance, that would be a different thing altogether."

"It ain't very comfortable for *me*."

"What do you mean? Mr. Furze sent for you, and you told him what you saw with your own eyes."

"Ah! you'd better mind wot you're sayin', Mrs. Furze, and you needn't put it in that way. Jist you look 'ere: I ain't very particklar myself, I ain't, but it may come to takin' my oath, and, to tell yer the truth, five shillin' don't pay me."

"But we are not going to prosecute."

"No, not now, but you may, and I shall have to stick to it, and maybe have to be brought up. Besides, it was put straight to me by the guvnor, and Mr. Tom was there a-lookin' at me right in my face. As I say, five shillin' don't pay me."

"Well, we shall not let the matter drop. We shall keep our eyes open : you may be sure of that, Jim. I daresay you have been worried over the business. Here's another five shillings for you."

Again Jim refrained from thanking her, but slowly put on his cap and left the house.

CHAPTER XVI.

MR. FURZE tried several experiments during the next two or three weeks. It was his custom to look after his shop when Tom went to his meals, and on those rare occasions when he had to go out during Tom's absence, Orkid Jim acted as a substitute. Whenever Mr. Furze found a sovereign in the till he quietly marked it with his knife or a file, but it was invariably handed over to him in the evening. On a certain Wednesday afternoon, Tom being at his dinner, Mr. Furze was summoned to the Bell by a message from Mr. Eaton, and Jim was ordered to come immediately. He usually went round to the front door. He preferred to walk down the lane from the foundry, and when the back rooms were living rooms, passage through them was of course forbidden. As the summons, however, was urgent, he came the

shortest way, and, looking in through the window
which let in some borrowed light from the back of
the shop to the warehouse behind, he saw Mr.
Furze, penknife in hand, at the till. Wondering
what he could be doing, Jim watched him for a
moment. As soon as Mr. Furze's back was
turned he went to the till, took out a sovereign
which was in it, closely examined it, discovered a
distinct though faint cross at the back of his
Majesty George the Third's head, pondered a
moment, and then put the coin back again. He
looked very abstruse, rubbed his chin, and finally
smiled after his fashion. Tom's shop coat and
waistcoat were hung up just inside the counting-
house. Jim went to them and turned the waistcoat pockets inside out. To put the sovereign in
an empty pocket would be dangerous. Tom would
discover it as soon as he returned, and would probably inform Mr. Furze at once. A similar test
for the future would then be impossible. Jim
thought of a better plan, and it was strange that
so slow a brain was so quick to conceive it. Along
one particular line, however, that brain, otherwise
so dull, was even rapid in its movements. It was

Mr. Furze's practice to pay wages at half-past five on Saturday afternoon, and he paid them himself. He generally went to his tea at six on that day, Tom waiting till he returned. On the following Saturday at half-past six Jim came into the shop.

"I met Eaton's man a minute ago as I wur goin' 'ome. He wanted to see the guvnor particklar, he said."

This was partly true, but the "particklar" was not true.

"I told him the guvnor warn't in, but you was there. He said he was goin' to the Bell, but he'd call again if he had time. You'd better go and see wot it is."

Tom took off his black apron and his shop coat and waistcoat, put them up in the usual place, and went out, leaving Jim in charge. Jim instantly went to the till. There were several sovereigns in it, for it had been a busy day. He turned them over, and again recognised the indubitable cross. With a swift promptitude utterly beyond his ordinary self, he again went to Tom's waistcoat—Tom always put gold in his waistcoat pocket—took out a sovereign of the thirty shillings there, put it in his own pocket, and replaced it by the marked sovereign. Just before the shop closed, the cash was taken to Mr. Furze. He tied it carefully in a bag, carried it home, turned it over, and the sovereign was absent. Meanwhile Orkid Jim had begun to reflect that the chain of evidence was not complete. He knew Tom's habits perfectly, and one of them was to buy his Sunday's dinner on Saturday night. He generally went to a small butcher near his own house. Jim followed him, having previously exchanged his own sovereign for twenty shillings in silver. As soon as Tom had left the butcher's shop Jim walked in. He was well known.

"Mr. Butterfield, you 'aven't got a sovereign, 'ave you, as you could give me for twenty shillings in silver?"

"Well, that's a rum 'un, Mr. Jim: generally it's t'other way: you want the silver for the gold. Besides, we don't take many sovereigns here—we ain't like people in the High Street."

"Mr. Butterfield, it's jist this: we've 'ad over-work at the guvnor's, and I'm a-goin' to put a sovereign by safe come next Whitsuntide, when I'm a-goin' to enjoy myself. I don't get much enjoyment, Mr. Butterfield, but I mean to 'ave it then."

"All right, Mr. Jim. I've only two sovereigns, and there they are. There's a bran-new one, and there's the other."

"I don't like bran-new nothin's, Mr. Butterfield. I ain't a Radical, I ain't. Wy, I've seed in my time an election last a week, and beer a-runnin' down the gutters. It was the only chance a poor man 'ad. Wot sort of a chance 'as he got now? There's nothin' to be 'ad now unless yer sweat for it: that's Radicalism, that is, and if I 'ad my way I'd upset the b——y Act, and all the lot of 'em. No, thank yer, Mr. Butterfield, I'll 'ave the old sovereign; where did he come from now, I wonder."

"Come from? Why, from your shop. Mr. Catchpole has just paid it me. You needn't go a-turnin' of it over and a-smellin' at it, Mr. Jim; it's as good as you are."

"Good! I worn't a-thinkin' about that. I wor jist a-lookin' at the picter of his blessed

Majesty King George the Third, and the way he wore his wig. Kewrus, ain't it? Now, somebody's been and scratched 'im jist on the neck. Do yer see that ere cross?"

"You seem awful suspicious, Mr. Jim. Give it me back again. I don't want you to have it."

"Lord! suspicious! 'Ere's your twenty shillin's, Mr. Butterfield. I wish I'd a 'undred sovereigns as good as this." And Mr. Jim departed.

Mr. Furze lost no time in communicating his discovery to his wife.

"Furze," she said, "you're a fool: where's the sovereign? You haven't got it, but how are you to prove now that he has got it? We are just where we were before. You ought to have taxed him with it at once, and have had him searched."

Mr. Furze was crestfallen, and made no reply. The next morning at church he was picturing to himself incessantly the dreadful moment when he would have to do something so totally unlike anything he had ever done before.

On the Sunday afternoon Jim appeared at the

Terrace, and Phœbe, who was not very well, and was at home, announced that he wished to see Mr. Furze.

"What can the man want? Tell him I will come down."

"I think," said Mrs. Furze, "Jim had better come up here."

Mr. Furze was surprised, but, as Phœbe was waiting, he said nothing, and Jim came up.

"Beg pardon for interruptin' yer on Sunday arternoon, but I've 'eerd as yer ain't satisfied with Mr. Catchpole, and I thought I'd jist tell yer as soon as I could as yesterday arternoon, while I was mindin' the shop, and he was out, I 'ad to go to the till, and it jist so 'appened, as I was a-givin' change, I was a-lookin' at a George the Third sovereign there, and took particklar notice of it. There was a mark on it. That werry sovereign was changed by Mr. Catchpole at Butterfield's that night, and 'ere it is. I 'ad to go in there, as I wanted a sovereign for a lot of silver, and he giv it to me."

"Can Butterfield swear that Catchpole gave it him?" said Mrs. Furze, quite calmly.

"Of course he can, marm; that's jist wot I asked him."

"That will do, Jim; you can go," said Mrs. Furze.

Jim looked at her, loitered, played with his cap, and seemed unwilling to leave.

"I'm comin' up to-morrow mornin', marm, just to 'ave one more look at that biler." He then walked out.

"I suppose I must prosecute now," said Mr. Furze.

"Prosecute! Nothing of the kind. What is your object? It is to get rid of him, and let Catharine see what he is. Suppose you prosecute and break down, where will you be, I should like to know? If you succeed, you won't be a bit better off than you are now. Discharge him. Everybody will know why, and will say how kind and forgiving you are, and Catharine cannot say we have been harsh to him."

Mr. Furze was uneasy. He had a vague feeling that everything was not quite right; but he said nothing, and mutely assented to his wife's proposals.

" Then I am to give him notice to-morrow ? "

" You cannot keep him after what has happened. You must give him a week's wages and let him go."

" Who is to take his place ? "

" Why do you not try Jim ? He is rough, it is true, but he knows the shop. He can write well enough for that work, and all you want is somebody to be there when you are out."

Mr. Furze shuddered. That was not all he wanted, but he had hardly allowed himself, as we have already seen, to confess his weakness.

" It might be as well, perhaps," added Mrs. Furze, " to have Tom up to-morrow and talk to him here."

" That will be much better."

It was now tea-time, and immediately afterwards Mr. and Mrs. Furze went to church.

Soon after nine on the following morning, and before Mr. Furze had left, Jim appeared with another request " to see the missus."

" I'll go downstairs," she said. " He wants to see me about the boiler."

There was nobody but Jim in the kitchen.

" Well, Jim ? "

" Well, marm."

" What have you got to say ? "

" No, marm, it's wot 'ave you got to say ? "

" It is very shocking about Mr. Catchpole, is it not ? But, then, we are not surprised, you know ; we have partly suspected something for a long time, as I have told you."

" 'Ave you really ? Well, then, it's a good thing as he's found out."

" I am very sorry. He has been with us so long, and we thought him such a faithful servant."

" You're sorry, are you ? Yes, of course you are. Wot are yer goin' to do with him ? "

" We shall not prosecute."

" No, marm, you take my advice, don't yer do that ; it wouldn't do nobody no good."

" We shall discharge him at once."

" Yes, that's all right ; but don't you prosecute 'im on no account, mind that. *Mis-sis* Furze," said Jim, deliberately, turning his head, and with his eyes full upon her in a way she did not like, " wot am I a-goin' to get out of this ? "

" Why, you will be repaid, I am sure, by Mr.

Furze for all the time and trouble you have taken."

"Now, marm, I ain't a-goin' to say nothin' as needn't be said, but I know that Tom's been a-makin' up to Miss Catharine, and yer know that as soon as yer found that out yer come and spoke to me. Mind that, marm; it was yer as come and spoke to me; it wasn't me as spoke fust, was it?" Jim was unusually excited. "And arter yer spoke to me, yer spoke to me agin—agin I say it—arter I told you as I seed Joe pay the money, and then I brought yer that ere sovereign."

Mrs. Furze sat down. In one short minute she lived a lifetime, and the decision was taken which determined her destiny. She resolved that she would *not* tread one single step in one particular direction, nor even look that way. She did not resolve to tell a lie, or, in fact, to do anything which was not strictly defensible and virtuous. She simply refused to reflect on the possibility of perjury on Jim's part. Refusing to reflect on it, she naturally had no proof of it; and, having no proof of it, she had no ground for believing that she was not perfectly innocent and upright—a

very pretty process, much commoner than perhaps
might be suspected. After the lapse of two or
three hours there was in fact no test by which to
distinguish the validity of this belief from that of
her other beliefs, nor indeed, it may be said, from
that of the beliefs in which many people live, and
for the sake of which they die.

"It is true, Jim," said Mrs. Furze, after a pause,
"that we thought Tom had so far forgotten himself
as to make proposals to Miss Catharine, but this
was a mere coincidence. It is extremely fortunate
that we have discovered just at this moment what
he really is ; most fortunate. I have not the least
doubt that he is a very bad character ; your evidence is most decisive, and, as we owe so much to
you, we think of putting you in Tom's place."

Jim had advanced with wariness, and occupied
such a position that he could claim Mrs. Furze as
an accomplice, or save appearances, if it was more
prudent to do so. The reward was brilliant, and
he saw what course he ought to take.

"Thank yer, marm ; it was very lucky ; now I
may speak freely I may say as I've 'ad my eyes on
Mr. Catchpole ever so long. I told yer as much

afore, and this ain't the fust time as he's robbed yer, but I couldn't prove it, and it worn't no good my sayin' wot I worn't sure of."

This, then, is the way in which Destiny rewards those who refuse to listen to the Divine Voice. Destiny supplies them with reasons for discrediting it. Mrs. Furze was more than ever thankful to Jim ; not so much because of these additional revelations, but because she was still further released from the obligation to turn her eyes. Had not Jim said it once, twice, and now thrice ? Who could condemn her ? She boldly faced herself, and asked herself what authority this other self possessed which, just for a moment, whispered something in her ear. What right had it thus to interrogate her ? What right had it to hint at some horrid villainy ? "None, none," it timidly answered, and was silent. The business of this other self is suggestion only, and, if it be resisted, it is either dumb or will reply just as it is bidden.

"You can tell Mr. Catchpole his master wishes to see him here."

"Thankee, marm ; good mornin'."

Tom came up to the Terrace much wondering,

and was shown into the dining-room by Phœbe not a little suspicious. Mr. Furze sat back in the easy-chair with his elbows on the arms and his hands held up and partly interlaced. It was an attitude he generally assumed when he was grave or wished to appear so. He had placed himself with his back to the light. Mrs. Furze sat in the window. Mr. Furze began with much hesitation.

"Sit down, Mr. Catchpole. I am sorry to be obliged to impart to you a piece—a something— which is very distressing. For some time, I must say, I have not been quite satisfied with the—the affairs—business—at the shop, and the case of Humphries' account made me more anxious. I could not tell who the—delinquent—might be, and, under advice, under advice, I resorted to the usual means of detection, and the result is that a marked coin placed in the till on Saturday was changed by you on Saturday night."

A tremendous blow steadies some men, at least for a time. Tom quietly replied—

"Well, Mr. Furze, what then?"

"What then?" said Mrs. Furze, with a little titter; "the evidence seems complete."

"A marked coin," continued Mr. Furze. "I may say at once that I do not propose to prosecute, although if I were to take proceedings and to produce the evidence of Jim and his brother with regard to Humphries, I should obtain a conviction. But I cannot bring myself to—to—the—forget your past services, and I wish to show no unchristian malice, even for such a crime as yours. You are discharged, and there are a week's wages."

"I am not sure," said Mrs. Furze, "that we are not doing wrong in the eye of the law, and that we might not ourselves be prosecuted for conniving at a felony."

Tom was silent for a moment, but it never entered into his head to ask for corroboration or any details.

"I will ask you both "—he spoke with deliberation and emphasis—" do you, both of you, believe I am a thief?"

"Really," said Mrs. Furze, " what a question to put! Two men declare money was paid to you for which you never accounted, and a marked sovereign, to which you had no right, was in your possession last Saturday evening. You seem rather absurd, Mr. Catchpole."

"Mrs. Furze, I repeat my question: do you believe I am a thief?"

"We are not going to prosecute you: let that be enough for you; I decline to say any more than it suits me to say: you have had the reasons for dismissal; ask yourself whether they are conclusive or not, and what the verdict of a jury would be."

"Then I tell you, Mrs. Furze, and I tell you, Mr. Furze, before the all-knowing God, who is in this room at this moment, that I am utterly innocent, and that somebody has wickedly lied."

"Mr. Catchpole," replied Mrs. Furze, "the introduction of the sacred name in such a conjunction is, I may say, rather shocking, and even blasphemous. Here is your money: you had better go."

Tom left the money and walked out of the room.

"Good-bye, Phœbe."

"Are you going to leave, Tom?"

"Discharged!"

" I knew there was some villainy going on," said Phœbe, greatly excited, as she took Tom's hand and wrung it, " but you aren't really going for good ? "

" Yes ; " and he was out in the street.

" H'm," said Mr. Furze, " it's very disagreeable. I don't quite like it."

" Don't quite like it ?—why, what *would* you have done ? would you have had Catharine marry him ?   I have no patience with you, Furze ! "

Mr. Furze subsided, but he did not move to go to his business, and Mrs. Furze went down into the kitchen.   Mr. Eaton had called at the shop at that early hour wishing to see Mr. Furze or Tom. He was to return shortly, and Mr. Orkid Jim, not knowing exactly what to do with such a customer, and, moreover, being rather curious, had left a boy in charge and walked back to the Terrace.

" There's Jim again at the door," said Mrs. Furze to Phœbe ; " let him in."

" Excuse me, ma'am, but never will I go to the door to let that man in again as long as I live."

" Phœbe ! do you know what you are saying ? I direct you to let him in."

"No, ma'am ; you may direct, but I sha'n't. Nothing shall make me go to the door to the biggest liar and scoundrel in this town, and if you don't know it yourself, Mrs. Furze, you ought."

"You do not expect me to stand this, Phœbe? You will have a month's wages and go to-night."

"This morning, ma'am, if you please."

Before noon her box was packed, and she too had departed.

CHAPTER XVII.

TOM began to understand, as soon as he left the Terrace, that a consciousness of his own innocence was not all that was necessary for his peace of mind. What would other people say? There was a damning chain of evidence, and what was he to do for a living with no character?

He did not return home nor to the shop. He took the road to Chapel Farm. He did not go to the house direct, but went round it, and walked about, and at last found himself on the bridge. It was there that he met Catharine after her jump into the water; it was there, although he knew nothing about it, that she parted from Mr. Cardew. It was no thundery, summer day now, but cold and dark. The wind was north-east, persistent with unvarying force; the sky was covered with an almost uniform sheet of heavy grey clouds, with no form or beauty in them ; there was nothing in the heavens or earth which seemed to have any relationship with man or to show any interest in him. Tom was not a philosopher, but some of his misery was due to a sense of carelessness and injustice somewhere in the government of the world. He was religious after his fashion, but the time had passed when a man could believe, as his forefathers believed, that the earth is a school of trial, and that after death is the judgment. What had he done to be visited thus ? How was his integrity to be discovered ? He had often thought that it was possible that a man should be convicted of some dreadful crime ; that he should be execrated, not only by the whole countryside, but by his own wife and children; that his descendants for ages might curse him as the solitary ancestor who had brought disgrace into the family, and that he might be innocent. There might be hundreds of such; doubtless there have been. Perhaps, even worse, there have been men who have been misinterpreted, traduced, forsaken, because they have been compelled for a reason sacredly secret to take a certain course which seemed disreputable, and the word which would have explained everything they have loyally sworn, for the sake of a friend, never to speak, and it has remained unspoken for ever. As he stood leaning over the parapet he saw Catharine coming along the path. She did not attempt to avoid him, for she wondered what he could be doing. He told her the whole story. " Miss Catharine, there is just one thing I want to know : do you believe I am guilty ? "

" I know you are not."

" Thank God for that."

Both remained silent for a minute or two. At last Tom spoke.

" Oh, Miss Catharine, this makes it harder to bear. You are the one person, perhaps, in the world now who has any faith in me ; there is, perhaps, no human being at this moment, excepting yourself, who, after having heard what you have heard, would at once put it all aside. What do you suppose I think of you now ? If I loved you before, what must my love now be ? Miss Catharine, I could tear out my heart for you, and if you can trust me so much, why can you not love me too ? What is it that prevents your love ?

Why cannot I alter it? And yet, what am I saying? You may think me honest, but how can I expect you to take a discharged felon!"

Catharine knew what Tom did not know. She was perfectly sure that the accusation against him was the result of the supposed discovery of their love for one another. If she had denied it promptly nothing perhaps would have happened. It was all due to her, then. She gazed up the stream; the leaden clouds drove on; the leaden water lay rippled; the willows and the rushes, vexed with the bitter blast, bent themselves continually. She turned and took her ring off her finger.

"It can never be," she slowly said; "here is my ring; you may keep it, but while I am alive you must never wear it."

Tom took it mechanically, bent his head over the parapet, and his anguish broke out in sobs and tears. Catharine took his hand in hers, leaned over him, and whispered:

"Tom, listen—I shall never be any man's wife."

Before he could say another word she had gone, and he felt that he should never see her again.

What makes the peculiar pang of parting? The coach comes up ; the friend mounts ; there is the wave of a handkerchief. I follow him to the crest of the hill ; he disappears, and I am left to walk down the dusty lane alone. Am I melancholy simply because I shall not see him for a month or a year ? She whom I have loved for half a life lies dying. I kiss her and bid her good-bye. Is the bare loss the sole cause of my misery, my despair, breeding that mad longing that I myself might die ? In all parting there is something infinite. We see in it a symbol of the order of the universe, and it is because that death-bed farewell stands for so much that we break down. " If it pleases God," says Swift to Pope, "to restore me to my health, I shall readily make a third journey ; if not, we must part *as all human creatures have parted."* As all human creatures have parted ! Swift did not say that by way of consolation.

Tom turned homewards. Catharine's last words were incessantly in his mind. What they meant he knew not and could not imagine, but in the midst of his trouble rose up something not worth calling joy, a little thread of water in the waste : it was a little relief that nobody was preferred before him, and that nobody would possess what to him was denied. He told his father, and found his faith unshakable. There was a letter for him in a handwriting he thought he knew, but he was not quite sure. It was as follows:—

"DEAR MR. CATCHPOLE,—I hope you will excuse the liberty I have taken in writing to you. I have left my place at the Terrace. I cannot help sending these few lines to say that Orkid Jim has been causing mischief here, and if he's had anything to do with your going he's a liar. It was all because I wouldn't go to the door and let him in, and gave missus a bit of my mind about him that I had notice. I wasn't sorry, however, for my cough is bad, and I couldn't stand running up and down those Terrace stairs. It was different at the shop. I thought I should just like to let you know that whatever missus and master may say, *I'm* sure you have done nothing but what is quite straight.

"Yours truly,

"PHŒBE CROWHURST."

Tom was grateful to Phœbe, and he put her letter in his pocket : it remained there for some time : it then came out with one or two other papers, was accidentally burnt with them, and was never answered. Day after day poor Phœbe watched the postman, but nothing came. She wondered if she had made any mistake in the address, but she had not the courage to write again. " He may be very much taken up," thought she, " but he might have sent me just a line ; " and then she felt ashamed, and wished she had not written, and would have given the world to have her letter back again. She had been betrayed into a little tenderness which met with no response. She was only a housemaid, and yet when she said to herself that maybe she had been too forward, the blood came to her cheeks ; beautifully, too beautifully white they were. Poor Phœbe !

Tom met Mr. Cardew in Eastthorpe the evening after the interview with Catharine, and told him his story.

" I am ruined," he said : " I have no character."

" Wait a minute ; come with me into the Bell where my horse is."

They went into the coffee-room, and Mr. Cardew took a sheet of note-paper and wrote :—

" MY DEAR ROBERT,—The bearer of this note, Mr. Thomas Catchpole, is well known to me as a perfectly honest man, and he thoroughly understands his business. He is coming to London, and I hope you will consider it your duty to obtain remunerative employment for him. He has been wickedly accused of a crime of which he is as innocent as I am, and this is an additional reason why you should exert yourself on his behalf.

     " Your affectionate cousin,

        " THEOPHILUS CARDEW.

" To ROBERT BERDOE, Esq.,
    " Clapham Common."

Mr. Cardew married a Berdoe, it will be remembered, and this Robert Berdoe was a wealthy wholesale ironmonger, who carried on business in Southwark.

" You had better leave Eastthorpe, Mr. Catchpole, and take your father with you. Are you in want of any money ? "

" No, sir, thank you ; I have saved a little. I cannot speak very well, Mr. Cardew ; you know I cannot : I cannot say to you what I ought."

" I want no thanks, my dear friend. What I do is a simple duty. I am a minister of God's Word, and I know no obligation more pressing which He has laid upon me than that of bearing witness to the truth."

Mr. Cardew went off as usual away from what was before him.

" The duty of Christ's minister is, generally speaking, *to take the other side*—that is to say, to resist the verdicts passed by the world upon men and things. Preaching mere abstractions, too, is not by itself of much use. What we are bound to do is not only to preserve the eternal standard, but to measure actual human beings and human deeds by it. I sometimes think, too, it is of more importance to say *this is right* than to say *this is wrong*, to save that which is true than to assist into perdition that which is false. Especially ought we to defend character unjustly assailed. A character is something alive, a soul ; to rescue it is the salvation of a soul ! "

He stopped and seemed to wake up suddenly.

" Good-bye ! God's blessing on you." He shook Tom's hand, and was going out of the yard.

" There is just one thing more, sir : I do not want to leave Eastthorpe with such a character behind me—to leave in the dark, one may say, and not defend myself. It looks as if it were an admission I was wrong. I should, above every-thing, like to get to the bottom of it, and see who is the liar or what the mistake is."

" Nobody would listen to you, and if you were to make a noise Mr. Furze might prosecute, and with the evidence he has we do not know what the end might be ; I will do my part, as I am bound to do, to set you right. But, above every-thing, Mr. Catchpole, endeavour to put yourself where the condemnation of the world and even crucifixion by it are of no consequence." Mr. Cardew gave Tom one more shake of the hand, mounted his horse, and rode off. He had asked Tom for no proofs : he had merely heard the tale and had given his certificate.

Mr. Furze distinctly enjoined Orkid Jim to hold his tongue. Neither Mr. nor Mrs. Furze wished to appear in court, and they were uncertain what Catharine might do if they went any further. Mr. Orkid Jim had the best of reasons for silence, but Mr. Humphries, the builder, of course repeated what he himself knew, and so it went about that Tom was wrong in his accounts, and all Eastthorpe affirmed him to be little better than a rascal. Mr. Cardew, with every tittle of much stronger and apparently irresistible testimony before him, never for a moment considered it as a feather's weight in the balance.

"But the facts, my good sir, the facts; the facts —there they are: the receipt to the bill; Jim's declaration; his brother's declaration; the marked coin; the absolute proof that Catchpole gave it to Butterfield, and he could not, as some may think, have changed silver of his own for it, for Mr. Furze paid him in gold, and there was not twenty shillings worth of silver in the till; what *have* you got to say? Do you tell me all this may be accident and coincidence? If you do, we may just as well give up reasoning and the whole of our criminal procedure."

Mr. Cardew did know the facts, *the* facts, and

relying on them he delivered his judgment. Catharine, Phœbe, and Tom's father agreed with him—four jurors out of one thousand of full age ; but the four were right and the nine hundred odd were wrong. In the four dwelt what aforetime would have been called Faith, nothing magical, nothing superstitious, but really the noblest form of reason, for it is the ability to rest upon the one reality which is of value, neglecting all delusive appearances which may apparently contradict it.

Tom left Eastthorpe the next morning, and on that day Catharine received the following letter from her mother :—

"MY DEAR CATHARINE,—I write to tell you that we have made an awful discovery. Catchpole has appropriated money belonging to your father, and the evidence against him is complete. (Mrs. Furze then told the story.) You will now, my dear Catharine, be able, I hope, to do justice to your father and mother, and to understand their anxiety that you should form no connection with a man like this. It is true that on the morning when we spoke to you we did not know the extent of his guilt, but we had suspected him for some time. It is quite providential that the disclosure comes at the present moment, and I hope it will detach you from him for ever. Your father and I send our love, and please assure Mr. and Mrs. Bellamy of our regard.

"Your affectionate mother,

"AMELIA FURZE."

On the same morning Mr. Furze received the following note from Mr. Cardew :—

"DEAR SIR,—I regret to hear that a false charge has been preferred against my friend Mr. Catchpole. By my advice he has left Eastthorpe without any attempt to defend himself, but I consider it my duty to tell you he is innocent ; that you have lost a faithful servant, and, what is worse, you have done him harm, not only in body, but in soul, for there are not many men who can be wrongfully accused and remain calm and resigned. You ask me on what evidence I acquit him. I know the whole story, but I also know him, and I know that he cannot lie. I beg you to consider what you do in branding as foul that which God has made good. I offer no apology for thus addressing you, for I am a minister of God's Word, and I have to do all that He bids. I should consider I was but a poor servant of the Most High if I did not protest against wrong-doing face to face with the doer of it.

> "Faithfully yours,
> "Theophilus Cardew."

Both Mr. and Mrs. Furze were greatly incensed, and Mr. Cardew received the following reply, due rather to Mrs. than to Mr. Furze :—

"Sir,—I am greatly surprised at the receipt of your letter You have taken up the cause of a servant against his master, and a dishonest servant, too : you have taken it up with only an imperfect acquaintance with the case, and knowing nothing of it except from his representation. If you were the clergyman of this parish I might, perhaps, recognise your right to address me, although I am inclined to believe that the clergy do far more harm than good by meddling with matters outside

their own sphere. How can we listen with respect
to a minister who is occupied with worldly affairs
rather than with those matters which befit his
calling and concern our salvation? Sir, I must
decline any discussion with you as to Mr. Catchpole's innocence or guilt, and respectfully deny
your right to interfere.

> " I am, sir,
>
> " Your obedient servant,
>
> "J. FURZE."

Catharine's first impulse was to go home instantly
and vindicate Tom, but she did not move, and the
letter remained unanswered. What could she say
to her own parents which would meet the case or
would be worthy of such a conspiracy? She would
not be believed, and no good would be done. A
stronger reason for not speaking was a certain pride
and a determination to retaliate by silence, but the
strongest of all reasons was a kind of collapse after
she arrived at Chapel Farm, and the disappearance
of all desire to fight. Her old cheerfulness began
to depart, and a cloud to creep over her like the
shadow of an eclipse. Young as she was, strange

thoughts possessed her. The interval between the present moment and death appeared annihilated ; life was a mere span ; a day would go by, and then a week, and in a few months, which could easily be counted, would come the end ; nay, it was already out there, visible, approaching, and when she came to think what death really meant, the difference between right and wrong was worth nothing. Terrors vague and misty possessed her, all the worse because they were not substantial. She could not put into words what ailed her, and she wrestled with shapeless, clinging forms which she could hardly discern, and could not disentangle from her, much less overthrow. They wound themselves about her, and, although they were but shadows, they made her shriek, and at times she fainted under their grasp, and thought she could not survive. She had no peace. If soldiers lie dead upon a battle-field there is an end of them ; new armies may be raised, but the enemy is at any rate weaker by those who are killed. It is not quite the same with our ghostly foes, for they rise into life after we think they are buried, and often with greater strength than ever.

There is something awful in the obstinacy of the assaults upon us. Day after day, night after night, and perhaps year after year, the wretched citadel is environed, and the pressure of the attack is unremitting, while the force which resists has to be summoned by a direct effort of the will, and the moment that effort relaxes the force fails, and the besiegers swarm upon the fortifications. That which makes for our destruction, everything that is horrible, seems spontaneously active, and the opposition is an everlasting struggle.

At last the effect upon Catharine's health was so obvious that Mrs. Bellamy was alarmed, and went over to Eastthorpe to see Mrs. Furze. Mrs. Furze in her own mind instantly concluded that Tom was the cause of her daughter's trouble, but she did not mean to admit it to her. In a sense Tom was the cause ; not that she loved him, but because her refusal of him brought it vividly before her that her life would be spent without love, or, at least, without a love which could be acknowledged. It was a crisis, for the pattern of her existence was henceforth settled, and she was to live not only without that which is sweetest for woman, but with no definite object before her. The force in woman is so great that something with which it can grapple, on which it can expend itself, is a necessity, and Catharine felt that her strength would have to occupy itself in twisting straws. It is really this which is the root of many a poor girl's suffering. As the world is arranged at present, there is too much power for the mills which have to be turned by it.

Mrs. Furze requested Mrs. Bellamy to send back Catharine at once in order that a doctor might be consulted. She returned: she did not really much care where she was; and to the doctor she went. Dr. Turnbull was the gentleman selected.

CHAPTER XVIII.

DR. TURNBULL was the doctor who, it will be remembered, lived in the square near the church. There was another doctor in Eastthorpe, Mr. Butcher, of whom we have heard, but Dr. Turnbull's reputation as a doctor was far higher than Mr. Butcher's. What Eastthorpe thought of Dr. Turnbull as a man is another matter. Mr. Butcher was married, church-going, polite, smiling to everybody, and when he called he always said, "Well, and how are *we?*" in such a nice way, identifying himself with his patient. But even Eastthorpe had not much faith in him, and in very serious cases always preferred Dr. Turnbull. Eastthorpe had remarked that Mr. Butcher's medicines had a curious similarity. He believed in two classes of diseases—sthenic and asthenic. For the former he prescribed bleeding and purgatives ; for the latter he " threw in " bark and iron, and ordered port wine. Eastthorpe thought him very fair for colds, measles, chicken-pox, and for rashes of all sorts, and so did all the country round. He generally attended everybody for such complaints, but as Mr. Gosford said after his recovery from a dangerous attack, " when it come to a stoppage, I thought I'd better have Turnbull," and Mr. Gosford sent for him promptly.

Dr. Turnbull was born three or four years before the outbreak of the French Revolution. He was consequently a little older than the great Dr. Elliotson, whose memory some of us still piously cherish, and Dr. Elliotson and he were devoted friends. Dr. Turnbull was tall, thin, upright, with undimmed grey eyes and dark hair, which had hardly yet begun to turn in colour, but was a little worn off his forehead. He had a curiously piercing look in his face, so that it was impossible if you told him an untruth not to feel that you were detected. He never joked or laughed in the sick-room or in his consulting-room, and his words were few. But what was most striking in him was his mute power of command, so that everybody in contact with him did his bidding without any effort on his part. He kept three servants—two women and a man. They were very good servants, but all three had been pronounced utterly intractable before they went to him. Master and mistress dared not speak to them; but with Dr. Turnbull they were suppressed as completely as if he had been Napoleon and they had been privates. He was kind to them, it is true, but at times very severe, and they could neither reply to him nor leave him. He did not affect the dress nor the manners of the doctors who preceded him. He wore a simple, black necktie, a shirt with no frill, and a black frock-coat. The poor worshipped him, as well they might, for his generosity to them was unexampled, and he took as much pains with them and was as kind to them as if they were the first people in Eastthorpe. He was perhaps even gentler with the poor than with the rich. He was very apt to be contemptuous, and to snarl when called to a rich man suffering from some trifling disorder, who thought that his wealth justified a second opinion, but he watched the whole night through with the tenderness of a woman by the bedside of poor Phœbe Crowhurst when she had congestion of the lungs before she lived with Mrs. Furze. He saved that girl and would not take a sixpence, and when the mother, overcome with gratitude, actually fell on her knees before him and clung to him and sobbed and could not speak, he lifted her up with a "Nonsense, my good woman!" and quickly departed. He was a materialist, and described himself as one: he disbelieved in what he called the soap-bubble theory, that somewhere in us there is something like a bubble, which controls everything, and is everything, and escapes invisible and gaseous to some other place after death. Consequently he never went to church. He was not openly combative, but Eastthorpe knew his heresies, and was taught to shudder at them. His professionally religious neighbours of course put him in hell in the future, but the common people did not go so far as that, although they could not believe him saved. They somehow confounded his denial of immortality with his own mortality, and imagined he would be at an end when he was put into the grave. As time wore on the attitude, even of the clergy, towards the doctor was gradually changed. They hastened to recognise him on week-days as he walked in his rapid, stately manner through the streets, although if they saw him on Sundays they considered it more becoming to avoid him. He was, as we have seen, a materialist, but yet he was the most spiritual person in the whole district. He took the keenest interest in science ; he was generous, and a believer in a spiritualism infinitely beyond that of most of his neighbours, for they had not a single spiritual interest. He was spiritual in his treatment of disease. He was before his age by half a century, and instead of "throwing in" drugs after the fashion of Butcher, he prescribed fresh air, rest, and change, and, above everything, administered his own powerful individuality. He did not follow his friend Elliotson into mesmerism, but he had a mesmerism of his own, subduing all terror and sanative like light. Mr. Gosford was not capable of great expression, but he was always as expressive as he could be when he told the story of that dreadful illness.

"He come into the room and ordered all the

physic away, and then he sat down beside me, and it was just afore hay-harvest, and I was in mortal fright, and I said to him, ' Oh, doctor, I shall die.' Never shall I forget what I had gone through that night, for I'd done nothing but see the grave afore me, and I was lying in it a-rotting. Well, he took my hand, and he said, ' Why, for that matter, my friend, I must die too ; but there's nothing in it ; you won't complain when you find out what death is. You won't die yet, though, and you'll get this lot of hay in at any rate ; what a heavy crop it is ! ' and he opened the winder and looked out. The way he spoke was wonderful, and what it was which come into me when he said, ' *I must die too*,' I don't know, but all my terrors went away, and I lay as calm as a child. 'Fore God I did, as calm as a child, and I felt the wind upon me across the meadow while he stood look-ing at it, and I could almost have got up that minute. I warn't out of bed for a fortnight, but I did go out into the hayfield, as he said."

Why did Dr. Turnbull come to Eastthorpe? Nobody ever knew while he lived. The question had been put at least some thousands of times, and all kinds of inquiries made, but with no result. The real reason, discovered afterwards, was simply that he had bad health, and that he had fled from temptation in the shape of a woman whom he loved, but whom duty, as he interpreted it, forbade him to marry, because he considered it wicked to run the risk of bringing diseased children into the world.

This was the man to whom Catharine went. Mrs. Furze went with her. He was perfectly acquainted with Mrs. Furze, and had seen Catharine, but had never spoken to her. Mrs. Furze told her story, which was that Catharine had no appetite, and was wasting, from no assignable cause. The doctor sounded her carefully, and then sat down without speaking. There was undoubtedly a weakness in one lung, but he was not satisfied. He knew how difficult it is to get people to tell the real truth to a physician, and that, if a third person is present, it is impossible. He therefore asked Mrs. Furze if she would step into the next room. "A girl," he said, "will not say all she has to say even to her mother." Mrs. Furze did not quite like it, but obeyed.

"Miss Furze," said the doctor, "I imagine you are a person who would not like to be deceived : you have a slight tenderness in the chest ; there is no reasonable cause for alarm, but you will have to be careful."

Catharine's face lighted up a little when the last sentence was half finished, and the careful observer noticed it instantly.

"That, however, is not the cause of your troubles : there is something on your mind. I never make any inquiries in such cases, because I know if I did I should be met with evasions."

Catharine's eyes were on the floor. After a long pause she said—

"I am wretched : I have no pleasure in life; that is all I can say."

"If there is no definite cause for it—mind, I say that—I may do something to relieve your distress. When people have no pleasure in living, and there is no concrete reason for it, they are out of health, and argument is of no avail. If a man does not find that food and light and the air are pleasant, it is of no use to debate with himself. Have you any friends at a distance?"

" None."

" What occupation have you ? "

" None."

" It is not often that people are so miserable that they are unable to make others less miserable. If instead of thinking about yourself you were to think a little about those who are worse, if you would just consider that you have duties and attempt to do them, the effort might be a mere dead lift at first, but it would do you good, and you would find a little comfort in knowing at the end of the day that, although it had brought no delight to you, it had through you been made more tolerable to somebody. Disorders of the type with which you are afflicted are terribly selfish. Mind, I repeat it, I presuppose nothing but general depression. If it is more than that I can be of no use."

Catharine was dumb, and Dr. Turnbull's singular power of winning confidence was of no avail to extract anything more from her.

" I am sorry you cannot leave home. I shall give you no medicine. With regard to the chest, the single definite point, you know what precautions to take; as to the nervous trouble, do not discuss, ponder, or even directly attack, but turn the position, if I may so speak, by work and a determination to be of some use. If you were tempted by what you call wicked thoughts you would not nurse them. It is a great pity that people are so narrow in their notions of what wicked thoughts are. Every thought which maims you is wicked, horribly wicked, I call it. By the way, going to another subject, that poor girl, Phœbe Crowhurst, who lived at your house, is very ill again. She would like to see you."

Catharine left, and Mrs. Furze came in.

" Has anything unsettled your daughter lately?"

" No, nothing particular."

She thought of Tom, but to save Catharine's life she would not have acknowledged that it was possible for a Catchpole to have power to disturb a Furze. Had it been Mr. Colston now, the case would have been different.

" She needs care, but there is nothing serious the matter with her. She ought to go away, but I understand she has no friends at a distance with whom she can stay. Give her a little wine."

" Any medicine ? "

" No, none ; I should like to see her again soon ; good morning."

Phœbe's home was near Abchurch, and Catharine went over to Abchurch to see her, not without remonstrance on the part of Mrs. Furze, Phœbe having been discharged in disgrace. Her father was an agricultural labourer, and lived in a little four-roomed, whitewashed cottage about a mile and a half out of the village. The living-room faced the north-east, the door opening direct on the little patch of garden, so that in winter, when the wind howled across the level fields, it was scarcely warmer indoors than outside, and rags and dish-clouts had to be laid on the door-sill to prevent the entrance of the snow and rain. At the back was a place, half outhouse, half kitchen, which had once had a brick floor, but the bricks had disappeared. Upstairs, over the living-room, was a bedroom, with no fireplace, and a very small casement window, where the mother and three children slept, the oldest a girl of about fourteen, the second a boy of twelve, and the third a girl of three or four, for the back bedroom over the out-

house had been given up to Phœbe since she was
ill.   The father slept below on the floor.   Phœbe's
room also had no fireplace, and great patches of
plaster had been brought down by the rain on the
south-west side.   Just underneath the window was
the pigstye.   Outside nothing had been done to
the house for years.   It was not brick built, and
here and there the laths and timber were bare, and
the thatch had almost gone.   Houses were very
scarce on the farms in that part, and landlords
would not build.   The labourers consequently were
driven into Abchurch, and had to walk, many of
them, a couple of miles each way daily.   Miss
Diana Eaton, eldest daughter of the Honourable
Mr. Eaton, had made a little sketch in water-colour
of the cottage.   It hung in the great drawing-room,
and was considered most picturesque.

"Lovely!   What a dear old place!" said the
guests.

"It makes one quite enamoured of the country,"
exclaimed Lady Fanshawe, one of the most determined diners-out in Mayfair.   "I never look at a
scene like that without wishing I could give up
London altogether.   I am sure I could be content.

It would be so charming to get rid of conventionality and be perfectly natural. You really ought to send that drawing to the Academy, Miss Eaton."

That we should take pleasure in pictures of filthy, ruined hovels, in which health and even virtue are impossible, is a strange sign of the times. It is more than strange; it is an omen and a prophecy that people will go into sham ecstasies over one of these pigstyes so long as it is in a gilt frame; that they will give a thousand guineas for its light and shade—light, forsooth!—or for its Prout-like quality, or for its quality of this, that, and the other, while inside the real stye, at the very moment when the auctioneer knocks down the drawing amidst applause, lies the mother dying from dirt fever; the mother of six children starving and sleeping there—starving, save for the parish allowance, for the snow is on the ground and the father is out of work.

Crowhurst's wages were ten shillings a week, and the boy earned half a crown, but in the winter there was nothing to do for weeks together. All this, however, was accepted as the established

order of things. It never entered into the heads
of the Crowhursts to revolt. They did not revolt
against the moon because she was sometimes full
and lit everybody comfortably, and at other times
was new and compelled the use of rushlights. It
was so ordained.

Half a mile beyond the cottage was a chapel.
It stood at a cross-road, and no houses were near
it. It had stood there for 150 years, gabled, red
brick, and why it was put there nobody knew.
Round it were tombstones, many totally dis-
figured, and most of them awry. The grass was
always long and rank, full of dandelions, sorrel,
and docks, excepting once a year in June when it
was cut, and then it looked raw and yellow. Here
and there was an unturfed, bare hillock, marking a
new grave, and that was the only mark it would
have, for people who could afford anything more
did not attend the chapel now. The last "respectable family" was a farmer's hard by, but he and
his wife had died, and his sons and daughters went
to church. The congregation, such as it was, con-
sisted nominally of about a dozen labourers and
their wives and children, but no more than half of

them came at any one time. The windows had painted wooden shutters, which were closed during the week to protect the glass from stone-throwing, and the rusty iron gate was always locked, save on Sundays. The gate, the door, and the shutters were unfastened just before the preacher came, and the horrible chapel smell and chapel damp hung about the place during the whole service. When there was a funeral of any one belonging to the congregation the Abchurch minister had to conduct it, and it was necessarily on Sunday, to his great annoyance. Nobody could be buried on any other day, because work could not be intermitted; no labourer could stay at home when wife or child was dying; he would have lost his wages, and perhaps his occupation. He thought himself lucky if they died in the night.

The chapel was "supplied," as it was called, by an Abchurch deacon or Sunday-school teacher, who came over, prayed, preached, gave out hymns, and went away. That was nearly all that Cross Lanes knew of the "parent cause." The supplies were constantly being changed, and if it was very bad weather they stayed at home. On very rare

occasions the Abchurch minister appeared on
Sunday evenings in summer, but that was only
when he wanted rest, and could deliver the
Abchurch sermon of the morning, and could
obtain a substitute at home.

Crowhursts had been buried at Cross Lanes
ever since it existed, but the present Crowhursts
knew nothing of their ancestors beyond the
generation immediately preceding. What was
there to remember, or if there was anything
worth remembering, why should they remember
it? Life was blank, blind, dull as the brown clay
in the sodden fields in November; nevertheless,
the Light which lighteth every man that cometh
into the world shone into the Crowhurst cottage
—that Light greater than all lights which can be
lit by priest or philosopher, as the sun is greater
than all our oil-lamps, gas, and candles. When
Phœbe first had congestion of the lungs, not a
single note of murmuring at the trouble caused
escaped a soul in the household. The mother
sat up with her at night, and a poor woman
half a mile off came in during the day and saw
that things went all straight. To be sure, there

was Dr. Turnbull. It was a long way out of his rounds, but he knew the Crowhursts well, and, as we have said, he watched over Phœbe as carefully as if she had been the daughter of a duke. Now Phœbe was ill again, but Dr. Turnbull was again there, and although her cough was incessant, the care of father, mother, brother, and sister was perfect in its tenderness, and their self-forgetfulness was complete. It was not with them as with a man known to the writer of this history. His wife, whom he professed to love, was dying of consumption. "I do not deny she suffers," he said ; "but nobody thinks of *me*." The sympathy of the agricultural poor with one another is hardly credible to fine people who live in towns. If we could have a record of the devotion of those women who lie forgotten under the turf round country churches throughout England, it would be better worth preserving than nine-tenths of our literature and histories. Surely in some sense they still *are*, and their love cannot have been altogether a thing of no moment to the Power that made them!

Catharine had never been to Phœbe's home

before. At the Terrace she was smart, attractive, and as particular as her mistress about her clothes. Nobody ever saw Phœbe with untidy shoes or stockings, and even in the morning, before she was supposed to be dressed, her little feet were as neat as if she had nothing to do but to sit in a drawing-room. She was now lying on a stump bedstead with a patchwork coverlet over her, and to protect her from the draughts an old piece of carpet had been nailed on a kind of rough frame and placed between her and the door. Catharine's first emotion when she entered was astonishment and indignation. Therein she showed her ignorance and stupidity. The owner of the cottage did not force the Crowhursts to live in it. It was not he who directed that a girl dying of consumption should lie close to a damp wall in a room eight feet square with no ventilation. He had the cottage, the Crowhursts, presumably, were glad to get it, and he conferred a favour on them.

"Oh, Miss Catharine," said Phœbe, "this is kind of you! To think of your coming over from Eastthorpe to see me, and after what happened

between me and Mrs. Furze! Miss Catharine,
I didn't mean to be rude, but that Orkid Jim is
a liar, and it's my belief that he's at the bottom
of the mischief with Tom. You haven't heard
of Tom, I suppose, Miss?"

"Yes, he is in London. He is doing very
well."

"Oh, I am very thankful. I am afraid you
will find the room very close, Miss. Don't stay
if you are uncomfortable."

Catharine replied by taking a chair and sitting
by the bedside. There was somewhat in Phœbe's
countenance, Catharine knew not what, but it
went to her heart, and she bent down and kissed
her upon the forehead. They had always been
half-friends when Phœbe was at the Terrace.
The poor girl's eyes filled with tears, and a smile
came over her face like the sunshine following
the shadow of a cloud sweeping over the hillside.
Mrs. Crowhurst came into the room.

"Why, mother, what are you doing here?
You ought to be abed. Where is Mrs. Dunsfold?"

"Mrs. Dunsfold is laid up with the rheumatics,

my dear. But don't you bother; we can manage very well. I will stay with you at night, and just have a bit of sleep in the mornings. Your sister can manage after I've seen to father's breakfast and while I'm a-lying down, and if she wants me, she's only got to call."

The mother looked worn and anxious, as though, even with Mrs. Dunsfold's assistance, her rest had been insufficient.

"Mrs. Crowhurst," said Catharine, "go to bed again directly. If you do not, you will be ill too. I will stay with Phœbe, at least for to-night, if anybody can be found to go to Eastthorpe to tell my mother I shall not be home."

"Miss Catharine! to think of such a thing! I'm sure you sha'n't," replied Mrs. Crowhurst; but Catharine persisted, and a message was sent by Phœbe's brother, who, although so young, knew the way perfectly well, and could be trusted.

The evening and the darkness drew on, and everything gradually became silent. Excepting Phœbe's cough, not a sound could be heard save the distant bark of some farmyard dog. As the air outside was soft and warm, Catharine opened the window, after carefully protecting her patient. Phœbe was restless.

"Shall I read to you?"

"Oh, please, Miss; but there is nothing here for you to read but the Bible and a hymn-book."

"Well, I will read the Bible. What would you like?"

Phœbe chose neither prophecy, psalm, nor epistle, but the last three chapters of St. Matthew. She, perhaps, hardly knew the reason why, but she could not have made a better choice. When we come near death, or near something which may be worse, all exhortation, theory, promise, advice, dogma fail. The one staff which, perhaps, may not break under us, is the victory achieved in the like situation by one who has preceded us; and the most desperate private experience cannot go beyond the garden of Gethsemane. The hero is a young man filled with dreams and an ideal of a heavenly kingdom which he was to establish on earth. He is disappointed by the time he is thirty. He has not a friend who understands him, save in so far as the love of two or three poor women is understanding. One of his

disciples denies him, another betrays him, and
in the presence of the hard Roman tribunal all
his visions are nothing, and his life is a failure.
He is to die a cruel death ; but the bitterness
of the cup must have been the thought that
in a few days—or at least in a few months or
years—everything would be as if he had never
been. This is the pang of death, even to the
meanest. "He that goeth down to the grave,"
says Job, "shall return no more to his house,
neither shall his place know him any more." A
higher philosophy would doubtless set no store
on our poor personality, and would even rejoice
in the thought of its obliteration or absorption,
but we cannot always lift ourselves to that level,
and the human sentiment remains. Catharine
read through the story of the conflict, and when
she came to the resurrection she felt, and Phœbe
felt, after her fashion, as millions have felt before,
that this was the truth of death. It may be a
legend, but the belief in it has carried with it
other beliefs which are vital.

The reading ceased, and Phœbe fell asleep for a
little. She presently waked and called Catharine.

"Miss Catharine," she whispered, drawing Catharine's hand between both her own thin hands, " I have something to say to you. Do you know I loved Tom a little; but I don't think he loved me. His mind was elsewhere; I saw where it was, and I don't wonder. It makes no difference, and never has, in my thoughts, either of him or of you. It will be better for him in every way, and I am glad for his sake. But when I am gone—and I sha'n't feel ashamed at his knowing it—please give him my Bible; and you may, if you like, put a piece of my hair in that last chapter you have been reading to-night."

"Phœbe, my Phœbe, listen," said Catharine: "I shall never be Tom's wife."

"Are you sure?"

"As sure as that I am here with my head on your pillow."

"I am sorry."

She then became silent, and so continued for two hours. Catharine thought she was asleep, but a little after dawn her mother came into the room. She knew better, and saw that the silence was not sleep, but the insensibility of death. In a few minutes she hurried Catharine downstairs, and when she was again admitted Phœbe lay dead, and her pale face, unutterably peaceful and serious, was bound up with a white neckerchief. The soul of the poor servant-girl had passed away —only a servant-girl—and yet there was something in that soul equal to the sun whose morning rays were pouring through the window. She lies at the back of the meeting-house, amongst her kindred, and a little mound was raised over her. Her father borrowed the key of the gate every now and then, and, after his work was over, cut the grass where his child lay, and prevented the weeds from encroaching ; but when he died, not long after, his wife had to go into the workhouse, and in one season the sorrel and dandelions took possession, and Phœbe's grave became like all the others—a scarcely distinguishable undulation in the tall, rank herbage.

CHAPTER XIX.

CATHARINE left the cottage that afternoon, and began to walk home to Eastthorpe. She thought, as she went along, of Phœbe's confession. She had loved Tom, but had reached the point of perfect acquiescence in any award of destiny, provided only he could be happy. She had faced sickness and death without a murmur ; she had no theory of duty, no philosophy, no religion, as it is usually called, save a few dim traditional beliefs, and she was the daughter of common peasants ; but she had attained just the one thing essential which religion and philosophy ought to help us to obtain, and, if they do not help us to obtain it, they are nothing. She lived not for herself, nor in herself, and it was not even justice to herself which she demanded. She had not become what she was because death was before her. Death and the prospect of death do not work any change. Catharine called to mind Phœbe's past life : it was all of a piece, and countless little incidents unnoticed at the time obtained a significance and were interpreted. She knew herself to be Phœbe's superior intellectually, and that much had been presented to her which was altogether over Phœbe's horizon. But in all her purposes, and in all her activity, she seemed to have had self for a centre, and she felt that she would gladly give up every single advantage she possessed if she could but depose that self and enthrone some other divinity in its place. Oh the bliss of waking up in the morning with the thoughts turned outwards instead of inwards ! Her misery which so weighed upon her might perhaps depart if she could achieve that conquest. She remembered one of Mr. Cardew's first sermons, when she was at Miss Ponsonby's, the sermon of which we have heard something, and she cried to herself, "Who shall deliver me from the body of this death !"

Strange, but true, precisely at that moment the passion for Mr. Cardew revived with more than its old intensity. Fresh from a deathbed, ponder-

ing over what she had learned or thought she had
learned there—the very lesson which ought to
have taught her to give up Mr. Cardew—she
loved him more than ever, and was less than
ever able to banish his image from her. She
turned out of her direct road and took that
which led past his house—swept that way as
irresistibly as a mastless hull is swept by the
tide. She knew that Mr. Cardew was in the
habit of walking out in the afternoon, and she
knew the path he usually took. She had not
gone far before she met him. She explained
what her errand had been, and added that she
preferred the bypath because she was able to
avoid the dusty Eastthorpe lane.

"I do not know those Crowhursts," said Mr.
Cardew; "they are Dissenters, I believe."

The subject dropped, and Catharine had not
another word to say about Phœbe.

"You look fatigued and as if you were not very
well."

"Nothing particular; a little cough at times,
but the doctor says it is of no consequence, if I
only take care."

"You have been up all night, and you are now going to walk back to Eastthorpe?"

"Yes, the walk will refresh me."

He did not ask her to go to his house. Catharine noticed the omission; hoped he would not—knew he would not.

"Have you heard anything of your father's assistant, Mr. Catchpole?"

"Yes, he likes that situation which you obtained for him so kindly."

"Is he quite happy?"

"Yes, I believe so."

"I encountered Mr. Colston, junior, a few minutes ago. He was on his way to Eastthorpe. I am afraid I was rather rude to him, for, to tell you the truth, I did not want his society. He is not an interesting young man. Do you care anything for him?"

"Nothing."

"I should like to see the picture you have formed of the man for whom you would care. I do not remember"—speaking slowly and dreamily—"ever to have seen a woman who would frame a loftier ideal."

He unconsciously came nearer to her; his arm moved into hers, and she did not resist.

"What is the use of painting pictures when reality is unattainable?"

"Unattainable! Yes, just what I imagined: you paint something unattainable to ordinary mortality. It is strange that most men and women, even those who more or less in all they do strive after perfection, seem to be satisfied with so little when it comes to love and marriage. The same sculptor, who unweariedly refines day after day to put in marble the image which haunts him, forms no such image of a woman whom he seeks unceasingly, or, if he does, he descends on one of the first twenty he meets and thinks he adores her. There is some strong thwarting power which prevents his search after the best, and it is as if Nature had said that we should not pick and choose. But the consequences are tremendous. I honour you for your aspirations."

"You give me credit for a strength I do not possess, Mr. Cardew. I said 'unattainable.' That was all. I did not say how."

They had come to a gate which led out of

the field into the road, and they paused there.
They leaned against the gate, and Mr. Cardew,
although his arm was withdrawn from Catharine's,
had placed it upon the top rail so that she felt it.
The pressure would not have moved an ounce
weight ; there were half a dozen thicknesses of
wool and linen between the arm and her shoulder,
but the encircling touch sent a quiver through
every nerve in her and shook her like electricity.
She stood gazing on the ground, digging up the
blades of grass with her foot.

" Do you mean," said Mr. Cardew, " that you
have ever seen him, and that——— "

The pressure behind her was a little more
obvious : he bent his head nearer to hers, looked
in her face, and she leaned back on the arm
heavily.   Suddenly, without a word, she put both
her hands to her head, pushed aside her hair, and
stood upright as a spear.

"Good-bye," she said, with her eyes straight
on his.   Another second and she had passed
through the gate, and was walking fast along the
road homewards alone.   She heard behind her
the sound of wheels, and an open carriage over-

took her. It was Dr. Turnbull's, and of course he stopped.

"Miss Furze, you are taking a long walk."

She told him she had been to see Phœbe, and of her death.

"You must be very tired : you must come with me."

She would have preferred solitude, but he insisted on her accompanying him, and she consented.

"I believe I saw Mr. Cardew in the meadow : I have just called on his wife."

"Is she ill ? "

"Yes, not seriously, I hope. You know Mr. Cardew ? "

"Yes, a little. I have heard him preach, and have been to his house when I was living at Abchurch."

"A remarkable man in many ways, and yet not a man whom I much admire. He thinks a good deal, and when I am in company with him I am unaccountably stimulated, but his thinking is not directed upon life. My notion is that our intellect is intended to solve real difficulties which

confront us, and that all intellectual exercise upon
what does not concern us is worse than foolish.
My brain finds quite enough to do in contriving
how to remove actual hard obstacles which lie in
the way of other people's happiness and my
own."

"His difficulties may be different from yours."

"Certainly, but they are to a great extent
artificial, and all the time spent upon them is so
much withdrawn from the others which are real.
He goes out into the fields reading endless books,
containing records of persons in various situations.
He is not like any one of those persons, and he
never will be in any one of those situations. The
situation in which he found himself that morning
at home, or that in which a poor neighbour found
himself, is that which to him is important. It is
a pernicious consequence of the sole study of extraordinary people that the customary standards
of human action are deposed, and other standards
peculiar to peculiar creatures under peculiar
circumstances are set up. I have known Cardew
do very curious things at times. I do not believe
for one moment he thought he was doing wrong,

but nevertheless, if any other man had done them, I should have had nothing more to say to him."

" Perhaps he ought to have his own rules. He may not be constituted as we are."

" My dear Miss Furze, as a physician, let me give you one word of solemn counsel. Nothing is more dangerous, physically and mentally, than to imagine we are not as other people. Strive to consider yourself, not as Catharine Furze, a young woman apart, but as a piece of common humanity and bound by its laws. It is infinitely healthier for you. Never, under any pretext whatever, allow yourself to do what is exceptional. If you have any originality, it will better come out in an improved performance of what everybody ought to do, than in the indulgence in singularity. For one person, who, being a person of genius, has been injured by what is called conventionality—I do not, of course, mean foolish conformity to what is absurd—thousands have been saved by it, and self-separation means mischief. It has been the beginning even of insanity in many cases which have come under my notice." The doctor paused a little.

"I am glad Mrs. Cardew is better," said Catharine. "I did not know she had been ill."

"There is a woman for you—a really wonderful woman, unobtrusive, devoted to her husband, almost annihilating herself for him, and, what is very noteworthy, she denies herself in studies to which she is much attached, and for which she has a remarkable capacity, merely in order that she may the better sympathise with him. Then her care of the poor in his parish makes her almost a divinity to them. While he is luxuriating amongst the cowslips, in what he calls thinking, she is teaching the sick people patience and nursing them. She is a saint, and he does not know half her worth. It would do you a world of good now, Miss Furze, to live with her for six months if she were alone, but I am not quite sure that his influence on you would be wholesome. I was alarmed about her, but she will not die yet if I can help it. I want her to recover for her own sake, but also for her husband's and for her friends' sake. Perhaps I was a little too severe upon the husband, for I believe he does really love her very much; at least, if he does not, he ought."

"Ought? Do yóu think, Dr. Turnbull, a man ought to love what he cannot love?"

"Yes, but I must explain myself. I have no patience with people who seem to consider that they may yield themselves to something they know not what, and allow themselves to be swayed by it. A man marries a woman whom he loves. Is it possible that she, of all women in the world, is the one he would love best if he were to know all of them? Is it likely that he would have selected this one woman if he had seen, say, fifty more before he had married her? Certainly not; and when he sees other women afterwards, better than the one he has chosen, he naturally admires them. If he does not he is a fool, but he is bound to check himself. He puts them aside and is obliged to be satisfied with his wife. If it were permissible in him in such a case to abandon her, a pretty chaos we should be in. It is clearly his duty, and quite as clearly in his power, to be thus contented—at least, in nine cases out of ten. He *may*—and this is my point—he *may* wilfully turn away from what is admirable in his own house, or he may turn towards it. He is as responsible for turning away from it, or turning towards it, as he is for any of his actions. If he says he cannot love a wife who is virtuous and good, I call him not only stupid, but wicked—yes, wicked : people in Eastthorpe will tell you I do not know what that word means, because I do not go to church, and do not believe in what they do not believe themselves, but still I say wicked—wicked because he *can* love his wife, just as he can refrain from robbing his neighbour, and wicked because there is a bit of excellence stuck down before him for *him* to value. It is not intended for others, but for *him*, and he deserts the place appointed him by Nature if he neglects it."

"You have wonderful self-control, Dr. Turnbull. I can understand that a man might refrain from open expression of his love for a woman, whatever his passion for her might be, for, if he did not so restrain himself, he might mar the peace of some other person who was better than himself, and better deserved that his happiness should not be wrecked ; but as for love, it may be beyond him to suppress it."

"Well, Miss Furze," replied the doctor, smiling,

" we are going beyond our own experience, I hope.
However, what I have said is true. I suppose it
is because it is my business to cure disease that I
always strive to extend the realm of what is *subject*
to us. You seem to be fond of an argument.
Some day we will debate the point how far the
proper appreciation even of a picture or a melody
is within our own power. But I am a queer kind
of doctor. I have never asked you how you are,
and you are one of my patients."

" Better."

" That is good, but you must be careful, especially in the evening. It was not quite prudent
to sit up last night at the Crowhursts', but yet, on
the whole, it was right. No, you shall not get
down here ; I will drive you up to the Terrace."

He drove her home, and she went upstairs to
lie down.

" Commonplace rubbish ! " she said to herself ;
" what I used to hear at Miss Ponsonby's, but
dressed up a little better, the moral prosing of
an old man of sixty who never knew what it was
to have his pulse stirred ; utterly incapable of
understanding Mr. Cardew, one of whose ideas

moves me more than volumes of Turnbull copy-book."

Pulse stirred! The young are often unjust to the old in the matter of pulsation, and the world in general is unjust to those who prefer to be silent, or to whom silence is a duty. Dr. Turnbull's pulse was unmistakably stirred on a certain morning thirty years ago, when he crept past a certain door in Bloomsbury Square very early. The blinds were still all drawn down, but he lingered and walked past the house two or three times. He had come there to take a last look at the bricks and mortar of that house before he went to Eastthorpe, under vow till death to permit no word of love to pass his lips, to be betrayed into no emotion warmer than that of man to man. His pulse was stirred, too, when he read the announcement of her marriage in the *Times* five years afterwards, and then in a twelvemonth the birth of her first child. How he watched for that birth! Ten days afterwards she died. He went to the funeral, and after the sorrowing husband and parents had departed he remained, and the most scalding tears shed by the grave were his. It was not exactly moral prosing, but rather inextinguishable fire just covered with a sprinkling of grey ash.

With that dreadful capacity which some people possess for the realisation of that which is not present, the parting with Mr. Cardew came before Catharine as she shut her eyes on her pillow: the arm was behind her — she actually felt it; his eyes were on hers; she was on fire, and once more, as she had done before, she cursed herself for what she almost called her cowardice in leaving him. She wrestled with her fancies, turned this way and that way: at times they sent the blood hot into her face, and she rose and plunged it into cold water. She was weary, but sleep was impossible. "Commonplace rubbish!" she repeated: "of what use is it to me?" She was young. When we grow old we find that what is commonplace is true. *We must learn to bear our troubles patiently*, says the copper-plate line for small text, and the revolving years bring nothing more. She heard outside a long-drawn breath, apparently just under the door. She opened it, and found Alice, her retriever. Alice came in, sat down by the chair, and put her head on her mistress's lap, looking up to her with large, brown, affectionate eyes which almost spoke. There is something very touching in the love of a dog. It is independent of all our misfortunes, mistakes, and sins. It may not be of much account, but it is constant, and it is a love for *me*, and does not desert me for anything accidental, not even if I am criminal. That is because a dog is a dog, it may be said ; if it had a proper sense of sin it would instantly leave the house. Perhaps so, perhaps not : it may be that with a proper sense of sin it would still continue to love me. Anyhow, it loves me now, and I take its fidelity to be significant of something beyond sin. Alice had a way of putting her feet on her mistress's lap, as if she asked to be noticed. When no notice was taken she generally advanced her nose to Catharine's face—a very disagreeable habit, Mrs. Furze thought, but Catharine never would check it. The poor beast was more than usually affectionate to-day, and just turned Catharine's gloom into tears. She was disturbed by a note from Dr.

Turnbull. He thought that what she needed was rest, and she was to go to bed and take his medicine. This she did, and she fell into a deep slumber from which she did not wake till morning.

Mr. Cardew, when Catharine left him, walked homewards, but he went a long distance out of his way, much musing. As he went along something came to him—the same Something which had so often restrained Catharine. It smote him as the light from heaven smote Saul of Tarsus journeying to Damascus. His eyes were opened; he crept into an outhouse in the fields, and there alone in an agony he prayed. It was almost dark when he reached his own gate, and he went up to his wife's bedroom, where she lay ill. He sat down by the bed: some of her flowers were on a little table at her side.

"I am so ignorant of flowers, Doss (the name he called her before they were married); you really *must* teach me."

"You know enough about them."

He took her hand in his, put his head on the pillow beside her, and she heard a gasp which sounded a little hysterical.

"What is the matter, my dear? You are tired. You have walked a long way."

She turned round, and then without another word he rose a little, leaned over her, and kissed her passionately. She never knew what his real history during the last year or two had been. He outlived her, and one of his sorrows when she was lying in the grave was that he had told her nothing. He was wrong to be silent. A man with any self-respect will not be anxious to confess his sins, save when reparation is due to others. If he be completely ashamed of them he will hold his tongue about them. But the perfect wife may know them. She will not love him the less: he will love her the more as the possessor of his secrets, and the consciousness of her knowledge of him and of them will strengthen and often, perhaps, save him.

CHAPTER XX.

MRS. CARDEW recovered, but Dr. Turnbull recommended that as soon as she could be moved she should have an entire change, and at the end of the autumn she and her husband went abroad.

That winter was a bad winter for Mr. Furze. The harvest had been the worst known for years: farmers had no money; his expenses had increased; many of his customers had left him, and Catharine's cough had become so much worse that, except on fine days, she was not allowed to go out of doors. For the first time in his life he was obliged to overdraw his account at the bank, and when his wife questioned him about his troubles he became angry and vicious. One afternoon he had a visit from one of the partners in the bank, who politely informed him that no further

advances could be made. It was near Christmas,
and it was Mr. Furze's practice at Christmas to
take stock. He set to work, and his balance-
sheet showed that he was a poorer man by three
hundred pounds than he was a twelvemonth
before. Catharine did not see him on the night
on which he made this discovery. He came home
very late, and she had gone to bed. At breakfast
he was unlike himself—strange, excited, and with
a hunted, terrified look in the eyes which alarmed
her. It was not so much the actual loss which
upset him as the old incapacity of dealing with
the unusual. Oh, for one hour with Tom! What
should he do? Should he retrench? Should he
leave the Terrace? Should he try and borrow
money? A dizzy whirl of a dozen projects
swung round and round in his brain, and he
could resolve on nothing. He pictured most
vividly and imagined most vividly the consequences of bankruptcy. His intellectual activity
in that direction was amazing, and if one-tenth
part of it could have been expended on the
consideration of the next best thing to be done,
not only would he have discovered what the next

best thing was, but the dreadful energy of his imagination would have been enfeebled. He was sitting at his desk at the back of the shop with his head propped on his elbows, when he heard a soft footstep behind him. He turned round : it was Catharine.

"Dearest father," she said, "what is the matter ? Why do you not tell me?"

"I am a ruined man. The bank refuses to make any further advances to me, and I cannot go on."

Catharine was not greatly surprised.

"Look at that," he said. "I don't know what to do ; it is as if my head were going wrong. If I had lost a lot of money through a bad debt it would be different, but it is not that : the business has been going down bit by bit. There is nothing before us but starvation."

Catharine glanced at the abstract of the balance-sheet.

"You must call your creditors together and make a proposal to them. You will then start fair, and we will reduce our expenses. Nothing will be easier. We will live at the shop again ; you will be able to look after things properly, and everything will go right—it will, indeed, father."

She was very tender with him, and her love and counsel revived his spirits. Suddenly she was seized with a fit of coughing, and had to sit down. He thought he saw a red stain on the pockethandkerchief she put to her mouth.

"You shall not stay in this cold shop, my dear ; you ought not to have come out."

"Nonsense, father ! There is nothing the matter. Have you a list of your creditors ? "

"Yes ; there it is."

She glanced at it, and to her amazement saw Mr. Cardew's name down for £100.

"Mr. Cardew, father ? "

"Yes ; he came in one day, and said that he had some money lying idle, and did not know what to do with it. I was welcome to it if I wanted it for the business."

A statement was duly prepared by Mr. Askew, Mr. Furze's solicitor ; the usual notice was sent round, and the meeting took place in a room at the Bell. A composition of seven-and-sixpence in the pound was offered, to be paid within a twelvemonth, with a further half-crown in two years' time, the debtor undertaking to give up his house in the Terrace.

"Considering," said the lawyer, "that the debts owing to the estate are nearly all good, although just now it is difficult to realise, I think, gentlemen, you are safe, and I may add that this seems to me a very fair proposal. My client, I may say, would personally have preferred a different course, and would have liked to bind himself to pay in full at some future time, but I cannot advise any such promise, for I do not think he would be able to keep it."

"I shall want some security for the half-crown," said Mr. Crook, representative of the firm of Jenkins, Crook and Hardman, iron merchants in Staffordshire.

"Can't say as I'm satisfied," said Mr. Nagle, brass founder. "The debtor takes an expensive house without any warranty, and he cannot expect much consideration. I must have ten shillings now. Times are bad for us as well as for him."

Mr. Furze turned very white and rose to speak, but Mr. Askew pulled him down.

"I beg, gentlemen, you will not take extreme measures. Ten shillings now would mean a sale of furniture, and perhaps ruin. My client has been a good customer to you."

"I am inclined to agree with Mr. Nagle," said Mr. Crook. "Sentiment is all very well, but I do not see why we should make the debtor a present of half a crown for a couple of years. For my own part, if I want to be generous with my money, I have plenty of friends of my own to whom to give it."

There was a pause, but it was clear that Mr. Nagle's proposal would be carried.

"I am authorised," said a tall gentleman at the back of the room, whom Mr. Askew knew to be Mr. Carruthers, of Cambridge, head of the firm of Carruthers, Doubleday, Carruthers and Pearse, one of the most respectable legal firms in the county, "to offer payment in full at once."

"It is a pity," said Mr. Nagle, "that this offer could not have been made before. We might have been saved the trouble of coming here."

"Pardon me," replied Mr. Carruthers; "my client has been abroad for some time, and did not return till last night."

The February in which the meeting of Mr.
Furze's creditors took place was unusually wet.
There had been a deep snow in January, with the
wind from the north-east. The London coaches
had, many of them, been stopped both on the
Norwich, Cambridge, and Great North roads. The
wind had driven with terrible force across the flat
country, piling up the snow in great drifts, and
curling it in fantastic waves which hung suspended
over the hedges and entirely obliterated them.
Between Eaton Socon and Huntingdon one of the
York coaches was fairly buried, and the passengers,
after being near death's door with cold and hunger,
made their way to a farmhouse which had great
difficulty in supplying them with provisions. Coals
rose in Abchurch and Eastthorpe to four pounds a
ton, and just before the frost broke there were not
ten tons in both places taken together. Suddenly
the wind went round by the east to the south-west,
and it began to rain heavily, not only in the
Eastern Midlands, but far away in the counties to
the west and south-west through which the river
ran. The snow and ice melted very quickly, and
then came a flood, the like of which had not been

seen in those parts before. The outfall has been
improved since that time, so that in all probability
no such flood will happen again. The water, of
course, went all over the low-lying meadows. For
miles and miles on either bank it spread into vast
lakes, and the only mark by which to distinguish
the bed of the stream was the greater rush and the
roar. Cottages were surrounded, and people were
rescued by boats. Every sluice and mill-dam were
opened, but the torrent poured past them, and at
Cottington Mill it swept from millpool to tail right
over the road which divided them, and washed
away nearly the whole garden. When the rain
ceased the worst had to come, for the upper waters
did not reach Eastthorpe until three or four days
later. Then there was indeed a sight to be seen!
The southern end of Eastthorpe High Street was
actually two feet under water, and a man in a boat
—event to be recorded for ever in the Eastthorpe
annals—went from the timber-yard on one side of
the street through the timber-yard gates and into
the coal-yard opposite. Parts of haystacks, trees,
and dead bodies of sheep and oxen drove down on
the yellow, raging waves, and were caught against

the abutments of the bridge. At one time it was thought that it must give way, for the arches were choked; the water was inches higher on the west side than on the east, and men with long poles stood on the parapet to break up the obstructions.

At last the flood began to subside, and on the afternoon of the day of the creditors' meeting Mr. Orkid Jim appeared at the boathouse at the bottom of Rectory Lane and asked to be taken across. The stream was still very strong, but the meadows were clear, and some repair was necessary to the ironwork of a sluice-gate just opposite, which Jim wished to inspect before the men were set to work.

"Don't know as it's safe, Mr. Jim," said the boatman. "It's as much as ever I can get through. It goes uncommon strong against the willows there."

"You'll get through all right. I'll give yer a hand. I don't care to go a mile round over the bridge."

"Yes, that's all very well, Mr. Jim, but I don't want my boat smashed."

"Smashed! I am a lucky one, I am. No harm comes to any boat or trap as long as I'm in it."

The boatman consented. Just as he was about to push off, another man came down and asked for a passage. It was Tom Catchpole. Jim stared, but said nothing to him. The boatman also knew Tom, but did not speak. Jim now had half a mind to alter his intention of crossing.

"I don't know as I'll go," said he. "It does look queer, and no mistake."

"Well, don't keep me a-waitin', that's all."

Jim took his seat and went to the stern. Tom sat in the bow, and the boatman took the sculls. He had to make for a point far above the island, so as to allow for the current, and he just succeeded in clearing it. He then began to drift down to the landing-place in the comparatively still water between the island and the mainland. Jim stood up with a boat-hook in his hand and laid hold of an overhanging willow in order to slacken their progress, but the hook stuck in the wood, and in an instant the boat was swept from under him and he was in the water. He went down like a stone, for he could not swim, but rose again just as he was passing. Tom leaned over the side, managed to catch him by the coat-collar and hold his head above water. Fortunately the boat had swung round somewhat, and in a few seconds struck the bank. It was made fast, and in an instant Jim was dragged ashore and was in safety.

"That's a narrow squeak for you, Mr. Jim. If it hadn't been for Mr. Catchpole you'd have been in another world by this time."

Jim was perfectly sensible, but his eyes were fixed on Tom with a strange, steady stare.

"Hadn't you better be moving and take off them things?"

Still he did not stir; but at last, without a word, he turned round and slowly walked away.

"That's a rum customer," observed the boat-man; "he might have thanked us at least, and he hasn't paid me. Howsomever, I sha'n't forget it the next time I see him."

Tom made no reply: gave the man double his usual fare, and went across the meadow. He had no particular object in coming to Eastthorpe, excepting that he had heard there was to be a meeting of Mr. Furze's creditors, and he could not rest until he knew the result. He avoided the

main street as much as possible, but he intended
to obtain his information from Mr. Nagle at the
Bell.

As to Jim, he went home, changed his clothes,
and went out again. He walked up and down
the street, and presently met Tom.

" Mr. Catchpole," he said, " will you please come
along o' me ? "

There was something of authority in the tone of
Jim's voice, and yet something which forbade all
fear.   Tom followed him in silence, and they went
to the Terrace.   Mr. Furze was not at home, but
Jim knew he would be back directly, and they
waited in the kitchen, Tom much wondering, but
restrained by some strange compulsion—he could
not say what—not only to remain, but to refrain
from asking any questions.   Directly Mr. Furze
returned, Jim went upstairs, with Tom behind
him, and to the amazement of Mr. and Mrs. Furze
presented him in the dining-room.

" What is the meaning of this ? " said Mrs.
Furze.

" Mrs. Furze," said Jim, " will you please excuse

me, and allow me to speak for this once? I don't see Miss Catharine here. I want yer to send for her. Wot I've got to say, I mean to say afore you all."

Catharine was in her bedroom. She came down wrapped up in a shawl, and Jim stood up.

"Mr. Furze, Mrs. Furze, Miss Catharine, and you, Mr. Catchpole, you see afore you the biggest liar as ever was, and one as deserves to go to hell, if ever any man did. Everything agin Mr. Catchpole was all trumped up, for he never had Humphries' money, and it was me as put the marked sovereign in his pocket. I was tempted by the devil and by—but the Lord 'as 'ad mercy on me and 'as saved my body and soul this day. I can't speak no more, but 'ere I am if I'm to be locked up and transported as I deserve."

"Never," said Tom.

"You say never, Mr. Catchpole. Very well, then: on my knees I axes your pardon, and you won't see me agin." Jim actually knelt down. "May the Lord forgive me, and do you forgive me, Mr. Catchpole, for being such a——" (Jim was about to use a familiar word, but checked himself, and contented himself with one which is blasphemous but also orthodox)—such a damned sinner."

He rose, walked out, left Eastthorpe that night, and nothing more was heard of him for years. Then there came news from an Eastthorpe man, who had gone to America, that Jim was at work at Pittsburg ; that he was also a preacher of God's Word, and that by God's grace he had brought hundreds to a knowledge of their Saviour.

This story may be deemed impossible by the ordinary cultivated reader, but he will please to recollect John Bunyan's account of the strange behaviour of Mr. Tod. " At a summer assizes holden at Hertford," says Bunyan, " while the judge was sitting up on the bench, comes this old Tod into court, clothed in a green suit, with his leathern girdle in his hand, his bosom open, and all in a dung sweat, as if he had run for his life ; and being come in, he spake aloud as follows : ' My Lord,' said he, ' here is the veriest rogue that breathes upon the face of the earth. I have been a thief from a child. When I was but a little one I gave myself to rob orchards, and to do other such like wicked things, and I have continued a thief ever since. My Lord, there has not been a robbery committed these many years, within so many miles of this place, but I have been either at it, or privy to it!' The judge thought the fellow was mad, but, after some conference with some of the justices, they agreed to indict him; and so they did of several felonious actions; to all of which he heartily confessed guilty, and so was hanged with his wife at the same time." I can also assure my incredulous literary friends that years ago it was not uncommon for men and women suddenly to awake to the fact that they had been sinners, and to determine that henceforth they would keep God's commandments by the help of Jesus Christ and the Holy Spirit. What is more extraordinary is that they did keep God's commandments for the rest of their lives. Fear of hell fire and hope of heaven may have had something to do with their reformation, but these were not the sole motives, and even if they were, the strength of mind necessary in order to sacrifice the present for the sake of something remote—a capacity which lies, we are told, at the basis of all virtue—was singular.

CHAPTER XXI.

TOM was restored to his former position, and Mr. Furze's business began to improve. Arrangements were made for the removal from the Terrace, and they were eagerly pressed forward by Catharine. Her mother pleaded that they could not leave till June; that even in June they would sacrifice a quarter's rent, but Catharine's reply was that they would pay no more if they went beforehand. Her father was anxious to please her, and the necessary alterations at the shop were taken in hand at once, and towards the beginning of May were completed. She was not allowed to move to the High Street with her father and mother; it was thought that the worry and fatigue would be too much for her, and it was settled, as the weather was wonderfully warm and bright for the time of year, that she should go over to Chapel Farm for a week. At the end of the week she would find the furniture all in its place and her room quite straight. Mrs. Bellamy called for her, and she reached the farm in safety, and looking better. The next morning she begged to be taken for a drive. Mr. Bellamy had to go over to Thingleby, and she was able to go with him. It was a lovely sunny day, one of those days which we sometimes have in May, summer days in advance of the main body, and more beautiful, perhaps, than any that follow, because they are days of anticipation and hope, our delight in the full midsummer being sobered by the thought of approaching autumn and winter. When they reached the bridge Mr. Bellamy remembered that he had forgotten his cheque-book and his money, and it was of no use to go to Thingleby without them.

"Botheration! I must go back, my dear."

"Leave me here, Mr. Bellamy; you won't be long. Let me get out, though, and just turn the mare aside off the road on to the grass against the gate; she will be quite quiet."

"Had you not better sit still? I shall be back in a quarter of an hour."

" If you do not mind, dear Mr. Bellamy, I should so like to stand on the bridge. I cannot let the gig stay there."

" Well, my dear, you shall have your own way. You know," he said, laughing, " I've long ago given up asking why my Catharine wants anything whatsomever. If she wishes it that's enough for me."

Catharine dismounted, and Mr. Bellamy walked back. She went to the parapet and once more looked up the stream. Once more, as on a memorable day in August, the sun was upon the water. Then the heat was intense, and the heavy cumulus clouds were charged with thunder and lightning. Now the sun shone with nothing more than warmth, and though the clouds, the same clouds, hung in the south-west, there was no fire in them, nothing but soft, warm showers. She looked and looked, and tears came into her eyes—tears of joy. Never had a day been to her what that day was. She felt as if she lay open to all the life of spring which was pouring up through the earth, and it swept into her as if she were one of those bursting exultant chestnut buds, the sight of which she loved so in April and May. Always for years when the season came round had she gathered one of those buds and carried it home, and it was more to her than any summer flower. The bliss of life passed over into contentment with death, and her delight was so great that she could happily have lain down amid the hum of the insects to die on the grass.

When they came back to the farm Mr. Bellamy observed to his wife that he had not seen Catharine looking better or in better spirits for months. Mrs. Bellamy said nothing, but on the following morning Catharine was certainly not so well. It was intended that she should go home that day, but it was wet, and a message was sent to East-thorpe to explain why she did not come. The next day she was worse, and Mrs. Bellamy went to Eastthorpe and counselled Mr. and Mrs. Furze to come to the Farm, and bring Dr. Turnbull with them. They all three came at once, and found Catharine in bed. She was feverish, and during the night had been slightly delirious. The doctor examined her carefully, and after the examination was over she turned to him and said—

"I want to hear the truth; I can bear it. Am I to die?"

"I know you can bear it. No man could be certain; but I believe the end is near."

"How much time have I?"

He sat down by the bedside. "Perhaps a day, perhaps a week. Is there anybody you wish to see?"

"I should like to see Mr. Cardew."

"Mr. Cardew!" said Dr. Turnbull to himself; "I fancied she would not care to have a clergyman with her; I thought she was a little beyond that kind of thing, but when people are about to die even the strongest are a little weak."

"She always liked Mr. Cardew's preaching," said Mrs. Furze, sobbing, but I wish she had asked for her own rector. It isn't as if Mr. Cardew were her personal friend."

It was Saturday evening when the message was dispatched to Abchurch, but Mr. Cardew was fortunately able to secure a substitute for the morrow. Sunday morning came. Mrs. Furze, who had been sitting up all night, drew down the blinds at dawn, but Catharine asked, not only that they might be drawn up again, but that her bed might be shifted a little so that she might look out across the meadow and towards the bridge. "The view that way is so lovely," said she. It was again a triumphal spring day, and light and warmth streamed into the sick chamber.

Presently her mother went to take a little rest, and Mr. Cardew was announced almost immediately afterwards. He came upstairs, and Mrs. Bellamy, who had taken Mrs. Furze's place, left the room. She did not think it proper to intrude when the clergyman visited anybody who was dying. Mr. Cardew remained standing and speechless.

"Sit down, Mr. Cardew. I felt that I should like to see you once more."

He sat down by the bedside.

"Do you mind opening the window and drawing up the blind again? It has fallen a little. That is better: now I can see the meadows and away towards the bridge foot. Will you give me a glass of water?"

She drank the water: he looked steadily at her, and he knew too well what was on her face. Her hand dropped on the bed : he fell on his knees beside her with that hand in his, but still he was dumb, and not a single article of his creed which he had preached for so many years presented itself to him : forgiveness, the atonement, heaven—it had all vanished.

" Mr. Cardew, I want to say something."

" Wait a moment, let me tell you—*you have saved me.*"

She smiled, her lips moved, and she whispered—

" *You* have saved *me.*"

By their love for each other they were both saved. The disguises are manifold which the Immortal Son assumes in the work of our redemption.

Tom henceforth wore the ring on his finger. Mr. Cardew resigned his living, and did not preach for many years. When pressed for an explanation he generally gave his health as an excuse. Later in life he took up his work again in a far distant, purely agricultural parish, but his sermons were of the simplest kind—exhortations to pity, considera- tion, gentleness, and counsels as to the common duties of life. He spent much of his time in visiting his parishioners and in helping them in their difficulties. Mrs. Cardew, as we have said, died before him, but no woman ever had a husband more tender and devoted than hers in these later years. He had changed much, and she knew it, but she did not know exactly how, nor did she know the reason. It was not the kind of change which comes from a new theory or a new principle: it was something deeper. Some men are determined by principles, and others are drawn and directed by a vision or a face. Before Mr. Cardew was set for evermore the face which he saw white and saintly at Chapel Farm that May Sunday morning when death had entered, and it controlled and moulded him with an all-pervading power more subtle and penetrating than that which could have been exercised by theology or ethics.

The Gresham Press,
UNWIN BROTHERS,
CHILWORTH AND LONDON.

CLARA HOPGOOD

Bibliographical note:

this facsimile has been made from a copy in the
Yale University Library
(Ip.W586.896)

CLARA HOPGOOD

BY

MARK RUTHERFORD

EDITED BY HIS FRIEND

REUBEN SHAPCOTT

London

T. FISHER UNWIN

PATERNOSTER SQUARE

MDCCCXCVI.

CLARA HOPGOOD

CHAPTER I

ABOUT ten miles north-east of Eastthorpe lies the town of Fenmarket, very like East-thorpe generally ; and as we are already familiar with Eastthorpe, a particular descrip-tion of Fenmarket is unnecessary. There is, however, one marked difference between them. Eastthorpe, it will be remembered, is on the border between the low uplands and the Fens, and has one side open to soft, swelling hills. Fenmarket is entirely in the Fens, and all the roads that lead out of it are alike level, monotonous, straight, and flanked by deep

A

and stagnant ditches. The river, also, here is broader and slower; more reluctant than it is even at Eastthorpe to hasten its journey to the inevitable sea. During the greater part of the year the visitor to Fenmarket would perhaps find it dull and depressing, and at times, under a grey, wintry sky, almost unendurable; but nevertheless, for days and weeks it has a charm possessed by few other landscapes in England, provided only that behind the eye which looks there is something to which a landscape of that peculiar character answers. There is, for example, the wide, dome-like expanse of the sky, there is the distance, there is the freedom and there are the stars on a clear night. The orderly, geometrical march of the constellations from the extreme eastern horizon across the meridian and down to the west has a solemn majesty, which is only partially discernible when their course is interrupted by broken country.

On a dark afternoon in November 1844,

two young women, Clara and Madge Hopgood, were playing chess in the back parlour of their mother's house at Fenmarket, just before tea. Clara, the elder, was about five-and-twenty, fair, with rather light hair worn flat at the side of her face, after the fashion of that time. Her features were tolerably regular. It is true they were somewhat marred by an uneven nasal outline, but this was redeemed by the curved lips of a mouth which was small and rather compressed, and by a definite, symmetrical and graceful figure. Her eyes were grey, with a curious peculiarity in them. Ordinarily they were steady, strong eyes, excellent and renowned optical instruments. Over and over again she had detected, along the stretch of the Eastthorpe road, approaching visitors, and had named them when her companions could see nothing but specks. Occasionally, however, these steady, strong, grey eyes utterly changed. They were the same eyes, the same colour, but they ceased to be mere optical instruments and became instruments of expression, transmissive of radiance to such a degree that the light which was reflected from them seemed insufficient to account for it. It was also curious that this change, though it must have been accompanied by some emotion, was just as often not attended by any other sign of it. Clara was, in fact, little given to any display of feeling.

Madge, four years younger than her sister, was of a different type altogether, and one more easily comprehended. She had very heavy dark hair, and she had blue eyes, a combination which fascinated Fenmarket. Fenmarket admired Madge more than it was admired by her in return, and she kept herself very much to herself, notwithstanding what it considered to be its temptations. If she went shopping she nearly always went with her sister; she stood aloof from all the small gaieties of the town; walked swiftly through its streets, and repelled, frigidly and decisively, all offers, and they were not a few, which had been made to her by the sons of the Fenmarket tradesfolk. Fenmarket pronounced her 'stuck-up,' and having thus labelled her, considered it had exhausted her. The very important question, Whether there was anything which naturally stuck up? Fenmarket never asked. It was a great relief to that provinical little town in 1844, in this and in other cases, to find a word which released it from further mental effort and put out of sight any troublesome, straggling, indefinable qualities which it would otherwise have been forced to examine and name. Madge was certainly stuck-up, but the projection above those around her was not artificial. Both she and her sister found the ways of Fenmarket were not to their taste. The reason lay partly in their nature and partly in their history.

Mrs Hopgood was the widow of the late manager in the Fenmarket branch of the bank of Rumbold, Martin & Rumbold, and when her husband died she had of course to leave the Bank Buildings. As her income was somewhat straitened, she was obliged to take

a small house, and she was now living next
door to the 'Crown and Sceptre,' the principal
inn in the town. There was then no fringe
of villas to Fenmarket for retired quality; the
private houses and shops were all mixed
together, and Mrs Hopgood's cottage was
squeezed in between the ironmonger's and
the inn. It was very much lower than
either of its big neighbours, but it had a
brass knocker and a bell, and distinctly
asserted and maintained a kind of aristocratic
superiority.

Mr Hopgood was not a Fenmarket man.
He came straight from London to be
manager. He was in the bank of the
London agents of Rumbold, Martin &
Rumbold, and had been strongly recommended by the city firm as just the
person to take charge of a branch which
needed thorough reorganisation. He succeeded, and nobody in Fenmarket was more
respected. He lived, however, a life apart
from his neighbours, excepting so far as business was concerned. He went to church once

on Sunday because the bank expected him to go, but only once, and had nothing to do with any of its dependent institutions. He was a great botanist, very fond of walking, and in the evening, when Fenmarket generally gathered itself into groups for gossip, either in the street or in back parlours, or in the 'Crown and Sceptre,' Mr Hopgood, tall, lean and stately, might be seen wandering along the solitary roads searching for flowers, which, in that part of the world, were rather scarce. He was also a great reader of the best books, English, German and French, and held high doctrine, very high for those days, on the training of girls, maintaining that they need, even more than boys, exact discipline and knowledge. Boys, he thought, find health in an occupation; but an uncultivated, unmarried girl dwells with her own untutored thoughts, which often breed disease. His two daughters, therefore, received an education much above that which was usual amongst people in their position, and each of them —an unheard of wonder in Fenmarket

—had spent some time in a school in Weimar. Mr Hopgood was also peculiar in his way of dealing with his children. He talked to them and made them talk to him, and whatever they read was translated into speech ; thought, in his house, was vocal.

Mrs Hopgood, too, had been the intimate friend of her husband, and was the intimate friend of her daughters. She was now nearly sixty, but still erect and graceful, and everybody could see that the picture of a beautiful girl of one-and-twenty, which hung opposite the fireplace, had once been her portrait. She had been brought up, as thoroughly as a woman could be brought up, in those days, to be a governess. The war prevented her education abroad, but her father, who was a clergyman, not too rich, engaged a French emigrant lady to live in his house to teach her French and other accomplishments. She consequently spoke French perfectly, and she could also read and speak Spanish fairly well, for the French lady had spent some years in Spain.

Mr Hopgood had never been particularly in earnest about religion, but his wife was a believer, neither High Church nor Low Church, but inclined towards a kind of quietism not uncommon in the Church of England, even during its bad time, a reaction against the formalism which generally prevailed. When she married, Mrs Hopgood did not altogether follow her husband. She never separated herself from her faith, and never would have confessed that she had separated herself from her church. But although she knew that his creed externally was not hers, her own was not sharply cut, and she persuaded herself that, in substance, his and her belief were identical. As she grew older her relationship to the Unseen became more and more intimate, but she was less and less inclined to criticise her husband's freedom, or to impose on the children a rule which they would certainly have observed, but only for her sake. Every now and then she felt a little lonely; when, for example, she read one or two books which were particularly her own;

when she thought of her dead father and
mother, and when she prayed her solitary
prayer. Mr Hopgood took great pains
never to disturb that sacred moment. Indeed, he never for an instant permitted a
finger to be laid upon what she considered
precious. He loved her because she had the
strength to be what she was when he first
knew her and she had so fascinated him. He
would have been disappointed if the mistress
of his youth had become some other person,
although the change, in a sense, might have
been development and progress. He did
really love her piety, too, for its own sake.
It mixed something with her behaviour to him
and to the children which charmed him, and
he did not know from what other existing
source anything comparable to it could be
supplied. Mrs Hopgood seldom went to
church. The church, to be sure, was horribly
dead, but she did not give that as a reason.
She had, she said, an infirmity, a strange
restlessness which prevented her from sitting
still for an hour. She often pleaded this ex-

cuse, and her husband and daughters never, by word or smile, gave her the least reason to suppose that they did not believe her.

CHAPTER II

BOTH Clara and Madge went first to an English day-school, and Clara went straight from this school to Germany, but Madge's course was a little different. She was not very well, and it was decided that she should have at least a twelvemonth in a boarding-school at Brighton before going abroad. It had been very highly recommended, but the head-mistress was Low Church and aggressive. Mr Hopgood, far away from the High and Low Church controversy, came to the conclusion that, in Madge's case, the theology would have no effect on her. It was quite impossible, moreover, to find a school which would be just what he could wish it to be. Madge, accordingly, was sent to Brighton, and was introduced into a new world. She was just beginning to ask herself *why* certain things were right and other things were wrong, and the Brighton answer was that the former were directed by revelation and the latter forbidden, and that the 'body' was an affliction to the soul, a means of 'probation,' our principal duty being to 'war' against it.

Madge's bedroom companion was a Miss Selina Fish, daughter of Barnabas Fish, Esquire, of Clapham, and merchant of the City of London. Miss Fish was not traitorous at heart, but when she found out that Madge had not been christened, she was so overcome that she was obliged to tell her mother. Miss Fish was really unhappy, and one cold night, when Madge crept into her neighbour's bed, contrary to law, but in accordance with custom when the weather was very bitter, poor Miss Fish shrank from her, half-believing that something dreadful might happen if she should by any chance touch unbaptised, naked flesh. Mrs Fish told her daughter that perhaps Miss Hopgood might be a Dissenter, and that although Dissenters were to be pitied, and even to be condemned, many of them were undoubtedly among the redeemed, as for example, that man of God, Dr Doddridge, whose *Family Expositor* was read systematically at home, as Selina knew. Then there were Matthew Henry, whose commentary her father preferred to any other, and the venerable saint, the Reverend William Jay of Bath, whom she was proud to call her friend. Miss Fish, therefore, made further inquiries gently and delicately, but she found to her horror that Madge had neither been sprinkled nor immersed! Perhaps she was a Jewess or a heathen! This was a happy thought, for then she might be converted. Selina knew what interest her mother took in missions to heathens and Jews; and if Madge, by the humble instrumentality of a child, could be brought to the foot of the Cross, what would her mother and father say? What would they not say? Fancy taking Madge to Clapham in a nice white dress—it should be white, thought Selina—and presenting her as a saved lamb!

The very next night she began,—

'I suppose your father is a foreigner?'

'No, he is an Englishman.'

'But if he is an Englishman you must have been baptised, or sprinkled, or immersed, and your father and mother must belong to church or chapel. I know there are thousands of wicked people who belong to neither, but they are drunkards and liars and robbers, and even they have their children christened.'

'Well, he is an Englishman,' said Madge, smiling.

'Perhaps,' said Selina, timidly, 'he may be—he may be—Jewish. Mamma and papa pray for the Jews every morning. They are not like other unbelievers.'

'No, he is certainly not a Jew.'

'What is he, then?'

'He is my papa and a very honest, good man.'

'Oh, my dear Madge! honesty is a broken reed. I have heard mamma say that she is more hopeful of thieves than honest people who think they are saved by works, for the thief who was crucified went to heaven, and if he had been only an honest man he never would have found the Saviour and would have gone to hell. You father must be something.'

'I can only tell you again that he is honest and good.'

Selina was confounded. She had heard of those people who were *nothing*, and had always considered them as so dreadful that she could not bear to think of them. The efforts of her father and mother did not extend to them; they were beyond the reach of the preacher—mere vessels of wrath. If Madge had confessed herself Roman Catholic, or idolator, Selina knew how to begin. She would have pointed out to the Catholic how unscriptural it was to suppose that anybody could forgive sins excepting God, and she would at once have been able to bring the idolator to his knees by exposing the absurdity of worshipping bits of wood and stone; but with a person who was nothing she could not tell what to do. She was puzzled to understand what right Madge had to her name. Who had any authority to say she was to be called Madge Hopgood? She determined at last to pray to God and again ask her mother's help.

She did pray earnestly that very night, and had not finished until long after Madge had said her Lord's Prayer. This was always said night and morning, both by Madge and Clara. They had been taught it by their mother. It was, by the way, one of poor Selina's troubles that Madge said nothing but the Lord's Prayer when she lay down and when she rose; of course, the Lord's Prayer was the best—how could it be otherwise, seeing that our Lord used it?—but those who supplemented it with no petitions of their own were set down as formalists, and it was always suspected that they had not received the true enlightenment from above. Selina cried to God till the counterpane was wet with her tears, but it was the answer from her mother which came first, telling her that however praiseworthy her intentions

B

might be, argument with such a *dangerous* infidel as Madge would be most perilous, and she was to desist from it at once. Mrs Fish had by that post written to Miss Pratt, the schoolmistress, and Selina no doubt would not be exposed to further temptation. Mrs Fish's letter to Miss Pratt was very strong, and did not mince matters. She informed Miss Pratt that a wolf was in her fold, and that if the creature were not promptly expelled, Selina must be removed into safety. Miss Pratt was astonished, and instantly, as her custom was, sought the advice of her sister, Miss Hannah Pratt, who had charge of the wardrobes and household matters generally. Miss Hannah Pratt was never in the best of tempers, and just now was a little worse than usual. It was one of the rules of the school that no tradesmen's daughters should be admitted, but it was very difficult to draw the line, and when drawn, the Misses Pratt were obliged to admit it was rather ridiculous. There was much debate over an application by an auctioneer.

He was clearly not a tradesman, but he sold chairs, tables and pigs, and, as Miss Hannah said, used vulgar language in recommending them. However, his wife had money; they lived in a pleasant house in Lewes, and the line went outside him. But when a druggist, with a shop in Bond Street, proposed his daughter, Miss Hannah took a firm stand. What is the use of a principle, she inquired severely, if we do not adhere to it? On the other hand, the druggist's daughter was the eldest of six, who might all come when they were old enough to leave home, and Miss Pratt thought there was a real difference between a druggist and, say, a bootmaker.

'Bootmaker!' said Miss Hannah with great scorn. 'I am surprised that you venture to hint the remotest possibility of such a contingency.'

At last it was settled that the line should also be drawn outside the druggist. Miss Hannah, however, had her revenge. A tanner in Bermondsey with a house in Bedford Square, had sent two of his children to Miss Pratt's seminary. Their mother found out that they had struck up a friendship with a young person whose father compounded prescriptions for her, and when she next visited Brighton she called on Miss Pratt, reminded her that it was understood that her pupils would 'all be taken from a superior class in society,' and gently hinted that she could not allow Bedford Square to be contaminated by Bond Street. Miss Pratt was most apologetic, enlarged upon the druggist's respectability, and more particularly upon his well-known piety and upon his generous contributions to the cause of religion. This, indeed, was what decided her to make an exception in his favour, and the piety also of his daughter was 'most exemplary.' However, the tanner's lady, although a shining light in the church herself, was not satisfied that a retail saint could produce a proper companion for her own offspring, and went away leaving Miss Pratt very uncomfortable.

'I warned you,' said Miss Hannah; 'I told you what would happen, and as to Mr Hopgood, I suspected him from the first. Besides, he is only a banker's clerk.'

'Well, what is to be done?'

'Put your foot down at once.' Miss Hannah suited the action to the word, and put down, with emphasis, on the hearthrug a very large, plate-shaped foot cased in a black felt shoe.

'But I cannot dismiss them. Don't you think it will be better, first of all, to talk to Miss Hopgood? Perhaps we could do her some good.'

'Good! Now, do you think we can do any good to an atheist? Besides, we have to consider our reputation. Whatever good we might do, it would be believed that the infection remained.'

'We have no excuse for dismissing the other.'

'Excuse! none is needed, nor would any be justifiable. Excuses are immoral. Say at once —of course politely and with regret—that the school is established on a certain basis. It will be an advantage to us if it is known why these girls do not remain. I will dictate the letter, if you like.'

Miss Hannah Pratt had not received the education which had been given to her younger sister, and therefore, was nominally subordinate, but really she was chief. She considered it especially her duty not only to look after the children's clothes, the servants and the accounts, but to maintain *tone* everywhere in the establishment, and to stiffen her sister when necessary, and preserve in proper sharpness her orthodoxy, both in theology and morals.

Accordingly, both the girls left, and both knew the reason for leaving. The druggist's faith was sorely tried. If Miss Pratt's had been a worldly seminary he would have thought nothing of such behaviour, but he did not expect it from one of the faithful. The next Sunday morning after he received the news, he stayed at home out of his turn to make up any medicines which might be urgently required, and sent his assistant to church.

As to Madge, she enjoyed her expulsion as a great joke, and her Brighton experiences were the cause of much laughter. She had learned a good deal while she was away from home, not precisely what it was intended she should learn, and she came back with a strong, insurgent tendency, which was even more noticeable when she returned from Germany. Neither of the sisters lived at the school in Weimar, but at the house of a lady who had been recommended to Mrs Hopgood, and by this lady they were introduced to the great German classics. She herself was an enthusiast for Goethe, whom she well remembered in his old age, and Clara and Madge, each of them in turn, learned to know the poet as they would never have known him in England. Even the town taught them much about him, for in many ways it was expressive of him and seemed as if it had shaped itself for him. It was a delightful time for them. They enjoyed the society and constant mental stimulus; they loved the beautiful park;

not a separate enclosure walled round like an English park, but suffering the streets to end in it, and in summer time there were excursions into the Thüringer Wald, generally to some point memorable in history, or for some literary association. The drawback was the contrast, when they went home, with Fenmarket, with its dulness and its complete isolation from the intellectual world. At Weimar, in the evening, they could see Egmont or hear Fidelio, or talk with friends about the last utterance upon the Leben Jesu; but the Fenmarket Egmont was a travelling wax-work show, its Fidelio psalm tunes, or at best some of Bishop's glees, performed by a few of the tradesfolk, who had never had an hour's instruction in music; and for theological criticism there were the parish church and Ram Lane Chapel. They did their best; they read their old favourites and subscribed for a German as well as an English literary weekly newspaper, but at times they were almost beaten.

Madge more than Clara was liable to depression.

No Fenmarket maiden, other than the Hopgoods, was supposed to have any connection whatever, or to have any capacity for any connection with anything outside the world in which 'young ladies' dwelt, and if a Fenmarket girl read a book, a rare occurrence, for there were no circulating libraries there in those days, she never permitted herself to say anything more than that it was 'nice,' or it was 'not nice,' or she 'liked it' or did 'not like it;' and if she had ventured to say more, Fenmarket would have thought her odd, not to say a little improper. The Hopgood young women were almost entirely isolated, for the tradesfolk felt themselves uncomfortable and inferior in every way in their presence, and they were ineligible for rectory and brewery society, not only because their father was merely a manager, but because of their strange ways. Mrs Tubbs, the brewer's wife, thought they were due to Germany. From what she knew of Germany she considered it most injudicious, and even morally wrong, to send girls there. She once made the acquaintance of a German lady at an hotel at Tunbridge Wells, and was quite shocked. She could see quite plainly that the standard of female delicacy must be much lower in that country than in England. Mr Tubbs was sure Mrs Hopgood must have been French, and said to his daughters, mysteriously, ' you never can tell who Frenchwomen are.'

'But, papa,' said Miss Tubbs, 'you know Mrs Hopgood's maiden name; we found that out. It was Molyneux.'

'Of course, my dear, of course; but if she was a Frenchwoman resident in England she would prefer to assume an English name, that is to say if she wished to be married.'

Occasionally the Miss Hopgoods were encountered, and they confounded Fenmarket sorely. On one memorable occasion there was a party at the Rectory: it was the annual party into which were swept all the unclassifiable odds-and-ends which could not be put into the two gatherings which included

the aristocracy and the democracy of the
place. Miss Clara Hopgood amazed everybody by 'beginning talk,' by asking Mrs
Greatorex, her hostess, who had been far away
to Sidmouth for a holiday, whether she had
been to the place where Coleridge was born,
and when the parson's wife said she had not,
and that she could not be expected to make
a pilgrimage to the birthplace of 'an infidel,
Miss Hopgood expressed her surprise, and
declared she would walk twenty miles any
day to see Ottery St Mary. Still worse,
when somebody observed that an Anti-Corn-
Law lecturer was coming to Fenmarket, and
the parson's daughter cried 'How horrid!'
Miss Hopgood talked again, and actually told
the parson that, so far as she had read upon
the subject—fancy her reading about the
Corn-Laws!—the argument was all one way,
and that after Colonel Thompson nothing new
could really be urged.

'What is so—' she was about to say 'objec-
tionable,' but she recollected her official position and that she was bound to be politic—

'so odd and unusual,' observed Mrs Greatorex to Mrs Tubbs afterwards, 'is not that Miss Hopgood should have radical views. Mrs Barker, I know, is a radical like her husband, but then she never puts herself forward, nor makes speeches. I never saw anything quite like it, except once in London ·at a dinner-party. Lady Montgomery then went on in much the same way, but she was a baronet's wife; the baronet was in Parliament; she received a good deal and was obliged to entertain her guests.'

Poor Clara! she was really very unobtrusive and very modest, but there had been constant sympathy between her and her father, not the dumb sympathy as between man and dog, but that which can manifest itself in human fashion.

CHAPTER III

CLARA and her father were both chess-players, and at the time at which our history begins, Clara had been teaching Madge the game for about six months.

'Check!' said Clara.

'Check! after about a dozen moves. It is of no use to go on; you always beat me. I should not mind that if I were any better now than when I started. It is not in me.'

'The reason is that you do not look two moves ahead. You never say to yourself, "Suppose I move there, what is she likely to do, and what can I do afterwards?"'

'That is just what is impossible to me. I cannot hold myself down; the moment I go beyond the next move my thoughts fly away, and I am in a muddle, and my head turns round. I was not born for it. I can do what is under my nose well enough, but nothing more.'

'The planning and the forecasting are the soul of the game. I should like to be a general, and play against armies and calculate the consequences of manœuvres.'

'It would kill me. I should prefer the fighting. Besides, calculation is useless, for when I think that you will be sure to move such and such a piece, you generally do not.'

'Then what makes the difference between the good and the bad player?'

'It is a gift, an instinct, I suppose.'

'Which is as much as to say that you give it up. You are very fond of that word instinct; I wish you would not use it.'

'I have heard you use it, and say you instinctively like this person or that.'

'Certainly; I do not deny that sometimes I am drawn to a person or repelled from him before I can say why; but I always force my-self to discover afterwards the cause of my attraction or repulsion, and I believe it is a duty to do so. If we neglect it we are little

better than the brutes, and may grossly
deceive ourselves.'

At this moment the sound of wheels was
heard, and Madge jumped up, nearly over-
setting the board, and rushed into the front
room. It was the four-horse coach from
London, which, once a day, passed through
Fenmarket on its road to Lincoln. It
was not the direct route from London to
Lincoln, but the *Defiance* went this way
to accommodate Fenmarket and other small
towns. It slackened speed in order to
change horses at the 'Crown and Sceptre,'
and as Madge stood at the window, a
gentleman on the box-seat looked at her
intently as he passed. In another minute he
had descended, and was welcomed by the
landlord, who stood on the pavement. Clara
meanwhile had taken up a book, but before
she had read a page, her sister skipped into
the parlour again, humming a tune.

'Let me see—check, you said, but it is
not mate.'

She put her elbows on the table, rested her

head between her hands, and appeared to con-
template the game profoundly.

'Now, then, what do you say to that?'

It was really a very lucky move, and Clara,
whose thoughts perhaps were elsewhere, was
presently most unaccountably defeated. Madge
was triumphant.

'Where are all your deep-laid schemes?
Baffled by a poor creature who can hardly put
two and two together.'

'Perhaps your schemes were better than
mine.'

'You know they were not. I saw the
queen ought to take that bishop, and never
bothered myself as to what would follow.
Have you not lost your faith in schemes?'

'You are very much mistaken if you
suppose that, because of one failure, or of
twenty failures, I would give up a principle.'

'Clara, you are a strange creature. Don't
let us talk any more about chess.'

Madge swept all the pieces with her hand
into the box, shut it, closed the board, and
put her feet on the fender.

'You never believe in impulses or in doing a thing just because here and now it appears to be the proper thing to do. Suppose anybody were to make love to you—oh! how I wish somebody would, you dear girl, for nobody deserves it more—' Madge put her head caressingly on Clara's shoulder and then raised it again. 'Suppose, I say, anybody were to make love to you, would you hold off for six months and consider, and consider, and ask yourself whether he had such and such virtues, and whether he could make you happy? Would not that stifle love altogether? Would you not rather obey your first impression and, if you felt you loved him, would you not say "Yes"?'

'Time is not everything. A man who is prompt and is therefore thought to be hasty by sluggish creatures who are never half awake, may in five minutes spend more time in consideration than his critics will spend in as many weeks. I have never had the chance, and am not likely to have it. I can only say that if it were to come to me, I should try

c

to use the whole strength of my soul. Precisely because the question would be so important, would it be necessary to employ
every faculty I have in order to decide it.
I do not believe in oracles which are supposed
to prove their divinity by giving no reasons
for their commands.'

'Ah, well, *I* believe in Shakespeare. His
lovers fall in love at first sight.'

'No doubt they do, but to justify yourself you have to suppose that you are a Juliet
and your friend a Romeo. They may, for
aught I know, be examples in my favour.
However, I have to lay down a rule for my
own poor, limited self, and, to speak the
truth, I am afraid that great men often do
harm by imposing on us that which is serviceable to themselves only; or, to put it perhaps more correctly, we mistake the real
nature of their processes, just as a person
who is unskilled in arithmetic would mistake
the processes of anybody who is very quick
at it, and would be led away by them.
Shakespeare is much to me, but the more he

is to me, the more careful I ought to be to discover what is the true law of my own nature, more important to me after all than Shakespeare's.'

'Exactly. I know what the law of mine is. If a man were to present himself to me, I should rely on that instinct you so much despise, and I am certain that the balancing, see-saw method would be fatal. It would disclose a host of reasons against any conclusion, and I should never come to any.'

Clara smiled. Although this impetuosity was foreign to her, she loved it for the good which accompanied it.

'You do not mean to say you would accept or reject him at once?'

'No, certainly not. What I mean is that in a few days, perhaps in a shorter time, something within me would tell me whether we were suited to one another, although we might not have talked upon half-a-dozen subjects.'

'I think the risk tremendous.'

'But there is just as much risk the other way. You would examine your friend, catalogue him, sum up his beliefs, note his behaviour under various experimental trials, and miserably fail, after all your scientific investigation, to ascertain just the one important point whether you loved him and could live with him. Your reason was not meant for that kind of work. If a woman trusts in such matters to the faculty by which, when she wishes to settle whether she is to take this house or that, she puts the advantages of the larger back kitchen on one side and the bigger front kitchen on the other, I pity her.'

Mrs Hopgood at this moment came downstairs and asked when in the name of fortune they meant to have the tea ready.

CHAPTER IV

FRANK PALMER, the gentleman whom we saw descend from the coach, was the eldest son of a wholesale and manufacturing chemist in London. He was now about five-and-twenty, and having just been admitted as a partner, he had begun, as the custom was in those days, to travel for his firm. The elder Mr Palmer was a man of refinement, something more than a Whig in politics, and an enthusiastic member of the Broad Church party, which was then becoming a power in the country. He was well-to-do, living in a fine old red-brick house at Stoke Newington, with half-a-dozen acres of ground round it, and, if Frank had been born thirty years later, he would probably have gone to Cambridge or Oxford. In those days, however, it was not the custom to send boys to the Universities,

unless they were intended for the law, divinity
or idleness, and Frank's training, which was
begun at St Paul's school, was completed there. He lived at home, going to
school in the morning and returning in the
evening. He was surrounded by every
influence which was pure and noble. Mr
Maurice and Mr Sterling were his father's
guests, and hence it may be inferred that
there was an altar in the house, and that the
sacred flame burnt thereon. Mr Palmer
almost worshipped Mr Maurice, and his
admiration was not blind, for Maurice connected the Bible with what was rational in
his friend. 'What! still believable : no need
then to pitch it overboard : here after all is
the Eternal Word !' It can be imagined
how those who dared not close their eyes to
the light, and yet clung to that book which
had been so much to their forefathers and
themselves, rejoiced when they were able to
declare that it belonged to them more than to
those who misjudged them and could deny that
they were heretics. The boy's education was

entirely classical and athletic, and as he was
quick at learning and loved his games, he
took a high position amongst his school-
fellows. He was not particularly reflective,
but he was generous and courageous, perfectly straightforward, a fair specimen of
thousands of English public-school boys. As
he grew up, he somewhat disappointed his
father by a lack of any real interest in the
subjects in which his father was interested.
He accepted willingly, and even enthusiastically,
the household conclusions on religion and
politics, but they were not properly his, for
he accepted them merely as conclusions and
without the premisses, and it was often even
a little annoying to hear him express some
free opinion on religious questions in a way
which showed that it was not a growth but
something picked up. Mr Palmer, senior,
sometimes recoiled into intolerance and
orthodoxy, and bewildered his son who, to
use one of his own phrases, 'hardly knew
where his father was.' Partly the reaction
was due to the oscillation which accompanies

serious and independent thought, but mainly it was caused by Mr Palmer's discontent with Frank's appropriation of a sentiment or doctrine of which he was not the lawful owner. Frank, however, was so hearty, so affectionate, and so cheerful, that it was impossible not to love him dearly.

In his visits to Fenmarket, Frank had often noticed Madge, for the 'Crown and Sceptre' was his headquarters, and Madge was well enough aware that she had been noticed. He had inquired casually who it was who lived next door, and when the waiter told him the name, and that Mr Hopgood was formerly the bank manager, Frank remembered that he had often heard his father speak of a Mr Hopgood, a clerk in a bank in London, as one of his best friends. He did not fail to ask his father about this friend, and to obtain an introduction to the widow. He had now brought it to Fenmarket, and within half an hour after he had alighted, he had presented it.

Mrs Hopgood, of course, recollected Mr Palmer perfectly, and the welcome to Frank was naturally very warm. It was delightful to connect earlier and happier days with the present, and she was proud in the possession of a relationship which had lasted so long. Clara and Madge, too, were both excited and pleased. To say nothing of Frank's appearance, of his unsnobbish, deferential behaviour which showed that he understood who they were and that the little house made no difference to him, the girls and the mother could not resist a side glance at Fenmarket and the indulgence of a secret satisfaction that it would soon hear that the son of Mr Palmer, so well known in every town round about, was on intimate terms with them.

Madge was particularly gay that evening. The presence of sympathetic people was always a powerful stimulus to her, and she was often astonished at the witty things and even the wise things she said in such company, although, when she was alone,

so few things wise or witty occurred to her.
Like all persons who, in conversation, do
not so much express the results of previous
conviction obtained in silence as the inspiration
of the moment, Madge dazzled everybody by
a brilliancy which would have been impossible
if she had communicated that which had
been slowly acquired, but what she left
with those who listened to her, did not
always seem, on reflection, to be so much as
it appeared to be while she was talking.
Still she was very charming, and it must
be confessed that sometimes her spontaneity
was truer than the limitations of speech
more carefully weighed.

'What makes you stay in Fenmarket,
Mrs Hopgood? How I wish you would
come to London!'

'I do not wish to leave it now; I have
become attached to it; I have very few
friends in London, and lastly, perhaps the
most convincing reason, I could not afford
it. Rent and living are cheaper here than
in town.'

'Would you not like to live in London, Miss Hopgood?'

Clara hesitated for a few seconds.

'I am not sure—certainly not by myself. I was in London once for six months as a governess in a very pleasant family, where I saw much society; but I was glad to return to Fenmarket.'

'To the scenery round Fenmarket,' interrupted Madge; 'it is so romantic, so mountainous, so interesting in every way.'

'I was thinking of people, strange as it may appear. In London nobody really cares for anybody, at least, not in the sense in which I should use the words. Men and women in London stand for certain talents, and are valued often very highly for them, but they are valued merely as representing these talents. Now, if I had a talent, I should not be satisfied with admiration or respect because of it. No matter what admiration, or respect, or even enthusiasm I might evoke, even if I were told that my services had been immense and that life had been changed through my instrumentality, I should feel the lack of quiet, personal affection, and that, I believe, is not common in London. If I were famous, I would sacrifice all the adoration of the world for the love of a brother—if I had one—or a sister, who perhaps had never heard what it was which had made me renowned.'

'Certainly,' said Madge, laughing, 'for the love of *such* a sister. But, Mr Palmer, I like London. I like the people, just the people, although I do not know a soul, and not a soul cares a brass farthing about me. I am not half so stupid in London as in the country. I never have a thought of my own down here. How should I? But in London there is plenty of talk about all kinds of things, and I find I too have something in me. It is true, as Clara says, that nobody is anything particular to anybody, but that to me is rather pleasant. I do not want too much of profound and eternal attachments. They are rather a burden. They involve profound and eternal attachment on my part; and I have always to be at my best; such watchfulness and such jealousy! I prefer a dressing-gown and slippers and bonds which are not so tight.'

'Madge, Madge, I wish you would sometimes save me the trouble of laboriously striving to discover what you really mean.'

Mrs Hopgood bethought herself that her daughters were talking too much to one another, as they often did, even when guests were present, and she therefore interrupted them.

'Mr Palmer, you see both town and country—which do you prefer?'

'Oh! I hardly know; the country in summer-time, perhaps, and town in the winter.'

This was a safe answer, and one which was not very original; that is to say, it expressed no very distinct belief; but there was one valid reason why he liked being in London in the winter.

'Your father, I remember, loves music. I

suppose you inherit his taste, and it is impossible to hear good music in the country.'

'I am very fond of music. Have you
heard "St Paul?" I was at Birmingham when
it was first performed in this country. Oh!
it *is* lovely,' and he began humming '*Be thou
faithful unto death.*'

Frank did really care for music. He went
wherever good music was to be had; he
belonged to a choral society and was in great
request amongst his father's friends at evening entertainments. He could also play the
piano, so far as to be able to accompany
himself thereon. He sang to himself when
he was travelling, and often murmured
favourite airs when people around him were
talking. He had lessons from an old Italian,
a little, withered, shabby creature, who was
not very proud of his pupil. 'He is a
talent,' said the Signor, 'and he will amuse
himself; good for a ballad at a party, but
a musician? no!' and like all mere 'talents'
Frank failed in his songs to give them just
what is of most value—just that which

separates an artistic performance from the vast region of well-meaning, respectable, but uninteresting commonplace. There was a curious lack in him also of correspondence between his music and the rest of himself. As music is expression, it might be supposed that something which it serves to express would always lie behind it ; but this was not the case with him, although he was so attractive and delightful in many ways. There could be no doubt that his love for Beethoven was genuine, but that which was in Frank Palmer was not that of which the sonatas and symphonies of the master are the voice. He went into raptures over the slow movement in the *C minor* Symphony, but no *C minor* slow movement was discernible in his character.

'What on earth can be found in "St Paul" which can be put to music?' said Madge. 'Fancy a chapter in the Epistle to the Romans turned into a duet !'

'Madge ! Madge ! I am ashamed of you,' said her mother.

'Well, mother,' said Clara, 'I am sure that some of the settings by your divinity, Handel, are absurd. "*For as in Adam all die*" may be true enough, and the harmonies are magnificent, but I am always tempted to laugh when I hear it.'

Frank hummed the familiar apostrophe '*Be not afraid.*'

'Is that a bit of "St Paul"?' said Mrs Hopgood.

'Yes, it goes like this,' and Frank went up to the little piano and sang the song through.

'There is no fault to be found with that,' said Madge, 'so far as the coincidence of sense and melody is concerned, but I do not care much for oratorios. Better subjects can be obtained outside the Bible, and the main reason for selecting the Bible is that what is called religious music may be provided for good people. An oratorio, to me, is never quite natural. Jewish history is not a musical subject, and, besides, you cannot have proper love songs in an oratorio, and in them music is at its best.'

Mrs Hopgood was accustomed to her daughter's extravagance, but she was, nevertheless, a little uncomfortable.

'Ah!' said Frank, who had not moved from the piano, and he struck the first two bars of '*Adelaide*.'

'Oh, please,' said Madge, 'go on, go on,' but Frank could not quite finish it.

She was sitting on the little sofa, and she put her feet up, lay and listened with her eyes shut. There was a vibration in Mr Palmer's voice not perceptible during his vision of the crown of life and of fidelity to death.

'Are you going to stay over Sunday?' inquired Mrs Hopgood.

'I am not quite sure; I ought to be back on Sunday evening. My father likes me to be at home on that day.'

'Is there not a Mr Maurice who is a friend of your father?'

'Oh, yes, a great friend.'

'He is not High Church nor Low Church?'

'No, not exactly.'

'What is he, then? What does he believe?'

' Well, I can hardly say; he does not
believe that anybody will be burnt in a brim-
stone lake for ever.'

' That is what he does not believe,' interposed Clara.

' He believes that Socrates and the great
Greeks and Romans who acted up to the
light that was within them were not sent to
hell. I think that is glorious, don't you?'

' Yes, but that also is something he does
not believe. What is there in him which is
positive? What has he distinctly won from
the unknown?'

'Ah, Miss Hopgood, you ought to hear
him yourself; he is wonderful. I do admire
him so much; I am sure you would like
him.'

' If you do not go home on Saturday,' said
Mrs Hopgood, ' we shall be pleased if you
will have dinner with us on Sunday; we
generally go for a walk in the afternoon.'

Frank hesitated, but at that moment
Madge rose from the sofa. Her hair
was disarranged, and she pushed its thick

folds backward. It grew rather low down on her forehead and stood up a little on her temples, a mystery of shadow and dark recess. If it had been electrical with the force of a strong battery and had touched him, he could not have been more completely paralysed, and his half-erect resolution to go back on Saturday was instantly laid flat.

'Thank you, Mrs Hopgood,' looking at Madge and meeting her eyes, 'I think it very likely I shall stay, and if I do I will most certainly accept your kind invitation.'

CHAPTER V

SUNDAY morning came, and Frank, being
in the country, considered himself absolved
from the duty of going to church, and
went for a long stroll. At half-past one
he presented himself at Mrs Hopgood's
house.

'I have had a letter from London,' said
Clara to Frank, 'telling me a most extraordinary story, and I should like to know
what you think of it. A man, who was
left a widower, had an only child, a
lovely daughter of about fourteen years
old, in whose existence his own was completely wrapped up. She was subject
at times to curious fits of self-absorption
or absence of mind, and while she was
under their influence she resembled a som-
nambulist rather than a sane human being

awake. Her father would not take her to a physician, for he dreaded lest he should be advised to send her away from home, and he also feared the effect which any recognition of her disorder might have upon her. He believed that in obscure and half-mental diseases like hers, it was prudent to suppress all notice of them, and that if he behaved to her as if she were perfectly well, she would stand a chance of recovery. Moreover, the child was visibly improving, and it was probable tnat the disturbance in her health would be speedily outgrown. One hot day he went out shopping with her, and he observed that she was tired and strange in her manner, although she was not ill, or, at least, not so ill as he had often before seen her. The few purchases they had to make at the draper's were completed, and they went out into the street. He took her hand-bag, and, in doing so, it opened and he saw to his horror a white silk pocket-handkerchief crumpled up in it, which he instantly recognised as one which had been shown him five minutes before, but he had not bought. The next moment a hand was on his shoulder. It was that of an assistant, who requested that they would both return for a few minutes. As they walked the half dozen steps back, the father's resolution was taken. "I am sixty," he thought to himself, "and she is fourteen." They went into the counting-house and he confessed that he had taken the handkerchief, but that it was taken by mistake and that he was about to restore it when he was arrested. The poor girl was now herself again, but her mind was an entire blank as to what she had done, and she could not doubt her father's statement, for it was a man's handkerchief and the bag was in his hands. The draper was inexorable, and as he had suffered much from petty thefts of late, had determined to make an example of the first offender whom he could catch. The father was accordingly prosecuted, convicted and sentenced to imprisonment. When his term had expired, his daughter, who, I am glad to say, never for an instant lost her faith in him, went away with him to a distant part of the country, where they lived under an assumed name. About ten years afterwards he died and kept his secret to the last; but he had seen the complete recovery and happy marriage of his child. It was remarkable that it never occurred to her that she might have been guilty, but her father's confession, as already stated, was apparently so sincere that she could do nothing but believe him. You will wonder how the facts were discovered. After his death a sealed paper disclosing them was found, with the inscription, "*Not to be opened during my daughter's life, and if she should have children or a husband who may survive her, it is to be burnt.*" She had no children, and when she died as an old woman, her husband also being dead, the seal was broken.'

'Probably,' said Madge, 'nobody except his daughter believed he was not a thief. For her sake he endured the imputation of common larceny, and was content to leave the world with only a remote chance that he would ever be justified.'

'I wonder,' said Frank, 'that he did not admit that it was his daughter who had taken the handkerchief, and excuse her on the ground of her ailment.'

'He could not do that,' replied Madge. 'The object of his life was to make as little of the ailment as possible. What would have been the effect on her if she had been made aware of its fearful consequences? Furthermore, would he have been believed? And then —awful thought, the child might have suspected him of attempting to shield himself at her expense! Do you think you could be capable of such sacrifice, Mr Palmer?'

Frank hesitated. 'It would—'

'The question is not fair, Madge,' said Mrs Hopgood, interrupting him. 'You are asking for a decision when all the materials to make up a decision are not present. It is wrong to question ourselves in cold blood as to what we should do in a great strait; for the emergency brings the insight and the power necessary to deal with it. I often fear lest, if such-and-such a trial were to befall me, I should miserably fail. So I should, furnished as I now am, but not as I should be under stress of the trial.'

'What is the use,' said Clara, 'of speculating whether we can, or cannot, do this or that? It *is* now an interesting subject for discussion whether the lie was a sin.'

'No,' said Madge, 'a thousand times no.'

'Brief and decisive. Well, Mr Palmer, what do you say?'

'That is rather an awkward question. A lie is a lie.'

'But not,' broke in Madge, vehemently, 'to save anybody whom you love. Is a contemptible little two-foot measuring-tape to be applied to such an action as that?'

'The consequences of such a philosophy, though, my dear,' said Mrs Hopgood, 'are rather serious. The moment you dispense with a fixed standard, you cannot refuse permission to other people to dispense with it also.'

'Ah, yes, I know all about that, but I am not going to give up my instinct for the sake of a rule. Do what you feel to be right, and let the rule go hang. Somebody, cleverer in logic than we are, will come along afterwards and find a higher rule which we have obeyed, and will formulate it concisely.'

'As for my poor self,' said Clara, 'I do not profess to know, without the rule, what is right and what is not. We are always trying to transcend the rule by some special pleading, and often in virtue of some fancied superiority. Generally speaking, the attempt is fatal.'

'Madge,' said Mrs Hopgood, 'your dogmatic decision may have been interesting, but it prevented the expression of Mr Palmer's opinion.'

Madge bent forward and politely inclined her head to the embarrassed Frank.

'I do not know what to say. I have never thought much about such matters. Is not what they call casuistry a science among Roman Catholics? If I were in a difficulty and could not tell right from wrong, I should turn Catholic, and come to you as my priest, Mrs Hopgood.'

'Then you would do, not what you thought right yourself, but what I thought right. The worth of the right to you is that it is your right, and that you arrive at it in your own way. Besides, you might not have time to consult anybody. Were you never compelled to settle promptly a case of this kind?'

'I remember once at school, when the mathematical master was out of the class-room, a boy named Carpenter ran up to the black-board and wrote "Carrots" on it. That was the master's nickname, for he was red-haired. Scarcely was the word finished, when Carpenter heard him coming along the passage. There was just time partially to rub out some of the big letters, but CAR remained, and Carpenter was standing at the board when "Carrots" came in. He was an excitable man, and he knew very well what the boys called him.

'"What have you been writing on the board, sir?"

'"Carpenter, sir."

'The master examined the board. The upper half of the second R was plainly perceptible, but it might possibly have been a P. He turned round, looked steadily at Carpenter for a moment, and then looked at us. Carpenter was no favourite, but not a soul spoke.

'"Go to your place, sir."

'Carpenter went to his place, the letters were erased and the lesson was resumed. I was greatly perplexed; I had acquiesced in a cowardly falsehood. Carrots was a great friend of mine, and I could not bear to feel that he was humbugged, so when we were outside I went up to Carpenter and told him he was an infernal sneak, and we had a desperate fight, and I licked him, and blacked both his eyes. I did not know what else to do.'

The company laughed.

'We cannot,' said Madge, 'all of us come to terms after this fashion with our consciences, but we have had enough of these discussions on morality. Let us go out.'

They went out, and, as some relief from the straight road, they turned into a field as they came home, and walked along a footpath which crossed the broad, deep ditches by planks. They were within about fifty yards of the last and broadest ditch, more a dyke than a ditch, when Frank, turning round, saw an ox, which they had not noticed, galloping after them.

'Go on, go on,' he cried, 'make for the plank.'

He discerned in an instant that unless the course of the animal could be checked it would overtake them before the bridge could be reached. The women fled, but Frank remained. He was in the habit of carrying a heavy walking-stick, the end of which he had hollowed out in his schooldays and had filled up with lead. Just as the ox came upon him, it laid its head to the ground, and Frank, springing aside, dealt it a tremendous, two-handed blow on the forehead with his knobbed weapon. The creature was dazed, it stopped and staggered, and in another instant Frank was across the bridge in safety. There was a little hysterical sobbing, but it was soon over.

'Oh, Mr Palmer,' said Mrs Hopgood, 'what presence of mind and what courage! We should have been killed without you.'

'The feat is not original, Mrs Hopgood. I saw it done by a tough little farmer last summer on a bull that was really mad. There was no ditch for him though, poor fellow, and he had to jump a hedge.'

'You did not find it difficult,' said Madge, 'to settle your problem when it came to you in the shape of a wild ox.'

'Because there was nothing to settle,' said Frank, laughing; 'there was only one thing to be done.'

'So you believed, or rather, so you saw,' said Clara. 'I should have seen half-a-dozen things at once—that is to say, nothing.'

'And I,' said Madge, 'should have settled it the wrong way: I am sure I should, even if I had been a man. I should have bolted.'

Frank stayed to tea, and the evening was musical. He left about ten, but just as the door had shut he remembered he had forgotten his stick. He gave a gentle rap and Madge appeared. She gave him his stick.

'Good-bye again. Thanks for my life.'

Frank cursed himself that he could not find the proper word. He knew there was something which might be said and ought to be said, but he could not say it. Madge held out her hand to him, he raised it to his lips and kissed it, and then, astonished at his boldness, he instantly retreated. He went to the 'Crown and Sceptre' and was soon in bed, but not to sleep. Strange, that the moment we lie down in the dark, images, which were half obscured, should become so intensely luminous! Madge hovered before Frank with almost tangible distinctness, and he felt his fingers moving in her heavy, voluptuous tresses. Her picture at last became almost painful to him and shamed him, so that he turned over from side to side to avoid it. He had never been thrown into the society

of women of his own age, for he had no
sister, and a fire was kindled within him
which burnt with a heat all the greater
because his life had been so pure. At last
he fell asleep and did not wake till late in
the morning. He had just time to eat his
breakfast, pay one more business visit in the
town, and catch the coach due at eleven
o'clock from Lincoln to London. As the
horses were being changed, he walked as
near as he dared venture to the windows of
the cottage next door, but he could see
nobody. When the coach, however, began
to move, he turned round and looked behind
him, and a hand was waved to him. He
took off his hat, and in five minutes he was
clear of the town. It was in sight a long
way, but when, at last, it disappeared, a
cloud of wretchedness swept over him as the
vapour sweeps up from the sea. What was
she doing? talking to other people, existing
for others, laughing with others! There were
miles between himself and Fenmarket. Life!
what was life? A few moments of living and

long, dreary gaps between. All this, however, is a vain attempt to delineate what was shapeless. It was an intolerable, unvanquishable oppression. This was Love; this was the blessing which the god with the ruddy wings had bestowed on him. It was a relief to him when the coach rattled through Islington, and in a few minutes had landed him at the 'Angel.'

CHAPTER VI

THERE was to be a grand entertainment
in the assembly room of the 'Crown and
Sceptre' in aid of the County Hospital. Mrs
Martin, widow of one of the late partners
in the bank, lived in a large house near
Fenmarket, and still had an interest in the
business. She was distinctly above anybody
who lived in the town, and she knew how
to show her superiority by venturing sometimes to do what her urban neighbours could
not possibly do. She had been known to
carry through the street a quart bottle of
horse physic although it was wrapped up
in nothing but brown paper. On her way
she met the brewer's wife, who was more
aggrieved than she was when Mrs Martin's
carriage swept past her in the dusty,
narrow lane which led to the Hall. Mrs

Martin could also afford to recognise in a measure the claims of education and talent. A gentleman came from London to lecture in the town, and showed astonished Fen-market an orrery and a magic lantern with dissolving views of the Holy Land. The exhibition had been provided in order to extinguish a debt incurred in repairing the church, but the rector's wife, and the brewer's wife, after consultation, decided that they must leave the lecturer to return to his inn. Mrs Martin, however, invited him to supper. Of course she knew Mr Hopgood well, and knew that he was no ordinary man. She knew also something of Mrs Hopgood and the daughters, and that they were no ordinary women. She had been heard to say that they were ladies, and that Mr Hopgood was a gentleman; and she kept up a distant kind of intimacy with them, always nodded to them whenever she met them, and every now and then sent them grapes and flowers. She had observed once or twice to Mrs Tubbs that Mr Hopgood was a remarkable person, who was quite scientific and therefore did not associate with the rest of the Fenmarket folk ; and Mrs Tubbs was much annoyed, particularly by a slight emphasis which she thought she detected in the 'therefore,' for Mr Tubbs had told her that one of the smaller London brewers, who had only about fifty public-houses, had refused to meet at dinner a learned French chemist who had written books. Mrs Martin could not make friends with the Hopgoods, nor enter the cottage. It would have been a transgression of that infinitely fine and tortuous line whose inexplicable convolutions mark off what is forbidden to a society lady. Clearly, however, the Hopgoods could be requested to co-operate at the 'Crown and Sceptre ;' in fact, it would be impolitic not to put some of the townsfolk on the list of patrons. So it came about that Mrs Hopgood was included, and that she was made responsible for the provision of one song and one recitation. For the song it was settled that Frank Palmer should be asked, as he would be in Fenmarket. Usually he came but once every half year, but he had not been able, so he said, to finish all his work the last time. The recitation Madge undertook.

The evening arrived, the room was crowded and a dozen private carriages stood in the 'Crown and Sceptre' courtyard. Frank called for the Hopgoods. Mrs Hopgood and Clara sat with presentation tickets in the second row, amongst the fashionable folk; Frank and Madge were upon the platform. Frank was loudly applauded in '*Il Mio Tesoro*,' but the loudest applause of the evening was reserved for Madge, who declaimed Byron's '*Destruction of Sennacherib*' with much energy. She certainly looked very charming in her red gown, harmonising with her black hair. The men in the audience were vociferous for something more, and would not be contented until she again came forward. The truth is, that the wily young woman had prepared herself beforehand for possibilities, but she artfully concealed her preparation. Looking on the ground and hesitating, she suddenly raised her head as if she had just remembered something, and then repeated Sir Henry Wotton's '*Happy Life*.' She was again greeted with cheers, subdued so as to be in accordance with the character of the poem, but none the less sincere, and in the midst of them she gracefully bowed and retired. Mrs Martin complimented her warmly at the end of the performance, and inwardly debated whether Madge could be asked to enliven one of the parties at the Hall, and how it could, at the same time, be made clear to the guests that she and her mother, who must come with her, were not even acquaintances, properly so called, but were patronised as persons of merit living in the town which the Hall protected. Mrs Martin was obliged to be very careful. She certainly was on the list at the Lord Lieutenant's, but she was in the outer ring, and she was not asked to those small and select little dinners which were given to Sir Egerton, the Dean of Peterborough, Lord Francis, and his brother, the county member. She decided, however, that she could make perfectly plain the conditions upon which the Hopgoods would be present, and the next day she sent Madge a little note asking her if she would 'assist in some festivities' at the Hall in about two months' time, which were to be given in celebration of the twenty-first birthday of Mrs Martin's third son. The scene from the 'Tempest,' where Ferdinand and Miranda are discovered playing chess, was suggested, and it was proposed that Madge should be Miranda, and Mr Palmer Ferdinand. Mrs Martin concluded with a hope that Mrs Hopgood and her eldest daughter would 'witness the performance.'

Frank joyously consented, for amateur theatricals had always attracted him, and in a few short weeks he was again at Fenmarket. He was obliged to be there for three or four days before the entertainment, in order to attend the rehearsals, which Mrs Martin had put under the control of a professional gentleman from London, and Madge and he were consequently compelled to make frequent journeys to the Hall.

At last the eventful night arrived, and a carriage was hired next door to take the party. They drove up to the grand entrance and were met by a footman, who directed Madge and Frank to their dressing-rooms, and escorted Mrs Hopgood and Clara to their places in the theatre. They had gone early in order to accommodate Frank and Madge, and they found themselves alone. They were surprised that there was nobody to welcome them, and a little more surprised when they found that the places allotted to them were rather in the rear. Presently two or three fiddlers were seen, who began to tune their instruments. Then some Fenmarket folk and some of the well-to-do tenants on the estate made their appearance, and took seats on either side of Mrs Hopgood and Clara. Quite at the back were the servants. At five minutes to eight the band struck up the overture to '*Zampa*,' and in the midst of it in sailed Mrs Martin and a score or two of fashionably-dressed people, male and female. The curtain ascended and Prospero's cell was seen. Alonso and his companions were properly grouped, and Prospero began,—

> 'Behold, Sir King,
> The wronged Duke of Milan, Prospero.'

The audience applauded him vigorously when he came to the end of his speech, but there was an instantaneous cry of 'hush!' when Prospero disclosed the lovers. It was really very pretty. Miranda wore a loose, simple, white robe, and her wonderful hair was partly twisted into a knot, and partly strayed down to her waist. The dialogue between the two was spoken with much dramatic feeling, and when Ferdinand came to the lines—

> 'Sir, she is mortal,
> But by immortal Providence she's mine,'

old Boston, a worthy and wealthy farmer, who sat next to Mrs Hopgood, cried out 'hear, hear!' but was instantly suppressed.

He put his head down behind the people in front of him, rubbed his knees, grinned, and then turned to Mrs Hopgood, whom he knew, and whispered, with his hand to his mouth,—

'And a precious lucky chap he is.'

Mrs Hopgood watched intently, and when Gonzalo invoked the gods to drop a blessed crown on the couple, and the applause was renewed, and Boston again cried 'hear, hear!' without fear of check, she did not applaud, for something told her that behind this stage show a drama was being played of far more serious importance.

The curtain fell, but there were loud calls for the performers. It rose, and they presented themselves, Alonso still holding the hands of the happy pair. The cheering now was vociferous, more particularly when a wreath was flung at the feet of the young princess, and Ferdinand, stooping, placed it on her head.

Again the curtain fell, the band struck up some dance music and the audience were treated to 'something light,' and roared with laughter at a pretty chambermaid at an inn who captivated and bamboozled a young booby who was staying there, pitched him overboard; 'wondered what he meant;' sang an audacious song recounting her many exploits, and finished with a *pas-seul.*

The performers and their friends were invited to a sumptuous supper, and the Fenmarket folk were not at home until half-past two in the morning. On their way back, Clara broke out against the juxtaposition of Shakespeare and such vulgarity.

'Much better,' she said, 'to have left the Shakespeare out altogether. The lesson of the sequence is that each is good in its way, a perfectly hateful doctrine to me.'

Frank and Madge were, however, in the best of humours, especially Frank, who had taken a glass of wine beyond his customary very temperate allowance.

'But, Miss Hopgood, Mrs Martin had to suit all tastes; we must not be too severe upon her.'

There was something in this remark most irritating to Clara; the word 'tastes,' for example, as if the difference between Miranda and the chambermaid were a matter of 'taste.' She was annoyed too with Frank's easy, cheery tones for she felt deeply what she said, and his mitigation and smiling latitudinarianism were more exasperating than direct opposition.

'I am sure,' continued Frank, 'that if we were to take the votes of the audience, Miranda would be the queen of the evening;' and he put the crown which he had brought away with him on her head again.

Clara was silent. In a few moments they were at the door of their house. It had begun to rain, and Madge, stepping out of the carriage in a hurry, threw a shawl over her head, forgetting the wreath. It fell into the gutter and was splashed with mud. Frank picked it up, wiped it as well as he could with his pocket-handkerchief, took it into the parlour and laid it on a chair.

CHAPTER VII

THE next morning it still rained, a cold rain from the north-east, a very disagreeable type of weather on the Fenmarket flats. Madge was not awake until late, and when she caught sight of the grey sky and saw her finery tumbled on the floor—no further use for it in any shape save as rags—and the dirty crown, which she had brought upstairs, lying on the heap, the leaves already fading, she felt depressed and miserable. The breakfast was dull, and for the most part all three were silent. Mrs Hopgood and Clara went away to begin their housework, leaving Madge alone.

'Madge,' cried Mrs Hopgood, 'what am I to do with this thing? It is of no use to preserve it; it is dead and covered with dirt.'

'Throw it down here.'

She took it and rammed it into the fire. At that moment she saw Frank pass. He was evidently about to knock, but she ran to the door and opened it.

'I did not wish to keep you waiting in the wet.'

'I am just off, but I could not help calling to see how you are. What! burning your laurels, the testimony to your triumph?'

'Triumph! rather transitory; finishes in smoke,' and she pushed two or three of the unburnt leaves amongst the ashes and covered them over. He stooped down, picked up a leaf, smoothed it between his fingers, and then raised his eyes. They met hers at that instant, as she lifted them and looked in his face. They were near one another, and his hands strayed towards hers till they touched. She did not withdraw; he clasped the hand, she not resisting; in another moment his arms were round her, his face was on hers, and he was swept into self-forgetfulness. Suddenly the horn of the coach about to start awoke him, and he murmured the line from one of his speeches of the night before—

'But by immortal Providence she's mine.'

She released herself a trifle, held her head back as if she desired to survey him apart from her, so that the ecstasy of union might be renewed, and then fell on his neck.

The horn once more sounded, she let him out silently, and he was off. Mrs Hopgood and Clara presently came downstairs.

'Mr Palmer came in to bid you good-bye, but he heard the coach and was obliged to rush away.'

'What a pity,' said Mrs Hopgood, 'that you did not call us.'

'I thought he would be able to stay longer.'

The lines which followed Frank's quotation came into her head,—

'Sweet lord, you play me false.'
'No, my dearest love,
I would not for the world.'

'An omen,' she said to herself; ' "he would not for the world." '

She was in the best of spirits all day long. When the housework was over and they were quiet together, she said,—

'Now, my dear mother and sister, I want to know how the performance pleased you.'

'It was as good as it could be,' replied her mother, 'but I cannot think why all plays should turn upon lovemaking. I wonder whether the time will ever come when we shall care for a play in which there is no courtship.'

'What a horrible heresy, mother,' said Madge.

'It may be so; it may be that I am growing old, but it seems astonishing to me sometimes that the world does not grow a little weary of endless variations on the same theme.'

'Never,' said Madge, 'as long as it does not weary of the thing itself, and it is not likely to do that. Fancy a young man and a young woman stopping short and exclaiming, "This is just what every son of Adam and daughter of Eve has gone through before;

why should we proceed?" Besides, it is the one emotion common to the whole world; we can all comprehend it. Once more, it reveals character. In *Hamlet* and *Othello*, for example, what is interesting is not solely the bare love. The natures of Hamlet and Othello are brought to light through it as they would not have been through any other stimulus. I am sure that no ordinary woman ever shows what she really is, except when she is in love. Can you tell what she is from what she calls her religion, or from her friends, or even from her husband?'

'Would it not be equally just to say women are more alike in love than in anything else? Mind, I do not say alike, but more alike. Is it not the passion which levels us all?'

'Oh, mother, mother! did one ever hear such dreadful blasphemy? That the loves, for example, of two such cultivated, exquisite creatures as Clara and myself would be nothing different from those of the barmaids next door?'

'Well, at anyrate, I do not want to see *my* children in love to understand what they are —to me at least.'

'Then, if you comprehend us so completely —and let us have no more philosophy—just tell me, should I make a good actress? Oh! to be able to sway a thousand human beings into tears or laughter! It must be divine.'

'No, I do not think you would,' replied Clara.

'Why not, miss? *Your* opinion, mind, was not asked. Did I not act to perfection last night?'

'Yes.'

'Then why are you so decisive?'

'Try a different part some day. I may be mistaken.'

'You are very oracular.'

She turned to the piano, played a few chords, closed the instrument, swung herself round on the music stool, and said she should go for a walk.

CHAPTER VIII

IT was Mr Palmer's design to send Frank abroad as soon as he understood the home trade. It was thought it would be an advantage to him to learn something of foreign manufacturing processes. Frank had gladly agreed to go, but he was now rather in the mood for delay. Mr Palmer conjectured a reason for it, and the conjecture was confirmed when, after two or three more visits to Fenmarket, perfectly causeless, so far as business was concerned, Frank asked for the paternal sanction to his engagement with Madge. Consent was willingly given, for Mr Palmer knew the family well; letters passed between him and Mrs Hopgood, and it was arranged that Frank's visit to Germany should be postponed till the summer. He was now frequently at Fen-

market as Madge's accepted suitor, and, as
the spring advanced, their evenings were
mostly spent by themselves out of doors.
One afternoon they went for a long walk,
and on their return they rested by a stile.
Those were the days when Tennyson was
beginning to stir the hearts of the young
people in England, and the two little green
volumes had just become a treasure in the
Hopgood household. Mr Palmer, senior,
knew them well, and Frank, hearing his
father speak so enthusiastically about them,
thought Madge would like them, and had
presented them to her. He had heard one
or two read aloud at home, and had looked
at one or two himself, but had gone no
further. Madge, her mother, and her sister
had read and re-read them.

'Oh,' said Madge, 'for that Vale in Ida.
Here in these fens how I long for something
that is not level! Oh, for the roar of—

> " The long brook falling thro' the clov'n ravine
> In cataract after cataract to the sea."

Go on with it, Frank.'

'I cannot.'

'But you know *Œnone?*'

'I cannot say I do. I began it—'

'Frank, how could you begin it and lay it down unfinished? Besides, those lines are some of the first; you *must* remember—

> " Behind the valley topmost Gargarus
> Stands up and takes the morning." '

'No, I do not recollect, but I will learn them; learn them for your sake.'

'I do not want you to learn them for my sake.'

'But I shall.'

She had taken off her hat and his hand strayed to her neck. Her head fell on his shoulder and she had forgotten his ignorance of *Œnone.* Presently she awoke from her delicious trance and they moved homewards in silence. Frank was a little uneasy.

'I do greatly admire Tennyson,' he said.

'What do you admire? You have hardly looked at him.'

'I saw a very good review of him. I will

look that review up, by the way, before I come down again. Mr Maurice was talking about it.'

Madge had a desire to say something, but she did not know what to say, a burden lay upon her chest. It was that weight which presses there when we are alone with those with whom we are not strangers, but with whom we are not completely at home, and she actually found herself impatient and half-desirous of solitude. This must be criminal or disease, she thought to herself, and she forcibly recalled Frank's virtues. She was so far successful that when they parted and he kissed her, she was more than usually caressing, and her ardent embrace, at least for the moment, relieved that unpleasant sensation in the region of the heart. When he had gone she reasoned with herself. What a miserable counterfeit of love, she argued, is mere intellectual sympathy, a sympathy based on books ! What did Miranda know about Ferdinand's 'views' on this or that subject? Love is something independent of 'views.' It is an attraction which has always been held to be inexplicable, but whatever it may be it is not 'views.' She was becoming a little weary, she thought, of what was called 'culture.' These creatures whom we know through Shakespeare and Goethe are ghostly. What have we to do with them? It is idle work to read or even to talk fine things about them. It ends in nothing. What we really have to go through and that which goes through it are interesting, but not circumstances and character impossible to us. When Frank spoke of his business, which he understood, he was wise, and some observations which he made the other day, on the management of his workpeople, would have been thought original if they had been printed. The true artist knows that his hero must be a character shaping events and shaped by them, and not a babbler about literature. Frank, also, was so susceptible. He liked to hear her read to him, and her enthusiasm would soon be his. Moreover, how gifted he was, unconsciously,

with all that makes a man admirable, with
courage, with perfect unselfishness! How
handsome he was, and then his passion for her!
She had read something of passion, but she
never knew till now what the white intensity
of its flame in a man could be. She was
committed, too, happily committed; it was
an engagement.

Thus, whenever doubt obtruded itself, she
poured a self-raised tide over it and concealed it. Alas! it could not be washed
away; it was a little sharp rock based beneath
the ocean's depths, and when the water ran
low its dark point reappeared. She was
more successful, however, than many women
would have been, for, although her interest
in ideas was deep, there was fire in her
blood, and Frank's arm around her made
the world well nigh disappear; her sur-
render was entire, and if Sinai had thundered
in her ears she would not have heard.
She was destitute of that power, which her
sister possessed, of surveying herself from
a distance. On the contrary, her emotion

enveloped her, and the safeguard of reflection on it was impossible to her.

As to Frank, no doubt ever approached him. He was intoxicated, and beside himself. He had been brought up in a clean household, knowing nothing of the vice by which so many young men are overcome, and woman hitherto had been a mystery to him. Suddenly he found himself the possessor of a beautiful creature, whose lips it was lawful to touch and whose heartbeats he could feel as he pressed her to his breast. It was permitted him to be alone with her, to sit on the floor and rest his head on her knees, and he had ventured to capture one of her slippers and carry it off to London, where he kept it locked up amongst his treasures. If he had been drawn over Fen-market sluice in a winter flood he would not have been more incapable of resistance.

Every now and then Clara thought she discerned in Madge that she was not entirely content, but the cloud-shadows swept past so rapidly and were followed by such dazzl-

ing sunshine that she was perplexed and
hoped that her sister's occasional moodi-
ness might be due to parting and absence,
or the anticipation of them. She never
ventured to say anything about Frank to
Madge, for there was something in her which
forbade all approach from that side. Once
when he had shown his ignorance of what
was so familiar to the Hopgoods, and Clara
had expected some sign of dissatisfaction
from her sister, she appeared ostentatiously
to champion him against anticipated criticism.
Clara interpreted the warning and was silent,
but, after she had left the room with her
mother in order that the lovers might be
alone, she went upstairs and wept many tears.
Ah! it is a sad experience when the nearest
and dearest suspects that we are aware of secret
disapproval, knows that it is justifiable, throws
up a rampart and becomes defensively belliger-
ent. From that moment all confidence is at
an end. Without a word, perhaps, the love
and friendship of years disappear, and in
the place of two human beings transparent

to each other, there are two who are opaque and indifferent. Bitter, bitter! If the cause of separation were definite disagreement upon conduct or belief, we could pluck up courage, approach and come to an understanding, but it is impossible to bring to speech anything which is so close to the heart, and there is, therefore, nothing left for us but to submit and be dumb.

CHAPTER IX

It was now far into June, and Madge and
Frank extended their walks and returned
later. He had come down to spend his last
Sunday with the Hopgoods before starting
with his father for Germany, and on the
Monday they were to leave London.

Wordsworth was one of the divinities at
Stoke Newington, and just before Frank
visited Fenmarket that week, he had heard
the *Intimations of Immortality* read with great
fervour. Thinking that Madge would be
pleased with him if she found that he knew
something about that famous Ode, and being
really smitten with some of the passages in
it, he learnt it, and just as they were about
to turn homewards one sultry evening he
suddenly began to repeat it, and declaimed
it to the end with much rhetorical power.

'Bravo!' said Madge, 'but, of all Wordsworth's poems, that is the one for which I
believe I care the least.'

Frank's countenance fell.

'Oh, me! I thought it was just what
would suit you.'

'No, not particularly. There are some
noble lines in it; for example—

> "And custom lie upon thee with a weight,
> Heavy as frost, and deep almost as life!"

But the very title—*Intimations of Immortality
from Recollections of Early Childhood*—is un-
meaning to me, and as for the verse which is
in everybody's mouth—

> "Our birth is but a sleep and a forgetting;"

and still worse the vision of "that immortal
sea," and of the children who "sport upon
the shore," they convey nothing whatever to
me. I find though they are much admired
by the clergy of the better sort, and by
certain religiously-disposed people, to whom
thinking is distasteful or impossible. Because

they cannot definitely believe, they fling themselves with all the more fervour upon these
cloudy Wordsworthian phrases, and imagine
they see something solid in the coloured
fog.'

It was now growing dark and a few heavy
drops of rain began to fall, but in a minute
or two they ceased. Frank, contrary to his
usual wont, was silent. There was something undiscovered in Madge, a region which
he had not visited and perhaps could not
enter. She discerned in an instant what she
had done, and in an instant repented. He
had taken so much pains with a long piece
of poetry for her sake : was not that better
than agreement in a set of propositions?
Scores of persons might think as she thought
about the ode, who would not spend a
moment in doing anything to gratify her.
It was delightful also to reflect that Frank
imagined she would sympathise with anything written in that temper. She recalled
what she herself had said when somebody
gave Clara a copy in 'Parian' of a Greek

statue, a thing coarse in outline and vulgar. Clara was about to put it in a cupboard in the attic, but Madge had pleaded so pathetically that the donor had in a measure divined what her sister loved, and had done her best, although she had made a mistake, that finally the statue was placed on the bedroom mantelpiece. Madge's heart overflowed, and Frank had never attracted her so powerfully as at that moment. She took his hand softly in hers.

'Frank,' she murmured, as she bent her head towards him, 'it is really a lovely poem.'

Suddenly there was a flash of forked lightning at some distance, followed in a few seconds by a roll of thunder increasing in intensity until the last reverberation seemed to shake the ground. They took refuge in a little barn and sat down. Madge, who was timid and excited in a thunderstorm, closed her eyes to shield herself from the glare.

The tumult in the heavens lasted for nearly two hours and, when it was over, Madge and

Frank walked homewards without speaking a word for a good part of the way.

'I cannot, cannot go to-morrow,' he suddenly cried, as they neared the town.

'You *shall* go,' she replied calmly.

'But, Madge, think of me in Germany, think what my dreams and thoughts will be —you here—hundreds of miles between us.'

She had never seen him so shaken with terror.

'You *shall* go ; not another word.'

'I must say something—what can I say? My God, my God, have mercy on me !'

'Mercy ! mercy !' she repeated, half unconsciously, and then rousing herself, exclaimed, 'You shall not say it ; I will not hear ; now, good-bye.'

They had come to the door ; he went inside ; she took his face between her hands, left one kiss on his forehead, led him back to the doorway and he heard the bolts drawn. When he recovered himself he went to the 'Crown and Sceptre' and tried to write a letter to her, but the words looked hateful, horrible on the paper, and they were not the words he wanted. He dared not go near the house the next morning, but as he passed it on the coach he looked at the windows. Nobody was to be seen, and that night he left England.

'Did you hear,' said Clara to her mother at breakfast, 'that the lightning struck one of the elms in the avenue at Mrs Martin's yesterday evening and splintered it to the ground?'

CHAPTER X

In a few days Madge received the following letter :—

'Frankfort, O. M.,
Hôtel Waidenbusch.

'My dearest Madge,—I do not know how to write to you. I have begun a dozen letters but I cannot bring myself to speak of what lies before me, hiding the whole world from me. Forgiveness! how is any forgiveness possible? But Madge, my dearest Madge, remember that my love is intenser than ever. What has happened has bound you closer to me. I *implore* you to let me come back. I will find a thousand excuses for returning, and we will marry. We had vowed marriage to each other and why should not our vows be fulfilled? Marriage, marriage *at once.* You will not, you *cannot*, no, you *cannot*, you must see you cannot refuse. My father wishes to make this town his head-quarters for ten days. Write by return for mercy's sake.—Your ever devoted

'FRANK.'

The reply came only a day late.

'MY DEAR FRANK,—Forgiveness! Who is to be forgiven? Not you. You believed you loved me, but I doubted my love, and I know now that no true love for you exists. We must part, and part forever. Whatever wrong may have been done, marriage to avoid disgrace would be a wrong to both of us in-finitely greater. I owe you an expiation; your release is all I can offer, and it is insufficient. I can only plead that I was deaf and blind. By some miracle, I cannot tell how, my ears and eyes are opened, and I hear and see. It is not the first time in my life that the truth has been revealed to me suddenly, supernaturally, I may say, as if in a vision, and I know the revelation is authentic. There must be no wavering, no half-measures, and I absolutely forbid another letter from you. If one arrives I must, for the sake of my own peace and resolution, refuse to read it. You have simply to announce to your father that the engagement is at an end, and give no reasons.— Your faithful friend

'MADGE HOPGOOD.'

Another letter did come, but Madge was true to her word, and it was returned unopened.

For a long time Frank was almost incapable of reflection. He dwelt on an event which might happen, but which he dared not name; and if it should happen! Pictures of his father, his home his father's friends, Fenmarket, the Hopgood household, passed before him with such wild rapidity and intermingled complexity that it seemed as if the reins had dropped out of his hands and he was being hurried away to madness.

He resisted with all his might this dreadful sweep of the imagination, tried to bring himself back into sanity and to devise schemes by which, although he was prohibited from writing to Madge, he might obtain news of her. Her injunction might not be final. There was but one hope for him, one possibility of extrication, one necessity — their marriage. It *must* be. He dared not think of what might be the consequences if they did not marry.

Hitherto Madge had given no explanation to her mother or sister of the rupture, but one morning—nearly two months had now passed—Clara did not appear at breakfast.

'Clara is not here,' said Mrs Hopgood; 'she was very tired last night, perhaps it is better not to disturb her.'

'Oh, no! please let her alone. I will see if she still sleeps.'

Madge went upstairs, opened her sister's door noiselessly, saw that she was not awake, and returned. When breakfast was over she rose, and after walking up and down the room once or twice, seated herself in the arm-chair by her mother's side. Her mother drew herself a little nearer, and took Madge's hand gently in her own.

'Madge, my child, have you nothing to say to your mother?'

'Nothing.'

'Cannot you tell me why Frank and you have parted? Do you not think I ought to know something about such an event in the life of one so close to me?'

'I broke off the engagement: we were not suited to one another.'

'I thought as much; I honour you; a thousand times better that you should separate now than find out your mistake afterwards when it is irrevocable. Thank God, He has given you such courage! But you must have suffered—I know you must;' and she tenderly kissed her daughter.

'Oh, mother! mother!' cried Madge, 'what is the worst — at least to — you—the worst that can happen to a woman?'

Mrs Hopgood did not speak; something

presented itself which she refused to recognise, but she shuddered. Before she could recover herself Madge broke out again,—

'It has happened to me; mother, your daughter has wrecked your peace for ever!'

'And he has abandoned you?'

'No, no; I told you it was I who left him.'

It was Mrs Hopgood's custom, when any evil news was suddenly communicated to her, to withdraw at once if possible to her own room. She detached herself from Madge, rose, and, without a word, went upstairs and locked her door. The struggle was terrible. So much thought, so much care, such an education, such noble qualities, and they had not accomplished what ordinary ignorant Fenmarket mothers and daughters were able to achieve! This fine life, then, was a failure, and a perfect example of literary and artistic training had gone the way of the common wenches whose affiliation cases figured in the county newspaper. She was shaken and bewildered. She was neither orthodox nor secular. She was too strong to be afraid that what she disbelieved could be true, and yet a fatal weakness had been disclosed in what had been set up as its substitute. She could not treat her child as a sinner who was to be tortured into something like madness by immitigable punishment, but, on the other hand, she felt that this sorrow was unlike other sorrows and that it could never be healed. For some time she was powerless, blown this way and that way by contradictory storms, and unable to determine herself to any point whatever. She was not, however, new to the tempest. She had lived and had survived when she thought she must have gone down. She had learned the wisdom which the passage through desperate straits can bring. At last she prayed and in a few minutes a message was whispered to her. She went into the breakfast-room and seated herself again by Madge. Neither uttered a word, but Madge fell down before her, and, with a great cry, buried her face in her mother's lap. She remained kneeling for some time waiting for a rebuke, but none came. Presently she felt smoothing hands on her head and the soft impress of lips. So was she judged.

CHAPTER XI

It was settled that they should leave Fen-market. Their departure caused but little surprise. They had scarcely any friends, and it was always conjectured that people so peculiar would ultimately find their way to London. They were particularly desirous to conceal their movements, and therefore determined to warehouse their furniture in town, to take furnished apartments there for three months, and then to move elsewhere. Any letters which might arrive at Fenmarket for them during these three months would be sent to them at their new address; nothing probably would come afterwards, and as nobody in Fenmarket would care to take any trouble about them, their trace would become obliterated. They found some rooms near Myddelton Square, Pentonville, not a particularly cheerful place, but they wished to avoid a more distant suburb, and Pentonville was cheap. Fortunately for them they had no difficulty whatever in getting rid of the Fenmarket house for the remainder of their term.

For a little while London diverted them after a fashion, but the absence of household cares told upon them. They had nothing to do but to read and to take dismal walks through Islington and Barnsbury, and the gloom of the outlook thickened as the days became shorter and the smoke began to darken the air. Madge was naturally more oppressed than the others, not only by reason of her temperament, but because she was the author of the trouble which had befallen them. Her mother and Clara did everything to sustain and to cheer her. They possessed the rare virtue of continuous tenderness. The love, which with many is an inspiration, was with them their own selves, from which they could not be separated ; a harsh word could not therefore escape from them. It was as impossible as that there should be any failure in the pressure with which the rocks press towards the earth's centre. Madge at times was very far gone in melancholy. How different this thing looked when it was close at hand ; when she personally was to be the victim ! She had read about it in history, the surface of which it seemed scarcely to ripple ; it had been turned to music in some of her favourite poems and had lent a charm to innumerable mythologies, but the actual fact was nothing like the poetry or mythology, and threatened to ruin her own history altogether. Nor would it be her own history solely, but more or less that of her mother and sister.

Had she believed in the common creed, her attention would have been concentrated on the salvation of her own soul ; she would have found her Redeemer and would have been comparatively at peace ; she would have acknowledged herself convicted of infinite sin, and hell would have been opened before her, but above the sin and the hell she would have seen the distinct image of the Mediator abolishing both. Popular theology makes personal salvation of such immense importance that, in comparison therewith, we lose sight of the consequences to others of our misdeeds. The sense of cruel injustice to those who loved her remained with Madge perpetually.

To obtain relief she often went out of London for the day; sometimes her mother and sister went with her; sometimes she insisted on going alone. One autumn morning, she found herself at Letherhead, the longest trip she had undertaken, for there were scarcely any railways then. She wandered about till she discovered a footpath which took her to a mill-pond, which spread itself out into a little lake. It was fed by springs which burst up through the ground. She watched at one particular point, and saw the water boil up with such force that it cleared a space of a dozen yards in diameter from every weed, and formed a transparent pool just tinted with that pale azure which is peculiar to the living fountains which break out from the bottom of the chalk. She was fascinated for a moment by the spectacle, and reflected upon it, but she passed on. In about three-quarters of an hour she found herself near a church, larger than an ordinary village church, and, as she was tired, and the gate of the church porch was open, she entered and sat down. The sun streamed in upon her, and some sheep which had strayed into the churchyard from the adjoining open field came almost close to her, unalarmed, and looked in her face. The quiet was complete, and the air so still, that a yellow leaf dropping here and there from the churchyard elms—just beginning to turn—fell quiveringly in a straight path to the earth. Sick at heart and despairing, she could not help being touched, and she thought to herself how strange the world is—so transcendent both in glory and horror ; a world capable of such scenes as those before her, and a world in which such suffering as hers could be ; a world infinite both ways.

The porch gate was open because the organist was about to practise, and in another instant she was listening to the *Kyrie* from Beethoven's Mass in C. She knew it; Frank had tried to give her some notion of it on the piano, and since she had been in London she had heard it at St Mary's, Moorfields. She broke down and wept, but there was something new in her sorrow, and it seemed as if a certain Pity overshadowed her.

She had barely recovered herself when she saw a woman, apparently about fifty, coming towards her with a wicker basket on her arm. She sat down beside Madge, put her basket on the ground, and wiped her face with her apron.

'Marnin' miss! its rayther hot walkin', isn't it? I've come all the way from Darkin, and I'm goin' to Great Oakhurst. That's a longish step there and back again; not that this is the nearest way, but I don't like climbing them hills, and then when I get to Letherhead I shall have a lift in a cart.'

Madge felt bound to say something as the sunburnt face looked kind and motherly.

'I suppose you live at Great Oakhurst?'

'Yes. I do: my husband, God bless him! he was a kind of foreman at The Towers, and when he died I was left alone and didn't know what to be at, as both my daughters were out and one married; so I took the general shop at Great Oakhurst, as Longwood used to have, but it don't pay for I ain't used to it, and the house is too big for me, and there isn't nobody proper to mind it when I goes over to Darkin for anything.'

'Are you going to leave?'

'Well, I don't quite know yet, miss, but I thinks I shall live with my daughter in London. She's married a cabinetmaker in Great Ormond Street: they let lodgings, too. Maybe you know that part?'

'No, I do not.'

'You don't live in London, then?'

'Yes, I do. I came from London this morning.'

'The Lord have mercy on us, did you

though ! I suppose, then, you're a-visitin' here. I know most of the folk hereabouts.'

'No : I am going back this afternoon.'

Her interrogator was puzzled and her curiosity stimulated. Presently she looked in Madge's face.

'Ah ! my poor dear, you'll excuse me, I don't mean to be forward, but I see you've been a-cryin' : there's somebody buried here.'

'No.'

That was all she could say. The walk from Letherhead, and the excitement had been too much for her and she fainted. Mrs Caffyn, for that was her name, was used to fainting fits. She was often 'a bit faint' herself, and she instantly loosened Madge's gown, brought out some smelling-salts and also a little bottle of brandy and water. Something suddenly struck her. She took up Madge's hand : there was no wedding ring on it.

Presently her patient recovered herself.

'Look you now, my dear ; you aren't noways fit to go back to London to-day. If you was my child you shouldn't do it for

H

all the gold in the Indies, no, nor you sha'n't now. I shouldn't have a wink of sleep this night if I let you go, and if anything were to happen to you it would be me as 'ud have to answer for it.'

'But I must go; my mother and sister will not know what has become of me.'

'You leave that to me; I tell you again as you can't go. I've been a mother myself, and I haven't had children for nothing. I was just a-goin' to send a little parcel up to my daughter by the coach, and her husband's a-goin' to meet it. She'd left something behind last week when she was with me, and I thought I'd get a bit of fresh butter here for her and put along with it. They make better butter in the farm in the bottom there, than they do at Great Oakhurst. A note inside now will get to your mother all right; you have a bit of something to eat and drink here, and you'll be able to walk along of me just into Letherhead, and then you can ride to Great Oakhurst; it's only about two miles, and you can stay there all night.'

Madge was greatly touched; she took Mrs Caffyn's hands in hers, pressed them both and consented. She was very weary, and the stamp on Mrs Caffyn's countenance was indubitable; it was evidently no forgery, but of royal mintage. They walked slowly to Letherhead, and there they found the carrier's cart, which took them to Great Oakhurst.

CHAPTER XII

MRS CAFFYN's house was a roomy old cottage near the church, with a bow-window in which were displayed bottles of 'suckers,' and of Day & Martin's blacking, cotton stuffs, a bag of nuts and some mugs, cups and saucers. Inside were salt butter, washing-blue, drapery, treacle, starch, tea, tobacco and snuff, cheese, matches, bacon, and a few drugs, such as black draught, magnesia, pills, sulphur, dill-water, Dalby's Carminative, and steel-drops. There was also a small stock of writing-paper, string and tin ware. A boy was behind the counter. When Mrs Caffyn was out he always asked the customers who desired any article, the sale of which was in any degree an art, to call again when she returned. He went as far as those things which were put up in packets, such as what were called 'grits' for making gruel, and he was also authorised to venture on pennyworths of liquorice and peppermints, but the sale of half-a-dozen yards of cotton print was as much above him as the negotiation of a treaty of peace would be to a messenger in the Foreign Office. In fact, nobody, excepting children, went into the shop when Mrs Caffyn was not to be seen there, and, if she had to go to Dorking or Letherhead on business, she always chose the middle of the day, when the folk were busy at their homes or in the fields. Poor woman! she was much tried. Half the people who dealt with her were in her debt, but she could not press them for her money. During winter-time they were discharged by the score from their farms, but as they were not sufficiently philosophic, or sufficiently considerate for their fellows to hang or drown themselves, they were obliged to consume food, and to wear clothes, for which they tried to pay by instalments during spring, summer and autumn. Mrs Caffyn managed to make both ends meet by the help of two or three pigs, by great economy, and by letting some of her superfluous rooms. Great Oakhurst was not a show place nor a Spa, but the Letherhead doctor had once recommended her to a physician in London, who occasionally sent her a patient who wanted nothing but rest and fresh air. She also, during the shooting-season, was often asked to find a bedroom for visitors to The Towers.

She might have done better had she been on thoroughly good terms with the parson. She attended church on Sunday morning with tolerable regularity. She never went inside a dissenting chapel, and was not heretical on any definite theological point, but the rector and she were not friends. She had lived in Surrey ever since she was a child, but she was not Surrey born. Both her father and mother came from the north country, and migrated southwards when she was very young. They were better educated than the southerners amongst whom they came ; and although their daughter had no schooling beyond what was obtainable in a Surrey village of that time, she was distinguished by a certain superiority which she had inherited or acquired from her parents. She was never subservient to the rector after the fashion of her neighbours; she never curtsied to him, and if he passed and nodded she said 'Marnin', sir,' in just the same tone as that in which she said it to the smallest of the Great Oakhurst farmers. Her church-going was an official duty incumbent upon her as the proprietor of the only shop in the parish. She had nothing to do with church matters except on Sunday, and she even went so far as to neglect to send for the rector when one of her children lay dying. She was attacked for the omission, but she defended herself.

'What was the use when the poor dear was only seven year old? What call was there for him to come to a blessed innocent like that? I did tell him to look in when my husband was took, for I know as before we

were married there was something atween
him and that gal Sanders. He never would
own up to me about it, and I thought as
he might to a clergyman, and, if he did, it
would ease his mind and make it a bit better
for him afterwards ; but, Lord ! it warn't no
use, for he went off and we didn't so much
as hear her name, not even when he was
a-wandering. I says to myself when the parson
left, "What's the good of having you?"'

Mrs Caffyn was a Christian, but she was
a disciple of St James rather than of St Paul.
She believed, of course, the doctrines of the
Catechism, in the sense that she denied none,
and would have assented to all if she had been
questioned thereon ; but her belief that 'faith,
if it hath not works, is dead, being alone,' was
something very vivid and very practical.

Her estimate, too, of the relative values
of the virtues and of the relative sinfulness
of sins was original, and the rector therefore
told all his parishioners that she was little
better than a heathen. The common failings in that part of the country amongst

the poor were Saturday-night drunkenness and looseness in the relations between the young men and young women. Mrs Caffyn's indignation never rose to the correct boiling point against these crimes. The rector once ventured to say, as the case was next door to her,—

'It is very sad, is it not, Mrs Caffyn, that Polesden should be so addicted to drink. I hope he did not disturb you last Saturday night. I have given the constable directions to look after the street more closely on Saturday evening, and if Polesden again offends he must be taken up.'

Mrs Caffyn was behind her own counter. She had just served a customer with two ounces of Dutch cheese, and she sat down on her stool. Being rather a heavy woman she always sat down when she was not busy, and she never rose merely to talk.

'Yes, it is sad, sir, and Polesden isn't no particklar friend of mine, but I tell you what's sad too, sir, and that's the way them people are mucked up in that cottage. Why, their living room opens straight on the road, and the wind comes in fit to blow your head off, and when he goes home o' nights, there's them children a-squalling, and he can't bide there and do nothing.'

'I am afraid, though, Mrs Caffyn, there must be something radically wrong with that family. I suppose you know all about the eldest daughter?'

'Yes, sir, I *have* heard it : it wouldn't be Great Oakhurst if I hadn't, but p'r'aps, sir, you've never been upstairs in that house, and yet a house it isn't. There's just two sleeping-rooms, that's all ; it's shameful, it isn't decent. Well, that gal, she goes away to service. Maybe, sir, them premises at the farm are also unbeknown to you. In the back kitchen there's a broadish sort of shelf as Jim climbs into o' nights, and it has a rail round it to keep you from a-falling out, and there's a ladder as they draws up in the day as goes straight up from that kitchen to the gal's bedroom door. It's downright disgraceful, and I don't believe the Lord

A'mighty would be marciful to neither of *us* if we was tried like that.'

Mrs Caffyn bethought herself of the 'us' and was afraid that even she had gone a little too far; 'leastways, speaking for myself, sir,' she added.

The rector turned rather red, and repented his attempt to enlist Mrs Caffyn.

'If the temptations are so great, Mrs Caffyn, that is all the more reason why those who are liable to them should seek the means which are provided in order that they may be overcome. I believe the Polesdens are very lax attendants at church, and I don't think they ever communicated.'

Mrs Polesden at that moment came in for an ounce of tea, and as Mrs Caffyn rose to weigh it, the rector departed with a stiff 'good-morning,' made to do duty for both women.

CHAPTER XIII

Mrs Caffyn persuaded Madge to go to bed at once, after giving her 'something to comfort her.' In the morning her kind hostess came to her bedside.

'You've got a mother, haven't you—leastways, I know you have, because you wrote to her.'

'Yes.'

'Well, and you lives with her and she looks after you?'

'Yes.'

'And she's fond of you, maybe?'

'Oh, yes.'

'That's a marcy; well then, my dear, you shall go back in the cart to Letherhead, and you'll catch the Darkin coach to London.'

'You have been very good to me; what have I to pay you?'

'Pay? Nothing! why, if I was to let you pay, it would just look as if I'd trapped you here to get something out of you. Pay! no, not a penny.

'I can afford very well to pay, but if it vexes you I will not offer anything. I don't know how to thank you enough.'

Madge took Mrs Caffyn's hand in hers and pressed it firmly.

'Besides, my dear,' said Mrs Caffyn, smoothing the sheets a little, 'you won't mind my saying it, I expex you are in trouble. There's something on your mind, and I believe as I knows pretty well what it is.'

Madge turned round in the bed so as no longer to face the light; Mrs Caffyn sat between her and the window.

'Look you here, my dear; don't you suppose I meant to say anything to hurt you. The moment I looked on you I was drawed to you like; I couldn't help it. I see'd what was the matter, but I was all the more drawed, and I just wanted you to know as it makes no differ- ence. That's like me; sometimes I'm drawed that way and sometimes t'other way, and it's never no use for me to try to go against it. I ain't a-going to say anything more to you ; God-A'mighty, He's above us all ; but p'r'aps you may be comin' this way again some day, and then you'll look in.'

Madge turned again to the light, and again caught Mrs Caffyn's hand, but was silent.

The next morning, after Madge's return, Mrs Cork, the landlady, presented herself at the sitting-room door and 'wished to speak with Mrs Hopgood for a minute.'

'Come in, Mrs Cork.'

'Thank you, ma'am, but I prefer as you should come downstairs.'

Mrs Cork was about forty, a widow with no children. She had a face of which it was impossible to recollect, when it had been seen even a dozen times, any feature except the eyes, which were steel-blue, a little bluer than the faceted head of the steel poker in her parlour, but just as hard. She lived in the basement with a maid, much like herself but a little more human. Although the fron

underground room was furnished Mrs Cork
never used it, except on the rarest occasions, and
a kind of apron of coloured paper hung over
the fireplace nearly all the year. She was
a woman of what she called regular habits.
No lodger was ever permitted to transgress
her rules, or to have meals ten minutes before
or ten minutes after the appointed time.
She had undoubtedly been married, but who
Cork could have been was a marvel. Why
he died, and why there were never any
children were no marvels. At two o'clock
her grate was screwed up to the narrowest
possible dimensions, and the ashes, potato
peelings, tea leaves and cabbage stalks were
thrown on the poor, struggling coals. No
meat, by the way, was ever roasted—it was
considered wasteful — everything was baked
or boiled. After half-past four not a bit
of anything that was not cold was allowed
till the next morning, and, indeed, from
the first of April to the thirty-first of
October the fire was raked out the moment
tea was over. Mrs Hopgood one night was

not very well and Clara wished to give her
mother something warm. She rang the bell
and asked for hot water. Maria came up
and disappeared without a word after receiv-
ing the message. Presently she returned.

'Mrs Cork, miss, wishes me to tell you as
it was never understood as 'ot water would
be required after tea, and she hasn't got any.'

Mrs Hopgood had a fire, although it
was not yet the thirty-first of October,
for it was very damp and raw. She had
with much difficulty induced Mrs Cork to
concede this favour (which probably would
not have been granted if the coals had not
yielded a profit of threepence a scuttleful),
and Clara, therefore, asked if she could not
have the kettle upstairs. Again Maria disappeared and returned.

'Mrs Cork says, miss, as it's very ill-
convenient as the kettle is cleaned up agin
to-morrow, and if you can do without it
she will be obliged.'

It was of no use to continue the contest,
and Clara bethought herself of a little 'Etna'

she had in her bedroom. She went to the druggist's, bought some methylated spirit, and obtained what she wanted.

Mrs Cork had one virtue and one weakness. Her virtue was cleanliness, but she persecuted the 'blacks,' not because she objected to dirt as dirt, but because it was unauthorised, appeared without permission at irregular hours, and because the glittering polish on varnished paint and red mahogany was a pleasure to her. She liked the dirt, too, in a way, for she enjoyed the exercise of her ill-temper on it and the pursuit of it to destruction. Her weakness was an enormous tom-cat which had a bell round its neck and slept in a basket in the kitchen, the best-behaved and most moral cat in the parish. At half-past nine every evening it was let out into the back-yard and vanished. At ten precisely it was heard to mew and was immediately admitted. Not once in a twelvemonth did that cat prolong its love making after five minutes to ten.

Mrs Hopgood went upstairs to her

room, Mrs Cork following and closing the door.

'If you please, ma'am, I wish to give you notice to leave this day week.'

'What is the matter, Mrs Cork?'

'Well, ma'am, for one thing, I didn't know as you'd bring a bird with you.'

It was a pet bird belonging to Madge.

'But what harm does the bird do? It gives no trouble; my daughter attends to it.'

'Yes, ma'am, but it worrits my Joseph—the cat, I mean. I found him the other mornin' on the table eyin' it, and I can't a-bear to see him urritated.'

'I should hardly have thought that a reason for parting with good lodgers.'

Mrs Hopgood had intended to move, as before explained, but she did not wish to go till the three months had expired.

'I don't say as that is everything, but if you wish me to tell you the truth, Miss Madge is not a person as I like to keep in the house. I wish you to know'—Mrs Cork

suddenly became excited and venomous—
'that I'm a respectable woman, and have
always let my apartments to respectable
people, and do you think I should ever let
them to respectable people again if it got
about as I had had anybody as wasn't respectable? Where was she last night? And do
you suppose as me as has been a married
woman can't see the condition she's in? I
say as you, Mrs Hopgood, ought to be
ashamed of yourself for bringing of such a
person into a house like mine, and you'll
please vacate these premises on the day named.'
She did not wait for an answer, but banged
the door after her, and went down to her
subterranean den.

Mrs Hopgood did not tell her children
the true reason for leaving. She merely said
that Mrs Cork had been very impertinent,
and that they must look out for other rooms.
Madge instantly recollected Great Ormond
Street, but she did not know the number,
and oddly enough she had completely forgotten Mrs Caffyn's name. It was a peculiar

name, she had heard it only once, she had not noticed it over the door, and her exhaustion may have had something to do with her loss of memory. She could not therefore write, and Mrs Hopgood determined that she herself would go to Great Oakhurst. She had another reason for her journey. She wished her kind friend there to see that Madge had really a mother who cared for her. She was anxious to confirm Madge's story, and Mrs Caffyn's confidence. Clara desired to go also, but Mrs Hopgood would not leave Madge alone, and the expense of a double fare was considered unnecessary.

When Mrs Hopgood came to Letherhead on her return, the coach was full inside, and she was obliged to ride outside, although the weather was cold and threatening. In about half an hour it began to rain heavily, and by the time she was in Pentonville she was wet through. The next morning she ought to have lain in bed, but she came down at her accustomed hour as Mrs Cork was more than usually disagreeable, and it was settled that they would leave at once if the rooms in Great Ormond Street were available. Clara went there directly after breakfast, and saw Mrs Marshall, who had already received an introductory letter from her mother.

CHAPTER XIV

THE Marshall family included Marshall and
his wife. He was rather a small man, with
blackish hair, small lips, and with a nose
just a little turned up at the tip. As we
have been informed, he was a cabinet-maker.
He worked for very good shops, and earned
about two pounds a week. He read books,
but he did not know their value, and often
fancied he had made a great discovery on
a bookstall of an author long ago superseded
and worthless. He belonged to a mechanic's
institute, and was fond of animal physiology;
heard courses of lectures on it at the institute,
and had studied two or three elementary hand-
books. He found in a second-hand dealer's
shop a model, which could be taken to pieces,
of the inside of the human body. He had
also bought a diagram of a man, showing the

circulation, and this he had hung in his bed-room, his mother - in - law objecting most strongly on the ground that its effect on his wife was injurious. He had a notion that the world might be regenerated if men and women were properly instructed in physio-logical science, and if before marriage they would study their own physical peculiarities, and those of their intended partners. The crossing of peculiarities nevertheless presented difficulties. A man with long legs surely ought to choose a woman with short legs, but if a man who was mathematical married a woman who was mathematical, the result might be a mathematical prodigy. On the other hand the parents of the prodigy might each have corresponding qualities, which, mixed with the mathematical tendency, would completely nullify it. The path of duty therefore was by no means plain. However, Marshall was sure that great cities dwarfed their inhabitants, and as he himself was not so tall as his father, and, moreover, suffered from bad digestion, and had a tendency to 'run to head,' he determined to select as his wife a 'daughter of the soil,' to use his own phrase, above the average height, with a vigorous constitution and plenty of common sense. She need not be bookish, 'he could supply all that himself.' Accordingly, he married Sarah Caffyn. His mother and Mrs Caffyn had been early friends. He was not mistaken in Sarah. She was certainly robust; she was a shrewd housekeeper, and she never read anything, except now and then a paragraph or two in the weekly newspaper, notwithstanding (for there were no children), time hung rather heavily on her hands. One child had been born, but to Marshall's surprise and disappointment it was a poor, rickety thing, and died before it was a twelvemonth old.

Mrs Marshall was not a very happy woman. Marshall was a great politician and spent many of his evenings away from home at political meetings. He never informed her what he had been doing, and if he had told her, she would neither have understood

nor cared anything about it. At Great
Oakhurst she heard everything and took
an interest in it, and she often wished with
all her heart that the subject which occupied
Marshall's thoughts was not Chartism but
the draining of that heavy, rush-grown bit
of rough pasture that lay at the bottom of
the village. He was very good and kind
to her, and she never imagined, before
marriage, that he ought to be more. She was
sure that at Great Oakhurst she would have
been quite comfortable with him but somehow, in London, it was different. 'I don't
know how it is,' she said one day, 'the
sort of husband as does for the country
doesn't do for London.'

At Great Oakhurst, where the doors were
always open into the yard and the garden,
where every house was merely a covered
bit of the open space, where people were
always in and out, and women never sat
down, except to their meals, or to do a little
stitching or sewing, it was really not necessary,
as Mrs Caffyn observed, that husband and

wife should 'hit it so fine.' Mrs Marshall
hated all the conveniences of London. She
abominated particularly the taps, and longed
to be obliged in all weathers to go out to
the well and wind up the bucket. She
abominated also the dust-bin, for it was a
pleasure to be compelled—so at least she
thought it now—to walk down to the muck-
heap and throw on it what the pig could
not eat. Nay, she even missed that corner
of the garden against the elder-tree, where
the pig-stye was, for 'you could smell the
elder-flowers there in the spring-time, and the
pig-stye wasn't as bad as the stuffy back room
in Great Ormond Street when three or four
men were in it.' She did all she could to
spend her energy on her cooking and clean-
ing, but 'there was no satisfaction in it,' and
she became much depressed, especially after
the child died. This was the main reason
why Mrs Caffyn determined to live with
her. Marshall was glad she resolved to come.
His wife had her full share of the common
sense he desired, but the experiment had

not altogether succeeded. He knew she was lonely, and he was sorry for her, although he did not see how he could mend matters. He reflected carefully, nothing had happened which was a surprise to him, the relationship was what he had supposed it would be, excepting that the child did not live and its mother was a little miserable. There was nothing he would not do for her, but he really had nothing more to offer her.

Although Mrs Marshall had made up her mind that husbands and wives could not be as contented with one another in the big city as they would be in a village, a suspicion crossed her mind one day that, even in London, the relationship might be different from her own. She was returning from Great Oakhurst after a visit to her mother. She had stayed there for about a month after her child's death, and she travelled back to town with a Letherhead woman, who had married a journeyman tanner, who formerly worked in the Letherhead tan-yard, and had now moved to Bermondsey, a horrid hole, worse than Great Ormond Street. Both Marshall and the tanner were at the 'Swan with Two Necks' to meet the covered van, and the tanner's wife jumped out first.

'Hullo, old gal, here you are,' cried the tanner, and clasped her in his brown, bark-stained arms, giving her, nothing loth, two or three hearty kisses. They were so much excited at meeting one another, that they forgot their friends, and marched off without bidding them good-bye. Mrs Marshall was welcomed in quieter fashion.

'Ah!' she thought to herself, 'Red Tom,' as the tanner was called, 'is not used to London ways. They are, perhaps, correct for London, but Marshall might now and then remember that I have not been brought up to them.'

To return, however, to the Hopgoods. Before the afternoon they were in their new quarters, happily for them, for Mrs Hopgood became worse. On the morrow she was seriously ill, inflammation of the lungs appeared, and in a week she was dead. What Clara and Madge suffered cannot be told here. Whenever anybody whom we love dies, we discover that although death is commonplace it is terribly original. We may have thought about it all our lives, but if it comes close to us, it is quite a new, strange thing to us, for which we are entirely unprepared. It may, perhaps, not be the bare loss so much as the strength of the bond which is broken that is the surprise, and we are debtors in a way to death for revealing something in us which ordinary life disguises. Long after the first madness of their grief had passed, Clara and Madge were astonished to find how dependent they had been on their mother. They were grown-up women accustomed to act for themselves, but they felt unsteady, and as if deprived of customary support. The reference to her had been constant, although it was often silent, and they were not conscious of it. A defence from the outside waste desert had been broken down, their mother had always seemed to intervene between them and the world, and now they were exposed and shelterless.

Three parts of Mrs Hopgood's little income was mainly an annuity, and Clara and Madge found that between them they had but seventy-five pounds a year.

CHAPTER XV

FRANK could not rest. He wrote again to Clara at Fenmarket; the letter went to Mrs Cork's, and was returned to him. He saw that the Hopgoods had left Fenmarket, and suspecting the reason, he determined at any cost to go home. He accordingly alleged ill-health, a pretext not altogether fictitious, and within a few days after the returned letter reached him he was back at Stoke Newington. He went immediately to the address in Pentonville which he found on the envelope, but was very shortly informed by Mrs Cork that 'she knew nothing whatever about them.' He walked round Myddelton Square, hopeless, for he had no clue whatever.

What had happened to him would scarcely, perhaps, have caused some young men much uneasiness, but with Frank the case was altogether different. There was a chance of discovery, and if his crime should come to light his whole future life would be ruined. He pictured his excommunication, his father's agony, and it was only when it seemed possible that the water might close over the ghastly thing thrown in it, and no ripple reveal what lay underneath, that he was able to breathe again. Immediately he asked himself, however, if he could live with his father and wear a mask, and never betray his dreadful secret. So he wandered home-ward in the most miserable of all conditions; he was paralysed by the intricacy of the coil which enveloped and grasped him.

That evening it happened that there was a musical party at his father's house; and, of course, he was expected to assist. It would have suited his mood better if he could have been in his own room, or out in the streets, but absence would have been inconsistent with his disguise, and might have led to betrayal. Consequently he was present, and the gaiety of the company and the excitement of his favourite exercise, brought about for a time forgetfulness of his trouble. Amongst the performers was a distant cousin, Cecilia Morland, a young woman rather tall and fully developed; not strikingly beautiful, but with a lovely reddish-brown tint on her face, indicative of healthy, warm, rich pulsations. She possessed a contralto voice, of a quality like that of a blackbird, and it fell to her and to Frank to sing. She was dressed in a fashion perhaps a little more courtly than was usual in the gatherings at Mr Palmer's house, and Frank, as he stood beside her at the piano, could not restrain his eyes from straying every now and then away from his music to her shoulders, and once nearly lost himself, during a solo which required a little unusual exertion, in watching the movement of a locket and of what was for a moment revealed beneath it. He escorted her amidst applause to a corner of the room, and the two sat down side by side.

'What a long time it is, Frank, since you and I sang that duet together. We have seen nothing of you lately.'

'Of course not ; I was in Germany.'

'Yes, but I think you deserted us before then. Do you remember that summer when we were all together at Bonchurch, and the part songs which astonished our neighbours just as it was growing dark? I recollect you and I tried together that very duet for the first time with the old lodging-house piano.'

Frank remembered that evening well.

'You sang better than you did to-night. You did not keep time : what were you dreaming about ? '

'How hot the room is ! Do you not feel it oppressive? Let us go into the conservatory for a minute.'

The door was behind them and they slipped in and sat down, just inside, and under the orange tree.

'You must not be away so long again. Now mind, we have a musical evening this day fortnight. You will come ? Promise ; and we must sing that duet again, and sing it properly.'

He did not reply, but he stooped down, plucked a blood-red begonia, and gave it to her.

'That is a pledge. It is very good of you.'

She tried to fasten it in her gown, underneath the locket, but she dropped a little black pin. He went down on his knees to find it; rose, and put the flower in its proper place himself, and his head nearly touched her neck, quite unnecessarily.

'We had better go back now,' she said, 'but mind, I shall keep this flower for a fortnight and a day, and if you make any excuses I shall return it faded and withered.'

'Yes, I will come.'

'Good boy; no apologies like those you sent the last time. No bad throat. Play me false, and there will be a pretty rebuke for you—a dead flower.'

Play me false! It was as if there were some stoppage in a main artery to his brain. *Play me false!* It rang in his ears, and for

a moment he saw nothing but the scene at
the Hall with Miranda. Fortunately for him,
somebody claimed Cecilia, and he slunk back
into the greenhouse.

One of Mr Palmer's favourite ballads was
The Three Ravens. Its pathos unfits it for
an ordinary drawing-room, but as the music
at Mr Palmer's was not of the common
kind, *The Three Ravens* was put on the list
for that night.

> ' *She was dead herself ere evensong time. With a down,*
>   *hey down, hey down,*
> *God send every gentleman*
> *Such hawks, such hounds, and such a leman. With a*
>   *down, hey down, hey down.*'

Frank knew well the prayer of that melody,
and, as he listened, he painted to himself,
in the vividest colours, Madge in a mean
room, in a mean lodging, and perhaps dying.
The song ceased, and one for him stood
next. He heard voices calling him, but he
passed out into the garden and went down
to the further end, hiding himself behind
the shrubs. Presently the inquiry for him

ceased, and he was relieved by hearing an instrumental piece begin.

Following on that presentation of Madge came self-torture for his unfaithfulness. He scourged himself into what he considered to be his duty. He recalled with an effort all Madge's charms, mental and bodily, and he tried to break his heart for her. He was in anguish because he found that in order to feel as he ought to feel some effort was necessary; that treason to her was possible, and because he had looked with such eyes upon his cousin that evening. He saw himself as something separate from himself, and although he knew what he saw to be flimsy and shallow, he could do nothing to deepen it, absolutely nothing! It was not the betrayal of that thunderstorm which now tormented him. He could have represented that as a failure to be surmounted; he could have repented it. It was his own inner being from which he revolted, from limitations which are worse than crimes, for who, by taking thought, can add one cubit to his stature?

CHAPTER XVI

THE next morning found Frank once more in Myddelton Square. He looked up at the house; the windows were all shut, and the blinds were drawn down. He had half a mind to call again, but Mrs Cork's manner had been so offensive and repellent that he desisted. Presently the door opened, and Maria, the maid, came out to clean the doorsteps. Maria, as we have already said, was a little more human than her mistress, and having overheard the conversation between her and Frank at the first interview, had come to the conclusion that Frank was to be pitied, and she took a fancy to him. Accordingly, when he passed her, she looked up and said,—'Good-morning.' Frank stopped, and returned her greeting.

'You was here the other day, sir, asking where them Hopgoods had gone.'

'Yes,' said Frank, eagerly, 'do you know what has become of them?'

'I helped the cabman with the boxes, and I heard Mrs Hopgood say "Great Ormond Street," but I have forgotten the number.'

'Thank you very much.'

Frank gave the astonished and grateful Maria half-a-crown, and went off to Great Ormond Street at once. He paced up and down the street half a dozen times, hoping he might recognise in a window some ornament from Fenmarket, or perhaps that he might be able to distinguish a piece of Fenmarket furniture, but his search was in vain, for the two girls had taken furnished rooms at the back of the house. His quest was not renewed that week. What was there to be gained by going over the ground again? Perhaps they might have found the lodgings unsuitable and have moved elsewhere. At church on Sunday he met his cousin Cecilia, who reminded him of his promise.

'See,' she said, 'here is the begonia. I put it in my prayer-book in order to preserve it when I could keep it in water no longer, and it has stained the leaf, and spoilt the Athanasian Creed. You will have it sent to you if you are faithless. Reflect on your emotions, sir, when you receive a dead flower, and you have the bitter consciousness also that you have damaged my creed without any recompense.'

It was impossible not to protest that he had no thought of breaking his engagement, although, to tell the truth, he had wished once or twice he could find some way out of it. He walked with her down the churchyard path to her carriage, assisted her into it, saluted her father and mother, and then went home with his own people.

The evening came, he sang with Cecilia, and it was observed, and he himself observed it, how completely their voices harmonised. He was not without a competitor, a handsome young baritone, who was much commended. When he came to the end of his performance everybody said what a pity it was that the following duet could not also be given, a duet which Cecilia knew perfectly well. She was very much pressed to take her part with him, but she steadily refused, on the ground that she had not practised it, that she had already sung once, and that she was engaged to sing once more with her cousin. Frank was sitting next to her, and she added, so as to be heard by him alone, 'He is no particular favourite of mine.'

There was no direct implication that Frank was a favourite, but an inference was possible, and at least it was clear that she preferred to reserve herself for him. Cecilia's gifts, her fortune, and her gay, happy face had made many a young fellow restless, and had brought several proposals, none of which had been accepted. All this Frank knew, and how could he repress something more than satisfaction when he thought that perhaps he might have been the reason why nobody as yet had been able to win her. She always called him Frank, for although they were not

first cousins, they were cousins. He generally called her Cecilia, but she was Cissy
in her own house. He was hardly close
enough to venture upon the more familiar
nickname, but to-night, as they rose to go
to the piano, he said, and the baritone sat
next to her,—

'Now, *Cissy*, once more.'

She looked at him with just a little start
of surprise, and a smile spread itself over her
face. After they had finished, and she never
sang better, the baritone noticed that she
seemed indisposed to return to her former
place, and she retired with Frank to the
opposite corner of the room.

'I wonder,' she said, 'if being happy in
a thing is a sign of being born to do it.
If it is, I am born to be a musician.'

'I should say it is; if two people are quite
happy in one another's company, it is as a
sign they were born for one another.'

'Yes, if they are sure they are happy. It
is easier for me to be sure that I am happier
with a thing than with a person.'

'Do you think so? Why?'

'There is the uncertainty whether the person is happy with me. I cannot be altogether happy with anybody unless I know I make him happy.'

'What kind of person is he with whom you *could* be without making him happy?'

The baritone rose to the upper F with a clash of chords on the piano, and the company broke up. Frank went home with but one thought in his head—the thought of Cecilia.

His bedroom faced the south-west, its windows were open, and when he entered, the wind, which was gradually rising, struck him on the face and nearly forced the door out of his hand; the fire in his blood was quenched, and the image of Cecilia receded. He looked out, and saw reflected on the low clouds the dull glare of the distant city. Just over there was Great Ormond Street, and underneath that dim, red light, like the light of a great house burning, was Madge Hopgood. He lay down, turning over from side to side in the vain hope that by change

of position he might sleep.   After about an
hour's feverish tossing, he just lost himself,
but not in that oblivion which slumber usually
brought him.   He was so far awake that
he saw what was around him, and yet, he
was so far released from the control of his
reason that he did not recognise what he saw,
and it became part of a new scene created
by his delirium.   The full moon, clearing
away the clouds as she moved upwards, had
now passed round to the south, and just
caught the white window - curtain farthest
from him.   He half-opened his eyes, his
mad dream still clung to him, and there was
the dead Madge before him, pale in death,
and holding a child in her arms !   He distinctly heard himself scream as he started up
in affright ; he could not tell where he was ;
the spectre faded and the furniture and hang-
ings transformed themselves into their familiar
reality.   He could not lie down again, and
rose and dressed himself.   He was not the
man to believe that the ghost could be a
revelation or a prophecy, but, nevertheless,

he was once more overcome with fear, a vague dread partly justifiable by the fact of Madge, by the fact that his father might soon know what had happened, that others also might know, Cecilia for example, but partly also a fear going beyond all the facts, and not to be accounted for by them, a strange, horrible trembling such as men feel in earthquakes when the solid rock shakes, on which everything rests.

CHAPTER XVII

WHEN Frank came downstairs to breakfast the conversation turned upon his return to Germany. He did not object to going, although it can hardly be said that he willed to go. He was in that perilous condition in which the comparison of reasons is impossible, and the course taken depends upon some chance impulse of the moment, and is a mere drift. He could not leave, however, in complete ignorance of Madge, and with no certainty as to her future. He resolved therefore to make one more effort to discover the house. That was all which he determined to do. What was to happen when he had found it, he did not know. He was driven to do something, which could not be of any importance, save for what must follow, but he was unable to bring himself even to consider what was to follow. He knew that at Fenmarket one or other of the sisters went out soon after breakfast to make provision for the day, and perhaps, if they kept up this custom, he might be successful in his search. He accordingly stationed himself in Great Ormond Street at about half-past nine, and kept watch from the Lamb's Conduit Street end, shifting his position as well as he could, in order to escape notice. He had not been there half an hour when he saw a door open, and Madge came out and went westwards. She turned down Devonshire Street as if on her way to Holborn. He instantly ran back to Theobalds Road, and when he came to the corner of Devonshire Street she was about ten yards from him, and he faced her. She stopped irresolutely, as if she had a mind to return, but as he approached her, and she found she was recognised, she came towards him.

'Madge, Madge,' he cried, 'I want to speak to you. I must speak with you.'

'Better not ; let me go.'

'I say I *must* speak to you.'

'We cannot talk here ; let me go.'

'I must ! I must ! come with me.'

She pitied him, and although she did not consent she did not refuse. He called a cab, and in ten minutes, not a word having been spoken during those ten minutes, they were at St Paul's. The morning service had just begun, and they sat down in a corner far away from the worshippers.

'Oh, Madge,' he began, 'I implore you to take me back. I love you. I do love you, and—and—I cannot leave you.'

She was side by side with the father of her child about to be born. He was not and could not be as another man to her, and for the moment there was the danger lest she should mistake this secret bond for love. The thought of what had passed between them, and of the child, his and hers, almost overpowered her.

'I cannot,' he repeated. 'I *ought* not. What will become of me ?'

She felt herself stronger; he was excited, but his excitement was not contagious. The string vibrated, and the note was resonant, but it was not a note which synchronised with her, and it did not stir her to respond. He might love her, he was sincere enough to sacrifice himself for her, and to remain faithful to her, but the voice was not altogether that of his own true self. Partly, at least, it was the voice of what he considered to be duty, of superstition and alarm. She was silent.

'Madge,' he continued, 'ought you to refuse? You have some love for me. Is it not greater than the love which thousands feel for one another. Will you blast your future and mine, and, perhaps, that of some-one besides, who may be very dear to you? *Ought* you not, I say, to listen?'

The service had come to an end, the organist was playing a voluntary, rather longer than usual, and the congregation was leaving, some of them passing near Madge and Frank, and casting idle glances on the

young couple who had evidently come neither
to pray nor to admire the architecture.
Madge recognised the well-known St Ann's
fugue, and, strange to say, even at such a
moment it took entire possession of her ; the
golden ladder was let down and celestial
visitors descended. When the music ceased
she spoke.

'It would be a crime.'

'A crime, but I —' She stopped him.

'I know what you are going to say. I
know what is the crime to the world ; but
it would have been a crime, perhaps a worse
crime, if a ceremony had been performed
beforehand by a priest, and the worst of
crimes would be that ceremony now. I
must go.' She rose and began to move
towards the door.

He walked silently by her side till they
were in St Paul's churchyard, when she took
him by the hand, pressed it affectionately and
suddenly turned into one of the courts that
lead towards Paternoster Row. He did not
follow her, something repelled him, and

when he reached home it crossed his mind that marriage, after such delay, would be a poor recompense, as he could not thereby conceal her disgrace.

CHAPTER XVIII

IT was clear that these two women could not live in London on seventy-five pounds a year, most certainly not with the prospect before them, and Clara cast about for something to do. Marshall had a brother-in-law, a certain Baruch Cohen, a mathematical instrument maker in Clerkenwell, and to him Marshall accidentally one day talked about Clara, and said that she desired an occupation. Cohen himself could not give Clara any work, but he knew a second-hand bookseller, an old man who kept a shop in Holborn, who wanted a clerk, and Clara thus found herself earning another pound a week. With this addition she and her sister could manage to pay their way and provide what Madge would want. The hours were long, the duties irksome and wearisome, and, worst of all, the conditions under which they were performed, were not only as bad as they could be, but their badness was of a kind to which Clara had never been accustomed, so that she felt every particle of it in its full force. The windows of the shop were, of course, full of books, and the walls were lined with them. In the middle of the shop also was a range of shelves, and books were stacked on the floor, so that the place looked like a huge cubical block of them through which passages had been bored. At the back the shop became contracted in width to about eight feet, and consequently the central shelves were not continued there, but just where they ended, and overshadowed by them were a little desk and a stool. All round the desk more books were piled, and some manœuvring was necessary in order to sit down. This was Clara's station. Occasionally, on a brilliant, a very brilliant day in summer, she could write without gas, but, perhaps, there were not a dozen such days in the year. By twisting herself sideways she could just catch a glimpse of a narrow line of sky over some heavy theology which was not likely to be disturbed, and was therefore put at the top of the window, and once when somebody bought the *Calvin Joann. Opera Omnia*, 9 *vol. folio, Amst.* 1671—it was very clear that afternoon—she actually descried towards seven o'clock a blessed star exactly in the middle of the gap the Calvin had left.

The darkness was very depressing, and poor Clara often shut her eyes as she bent over her day-book and ledger, and thought of the Fenmarket flats where the sun could be seen bisected by the horizon at sun-rising and sun-setting, and where even the southern Antares shone with diamond glitter close to the ground during summer nights. She tried to reason with herself during the dreadful smoke fogs ; she said to herself that they were only half-a-mile thick, and she carried herself up in imagination and beheld the unclouded azure, the filthy smother lying all beneath her, but her dream did not continue, and reality was

too strong for her. Worse, perhaps, than
the eternal gloom was the dirt. She was
naturally fastidious, and as her skin was thin
and sensitive, dust was physically a discomfort.
Even at Fenmarket she was continually washing
her hands and face, and, indeed, a wash was
more necessary to her after a walk than food
or drink. It was impossible to remain clean
in Holborn for five minutes; everything she
touched was foul with grime; her collar and
cuffs were black with it when she went home
to her dinner, and it was not like the honest,
blowing road-sand of Fenmarket highways, but
a loathsome composition of everything dis-
gusting which could be produced by millions
of human beings and animals packed together
in soot. It was a real misery to her and
made her almost ill. However, she managed
to set up for herself a little lavatory in the
basement, and whenever she had a minute at
her command, she descended and enjoyed the
luxury of a cool, dripping sponge and a
piece of yellow soap. The smuts began to
gather again the moment she went upstairs,

but she strove to arm herself with a little
philosophy against them. 'What is there in
life,' she moralised, smiling at her sermonis-
ing, 'which once won is for ever won? It
is always being won and always being lost.
Her master, fortunately, was one of the kindest
of men, an old gentleman of about sixty-five,
who wore a white necktie, clean every morning. He was really a *gentle*man in the true
sense of that much misused word, and not a
mere *trades*man; that is to say, he loved his
business, not altogether for the money it
brought him, but as an art. He was known
far and wide, and literary people were glad
to gossip with him. He never pushed his
wares, and he hated to sell them to anybody
who did not know their value. He amused
Clara one afternoon when a carriage stopped
at the door, and a lady inquired if he had a
Manning and Bray's *History of Surrey*. Yes,
he had a copy, and he pointed to the three
handsome, tall folios.

'What is the price?'

'Twelve pounds ten.'

'I think I will have them.'

'Madam, you will pardon me, but, if I were you, I would not. I think something much cheaper will suit you better. If you will allow me, I will look out for you and will report in a few days.'

'Oh! very well,' and she departed.

'The wife of a brassfounder,' he said to Clara; 'made a lot of money, and now he has bought a house at Dulwich and is setting up a library. Somebody has told him that he ought to have a county history, and that Manning and Bray is the book. Manning and Bray! What he wants is a Dulwich and Denmark Hill Directory. No, no,' and he took down one of the big volumes, blew the dust off the top edges and looked at the old book-plate inside, 'you won't go there if I can help it.' He took a fancy to Clara when he found she loved literature, although what she read was out of his department altogether, and his perfectly human behaviour to her prevented that sense of exile and loneliness which is so horrible to many a poor

creature who comes up to London to begin
therein the struggle for existence. She read
and meditated a good deal in the shop, but
not to much profit, for she was continually
interrupted, and the thought of her sister
intruded itself perpetually.

Madge seldom or never spoke of her
separation from Frank, but one night, when
she was somewhat less reserved than usual,
Clara ventured to ask her if she had heard
from him since they parted.

'I met him once.'

'Madge, do you mean that he found out
where we are living, and that he came to see
you?'

'No, it was just round the corner as I
was going towards Holborn.'

'Nothing could have brought him here but
yourself,' said Clara, slowly.

'Clara, you doubt?'

'No, no! I doubt you? Never!'

'But you hesitate; you reflect. Speak out.'

'God forbid I should utter a word which
would induce you to disbelieve what you know

to be right. It is much more important to believe earnestly that something is morally right than that it should be really right, and he who attempts to displace a belief runs a certain risk, because he is not sure that what he substitutes can be held with equal force. Besides, each person's belief, or proposed course of action, is a part of himself, and if he be diverted from it and takes up with that which is not himself, the unity of his nature is impaired, and he loses himself.'

'Which is as much as to say that the prophet is to break no idols.'

'You know I do not mean that, and you know, too, how incapable I am of defending myself in argument. I never can stand up for anything I say. I can now and then say something, but, when I have said it, I run away.'

'My dearest Clara,' Madge put her arm over her sister's shoulder as they sat side by side, 'do not run away now; tell me just what you think of me.'

Clara was silent for a minute.

'I have sometimes wondered whether you have not demanded a little too much of yourself and Frank. It is always a question of how much. There is no human truth which is altogether true, no love which is altogether perfect. You may possibly have neglected virtue or devotion such as you could not find elsewhere, overlooking it because some failing, or the lack of sympathy on some unimportant point, may at the moment have been prominent. Frank loved you, Madge.'

Madge did not reply; she withdrew her arm from her sister's neck, threw herself back in her chair and closed her eyes. She saw again the Fenmarket roads, that summer evening, and she felt once more Frank's burning caresses. She thought of him as he left St Paul's, perhaps broken-hearted. Stronger than every other motive to return to him, and stronger than ever, was the movement towards him of that which belonged to him.

At last she cried out, literally cried, with a vehemence which startled and terrified Clara,—

'Clara, Clara, you know not what you do! For God's sake forbear!' She was again silent, and then she turned round hurriedly, hid her face, and sobbed piteously. It lasted, however, but for a minute; she rose, wiped her eyes, went to the window, came back again, and said,—

'It is beginning to snow.'

The iron pillar bolted to the solid rock had quivered and resounded under the blow, but its vibrations were nothing more than those of the rigid metal; the base was unshaken and, except for an instant, the column had not been deflected a hair's-breadth.

CHAPTER XIX

Mr Cohen, who had obtained the situation indirectly for Clara, thought nothing more about it until, one day, he went to the shop, and he then recollected his recommendation, which had been given solely in faith, for he had never seen the young woman, and had trusted entirely to Marshall. He found her at her dark desk, and as he approached her, she hastily put a mark in a book and closed it.

'Have you sold a little volume called *After Office Hours* by a man named Robinson?'

'I did not know we had it. I have never seen it.'

'I do not wonder, but I saw it here about six months ago; it was up there,' pointing to a top shelf. Clara was about to mount the ladder, but he stopped her, and found what he wanted. Some of the leaves were torn.

'We can repair those for you; in about a couple of days it shall be ready.'

He lingered a little, and at that moment another customer entered. Clara went forward to speak to him, and Cohen was able to see that it was the *Heroes and Hero Worship* she had been studying, a course of lectures which had been given by a Mr Carlyle, of whom Cohen knew something. As the customer showed no signs of departing, Cohen left, saying he would call again.

Before sending Robinson's *After Office Hours* to the binder, Clara looked at it. It was made up of short essays, about twenty altogether, bound in dark-green cloth, lettered at the side, and published in 1841. They were upon the oddest subjects: such as, *Ought Children to learn Rules before Reasons? The Higher Mathematics and Materialism. Ought We to tell Those Whom We love what We*

*think about Them? Deductive Reasoning in
Politics. What Troubles ought We to Make
Known and What ought We to Keep Secret:
Courage as a Science and an Art.*

Clara did not read any one essay through,
she had no time, but she was somewhat
struck with a few sentences which caught
her eye ; for example—

'A mere dream, a vague hope, ought in
some cases to be more potent than a certainty
in regulating our action. The faintest vision
of God should be more determinative than
the grossest earthly assurance.'

'I knew a case in which a man had to
encounter three successive trials of all the
courage and inventive faculty in him. Failure
in one would have been ruin. The odds
against him in each trial were desperate, and
against ultimate victory were overwhelming.
Nevertheless, he made the attempt, and was
triumphant, by the narrowest margin, in every
struggle. That which is of most value to
us is often obtained in defiance of the laws
of probability.'

'What is precious in Quakerism is not so much the doctrine of the Divine voice as that of the preliminary stillness, the closure against other voices and the reduction of the mind to a condition in which it can *listen*, in which it can discern the merest whisper, inaudible when the world, or interest, or passion, are permitted to speak.'

'The acutest syllogiser can never develop the actual consequences of any system of policy, or, indeed, of any change in human relationship, man being so infinitely complex, and the interaction of human forces so incalculable.'

'Many of our speculative difficulties arise from the unauthorised conception of an *omnipotent* God, a conception entirely of our own creation, and one which, if we look at it closely, has no meaning. It is because God *could* have done otherwise, and did not, that we are confounded. It may be distressing to think that God cannot do any better, but it is not so distressing as to believe that He might have done better had He so willed.'

M

Although these passages were disconnected, each of them seemed to Clara to be written in a measure for herself, and her curiosity was excited about the author. Perhaps the man who called would say something about him.

Baruch Cohen was now a little over forty. He was half a Jew, for his father was a Jew and his mother a Gentile. The father had broken with Judaism, but had not been converted to any Christian church or sect. He was a diamond-cutter, originally from Holland, came over to England and married the daughter of a mathematical instrument maker, at whose house he lodged in Clerkenwell. The son was apprenticed to his maternal grandfather's trade, became very skilful at it, worked at it himself, employed a man and a boy, and supplied London shops, which sold his instruments at about three times the price he obtained for them. Baruch, when he was very young, married Marshall's elder sister, but she died at the birth of her first child and he had been a widower now for nine-

teen years. He had often thought of taking
another wife, and had seen, during these nineteen years, two or three women with whom he
had imagined himself to be really in love, and
to whom he had been on the verge of making
proposals, but in each case he had hung back,
and when he found that a second and a third
had awakened the same ardour for a time as
the first, he distrusted its genuineness. He
was now, too, at a time of life when a
man has to make the unpleasant discovery
that he is beginning to lose the right to
expect what he still eagerly desires, and
that he must beware of being ridiculous. It
is indeed a very unpleasant discovery. If
he has done anything well which was worth
doing, or has made himself a name, he may
be treated by women with respect or adula-
tion, but any passable boy of twenty is
really more interesting to them, and, un-
happily, there is perhaps so much of the
man left in him that he would rather see
the eyes of a girl melt when she looked at
him than be adored by all the drawing-

rooms in London as the author of the greatest poem since *Paradise Lost*, or as the conqueror of half a continent. Baruch's life during the last nineteen years had been such that he was still young, and he desired more than ever, because not so blindly as he desired it when he was a youth, the tender, intimate sympathy of a woman's love. It was singular that, during all those nineteen years, he should not once have been over-come. It seemed to him as if he had been held back, not by himself, but by some external power, which refused to give any reasons for so doing. There was now less chance of yielding than ever; he was reserved and self-respectful, and his manner towards women distinctly announced to them that he knew what he was and that he had no claims whatever upon them. He was some-thing of a philosopher, too; he accepted, therefore, as well as he could, without com-plaint, the inevitable order of nature, and he tried to acquire, although often he failed, that blessed art of taking up lightly and even with a smile whatever he was compelled to handle. 'It is possible,' he said once, 'to consider death too seriously.' He was naturally more than half a Jew; his features were Jewish, his thinking was Jewish, and he believed after a fashion in the Jewish sacred books, or, at anyrate, read them continuously, although he had added to his armoury defensive weapons of another type. In nothing was he more Jewish than in a tendency to dwell upon the One, or what he called God, clinging still to the expression of his forefathers although departing so widely from them. In his ethics and system of life, as well as in his religion, there was the same intolerance of a multiplicity which was not reducible to unity. He seldom explained his theory, but everybody who knew him recognised the difference which it wrought between him and other men. There was a certain concord in everything he said and did, as if it were directed by some enthroned but secret principle.

He had encountered no particular trouble since his wife's death, but his life had been unhappy. He had no friends, much as he longed for friendship, and he could not give any reasons for his failure. He saw other persons more successful, but he remained solitary. Their needs were not so great as his, for it is not those who have the least but those who have the most to give who most want sympathy. He had often made advances ; people had called on him and had appeared interested in him, but they had dropped away. The cause was chiefly to be found in his nationality. The ordinary Englishman disliked him simply as a Jew, and the better sort were repelled by a lack of geniality and by his inability to manifest a healthy interest in personal details. Partly also the cause was that those who care to speak about what is nearest to them are very rare, and most persons find conversation easy in proportion to the remoteness of its topics from them. Whatever the reasons may have been, Baruch now, no matter what the pressure from within might be, generally kept himself to himself. It was a mistake and he ought not to have retreated so far upon repulse. A word will sometimes, when least expected, unlock a heart, a soul is gained for ever, and at once there is much more than a recompense for the indifference of years.

After the death of his wife, Baruch's affection spent itself upon his son Benjamin, whom he had apprenticed to a firm of optical instrument makers in York. The boy was not very much like his father. He was indifferent to that religion by which his father lived, but he inherited an aptitude for mathematics, which was very necessary in his trade. Benjamin also possessed his father's rectitude, trusted him, and looked to him for advice to such a degree that even Baruch, at last, thought it would be better to send him away from home in order that he might become a little more self-reliant and independent. It was the sorest of trials to part with him, and, for some time after he left, Baruch's loneliness was intolerable. It was,

however, relieved by a visit to York perhaps once in four or five months, for whenever business could be alleged as an excuse
for going north, he managed, as he said,
'to take York on his way.'

The day after he met Clara he started for
Birmingham, and although York was certainly
not 'on his way,' he pushed forward to the
city and reached it on a Saturday evening.
He was to spend Sunday there, and on
Sunday morning he proposed that they should
hear the cathedral service, and go for a walk
in the afternoon. To this suggestion Benjamin
partially assented. He wished to go to the
cathedral in the morning, but thought his
father had better rest after dinner. Baruch
somewhat resented the insinuation of possible
fatigue consequent on advancing years.

'What do you mean?' he said; 'you know
well enough I enjoy a walk in the afternoon;
besides, I shall not see much of you,
and do not want to lose what little time I
have.'

About three, therefore, they started, and

presently a girl met them, who was introduced simply as 'Miss Masters.'

'We are going to your side of the water,' said the son ; 'you may as well cross with us.'

They came to a point where a boat was moored, and a man was in it. There was no regular ferry, but on Sundays he earned a trifle by taking people to the opposite meadow, and thus enabling them to vary their return journey to the city. When they were about two-thirds of the way over, Benjamin observed that if they stood up they could see the Minster. They all three rose, and without an instant's warning — they could not tell afterwards how it happened—the boat half capsized, and they were in eight or nine feet of water. Baruch could not swim and went down at once, but on coming up close to the gunwale he caught at it and held fast. Looking round, he saw that Benjamin, who could swim well, had made for Miss Masters, and, having caught her by the back of the neck, was taking her ashore. The

boatman, who could also swim, called out to
Baruch to hold on, gave the boat three or
four vigorous strokes from the stern, and
Baruch felt the ground under his feet.
The boatman's little cottage was not far off,
and, when the party reached it, Benjamin
earnestly desired Miss Masters to take off her
wet clothes and occupy the bed which was
offered her. He himself would run home—
it was not half-a-mile—and, after having
changed, would go to her house and send
her sister with what was wanted. He was
just off when it suddenly struck him that
his father might need some attention.

'Oh, father—' he began, but the boatman's
wife interposed.

'He can't be left like that, and he can't
go home; he'll catch his death o' cold, and
there isn't but one more bed in the house,
and that isn't quite fit to put a gentleman in.
Howsomever, he must turn in there, and my
husband, he can go into the back-kitchen
and rub himself down. You won't do yourself no good, Mr Cohen,' addressing the son,

whom she knew, 'by going back ; you'd better stay here and get into bed with your father.'

In a few minutes the boatman would have gone on the errand, but Benjamin could not lose the opportunity of sacrificing himself for Miss Masters. He rushed off, and in three-quarters of an hour had returned with the sister. Having learned, after anxious inquiry, that Miss Masters, so far as could be discovered, had not caught a chill, he went to his father.

'Well, father, I hope you are none the worse for the ducking,' he said gaily. 'The next time you come to York you'd better bring another suit of clothes with you.'

Baruch turned round uneasily and did not answer immediately. He had had a narrow escape from drowning.

'Nothing of much consequence. Is your friend all right ? '

'Oh, yes ; I was anxious about her, for she is not very strong, but I do not think she will come to much harm. I made them light a fire in her room.'

'Are they drying my clothes?'

'I'll go and see.'

He went away and encountered the elder Miss Masters, who told him that her sister, feeling no ill effects from the plunge, had determined to go home at once, and in fact was nearly ready. Benjamin waited, and presently she came downstairs, smiling.

'Nothing the matter. I owe it to you, however, that I am not now in another world.'

Benjamin was in an ecstasy, and considered himself bound to accompany her to her door.

Meanwhile, Baruch lay upstairs alone in no very happy temper. He heard the conversation below, and knew that his son had gone. In all genuine love there is something of ferocious selfishness. The perfectly divine nature knows how to keep it in check, and is even capable—supposing it to be a woman's nature—of contentment if the loved one is happy, no matter with what or with whom; but the nature only a little less than divine cannot, without pain, endure the

thought that it no longer owns privately
and exclusively that which it loves, even
when it loves a child, and Baruch was particularly excusable, considering his solitude.
Nevertheless, he had learned a little wisdom,
and, what was of much greater importance,
had learned how to use it when he needed
it. It had been forced upon him; it was
an adjustment to circumstances, the wisest
wisdom. It was not something without any
particular connection with him; it was rather
the external protection built up from within
to shield him where he was vulnerable; it
was the answer to questions which had been
put to *him*, and not to those which had
been put to other people. So it came to
pass that, when he said bitterly to himself
that, if he had at that moment being lying
dead at the bottom of the river, Benjamin
would have found consolation very near at
hand, he was able to reflect upon the folly
of self-laceration, and to rebuke himself for
a complaint against what was simply the
order of Nature, and not a personal failure.

His self-conquest, however, was not very permanent. When he left York the next morning, he fancied his son was not particularly grieved, and he was passive under the thought that an epoch in his life had come, that the milestones now began to show the distance to the place to which he travelled, and, still worse, that the boy who had been so close to him, and upon whom he had so much depended, had gone from him.

There is no remedy for our troubles which is uniformly and progressively efficacious. All that we have a right to expect from our religion is that gradually, very gradually, it will assist us to a real victory. After each apparent defeat, if we are bravely in earnest, we gain something on our former position. Baruch was two days on his journey back to town, and as he came nearer home, he recovered himself a little. Suddenly he remembered the bookshop and the book for which he had to call, and that he had intended to ask Marshall something about the bookseller's new assistant.

CHAPTER XX

MADGE was a puzzle to Mrs Caffyn. Mrs Caffyn loved her, and when she was ill had behaved like a mother to her. The newly-born child, a healthy girl, was treated by Mrs Caffyn as if it were her own grand-daughter, and many little luxuries were bought which never appeared in Mrs Marshall's weekly bill. Naturally, Mrs Caffyn's affection moved a response from Madge, and Mrs Caffyn by degrees heard the greater part of her history ; but why she had separated herself from her lover without any apparent reason remained a mystery, and all the greater was the mystery because Mrs Caffyn believed that there were no other facts to be known than those she knew. She longed to bring about a recon-ciliation. It was dreadful to her that Madge should be condemned to poverty, and that her infant should be fatherless, although there was a gentleman waiting to take them both and make them happy.

'The hair won't be dark like yours, my love,' she said one afternoon, soon after Madge had come downstairs and was lying on the sofa. 'The hair do darken a lot, but hers will never be black. It's my opinion as it'll be fair.'

Madge did not speak, and Mrs Caffyn, who was sitting at the head of the couch, put her work and her spectacles on the table. It was growing dusk; she took Madge's hand, which hung down by her side, and gently lifted it up. Such a delicate hand, Mrs Caffyn thought. She was proud that she had for a friend the owner of such a hand, who behaved to her as an equal. It was delightful to be kissed—no mere formal salutations—by a lady fit to go into the finest drawing-room in London, but it was a greater delight that Madge's talk suited her better than any she had heard at Great Oakhurst. It was natural she should rejoice when she discovered, unconsciously that she had a soul, to which the speech of the stars, though somewhat strange, was not an utterly foreign tongue.

She retained her hold on Madge's hand.

'May be,' she continued, 'it'll be like its father's. In our family all the gals take after the father, and all the boys after the mother. I suppose as *he* has lightish hair?'

Still Madge said nothing.

'It isn't easy to believe as the father of that blessed dear could have been a bad lot. I'm sure he isn't, and yet there's that Polesden gal at the farm, she as went wrong with Jim, a great ugly brute, and she herself warnt up to much, well, as I say, her child was the delicatest little angel as I ever saw. It's my belief as God-a-mighty mixes Hisself up in it more nor we think. But there *was* nothing amiss with him, was there, my sweet?'

Mrs Caffyn inclined her head towards Madge.

'Oh, no! Nothing, nothing.'

'Don't you think, my dear, if there's nothing atwixt you, as it was a flyin' in the face of Providence to turn him off? You were reglarly engaged to him, and I have heard you say he was very fond of you. I suppose there were some high words about something, and a kind of a quarrel like, and so you parted, but that's nothing. It might all be made up now, and it ought to be made up. What was it about?'

'There was no quarrel.'

'Well, of course, if you don't like to say anything more to me, I won't ask you. I don't want to hear any secrets as I shouldn't hear. I speak only because I can't abear to see you here when I believe as everything might be put right, and you might have a house of your own, and a good husband, and be happy for the rest of your days. It isn't too late for that now. I know what I know, and as how he'd marry you at once.'

'Oh, my dear Mrs Caffyn, I have no secret from you, who have been so good to me; I can only say I could not love him— not as I ought.'

'If you can't love a man, that is to say if

you can't *abear* him, it's wrong to have him, but if there's a child that does make a difference, for one has to think of the child and of being respectable. There's something in being respectable ; although, for that matter, I've see'd respectable people at Great Oakhurst as were ten times worse than those as aren't. Still, a-speaking for myself, I'd put up with a goodish bit to marry the man whose child wor mine.'

' For myself I could, but it wouldn't be just to him.'

' I don't see what you mean.'

' I mean that I could sacrifice myself if I believed it to be my duty, but I should wrong him cruelly if I were to accept him and did not love him with all my heart.'

' My dear, you take my word for it, he isn't so particklar as you are. A man isn't so particklar as a woman. He goes about his work, and has all sorts of things in his head, and if a woman makes him comfortable when he comes home, he's all right. I won't say as one woman is much the same as another

to a man—leastways to all men—but still they
are *not* particklar. Maybe, though, it isn't
quite the same with gentlefolk like yourself,
—but there's that blessed baby a-cryin'.'

Mrs Caffyn hastened upstairs, leaving Madge
to her reflections. Once more the old dialectic
reappeared. ' After all,' she thought, ' it is, as
Clara said, a question of degree. There are not
a thousand husbands and wives in this great
city whose relationship comes near perfection.
If I felt aversion my course would be clear,
but there is no aversion ; on the contrary, our
affection for one another is sufficient for a
decent household and decent existence undisturbed by catastrophes. No brighter sunlight
is obtained by others far better than myself.
Ought I to expect a refinement of relationship
to which I have no right? Our claims are
always beyond our deserts, and we are disappointed if our poor, mean, defective natures
do not obtain the homage which belongs to
those of ethereal texture. It will be a life with
no enthusiasms nor romance, perhaps, but it will
be tolerable, and what may be called happy,

and my child will be protected and educated. My child! what is there which I ought to put in the balance against her? If our sympathy is not complete, I have my own little oratory: I can keep the candles alight, close the door, and worship there alone.'

So she mused, and her foes again ranged themselves over against her. There was nothing to support her but something veiled, which would not altogether disclose or explain itself. Nevertheless, in a few minutes, her enemies had vanished, like a mist before a sudden wind, and she was once more victorious. Precious and rare are those divine souls, to whom that which is aërial is substantial, the only true substance; those for whom a pale vision possesses an authority they are forced unconditionally to obey.

CHAPTER XXI

MRS CAFFYN was unhappy, and made up her mind that she would talk to Frank herself. She had learned enough about him from the two sisters, especially from Clara, to make her believe that, with a very little management, she could bring him back to Madge. The difficulty was to see him without his father's knowledge. At last she determined to write to him, and she made her son-in-law address the envelope and mark it private. This is what she said :—

'DEAR SIR,—Although unbeknown to you, I take the liberty of telling you as M. H. is a-livin' here with me, and somebody else as I think you ought to see, but perhaps I'd better have a word or two with you myself, if not quite ill-convenient to you, and maybe you'll

be kind enough to say how that's to be done
to your obedient, humble servant,

                              'MRS CAFFYN.'

She thought this very diplomatic, inasmuch
as nobody but Frank could possibly suspect
what the letter meant.   It went to Stoke
Newington, but, alas! he was in Germany, and
poor Mrs Caffyn had to wait a week before she
received a reply.   Frank of course understood
it.   Although he had thought about Madge
continually, he had become calmer.   He saw,
it is true, that there was no stability in his
position, and that he could not possibly remain
where he was.   Had Madge been the commonest
of the common, and his relationship to her the
commonest of the common, he could not permit
her to cast herself loose from him for ever and
take upon herself the whole burden of his mis-
deed.   But he did not know what to do, and,
as successive considerations and reconsiderations
ended in nothing, and the distractions of a
foreign country were so numerous, Madge had
for a time been put aside, like a huge bill which

we cannot pay, and which staggers us. We therefore docket it, and hide it in the desk, and we imagine we have done something. Once again, however, the flame leapt up out of the ashes, vivid as ever. Once again the thought that he had been so close to Madge, and that she had yielded to him, touched him with peculiar tenderness, and it seemed impossible to part himself from her. To a man with any of the nobler qualities of man it is not only a sense of honour which binds him to a woman who has given him all she has to give. Separation seems unnatural, monstrous, a divorce from himself; it is not she alone, but it is himself whom he abandons. Frank's duty, too, pointed imperiously to the path he ought to take, duty to the child as well as to the mother. He determined to go home, secretly; Mrs Caffyn would not have written if she had not seen good reason for believing that Madge still belonged to him. He made up his mind to start the next day, but when the next day came, instructions to go immediately to Hamburg arrived from his father. There were rumours

of the insolvency of a house with which Mr
Palmer dealt ; inquiries were necessary which
could better be made personally, and if these
rumours were correct, as Mr Palmer believed
them to be, his agency must be transferred to
some other firm.   There was now no possibility
of a journey to England.   For a moment he
debated whether, when he was at Hamburg, he
could not slip over to London, but it would
be dangerous.   Further orders might come from
his father, and the failure to acknowledge
them would lead to evasion, and perhaps to
discovery.   He must, therefore, content himself
with a written explanation to Mrs Caffyn why
he could not meet her, and there should be one
more effort to make atonement to Madge.
This was what went to Mrs Caffyn, and to her
lodger :—

'DEAR MADAM, — Your note has reached
me here.   I am very sorry that my engage-
ments are so pressing that I cannot leave
Germany at present.   I have written to Miss
Hopgood.   There is one subject which I

cannot mention to her—I cannot speak to her about money. Will you please give me full information? I enclose £20, and I must trust to your discretion. I thank you heartily for all your kindness.—Truly yours,

'FRANK PALMER.'

'MY DEAREST MADGE,—I cannot help saying one more word to you, although, when I last saw you, you told me that it was useless for me to hope. I know, however, that there is now another bond between us, the child is mine as well as yours, and if I am not all that you deserve, ought you to prevent me from doing my duty to it as well as to you? It is true that if we were to marry I could never right you, and perhaps my father would have nothing to do with us, but in time he might relent, and I will come over at once, or, at least, the moment I have settled some business here, and you shall be my wife. Do, my dearest Madge, consent.'

When he came to this point his pen

stopped. What he had written was very smooth, but very tame and cold. However, nothing better presented itself; he changed his position, sat back in his chair, and searched himself, but could find nothing. It was not always so. Some months ago there would have been no difficulty, and he would not have known when to come to an end. The same thing would have been said a dozen times, perhaps, but it would not have seemed the same to him, and each succeeding repetition would have been felt with the force of novelty. He took a scrap of paper and tried to draft two or three sentences, altered them several times and made them worse. He then re-read the letter; it was too short; but after all it contained what was necessary, and it must go as it stood. She knew how he felt towards her. So he signed it after giving his address at Hamburg, and it was posted.

Three or four days afterwards Mrs Marshall, in accordance with her usual custom, went to see Madge before she was up. The child lay peacefully by its mother's side and Frank's letter was upon the counterpane. The resolution that no letter from him should be opened had been broken. The two women had become great friends and, within the last few weeks, Madge had compelled Mrs Marshall to call her by her Christian name.

'You've had a letter from Mr Palmer; I was sure it was his handwriting when it came late last night.'

'You can read it; there is nothing private in it.'

She turned round to the child and Mrs Marshall sat down and read. When she had finished she laid the letter on the bed again and was silent.

'Well?' said Madge. 'Would you say "No?"'

'Yes, I would.'

'For your own sake, as well as for his?'

Mrs Marshall took up the letter and read half of it again.

'Yes, you had better say "No." You will

find it dull, especially if you have to live in London.'

'Did you find London dull when you came to live in it?'

'Rather; Marshall is away all day long.'

'But scarcely any woman in London expects to marry a man who is not away all day.'

'They ought then to have heaps of work, or they ought to have a lot of children to look after; but, perhaps, being born and bred in the country, I do not know what people in London are. Recollect you were country born and bred yourself, or, at anyrate, you have lived in the country for the most of your life.'

'Dull! we must all expect to be dull.'

'There's nothing worse. I've had rheumatic fever, and I say, give me the fever rather than what comes over me at times here. If Marshall had not been so good to me, I do not know what I should have done with myself.'

Madge turned round and looked Mrs Marshall straight in the face, but she did not flinch.

'Marshall is very good to me, but I was

glad when mother and you and your sister
came to keep me company when he is not at
home. It tired me to have my meals alone :
it is bad for the digestion ; at least, so he says,
and he believes that it was indigestion that was
the matter with me. I should be sorry for
myself if you were to go away ; not that
I want to put that forward. Maybe I should
never see much more of you : he is rich :
you might come here sometimes, but he would
not like to have Marshall and mother and me
at his house.'

Not a word was spoken for at least a minute.

Suddenly Mrs Marshall took Madge's hand
in her own hands, leaned over her, and in that
kind of whisper with which we wake a sleeper
who is to be aroused to escape from sudden
peril, she said in her ear,—

'Madge, Madge : for God's sake leave him ! '

'I have left him.'

'Are you sure ? '

'Quite.'

'For ever ? '

'For ever ! '

Mrs Marshall let go Madge's hand, turned her eyes towards her intently for a moment, and again bent over her as if she were about to embrace her. A knock, however, came at the door, and Mrs Caffyn entered with the cup of coffee which she always insisted on bringing before Madge rose. After she and her daughter had left, Madge read the letter once more. There was nothing new in it, but formally it was something, like the tolling of the bell when we know that our friend is dead. There was a little sobbing, and then she kissed her child with such eagerness that it began to cry.

'You'll answer that letter, I suppose?' said Mrs Caffyn, when they were alone.

'No.'

'I'm rather glad. It would worrit you, and there's nothing worse for a baby than worritin' when it's mother's a-feedin it.'

Mr Caffyn wrote as follows :—

'DEAR SIR,—I was sorry as you couldn't come ; but I believe now as it was better as

you didn't.   I am no scollard, and so no more
from your obedient, humble servant,

'Mrs Caffyn.

'*P.S.*—I return the money, having no use
for the same.'

CHAPTER XXII

BARUCH did not obtain any very definite information from Marshall about Clara. He
was told that she had a sister; that they were
both of them gentlewomen; that their mother
and father were dead; that they were great
readers, and that they did not go to church
nor chapel, but that they both went sometimes
to hear a certain Mr A. J. Scott lecture. He
was once assistant minister to Irving, but was
now heretical, and had a congregation of his
own creating at Woolwich.

Baruch called at the shop and found Clara
once more alone. The book was packed up
and had being lying ready for him for two
or three days. He wanted to speak, but
hardly knew how to begin. He looked
idly round the shelves, taking down one

volume after another, and at last he said,—

'I suppose nobody but myself has ever asked for a copy of Robinson?'

'Not since I have been here.'

'I do not wonder at it; he printed only two hundred and fifty; he gave away five-and-twenty, and I am sure nearly two hundred were sold as wastepaper.'

'He is a friend of yours?'

'He was a friend; he is dead; he was an usher in a private school, although you might have supposed, from the title selected, that he was a clerk. I told him it was useless to publish, and his publishers told him the same thing.'

'I should have thought that some notice would have been taken of him; he is so evidently worth it.'

'Yes, but although he was original and reflective, he had no particular talent. His excellence lay in criticism and observation, often profound, on what came to him every day, and he was valueless in the literary market.

A talent of some kind is necessary to genius if it is to be heard. So he died utterly unrecognised, save by one or two personal friends who loved him dearly. He was peculiar in the depth and intimacy of his friendships. Few men understand the meaning of the word friendship. They consort with certain companions and perhaps very earnestly admire them, because they possess intellectual gifts, but of friendship, such as we two, Morris and I (for that was his real name) understood it, they know nothing.'

'Do you believe, that the good does not necessarily survive?'

'Yes and no; I believe that power every moment, so far as our eyes can follow it, is utterly lost. I have had one or two friends whom the world has never known and never will know, who have more in them than is to be found in many an English classic. I could take you to a little dissenting chapel not very far from Holborn where you would hear a young Welshman, with no education beyond that provided by a Welsh denominational college, who is a perfect orator and whose depth of insight is hardly to be matched, save by Thomas À Kempis, whom he much resembles When he dies he will be forgotten in a dozen years. Besides, it is surely plain enough to everybody that there are thousands of men and women within a mile of us, apathetic and obscure, who, if, an object worthy of them had been presented to them, would have shown themselves capable of enthusiasm and heroism. Huge volumes of human energy are apparently annihilated.'

'It is very shocking, worse to me than the thought of the earthquake or the pestilence.'

'I said " yes and no " and there is another side. The universe is so wonderful, so intricate, that it is impossible to trace the transformation of its forces, and when they seem to disappear the disappearance may be an illusion. Moreover, " waste " is a word which is applicable only to finite resources. If the resources are infinite it has no meaning.'

Two customers came in and Baruch was

obliged to leave. When he came to reflect, he was surprised to find not only how much he had said, but what he had said. He was usually reserved, and with strangers he adhered to the weather or to passing events. He had spoken, however, to this young woman as if they had been acquainted for years. Clara, too, was surprised. She always cut short attempts at conversation in the shop. Frequently she answered questions and receipted and returned bills without looking in the faces of the people who spoke to her or offered her the money. But to this foreigner, or Jew, she had disclosed something she felt. She was rather abashed, but presently her employer, Mr Barnes, returned and somewhat relieved her.

'The gentleman who bought *After Office Hours* came for it while you were out?'

'Oh! what, Cohen? Good fellow Cohen is; he it was who recommended you to me. He is brother-in-law to your landlord.' Clara was comforted; he was not a mere 'casual,' as Mr Barnes called his chance customers.

CHAPTER XXIII

ABOUT a fortnight afterwards, on a Sunday afternoon, Cohen went to the Marshalls'. He had called there once or twice since his mother-in-law came to London, but had seen nothing of the lodgers. It was just about tea-time, but unfortunately Marshall and his wife had gone out. Mrs Caffyn insisted that Cohen should stay, but Madge could not be persuaded to come downstairs, and Baruch, Mrs Caffyn and Clara had tea by themselves. Baruch asked Mrs Caffyn if she could endure London after living for so long in the country.

'Ah! my dear boy, I have to like it.'

'No, you haven't; what you mean is that, whether you like it, or whether you do not, you have to put up with it.'

'No, I don't mean that. Miss Hopgood, Cohen and me, we are the best of friends, but whenever he comes here, he allus begins to argue with me. Howsomever, arguing isn't everything, is it, my dear? There's some things, after all, as I can do and he can't, but he's just wrong here in his arguing; that wasn't what I meant. I meant what I said, as I had to like it.'

'How can you like it if you don't?'

'How can I? That shows you're a man and not a woman. Jess like you men. *You'd* do what you didn't like, I know, for you're a good sort—*and* everybody would know you didn't like it—but what would be the use of me a-livin' in a house if I didn't like it? —with my daughter and these dear, young women? If it comes to livin', you'd ten thousand times better say at once as you hate bein' where you are than go about all day long, as if you was a blessed saint and put upon.'

Mrs Caffyn twitched at her gown and pulled it down over her knees and brushed

the crumbs off with energy. She continued,
'I can't abide people who everlastin' make
believe they are put upon. Suppose I were
allus a-hankering every foggy day after
Great Oakhurst, and yet a-tellin' my daughter
as I knew my place was here ; if I was she,
I should wish my mother at Jericho.'

'Then you really prefer London to Great
Oakhurst?' said Clara.

'Why, my dear, of course I do. Don't
you think it's pleasanter being here with you
and your sister and that precious little creature,
and my daughter, than down in that dead-
alive place? Not that I don't miss my walk
sometimes into Darkin ; you remember that
way as I took you once, Baruch, across the
hill, and we went over Ranmore Common and
I showed you Camilla Lacy, and you said as
you knew a woman who wrote books who
once lived there? You remember them beech-
woods? Ah, it was one October ! Weren't
they a colour—weren't they lovely?'

Baruch remembered them well enough.
Who that had ever seen them could forget them?

'And it was I as took you! You wouldn't think it, my dear, though he's always a-arguin', I do believe he'd love to go that walk again, even with an old woman, and see them heavenly beeches. But, Lord, how I do talk, and you've neither of you got any tea.'

'Have you lived long in London, Miss Hopgood?' inquired Baruch.

'Not very long.'

'Do you feel the change?'

'I cannot say I do not.'

'I suppose, however, you have brought yourself to believe in Mrs Caffyn's philosophy?'

'I cannot say that, but I may say that I am scarcely strong enough for mere endurance, and I therefore always endeavour to find something agreeable in circumstances from which there is no escape.'

The recognition of the One in the Many had as great a charm for Baruch as it had for Socrates, and Clara spoke with the ease of a person whose habit it was to deal with principles and generalisations.

'Yes, and mere toleration, to say nothing

of opposition, at least so far as persons are concerned, is seldom necessary. It is generally thought that what is called dramatic power is a poetic gift, but it is really an indispensable virtue to all of us if we are to be happy.'

Mrs Caffyn did not take much interest in abstract statements. ' You remember,' she said, turning to Baruch, ' that man Chorley as has the big farm on the left-hand side just afore you come to the common ? He wasn't a Surrey man : he came out of the shires.'

' Very well.'

' He's married that Skelton girl ; married her the week afore I left. There isn't no love lost there, but the girl's father said he'd murder him if he didn't, and so it come off. How she ever brought herself to it gets over me. She has that big farm-house, and he's made a fine drawing-room out of the livin' room on the left-hand side as you go in, and put a new grate in the kitchen and turned that into the livin' room, and they does the cooking in the back kitchen, but for all that, if I'd been her,

I'd never have seen his face no more, and I'd have packed off to Australia.'

'Does anybody go near them?'

'Near them! of course they do, and, as true as I'm a-sittin' here, our parson, who married them, went to the breakfast. It isn't Chorley as I blame so much; he's a poor, snivellin' creature, and he was frightened, but it's the girl. She doesn't care for him no more than me, and then again, although, as I tell you, he's such a poor creature, he's awful cruel and mean, and she knows it. But what was I a-goin' to say? Never shall I forget that wedding. You know as it's a short cut to the church across the farmyard at the back of my house. The parson, he was rather late—I suppose he'd been giving himself a finishin' touch—and, as it had been very dry weather, he went across the straw and stuff just at the edge like of the yard. There was a pig under the straw—pigs, my dear,' turning to Clara, 'nuzzle under the straw so as you can't see them. Just as he came to this pig it started up and upset him, and

he fell and straddled across its back, and
the Lord have mercy on me if it didn't
carry him at an awful rate, as if he was a
jockey at Epsom races, till it come to a
puddle of dung water, and then down he
plumped in it. You never see'd a man in
such a pickle! I heer'd the pig a-squeakin'
like mad, and I ran to the door, and I called
out to him, and I says, "Mr Ormiston, won't
you come in here?" and though, as you know,
he allus hated me, he had to come. Mussy
on us, how he did stink, and he saw me
turn up my nose, and he was wild with rage,
and he called the pig a filthy beast. I says
to him as that was the pig's way and the pig
didn't know who it was who was a-ridin' it, and
I took his coat off and wiped his stockings,
and sent to the rectory for another coat, and
he crept up under the hedge to his garden,
and went home, and the people at church
had to wait for an hour. I was glad I was
goin' away from Great Oakhurst, for he
never would have forgiven me.'

There was a ring at the front door bell,

and Clara went to see who was there. It was a runaway ring, but she took the opportunity of going upstairs to Madge.

'She has a sister?' said Baruch.

'Yes, and I may just as well tell you about her now—leastways what I know—and I believe as I know pretty near everything about her. You'll have to be told if they stay here. She was engaged to be married, and how it came about with a girl like that is a bit beyond me, anyhow, there's a child, and the father's a good sort by what I can make out, but she won't have anything more to do with him.'

'What do you mean by "a girl like that."'

'She isn't one of them as goes wrong; she can talk German and reads books.'

'Did he desert her?'

'No, that's just it. She loves me, although I say it, as if I was her mother, and yet I'm just as much in the dark as I was the first day I saw her as to why she left that man.'

Mrs Caffyn wiped the corners of her eyes with her apron.

'It's gospel truth as I never took to anybody as I've took to her.'

After Baruch had gone, Clara returned.

'He's a curious creature, my dear,' said Mrs Caffyn, 'as good as gold, but he's too solemn by half. It would do him a world of good if he'd somebody with him who'd make him laugh more. He *can* laugh, for I've seen him forced to get up and hold his sides, but he never makes no noise. He's a Jew, and they say as them as crucified our blessed Lord never laugh proper.'

CHAPTER XXIV

BARUCH was now in love. He had fallen in love with Clara suddenly and totally. His tendency to reflectiveness did not diminish his passion : it rather augmented it. The men and women whose thoughts are here and there continually are not the people to feel the full force of love. Those who do feel it are those who are accustomed to think of one thing at a time, and to think upon it for a long time. 'No man,' said Baruch once 'can love a woman unless he loves God.' 'I should say,' smilingly replied the Gentile, 'that no man can love God unless he loves a woman.' 'I am right,' said Baruch, 'and so are you.'

But Baruch looked in the glass : his hair, jet black when he was a youth, was marked with grey, and once more the thought came

to him—this time with peculiar force — that
he could not now expect a woman to love him
as she had a right to demand that he should
love, and that he must be silent. He was
obliged to call upon Barnes in about a fortnight's time. He still read Hebrew, and he
had seen in the shop a copy of the Hebrew
translation of the *Moreh Nevochim* of Maimonides, which he greatly coveted, but could not
afford to buy. Like every true book-lover,
he could not make up his mind when he
wished for a book which was beyond his means
that he ought once for all to renounce it, and
he was guilty of subterfuges quite unworthy
of such a reasonable creature in order to de-
lude himself into the belief that he might
yield. For example, he wanted a new over-
coat badly, but determined it was more
prudent to wait, and a week afterwards very
nearly came to the conclusion that as he had
not ordered the coat he had actually accumulated a fund from which the *Moreh Nevochim*
might be purchased. When he came to the
shop he saw Barnes was there, and he

persuaded himself he should have a quieter moment or two with the precious volume when Clara was alone. Barnes, of course, gossiped with everybody.

He therefore called again in the evening, about half an hour before closing time, and found that Barnes had gone home. Clara was busy with a catalogue, the proof of which she was particularly anxious to send to the printer that night. He did not disturb her, but took down the Maimonides, and for a few moments was lost in revolving the doctrine, afterwards repeated and proved by a greater than Maimonides, that the will and power of God are co-extensive: that there is nothing which might be and is not. It was familiar to Baruch, but like all ideas of that quality and magnitude—and there are not many of them—it was always new and affected him like a starry night, seen hundreds of times, yet for ever infinite and original.

But was it Maimonides which kept him till the porter began to put up the shutters? Was he pondering exclusively upon God

P

as the folio lay open before him? He did think about Him, but whether he would have thought about Him for nearly twenty minutes if Clara had not been there is another matter.

'Do you walk home alone?' he said as she gave the proof to the boy who stood waiting.

'Yes, always.'

'I am going to see Marshall to-night, but I must go to Newman Street first. I shall be glad to walk with you, if you do not mind diverging a little.'

She consented and they went along Oxford Street without speaking, the roar of the carriages and waggons preventing a word.

They turned, however, into Bloomsbury, and were able to hear one another. He had much to say and he could not begin to say it. There was a great mass of something to be communicated pent up within him, and he would have liked to pour it all out before her at once. It is just at such times that we often take up as a means of expression and relief that which is absurdly inexpressive and irrelevant.

'I have not seen your sister yet; I hope I may see her this evening.'

'I hope you may, but she frequently suffers from headache and prefers to be alone.'

'How do you like Mr Barnes?'

The answer is not worth recording, nor is any question or answer which was asked or returned for the next quarter of an hour worth recording, although they were so interesting then. When they were crossing Bedford Square on their return Clara happened to say amongst other commonplaces,—

'What a relief a quiet space in London is.'

'I do not mind the crowd if I am by myself.'

'I do not like crowds; I dislike even the word, and dislike " the masses " still more. I do not want to think of human beings as if they were a cloud of dust, and as if each atom had no separate importance. London is often horrible to me for that reason. In the country it was not quite so bad.'

'That is an illusion,' said Baruch after a moment's pause.

'I do not quite understand you, but if it be an illusion it is very painful. In London human beings seem the commonest, cheapest things in the world, and I am one of them. I went with Mr Marshall not long ago to a Free Trade Meeting, and more than two thousand people were present. Everybody told me it was magnificent, but it made me very sad.' She was going on, but she stopped. How was it, she thought again, that she could be so communicative? How was it? How is it that sometimes a stranger crosses our path, with whom, before we have known him for more than an hour, we have no secrets? An hour? we have actually known him for centuries.

She could not understand it, and she felt as if she had been inconsistent with her constant professions of wariness in self-revelation.

'It is an illusion, nevertheless—an illusion of the senses. It is difficult to make what I mean clear, because insight is not possible beyond a certain point, and clearness does not come until penetration is complete and what we acquire is brought into a line with other acquisitions. It constantly happens that we are arrested short of this point, but it would be wrong to suppose that our conclusions, if we may call them so, are of no value.'

She was silent, and he did not go on. At last he said,—

'The illusion lies in supposing that number, quantity and terms of that kind are applicable to any other than sensuous objects, but I cannot go further, at least not now. After all, it is possible here in London for one atom to be of eternal importance to another.'

They had gone quite round Bedford Square without entering Great Russell Street, which was the way eastwards. A drunken man was holding on by the railings of the Square. He had apparently been hesitating for some time whether he could reach the road, and, just as Baruch and Clara came up to him, he made a lurch towards it, and nearly fell over them. Clara instinctively seized Baruch's arm in order to avoid the poor, staggering mortal ; they went once more to the right, and began to com-

plete another circuit. Somehow her arm had
been drawn into Baruch's, and there it remained.

'Have you any friends in London?' said
Baruch.

'There are Mrs Caffyn, her son and
daughter, and there is Mr A. J. Scott. He
was a friend of my father.'

'You mean the Mr Scott who was Irving's
assistant?'

'Yes.'

'An addition—' he was about to say, 'an
additional bond' but he corrected himself. 'A
bond between us; I know Mr Scott.

'Do you really? I suppose you know many
interesting people in London, as you are in
his circle.'

'Very few; weeks, months have passed
since anybody has said as much to me as
you have.'

His voice quivered a little, for he was trembling with an emotion quite inexplicable by
mere intellectual relationship. Something came
through Clara's glove as her hand rested on

his wrist which ran through every nerve and sent the blood into his head.

Clara felt his excitement and dreaded lest he should say something to which she could give no answer, and when they came opposite Great Russell Street, she withdrew her arm from his, and began to cross to the opposite pavement. She turned the conversation towards some indifferent subject, and in a few minutes they were at Great Ormond Street. Baruch would not go in as he had intended; he thought it was about to rain, and he was late. As he went along he became calmer, and when he was fairly indoors he had passed into a despair entirely inconsistent—superficially—with the philosopher Baruch, as inconsistent as the irrational behaviour in Bedford Square. He could well enough interpret, so he believed, Miss Hopgood's suppression of him. Ass that he was not to see what he ought to have known so well, that he was playing the fool to her; he, with a grown-up son, to pretend to romance with a girl! At that moment she might be mocking him, or, if she was too good for mockery, she might be contriving to avoid or to quench him. The next time he met her, he would be made to understand that he was *pitied*, and perhaps he would then learn the name of the youth who was his rival, and had won her. He would often meet her, no doubt, but of what value would anything he could say be to her. She could not be expected to make fine distinctions, and there was a class of elderly men, to which of course he would be assigned, but the thought was too horrible. . . .

Perhaps his love for Clara might be genuine ; perhaps it was not. He had hoped that as he grew older he might be able really to *see* a woman, but he was once more like one of the possessed. It was not Clara Hopgood who was before him, it was hair, lips, eyes, just as it was twenty years ago, just as it was with the commonest shop-boy he met, who had escaped from the counter, and was waiting at an area gate. It was terrible to him to find that he had so nearly lost his self-control, but upon this point he was unjust to himself, for we are often more distinctly aware of the strength of the temptation than of the authority within us, which falteringly, but decisively, enables us at last to resist it.

Then he fell to meditating how little his studies had done for him. What was the use of them? They had not made him any stronger, and he was no better able than other people to resist temptation. After twenty years' continuous labour he found himself capable of the vulgarest, coarsest faults and failings from which the remotest skiey influence in his begetting might have saved him.

Clara was not as Baruch. No such storm as that which had darkened and disheartened him could pass over her, but she could love, perhaps better than he, and she began to love him. It was very natural to a woman such as Clara, for she had met a man who had said to her that what she believed was really of some worth. Her father and mother had been very dear to her; her sister was very dear to her, but she had never received any such recognition as that which had now been offered to her : her own self had never been returned to her with such honour. She thought, too—why should she not think it?—of the future, of the release from her dreary occupation, of a happy home with independence, and she thought of the children that might be. She lay down without any misgiving. She was sure he was in love with her ; she did not know much of him, certainly, in the usual meaning of the word, but she knew enough. She would like to find out more of his history ; perhaps without exciting suspicion she might obtain it from Mrs Caffyn.

CHAPTER XXV

Mr Frank Palmer was back again in England. He was much distressed when he received that last letter from Mrs Caffyn, and discovered that Madge's resolution not to write remained unshaken. He was really distressed, but he was not the man upon whom an event, however deeply felt at the time, could score a furrow which could not be obliterated. If he had been a dramatic personage, what had happened to him would have been the second act leading to a fifth, in which the Fates would have appeared, but life seldom arranges itself in proper poetic form. A man determines that he must marry; he makes the shop-girl an allowance, never sees her or her child again, transforms himself into a model husband, is beloved by his wife

and family ; the woman whom he kissed as
he will never kiss his lawful partner, withdraws
completely, and nothing happens to him.

Frank was sure he could never love anybody as he had loved Madge, nor could
he cut indifferently that other cord which
bound him to her. Nobody in society expects
the same paternal love for the offspring of
a housemaid or a sempstress as for the child
of the stockbroker's or brewer's daughter,
and nobody expects the same obligations, but
Frank was not a society youth, and Madge
was his equal. A score of times, when his
fancy roved, the rope checked him as suddenly
as if it were the lasso of a South American
Gaucho. But what could he do? that was
the point. There were one or two things
which he could have done, perhaps, and one
or two things which he could not have done
if he had been made of different stuff, but
there was nothing more to be done which
Frank Palmer could do. After all, it was
better that Madge should be the child's
mother than that it should belong to some

peasant. At least it would be properly
educated. As to money, Mrs Caffyn had
told him expressly that she did not want
it. That might be nothing but pride, and
he resolved, without very‚ clearly seeing how,
and without troubling himself for the moment
as to details, that Madge should be entirely
and handsomely supported by him. Meanwhile it was of great importance that he
should behave in such a manner as to raise
no suspicion. He did not particularly care
for some time after his return from Germany
to go out to the musical parties to which
he was constantly invited, but he went as a
duty, and wherever he went he met his
charming cousin. They always sang together ;
they had easy opportunities of practising
together, and Frank, although nothing definite
was said to him, soon found that his family
and hers considered him destined for her.
He could not retreat, and there was no
surprise manifested by anybody when it was
rumoured that they were engaged. His story
may as well be finished at once. He and

Miss Cecilia Morland were married. A few
days before the wedding, when some legal
arrangements and settlements were necessary,
Frank made one last effort to secure an
income for Madge, but it failed. Mrs Caffyn
met him by appointment, but he could not
persuade her even to be the bearer of a
message to Madge. He then determined to
confess his fears. To his great relief Mrs
Caffyn of her own accord assured him that he
never need dread any disturbance or betrayal.

'There are three of us,' she said, 'as knows
you—Miss Madge, Miss Clara and myself—
and, as far as you are concerned, we are dead
and buried. I can't say as I was altogether
of Miss Madge's way of looking at it at
first, and I thought it ought to have been
different, though I believe now as she's
right, but,' and the old woman suddenly
fired up as if some bolt from heaven had
kindled her, 'I pity you, sir—*you*, sir, I say—
more nor I do her. You little know what
you've lost, the blessedest, sweetest, ah, and the
cleverest creature, too, as ever I set eyes on.

'But, Mrs Caffyn,' said Frank, with much emotion, 'it was not I who left her, you know it was not, and, and even—'

The word 'now' was coming, but it did not come.

'Ah,' said Mrs Caffyn, with something like scorn, '*I* know, yes, I do know. It was she, you needn't tell me that, but, God-a-mighty in heaven, if I'd been you, I'd have laid myself on the ground afore her, I'd have tore my heart out for her, and I'd have said, "No other woman in this world but you"—but there, what a fool I am! Good-bye, Mr Palmer.'

She marched away, leaving Frank very miserable, and, as he imagined, unsettled, but he was not so. The fit lasted all day, but when he was walking home that evening, he met a poor friend whose wife was dying.

'I am so grieved,' said Frank 'to hear of your trouble—no hope?'

'None, I am afraid.'

'It is very dreadful.'

'Yes, it is hard to bear, but to what is inevitable we must submit.'

This new phrase struck Frank very much, and it seemed very philosophic to him, a maxim for guidance through life. It did not strike him that it was generally either a platitude or an excuse for weakness, and that a nobler duty is to find out what is inevitable and what is not, to declare boldly that what the world oftentimes affirms to be inevitable is really evitable, and heroically to set about making it so. Even if revolt be perfectly useless, we are not particularly drawn to a man who prostrates himself too soon and is incapable of a little cursing.

As it was impossible to provide for Madge and the child now, Frank considered whether he could not do something for them in the will which he had to make before his marriage. He might help his daughter if he could not help the mother.

But his wife would perhaps survive him, and the discovery would cause her and her children much misery; it would damage his character with them and inflict positive moral mischief. The will, therefore, did not mention Madge, and it was not necessary to tell his secret to his solicitor.

The wedding took place amidst much rejoicing ; everybody thought the couple were most delightfully matched ; the presents were magnificent ; the happy pair went to Switzerland, came back and settled in one of the smaller of the old, red brick houses in Stoke Newington, with a lawn in front, always shaved and trimmed to the last degree of smoothness and accuracy, with paths on whose gravel not the smallest weed was ever seen, and with a hot-house that provided the most luscious black grapes. There was a grand piano in the drawing-room, and Frank and Cecilia became more musical than ever, and Waltham Lodge was the headquarters of a little amateur orchestra which practised Mozart and Haydn, and gave local concerts. A twelvemonth after the marriage a son was born and Frank's father increased Frank's share in the business. Mr Palmer had long ceased to take any interest in the Hopgoods. He considered that Madge had treated Frank shamefully in jilting him, but was convinced that he was fortunate in his escape. It was clear that she was unstable ; she probably threw him overboard for somebody more attractive, and she was not the woman to be a wife to his son.

One day Cecilia was turning out some drawers belonging to her husband, and she found a dainty little slipper wrapped up in white tissue paper. She looked at it for a long time, wondering to whom it could have belonged, and had half a mind to announce her discovery to Frank, but she was a wise woman and forbore. It lay underneath some neckties which were not now worn, two or three silk pocket handkerchiefs also discarded, and some manuscript books containing school themes. She placed them on the top of the drawers as if they had all been taken out in a lump and the slipper was at the bottom.

' Frank my dear,' she said after dinner, ' I emptied this morning one of the drawers in the attic. I wish you would look over the things and decide what you wish to keep. I have not examined them, but they seem to be mostly rubbish.'

He went upstairs after he had smoked his cigar and read his paper. There was the slipper! It all came back to him, that never-to-be-forgotten night, when she rebuked him for the folly of kissing her foot, and he begged the slipper and determined to preserve it for ever, and thought how delightful it would be to take it out and look at it when he was an old man. Even now he did not like to destroy it, but Cecilia might have seen it and might ask him what he had done with it, and what could he say? Finally he decided to burn it. There was no fire, however, in the room, and while he stood meditating, Cecilia called him. He replaced the slipper in the drawer. He could not return that evening, but he intended to go back the next morning, take the little parcel away in his pocket and burn it at his office. At breakfast some letters came which put everything else out of mind. The first thing he did that evening was to revisit the garret, but the slipper had gone. Cecilia had been there and had found it carefully folded up in the drawer. She pulled it out, snipped and tore it into fifty pieces, carried them downstairs, threw them on the dining-room fire, sat down before it, poking them further and further into the flames, and watched them till every vestige had vanished. Frank did not like to make any inquiries ; Cecilia made none, and thenceforward no trace existed at Waltham Lodge of Madge Hopgood.

CHAPTER XXVI

Baruch went neither to Barnes's shop nor
to the Marshalls for nearly a month. One
Sunday morning he was poring over the
Moreh Nevochim, for it had proved too
powerful a temptation for him, and he fell
upon the theorem that without God the
Universe could not continue to exist, for
God is its Form. It was one of those say-
ings which may be nothing or much to the
reader. Whether it be nothing or much
depends upon the quality of his mind.

There was certainly nothing in it particularly adapted to Baruch's condition at that
moment, but an antidote may be none the
less efficacious because it is not direct. It
removed him to another region. It was like
the sight and sound of the sea to the man

who has been in trouble in an inland city.
His self-confidence was restored, for he to
whom an idea is revealed becomes the idea,
and is no longer personal and consequently
poor.

His room seemed too small for him; he shut
his book and went to Great Ormond Street.
He found there Marshall, Mrs Caffyn, Clara
and a friend of Marshall's named Dennis.

'Where is your wife?' said Baruch to
Marshall.

'Gone with Miss Madge to the Catholic
chapel to hear a mass of Mozart's.'

'Yes,' said Mrs Caffyn. 'I tell them
they'll turn Papists if they do not mind.
They are always going to that place, and
there's no knowing, so I've hear'd, what
them priests can do. They aren't like our
parsons. Catch that man at Great Oakhurst
a-turnin' anybody.'

'I suppose,' said Baruch to Clara, 'it is
the music takes your sister there?'

'Mainly, I believe, but perhaps not entirely.'

'What other attraction can there be?'

'I am not in the least disposed to become a convert. Once for all, Catholicism is incredible and that is sufficient, but there is much in its ritual which suits me. There is no such intrusion of the person of the minister as there is in the Church of England, and still worse amongst dissenters. In the Catholic service the priest is nothing; it is his office which is everything; he is a mere means of communication. The mass, in so far as it proclaims that miracle is not dead, is also very impressive to me.'

'I do not quite understand you,' said Marshall, 'but if you once chuck your reason overboard, you may just as well be Catholic as Protestant. Nothing can be more ridiculous than the Protestant objection, on the ground of absurdity, to the story of the saint walking about with his head under his arm.'

The tea things had been cleared away, and Marshall was smoking. Both he and Dennis were Chartists, and Baruch had interrupted a debate upon a speech delivered at a

Chartist meeting that morning by Henry Vincent.

Frederick Dennis was about thirty, tall and rather loose-limbed. He wore loose clothes, his neck-cloth was tied in a big, loose knot, his feet were large and his boots were heavy. His face was quite smooth, and his hair, which was very thick and light brown, fell across his forehead in a heavy wave with just two complete undulations in it from the parting at the side to the opposite ear. It had a trick of tumbling over his eyes, so that his fingers were continually passed through it to brush it away. He was a wood engraver, or, as he preferred to call himself, an artist, but he also wrote for the newspapers, and had been a contributor to the *Northern Star*. He was well brought up and was intended for the University, but he did not stick to his Latin and Greek, and as he showed some talent for drawing he was permitted to follow his bent. His work, however, was not of first-rate quality, and consequently orders were not abundant. This was the reason why he had turned to literature. When he had any books to illustrate he lived upon what they brought him, and when there were no books he renewed his acquaintance with politics. If books and newspapers both failed, he subsisted on a little money which had been left him, stayed with friends as long as he could, and amused himself by writing verses which showed much command over rhyme.

'I cannot stand Vincent,' said Marshall, 'he is too flowery for me, and he does not belong to the people. He is middle-class to the backbone.'

'He is deficient in ideas,' said Dennis.

'It is odd,' continued Marshall, turning to Cohen, 'that your race never takes any interest in politics.'

'My race is not a nation, or, if a nation, has no national home. It took an interest in politics when it was in its own country, and produced some rather remarkable political writing.'

'But why do you care so little for what is going on now?'

'I do care, but all people are not born to be agitators, and, furthermore, I have doubts if the Charter will accomplish all you expect.'

'I know what is coming'—Marshall took the pipe out of his mouth and spoke with perceptible sarcasm—'the inefficiency of merely external remedies, the folly of any attempt at improvement which does not begin with the improvement of individual character, and that those to whom we intend to give power are no better than those from whom we intend to take it away. All very well, Mr Cohen. My answer is that at the present moment the stockingers in Leicester are earning four shillings and sixpence a week. It is not a question whether they are better or worse than their rulers. They want something to eat, they have nothing, and their masters have more than they can eat.'

'Apart altogether from purely material reasons,' said Dennis, 'we have rights; we are born into this planet without our consent, and, therefore, we may make certain demands.'

'Do you not think,' said Clara, 'that the repeal of the corn laws will help you?'

Dennis smiled and was about to reply, but Marshall broke out savagely,—

'Repeal of the corn laws is a contemptible device of manufacturing selfishness. It means low wages. Do you suppose the great Manchester cotton lords care one straw for their hands? Not they! They will face a revolution for repeal because it will enable them to grind an extra profit out of us.'

'I agree with you entirely,' said Dennis, turning to Clara, 'that a tax upon food is wrong; it is wrong in the abstract. The notion of taxing bread, the fruit of the earth, is most repulsive; but the point is—what is our policy to be? If a certain end is to be achieved, we must neglect subordinate ends, and, at times, even contradict what our own principles would appear to dictate. That is the secret of successful leadership.'

He took up the poker and stirred the fire.

'That will do, Dennis,' said Marshall, who was evidently fidgety. 'The room is rather warm. There's nothing in Vincent which irritates me more than those bits of poetry with which he winds up.

" God made the man—man made the slave,"

and all that stuff. If God made the man, God made the slave. I know what Vincent's little game is, and it is the same game with all his set. They want to keep Chartism religious, but we shall see. Let us once get the six points, and the Established Church will go, and we shall have secular education, and in a generation there will not be one superstition left.'

'Theological superstition, you mean?' said Clara.

'Yes, of course, what others are there worth notice?'

'A few. The superstition of the ordinary newspaper reader is just as profound, and the tyranny of the majority may be just as injurious as the superstition of a Spanish peasant, or the tyranny of the Inquisition.'

'Newspapers will not burn people as the

priests did and would do again if they had the power, and they do not insult us with fables and a hell and a heaven.'

'I maintain,' said Clara with emphasis, 'that if a man declines to examine, and takes for granted what a party leader or a newspaper tells him, he has no case against the man who declines to examine, or takes for granted what the priest tells him. Besides, although, as you know, I am not a convert myself, I do lose a little patience when I hear it preached as a gospel to every poor conceited creature who goes to your Sunday evening atheist lecture, that he is to believe nothing on one particular subject which his own precious intellect cannot verify, and the next morning he finds it to be his duty to swallow wholesale anything you please to put into his mouth. As to the tyranny, the day may come, and I believe is approaching, when the majority will be found to be more dangerous than any ecclesiastical establishment which ever existed.'

Baruch's lips moved, but he was silent. He

was not strong in argument. He was thinking about Marshall's triumphant inquiry whether God is not responsible for slavery. He would have liked to say something on that subject, but he had nothing ready.

'Practical people,' said Dennis, who had not quite recovered from the rebuke as to the warmth of the room, 'are often most unpractical and injudicious. Nothing can be more unwise than to mix up politics and religion. If you *do*,' Dennis waved his hand, 'you will have all the religious people against you. My friend Marshall, Miss Hopgood, is under the illusion that the Church in this country is tottering to its fall. Now, although I myself belong to no sect, I do not share his illusion; nay, more, I am not sure'—Mr Dennis spoke slowly, rubbed his chin and looked up at the ceiling—'I am not sure that there is not something to be said in favour of State endowment—at least, in a country like Ireland.'

'Come along, Dennis, we shall be late,' said Marshall, and the two forthwith took their departure in order to attend another meeting.

'Much either of 'em knows about it,' said Mrs Caffyn when they had gone. 'There's Marshall getting two pounds a week reg'lar, and goes on talking about people at Leicester, and he has never been in Leicester in his life ; and, as for that Dennis, he knows less than Marshall, for he does nothing but write for newspapers and draw for picture-books, never nothing what you may call work, and he does worrit me so whenever he begins about poor people that I can't sit still. *I* do know what the poor is, having lived at Great Oakhurst all these years.'

'You are not a Chartist, then?' said Baruch.

'Me—me a Chartist? No, I ain't, and yet, maybe, I'm something worse. What would be the use of giving them poor creatures votes? Why, there isn't one of them as wouldn't hold up his hand for anybody as would give him a shilling. Quite right of 'em, too, for the one thing they have to think about from morning to night is how to get a bit of something to fill their bellies, and they won't fill them by voting.'

'But what would you do for them?'

'Ah! that beats me! Hang somebody, but I don't know who it ought to be. There's a family by the name of Longwood, they live just on the slope of the hill nigh the Dower Farm, and there's nine of them, and the youngest when I left was a baby six months old, and their living-room faces the road so that the north wind blows in right under the door, and I've seen the snow lie in heaps inside. As reg'lar as winter comes Longwood is knocked off—no work. I've knowed them not have a bit of meat for weeks together, and him a-loungin' about at the corner of the street. Wasn't that enough to make him feel as if somebody ought to be killed? And Marshall and Dennis say as the proper thing to do is to give him a vote, and prove to him there was never no Abraham nor Isaac, and that Jonah never was in a whale's belly, and that nobody had no business to have more children than he could feed. And what goes on, and what must go on, inside such a place as Longwood's, with him and his wife, and with them boys and gals all huddled together— But I'd better hold my tongue. We'll let the smoke out of this room, I think, and air it a little.'

She opened the window, and Baruch rose and went home.

Whenever Mrs Caffyn talked about the labourers at Great Oakhurst, whom she knew so well, Clara always felt as if all her reading had been a farce, and, indeed, if we come into close contact with actual life, art, poetry and philosophy seem little better than trifling. When the mist hangs over the heavy clay land in January, and men and women shiver in the bitter cold and eat raw turnips, to indulge in fireside ecstasies over the divine Plato or Shakespeare is surely not such a virtue as we imagine it to be.

CHAPTER XXVII

BARUCH sat and mused before he went to bed. He had gone out stirred by an idea, but it was already dead. Then he began to think about Clara. Who was this Dennis who visited the Marshalls and the Hopgoods? Oh! for an hour of his youth! Fifteen years ago the word would have come unbidden if he had seen Clara, but now, in place of the word, there was hesitation, shame. He must make up his mind to renounce for ever. But, although this conclusion had forced itself upon him overnight as inevitable, he could not resist the temptation when he rose the next morning of plotting to meet Clara, and he walked up and down the street opposite the shop door that evening nearly a quarter of an hour, just before closing time, hoping that

she might come out and that he might have
the opportunity of overtaking her apparently
by accident. At last, fearing he might miss
her, he went in and found she had a companion
whom he instantly knew, before any introduction, to be her sister. Madge was not now
the Madge whom we knew at Fenmarket.
She was thinner in the face and paler. Nevertheless, she was not careless; she was even
more particular in her costume, but it was
simpler. If anything, perhaps, she was a little
prouder. She was more attractive, certainly,
than she had ever been, although her face
could not be said to be handsomer. The slight
prominence of the cheek-bone, the slight hollow
underneath, the loss of colour, were perhaps
defects, but they said something which had
a meaning in it superior to that of the tint
of the peach. She had been reading a book
while Clara was balancing her cash, and she
attempted to replace it. The shelf was a little
too high, and the volume fell upon the ground.
It contained Shelley's *Revolt of Islam*.

'Have you read Shelley?' said Baruch.

'Every line—when I was much younger.'

'Do you read him now?'

'Not much. I was an enthusiast for him when I was nineteen, but I find that his subject matter is rather thin, and his themes are a little worn. He was entirely enslaved by the ideals of the French Revolution. Take away what the French Revolution contributed to his poetry, and there is not much left.'

'As a man he is not very attractive to me.'

'Nor to me; I never shall forgive his treatment of Harriet.'

'I suppose he had ceased to love her, and he thought, therefore, he was justified in leaving her.'

Madge turned and fixed her eyes, unobserved, on Baruch. He was looking straight at the bookshelves. There was not, and, indeed, how could there be, any reference to herself.

'I should put it in this way,' she said, 'that he thought he was justified in sacrificing a woman for the sake of an *impulse*. Call this a defect or a crime—whichever you like—it

is repellent to me.   It makes no difference to
me to know that he believed the impulse to
be divine.'

'I wish,' interrupted Clara, 'you two would
choose less exciting subjects of conversation ;
my totals will not come right.'

They were silent, and Baruch, affecting to
study a Rollin's *Ancient History*, wondered,
especially when he called to mind Mrs Caffyn's
report, what this girl's history could have been.
He presently recovered himself, and it occurred
to him that he ought to give some reason
why he had called.   Before, however, he was
able to offer any excuse, Clara closed her
book.

'Now, it is right,' she said, 'and I am
ready.'

Just at that moment Barnes appeared, hot
with hurrying.

'Very sorry, Miss Hopgood, to ask you
to stay for a few minutes.   I recollected after
I left that the doctor particularly wanted those
books sent off to-night.   I should not like
to disappoint him.   I have been to the booking-

office, and the van will be here in about twenty
minutes. If you will make out the invoice
and check me, I will pack them.'

'I will be off,' said Madge. 'The shop
will be shut if I do not make haste.'

'You are not going alone, are you?' said
Baruch. 'May I not go with you, and cannot
we both come back for your sister?'

'It is very kind of you.'

Clara looked up from her desk, watched
them as they went out at the door and, for a
moment, seemed lost. Barnes turned round.

'Now, Miss Hopgood.' She started.

'Yes, sir.'

'*Fabricius, J. A. Bibliotheca Ecclesiastica in
qua continentur.*'

'I need not put in the last three words.'

'Yes, yes.' Barnes never liked to be corrected in a title. 'There's another *Fabricius
Bibliotheca* or *Bibliographia.* Go on—*Basili
opera ad MSS. codices,* 3 vols.'

Clara silently made the entries a little more
scholarly. In a quarter of an hour the parcel
was ready and Cohen returned.

'Your sister would not allow me to wait. She met Mrs Marshall; they said they should have something to carry, and that it was not worth while to bring it here. I will walk with you, if you will allow me. We may as well avoid Holborn.'

They turned into Gray's Inn, and, when they were in comparative quietude, he said,—

'Any Chartist news?' and then without waiting for an answer, 'By the way, who is your friend Dennis?'

'He is no particular friend of mine. He is a wood-engraver, and writes also, I believe, for the newspapers.'

'He can talk as well as write.'

'Yes, he can talk very well.'

'Do you not think there was something unreal about what he said?'

'I do not believe he is actually insincere. I have noticed that men who write or read much often appear somewhat shadowy.'

'How do you account for it?'

'What they say is not experience.'

'I do not quite understand. A man may

think much which can never become an experience in your sense of the word, and be very much in earnest with what he thinks ; the thinking is an experience.'

' Yes, I suppose so, but it is what a person has gone through which I like to hear. Poor Dennis has suffered much. You are perhaps surprised, but it is true, and when he leaves politics alone he is a different creature.'

' I am afraid I must be very uninteresting to you ? '

' I did not mean that I care for nothing but my friend's aches and pains, but that I do not care for what he just takes up and takes on.'

' It is my misfortune that my subjects are not very—I was about to say—human. Perhaps it is because I am a Jew.'

' I do not know quite what you mean by your "subjects," but if you mean philosophy and religion, they are human.'

' If they are, very few people like to hear anything about them. Do you know, Miss

Hopgood, I can never talk to anybody as I can to you.'

Clara made no reply. A husband was to be had for a look, for a touch, a husband whom she could love, a husband who could give her all her intellect demanded. A little house rose before her eyes as if by Arabian enchantment ; there was a bright fire on the hearth, and there were children round it ; without the look, the touch, there would be solitude, silence and a childless old age, so much more to be feared by a woman than by a man. Baruch paused, waiting for her answer, and her tongue actually began to move with a reply, which would have sent his arm round her, and made them one for ever, but it did not come. Something fell and flashed before her like lightning from a cloud overhead, divinely beautiful, but divinely terrible.

'I remember,' she said, 'that I have to call in Lamb's Conduit Street to buy something for my sister. I shall just be in time.' Baruch went as far as Lamb's Conduit Street with her. He, too, would have determined his own destiny if she had uttered the word, but the power to proceed without it was wanting and he fell back. He left her at the door of the shop. She bid him good-bye, obviously intending that he should go no further with her, and he shook hands with her, taking her hand again and shaking it again with a grasp which she knew well enough was too fervent for mere friendship. He then wandered back once more to his old room at Clerkenwell. The fire was dead, he stirred it, the cinders fell through the grate and it dropped out all together. He made no attempt to rekindle it, but sat staring at the black ashes, not thinking, but dreaming. Thirty years more perhaps with no change! The last chance that he could begin a new life had disappeared. He cursed himself that nothing drove him out of himself with Marshall and his fellow-men; that he was not Chartist nor revolutionary; but it was impossible to create in himself enthusiasm for a cause. He had tried before to become a patriot and had failed, and was conscious, during the trial, that he was pretending to be something he was not and could not be. There was nothing to be done but to pace the straight road in front of him, which led nowhere, so far as he could see.

CHAPTER XXVIII

A MONTH afterwards Marshall announced that he intended to pay a visit.

'I am going,' he said, 'to see Mazzini. Who will go with me?'

Clara and Madge were both eager to accompany him. Mrs Caffyn and Mrs Marshall chose to stay at home.

'I shall ask Cohen to come with us,' said Marshall. 'He has never seen Mazzini and would like to know him. Cohen accordingly called one Sunday evening, and the party went together to a dull, dark, little house in a shabby street of small shops and furnished apartments. When they knocked at Mazzini's door Marshall asked for Mr —— for, even in England, Mazzini had an assumed name which was always used when inquiries were made for him. They were shown upstairs into a rather mean room, and found there a man, really about forty, but looking older. He had dark hair growing away from his forehead, dark moustache, dark beard and a singularly serious face. It was not the face of a conspirator, but that of a saint, although without that just perceptible touch of silliness which spoils the faces of most saints. It was the face of a saint of the Reason, of a man who could be ecstatic for rational ideals, rarest of all endowments. It was the face, too, of one who knew no fear, or, if he knew it, could crush it. He was once concealed by a poor woman whose house was surrounded by Austrian soldiers watching for him. He was determined that she should not be sacrificed, and, having disguised himself a little, walked out into the street in broad daylight, went up to the Austrian sentry, asked for a light for his cigar and escaped. He was cordial in his reception of his visitors, particularly of Clara, Madge and Cohen, whom he had not seen before.

'The English,' he said, after some preliminary conversation, 'are a curious people. As a nation they are what they call practical and have a contempt for ideas, but I have known some Englishmen who have a religious belief in them, a nobler belief than I have found in any other nation. There are English women, also, who have this faith, and one or two are amongst my dearest friends.'

'I never,' said Marshall, 'quite comprehend you on this point. I should say that we know as clearly as most folk what we want, and we mean to have it.'

'That may be, but it is not Justice, as Justice which inspires you. Those of you who have not enough, desire to have more, that is all.'

'If we are to succeed, we must preach what the people understand.'

'Pardon me, that is just where you and I differ. Whenever any real good is done it is by a crusade; that is to say, the cross must be raised and appeal be made to something *above* the people. No system based on rights will stand. Never will society be permanent till it is founded on duty. If we consider our rights exclusively, we extend them over the rights of our neighbours. If the oppressed classes had the power to obtain their rights to-morrow, and with the rights came no deeper sense of duty, the new order, for the simple reason that the oppressed are no better than their oppressors, would be just as unstable as that which preceded it.'

'To put it in my own language,' said Madge, 'you believe in God.'

Mazzini leaned forward and looked earnestly at her.

'My dear young friend, without that belief I should have no other.'

'I should like, though,' said Marshall, 'to see the church which would acknowledge you and Miss Madge, or would admit your God to be theirs.'

'What is essential,' replied Madge, 'in a belief in God is absolute loyalty to a principle we know to have authority.'

'It may, perhaps,' said Mazzini, 'be more to me, but you are right, it is a belief in the supremacy and ultimate victory of the conscience.'

'The victory seems distant in Italy now,' said Baruch. 'I do not mean the millennial victory of which you speak, but an approximation to it by the overthrow of tyranny there.'

'You are mistaken ; it is far nearer than you imagine.'

'Do you obtain,' said Clara, 'any real help from people here? Do you not find that they merely talk and express what they call their sympathy?'

'I must not say what help I have received ; more than words, though, from many.'

'You expect, then,' said Baruch, 'that the Italians will answer your appeal?'

'If I had no faith in the people, I do not see what faith could survive.'

'The people are the persons you meet in the street.'

'A people is not a mere assemblage of uninteresting units, but it is not a phantom. A spirit lives in each nation which is superior to any individual in it. It is this which is the true reality, the nation's purpose and destiny, it is this for which the patriot lives and dies.'

'I suppose,' said Clara, 'you have no difficulty in obtaining volunteers for any dangerous enterprise?'

'None. You would be amazed if I were to tell you how many men and women at this very moment would go to meet certain death if I were to ask them.'

'Women?'

'Oh, yes; and women are of the greatest use, but it is rather difficult to find those who have the necessary qualifications.'

'I suppose you employ them in order to obtain secret information?'

'Yes; amongst the Austrians.'

The party broke up. Baruch manœuvred to walk with Clara, but Marshall wanted to borrow a book from Mazzini, and she stayed behind for him. Madge was outside in the street, and Baruch could do nothing but go to her. She seemed unwilling to wait, and Baruch and she went slowly homewards, thinking the others would overtake them. The conversation naturally turned upon Mazzini.

'Although,' said Madge, 'I have never seen him before, I have heard much about him and he makes me sad.'

'Why?'

'Because he has done something worth doing and will do more.'

'But why should that make you sad?'

'I do not think there is anything sadder than to know you are able to do a little good and would like to do it, and yet you are not permitted to do it. Mazzini has a world open to him large enough for the exercise of all his powers.'

'It is worse to have a desire which is intense but not definite, to be continually anxious to do something, you know not what, and always to feel, if any distinct task is offered, your incapability of attempting it.'

'A man, if he has a real desire to be of any service, can generally gratify it to some extent; a woman as a rule cannot, although a woman's enthusiasm is deeper than a man's. You can join Mazzini to-morrow, I suppose, if you like.'

'It is a supposition not quite justifiable, and if I were free to go I could not.'

'Why?'

'I am not fitted for such work; I have not sufficient faith. When I see a flag waving, a doubt always intrudes. Long ago I was forced to the conclusion that I should have to be content with a life which did not extend outside itself.'

'I am sure that many women blunder into the wrong path, not because they are bad, but simply because—if I may say so—they are too good.'

'Maybe you are right. The inability to obtain mere pleasure has not produced the misery which has been begotten of mistaken or baffled self-sacrifice. But do you mean to say that you would like to enlist under Mazzini?'

'No!'

Baruch thought she referred to her child, and he was silent.

'You are a philosopher,' said Madge, after a pause. 'Have you never discovered anything which will enable us to submit to be useless?'

'That is to say, have I discovered a religion? for the core of religion is the relationship of the individual to the whole, the faith that the poorest and meanest of us is a person. That is the real strength of all religions.'

'Well, go on; what do you believe?'

'I can only say it like a creed; I have no demonstration, at least none such as I would venture to put into words. Perhaps the highest of all truths is incapable of demonstration and can only be stated. Perhaps, also, the statement, at least to some of us, is a sufficient demonstration. I believe that inability to imagine a thing is not a reason for its non-existence. If the infinite is a conclusion which is forced upon me, the fact that I cannot picture it does not disprove it. I believe, also, in thought and the soul, and it is nothing to me that I cannot explain them by attributes belonging to body. That being so, the difficulties which arise from the perpetual and unconscious confusion of the qualities of thought and soul with those of body disappear. Our imagination represents to itself souls like pebbles, and asks itself what count can be kept of a million, but number in such a case is inapplicable. I believe that all thought is a manifestation of the Being, who is One, whom you may call God if you like, and that, as It never was created, It will never be destroyed.'

'But,' said Madge, interrupting him, 'although you began by warning me not to expect that you would prove anything, you can tell me whether you have any kind of basis for what you say, or whether it is all a dream.'

'You will be surprised, perhaps, to hear that mathematics, which, of course, I had to learn

for my own business, have supplied something
for a foundation. They lead to ideas which
are inconsistent with the notion that the
imagination is a measure of all things. Mind,
I do not for a moment pretend that I have
any theory which explains the universe. It
is something, however, to know that the sky
is as real as the earth.'

They had now reached Great Ormond
Street, and parted. Clara and Marshall were
about five minutes behind them. Madge
was unusually cheerful when they sat down
to supper.

'Clara,' she said, 'what made you so silent
to-night at Mazzini's?' Clara did not reply,
but after a pause of a minute or two, she asked
Mrs Caffyn whether it would not be possible
for them all to go into the country on
Whitmonday? Whitsuntide was late; it
would be warm, and they could take their
food with them and eat it out of doors.

'Just the very thing, my dear, if we could
get anything cheap to take us; the baby, of
course, must go with us.

'I should like above everything to go to Great Oakhurst.'

'What, five of us—twenty miles there and twenty miles back! Besides, although I love the place, it isn't exactly what one would go to see just for a day. No! Letherhead or Mickleham or Darkin would be ever so much better. They are too far, though, and, then, that man Baruch must go with us. He'd be company for Marshall, and he sticks up in Clerkenwell and never goes nowhere. You remember as Marshall said as he must ask him the next time we had an outing.'

Clara had not forgotten it.

'Ah,' continued Mrs Caffyn, 'I should just love to show you Mickleham.'

Mrs Caffyn's heart yearned after her Surrey land. The man who is born in a town does not know what it is to be haunted through life by lovely visions of the landscape which lay about him when he was young. The village youth leaves the home of his child-hood for the city, but the river doubling on itself, the overhanging alders and willows, the fringe of level meadow, the chalk hills bounding the river valley and rising against the sky, with here and there on their summits solitary clusters of beech, the light and peace of the different seasons, of morning, afternoon and evening, never forsake him. To think of them is not a mere luxury ; their presence modifies the whole of his life.

' I don't see how it is to be managed,' she mused ; ' and yet there's nothing near London as I'd give two pins to see. There's Richmond as we went to one Sunday ; it was no better, to my way of thinking, than looking at a picture. I'd ever so much sooner be a-walking across the turnips by the footpath from Darkin home.'

' Couldn't we, for once in a way, stay somewhere over-night ? '

' It might as well be two,' said Mrs Marshall ; ' Saturday and Sunday.'

' Two,' said Madge ; ' I vote for two.'

' Wait a bit, my dears, we're a precious awkward lot to fit in—Marshall and his wife ;

me and you and Miss Clara and the baby ;
and then there's Baruch, who's odd man, so
to speak ; that's three bedrooms. We sha'n't
do it— Otherwise, I was a-thinking—'

'What were you thinking ? ' said Marshall.

'I've got it,' said Mrs Caffyn, joyously.
'Miss Clara and me will go to Great Oakhurst on the Friday. We can easy enough
stay at my old shop. Marshall and Sarah,
Miss Madge, the baby and Baruch can go to
Letherhead on the Saturday morning. The
two women and the baby can have one of the
rooms at Skelton's, and Marshall and Baruch
can have the other. Then, on Sunday morning, Miss Clara and me we'll come over for
you, and we'll all walk through Norbury Park.
That'll be ever so much better in many ways.
Miss Clara and me, we'll go by the coach.
Six of us, not reckoning the baby, in that
heavy ginger-beer cart of Masterman's would
be too much.'

'An expensive holiday, rather,' said Marshall.

'Leave that to me ; that's my business.
I ain't quite a beggar, and if we can't take

our pleasure once a year, it's a pity. We aren't like some folk as messes about up to Hampstead every Sunday, and spends a fortune on shrimps and donkeys. No ; when I go away, it *is* away, maybe it's only for a couple of days, where I can see a blessed ploughed field ; no shrimps nor donkeys for me.'

CHARTER XXIX

So it was settled, and on the Friday Clara and Mrs Caffyn journeyed to Great Oak-hurst. They were both tired, and went to bed very early, in order that they might enjoy the next day. Clara, always a light sleeper, woke between three and four, rose and went to the little casement window which had been open all night. Below her, on the left, the church was just discernible, and on the right, the broad chalk uplands leaned to the south, and were waving with green barley and wheat. Underneath her lay the cottage garden, with its row of beehives in the north-east corner, sheltered from the cold winds by the thick hedge. It had evidently been raining a little, for the drops hung on the currant bushes, but the clouds had been driven by

the south-westerly wind into the eastern sky,
where they lay in a long, low, grey band.
Not a sound was to be heard, save every now
and then the crow of a cock or the short cry
of a just-awakened thrush. High up on the
zenith, the approach of the sun to the horizon
was proclaimed by the most delicate tints of
rose-colour, but the cloud-bank above him was
dark and untouched, although the blue which
was over it, was every moment becoming paler.
Clara watched ; she was moved even to tears
by the beauty of the scene, but she was stirred
by something more than beauty, just as he
who was in the Spirit and beheld a throne
and One sitting thereon, saw something more
than loveliness, although He was radiant with
the colour of jasper and there was a rainbow round about Him like an emerald to
look upon. In a few moments the highest
top of the cloud-rampart was kindled, and
the whole wavy outline became a fringe of
flame. In a few moments more the fire just
at one point became blinding, and in another
second the sun emerged, the first arrowy shaft

passed into her chamber, the first shadow was cast, and it was day. She put her hands to her face ; the tears fell faster, but she wiped them away and her great purpose was fixed. She crept back into bed, her agitation ceased, a strange and almost supernatural peace over-shadowed her and she fell asleep not to wake till the sound of the scythe had ceased in the meadow just beyond the rick-yard that came up to one side of the cottage, and the mowers were at their breakfast.

Neither Mrs Caffyn nor Clara thought of seeing the Letherhead party on Saturday. They could not arrive before the afternoon, and it was considered hardly worth while to walk from Great Oakhurst to Letherhead merely for the sake of an hour or two. In the morning Mrs Caffyn was so busy with her old friends that she rather tired herself, and in the evening Clara went for a stroll. She did not know the country, but she wandered on until she came to a lane which led down to the river. At the bottom of the lane she found herself at a narrow, steep, stone bridge. She had not been there more than three or four minutes before she descried two persons coming down the lane from Letherhead. When they were about a couple of hundred yards from her they turned into the meadow over the stile, and struck the river-bank some distance below the point where she was. It was impossible to mistake them ; they were Madge and Baruch. They sauntered leisurely ; presently Baruch knelt down over the water, apparently to gather something which he gave to Madge. They then crossed another stile and were lost behind the tall hedge which stopped further view of the footpath in that direction.

'The message then was authentic,' she said to herself. 'I thought I could not have misunderstood it.'

On Sunday morning Clara wished to stay at home. She pleaded that she preferred rest, but Mrs Caffyn vowed there should be no Norbury Park if Clara did not go, and the kind creature managed to persuade a pig-dealer to drive them over to Letherhead for

a small sum, notwithstanding it was Sunday.
The whole party then set out; the baby
was drawn in a borrowed carriage which also
took the provisions, and they were fairly out
of the town before the Letherhead bells had
ceased ringing for church. It was one of
the sweetest of Sundays, sunny, but masses
of white clouds now and then broke the heat.
The park was reached early in the forenoon,
and it was agreed that dinner should be
served under one of the huge beech trees
at the lower end, as the hill was a little too
steep for the baby-carriage in the hot sun.

'This is very beautiful,' said Marshall,
when dinner was over, 'but it is not what
we came to see. We ought to move upwards
to the Druid's grove.'

'Yes, you be off, the whole lot of you,'
said Mrs Caffyn. 'I know every tree there,
and I ain't going there this afternoon. Somebody must stay here to look after the baby;
you can't wheel her, you'll have to carry
her, and you won't enjoy yourselves much
more for moiling along with her up that hill.'

'I will stay with you,' said Clara.

Everybody protested, but Clara was firm. She was tired, and the sun had given her a headache. Madge pleaded that it was she who ought to remain behind, but at last gave way for her sister looked really fatigued.

'There's a dear child,' said Clara, when Madge consented to go. 'I shall lie on the grass and perhaps go to sleep.'

'It is a pity,' said Baruch to Madge as they went away, 'that we are separated; we must come again.'

'Yes, I am sorry, but perhaps it is better she should be where she is; she is not particularly strong, and is obliged to be very careful.'

In due time they all came to the famous yews, and sat down on one of the seats overlooking that wonderful gate in the chalk downs through which the Mole passes northwards.

'We must go,' said Marshall, 'a little bit further and see the oak.'

'Not another step,' said his wife. 'You can go if you like.'

'Content ; nothing could be pleasanter than to sit here,' and he pulled out his pipe ; 'but really, Miss Madge, to leave Norbury without paying a visit to the oak is a pity.'

He did not offer, however, to accompany her.

'It is the most extraordinary tree in these parts,' said Baruch ; 'of incalculable age and with branches spreading into a tent big enough to cover a regiment. Marshall is quite right.'

'Where is it ?'

'Not above a couple of hundred yards further ; just round the corner.'

Madge rose and looked.

'No ; it is not visible here ; it stands a little way back. If you come a little further you will catch a glimpse of it.'

She followed him and presently the oak came in view. They climbed up the bank and went nearer to it. The whole vale was underneath them and part of the weald with the Sussex downs blue in the distance. Baruch was not much given to raptures over scenery, but the indifference of Nature to the world's turmoil always appealed to him.

'You are not now discontented because you cannot serve under Mazzini?'

'Not now.'

There was nothing in her reply on the face of it of any particular consequence to Baruch. She might simply have intended that the beauty of the fair landscape extinguished her restlessness, or that she saw her own unfitness, but neither of these interpretations presented itself to him.

'I have sometimes thought,' continued Baruch, slowly, 'that the love of any two persons in this world may fulfil an eternal purpose which is as necessary to the Universe as a great revolution.'

Madge's eyes moved round from the hills and they met Baruch's. No syllable was uttered, but swiftest messages passed, question and answer. There was no hesitation on his part now, no doubt, the woman and the moment had come. The last question was put, the final answer was given; he took her hand in his and came closer to her.

'Stop!' she whispered, 'do you know my history?'

He did not reply, but fell upon her neck. This was the goal to which both had been journeying all these years, although with much weary mistaking of roads; this was what from the beginning was designed for both! Happy Madge! happy Baruch! There are some so closely akin that the meaning of each may be said to lie in the other, who do not approach till it is too late. They travel towards one another, but are waylaid and detained, and just as they are within greeting, one of them drops and dies.

They left the tree and went back to the Marshalls, and then down the hill to Mrs Caffyn and Clara. Clara was much better for her rest, and early in the evening the whole party returned to Letherhead, Clara and Mrs Caffyn going on to Great Oakhurst.

Madge kept close to her sister till they separated, and the two men walked together. On Whitmonday morning the Letherhead people came over to Great Oakhurst. They had to go back to London in the afternoon, but Mrs Caffyn and Clara were to stay till Tuesday, as they stood a better chance of securing places by the coach on that day. Mrs Caffyn had as much to show them as if the village had been the Tower of London. The wonder of wonders, however, was a big house, where she was well known, and its hot-houses. Madge wanted to speak to Clara, but it was difficult to find a private opportunity. When they were in the garden, however, she managed to take Clara unobserved down one of the twisted paths, under pretence of admiring an ancient mulberry tree.

'Clara,' she said, 'I want a word with you. Baruch Cohen loves me.'

'Do you love him?'

'Yes.'

'Without a shadow of a doubt?'

'Without a shadow of a doubt.'

Clara put her arm round her sister, kissed her tenderly and said,—

'Then I am perfectly happy.'

'Did you suspect it?'

'I knew it.'

Mrs Caffyn called them; it was time to be moving, and soon afterwards those who had to go to London that afternoon left for Letherhead. Clara stood at the gate for a long time watching them along the straight, white road. They came to the top of the hill; she could just discern them against the sky; they passed over the ridge and she went indoors. In the evening a friend called to see Mrs Caffyn, and Clara went to the stone bridge which she had visited on Saturday. The water on the upper side of the bridge was dammed up and fell over the little sluice gates under the arches into a clear and deep basin about forty or fifty feet in diameter. The river, for some reason of its own, had bitten into the western bank, and had scooped out a great piece of it into an island. The main current went round the island with a shallow, swift ripple, instead of going through the pool, as it might have done, for there was a clear channel for it. The centre and the region under the island were deep and still, but at the farther end, where the river in passing called to the pool, it broke into waves as it answered the appeal, and added its own contribution to the stream, which went away down to the mill and onwards to the big Thames. On the island were aspens and alders. The floods had loosened the roots of the largest tree, and it hung over heavily in the direction in which it had yielded to the rush of the torrent, but it still held its grip, and the sap had not forsaken a single branch. Every one was as dense with foliage as if there had been no struggle for life, and the leaves sang their sweet song, just perceptible for a moment every now and then in the variations of the louder music below them. It is curious that the sound of a weir is never uniform, but is perpetually changing in the ear even of a person who stands close by it. One of the arches of the bridge was dry, and Clara went down into it, stood at the edge and watched that wonderful sight— the plunge of a smooth, pure stream into the great cup which it has hollowed out for itself. Down it went, with a dancing, foamy fringe playing round it just where it met the surface ; a dozen yards away it rose again, bubbling and exultant.

She came up from the arch and went home as the sun was setting. She found Mrs Caffyn alone.

'I have news to tell you,' she said. 'Baruch Cohen is in love with my sister, and she is in love with him.'

'The Lord, Miss Clara ! I thought some-times that perhaps it might be you ; but there, it's better, maybe, as it is, for—'

'For what ? '

'Why, my dear, because somebody's sure to turn up who'll make you happy, but there aren't many men like Baruch. You see what I mean, don't you ? He's always a-reading books, and, therefore, he don't think so much of what some people would make

a fuss about. Not as anything of that kind
would ever stop me, if I were a man and saw
such a woman as Miss Madge. He's really
as good a creature as ever was born, and
with that child she might have found it hard
to get along, and now it will be cared for,
and so will she be to the end of their lives.'

The evening after their return to Great
Ormond Street, Mazzini was surprised by a
visit from Clara alone.

'When I last saw you,' she said, 'you told
us that you had been helped by women. I
offer myself.'

'But, my dear madam, you hardly know
what the qualifications are. To begin with,
there must be a knowledge of three foreign
languages, French, German and Italian, and the
capacity and will to endure great privation,
suffering and, perhaps, death.'

'I was educated abroad, I can speak German
and French. I do not know much Italian,
but when I reach Italy I will soon learn.'

'Pardon me for asking you what may
appear a rude question. Is it a personal

disappointment which sends you to me, or love for the cause? It is not uncommon to find that young women, when earthly love is impossible, attempt to satisfy their cravings with a love for that which is impersonal.'

'Does it make any difference, so far as their constancy is concerned?'

'I cannot say that it does. The devotion of many of the martyrs of the Catholic church was repulsion from the world as much as attraction to heaven. You must understand that I am not prompted by curiosity. If you are to be my friend, it is necessary that I should know you thoroughly.'

'My motive is perfectly pure.'

They had some further talk and parted. After a few more interviews, Clara and another English lady started for Italy. Madge had letters from her sister at intervals for eighteen months, the last being from Venice. Then they ceased, and shortly afterwards Mazzini told Baruch that his sister-in-law was dead.

All efforts to obtain more information from Mazzini were in vain, but one day when her name was mentioned, he said to Madge,—

'The theologians represent the Crucifixion as the most sublime fact in the world's history. It was sublime, but let us reverence also the Eternal Christ who is for ever being crucified for our salvation.'

'Father,' said a younger Clara to Baruch some ten years later as she sat on his knee, 'I had an Aunt Clara once, hadn't I?'

'Yes, my child.'

'Didn't she go to Italy and die there?'

'Yes.'

'Why did she go?'

'Because she wanted to free the poor people of Italy who were slaves.'

THE END

Colston & Company, Ltd., Printers, Edinburgh.